Author's biography:

David was born in 1936.

His father was killed in France in 1940, the early stages of
the war. David was evacuated at the age of four, returning home
almost six years later. He joined the Merchant Navy at sixteen,
emigrated from England to New Zealand at seventeen and was
recruited into the NZ Army at eighteen. He married at twenty one
and helped raise three children.

He arrived back in the UK in 1994. Two years later, at the
age of sixty, he started a Tour Boat business on the Brighton
Marina. Ten years later he was diagnosed with prostate cancer,
sold his business and retired the following year.
In 2009, at the age of 73 he walked around England for Cancer
Research UK and the ACRF (Australian Cancer Research
Federation).

His first book **The Big Walk,** was a day-to-day account of
the above walk and was published in 2012.
In 2014 he wrote **The Mud Pack,** his first fiction novel.
A year later he completed his third book, **If Only…!** a
romantic work.
The Rise of Merlin is the author's first venture into the
fantasy genre.

1

The Rise of Merlin

By

D. Austin Wilson.

Copyright © 284704360 on 22nd May, 2016 by David Wilson

For more about this author please visit: www.david-a-wilson.com

All paper used in the printing of this book has been made from wood grown in managed, sustainable forests.

ISBN: 978-1-5272-0035-7

Printed and bound in the UK.
A catalogue record of this book is available from the British Library

"Tell me with whom you associate, and I will tell you who you are."

GOETHE

To all my friends:
My life would have been the poorer
not knowing you.

PROLOGUE

Every year since the Industrial Revolution there has been technological progress; small steps at first, gradually developing into huge strides during the latter years of the 20th century and into the new millennium.

This technical evolution has produced such remarkable results that many 'everyday' items we utilize without a thought, would, a mere 30 years ago, have been regarded as astonishing. Go back a100 years and today's technological advances would be thought of as unbelievable.

Imagine therefore, what a terrifying world it would be if someone from the 6th century was suddenly thrust into our modern world.

This is exactly what happens to Merlin.

The Rise of Merlin

CHAPTER 1

Tom was late for school, but he dawdled as if he had all day to get there. Two boys about the same age called out as they cycled by. Tom looked up, waved and continued at his leisurely pace.

The school had swallowed the last of the stragglers by the time Tom arrived at the imposing entrance. He waited, kicking his feet on the old flint wall that concealed his presence from those within. He looked at his watch, the one aunt Kate had given him on his tenth birthday. Just five more minutes and the whole school would be at assembly in the main hall. It would be the safest time.

He sat down with his back to the wall and studied the scuffed toes on his old school shoes. They were not as old as they appeared; it was just that Tom was particularly hard on his footwear. His stepmother had bought him a new pair for his birthday, to replace the ones she had bought on his previous birthday. She hardly ever gave him presents, not that he could remember anyway, even at Christmas, it was always just clothes. The twins always got toys. He had worn the new shoes a few times, but finding them uncomfortable he'd changed back to his other pair. It was a change unnoticed by his disinterested stepmother.

Tom checked his watch again before peering around the wall to see if there was anyone at the school windows overlooking the playground. Reassured, he darted into the school ground and hurried over to one of the two long bike sheds near the school gates. Tom knew the bike he wanted. He spotted the smart black and silver mountain bike belonging to Jamie Sheriden straight away.

Jamie always had the smartest bike at the school, indeed everything Jamie had was always the best and he made no attempt to hide his good fortune. He would often boast about his large home with the swimming pool, his holidays abroad with his parents and would show off any expensive gifts he was given. Apart from a few hangers-on, it made Jamie Sheriden the most disliked child at the school. It salved Tom's conscience a little to know the missing bike would cause Jamie nothing more than a slight, temporary inconvenience.

Tom darted along the rows of bikes hoping the rich kid, for that was what everyone called him, had left his bike unlocked as usual. With relief, Tom saw the D shackle was still in its bracket. He quickly steered it out from the shed and pedalled out of the school grounds. He cycled to the junction on the outskirts of town before stopping to take off his school jacket and cap. He crammed them into his dark blue rucksack, then resumed his journey, turning off in the direction that would lead him towards his ultimate destination - Long Acre farm, near the town of Saltridge.

Today's escapade had been planned nine days ago, and for a boy of twelve Tom had prepared himself remarkably well. His main concern about the long journey was the risk of punctures, so early in the week he'd checked the wheel size on Jamie Sheridan's bike before purchasing an extra inner tube and a puncture repair kit from the local bike store. There was no need to buy a bicycle pump as one was already fitted on Jamie's bike. He had also prepared a larger than usual packed lunch and stored it, along with two bottles of water and a bottle of lemon squash, in his rucksack.

After the birth of her twins, Cynthia Watson, Tom's stepmother, hadn't the slightest interest in preparing school lunches for her stepson, so Tom had been left to do his own lunches ever since. Therefore, extra activity in the kitchen that morning went completely unnoticed.

Tom cycled steadily for some time. The twenty-one gears on Jamie's bike made the uphill going much easier, but the heat of the late morning sun was at last imposing itself and Tom was beginning to feel tired, hot and thirsty. He finally stopped at a crossroad to rest and eat. As he sat by the road munching a sandwich, he ruminated on the events leading up to the bike theft. He knew he was asking for more trouble. His main worry, however, was how aunt Kate and uncle Bill would receive him when he arrived at their door.

The slim, brown-haired youngster looked at his watch again and then at the signpost nearby. He knew he was heading in the right direction, but he also knew there was still a fair distance to travel. He quickly finished eating another sandwich and set off with renewed vigour towards his destination. As he rode he let his thoughts settle, once again, on his predicament. By his watch it was almost midday. Would Jamie Sheriden discover his mountain bike missing during lunchtime? Would anyone have seen him take it? What about the two welfare officers who were to see him at his home after school? Tom could only imagine the anger of his stepmother at his absence from the meeting. It would only take a phone call from her to discover he'd never attended school that day anyway... what then?

Tom suspected his aunt Kate would be the first to be told, for she seemed to have been kept well informed about all of his wayward behaviour, his constant truancy, his disobedience at home, his poor report from school and the recent shoplifting he'd not actually been involved in. Tom suspected his stepmother derived some pleasure from reporting anything remotely negative about him to his only relatives. But what would his aunt and uncle think? Maybe this time they'd want nothing more to do with him. Maybe this time they would turn him away from their door. Tom tried to dismiss this possibility, but although he was instinctively aware of their affection for him, the nagging thought persisted that on this occasion they might not be so forgiving.

It was the thought of meeting with council welfare officials that had finally made up Tom's mind to leave home, not that he hadn't considered the idea many times since the loss of his father. Tom knew there were concerns over his truancy and he suspected this was what the meeting was about. He also wondered if they might be thinking of placing him in care. Luckily he wouldn't be there to find out.

His thoughts turned once again to his aunt Kate and uncle Bill. What a wonderful holiday he'd had with them last summer! Tom loved nothing more than helping his uncle with all the many tasks around the farm. His greatest delight was sitting in the small trailer attached to the back of uncle Bill's motorbike, especially with Sam the sheep dog, who took every opportunity to jump in the cart with him, even when it was moving. His aunt thought it was dangerous and would often reproach her husband for allowing it. Tom, therefore, had been sworn to secrecy about the rides by his uncle, and this made it even more exciting.

The most memorable time for Tom was the Easter holidays he had spent on the farm when he made that remarkable discovery with his cousin, Felicity. Stumbling on to that hidden cave made his holiday extra special.

Felicity, or Fliss, as everyone called her, was a terrific sport, always ready to accompany her cousin wherever he went. She could climb and run as well as any boy Tom knew, yet she was his junior by almost twenty months. Fliss had sat beside Tom on the journey back to his home after the Easter holidays, and they had talked, laughed and teased each other until his uncle told the boisterous pair to quieten down. Tom recalled his cousin's tearful hug and the strange lump in his throat as he watched the car disappear down the road.

That was three months ago, but the strangest thing was, since that weekend, hardly a day went by without thoughts and images of the cave encroaching on his mind. Tom would try to ignore the persistent, nebulous intrusions, yet was always conscious of their mysterious presence.

He stopped at another intersection where a road sign showed he was now twelve and a half miles from Saltridge. He glanced at his watch again and realised he had been cycling for almost three hours. He could feel the growing stiffness in his young legs. He longed to rest, but his eagerness to reach the farm spurred him on. He knew he could have got there much sooner if he had travelled on the main road, but the direct route meant heavier traffic, and a greater chance of someone recognising him.

The country route he had chosen was the same his father had taken when they drove up to the farm together. Now, as he cycled along, those nostalgic memories surfaced; sitting next to his father in the car, wonderful occasions being together without his stepmother; times when their shared confidences, their chats, their laughter, created a special feeling of closeness for Tom. Now they were just vague, but precious memories, of a place in time that would always be with him.

It was early afternoon and for the past hour a build-up of clouds provided the young traveller with some relief from the hot sun. He managed to continue at a good pace, finally reaching the turn-off he thought his father had taken to his aunt and uncle's property. Being unsure, he stopped outside a roadside garage to ask a silver-haired man in greasy blue overalls about the whereabouts of Long Acre farm.

The man, crouched over the open bonnet of a car, grinned at the boy, then straightened up with some effort. "Oh, ya mean Billy Watson's place. 'E was in 'ere a couple a days ago 'bout 'is tractor... Ooh are you anyway?"

Tom told him. The man nodded and pointed to the turn-off. "Down that way, son, 'bout four and 'alf miles."

Tom thanked the man and quickly rode off again, anxious to reach his destination and the home he loved. It wasn't long before Tom found himself on the familiar tree-lined drive of Long Acre farm. He stopped at the disused implement shed and hid the bike under an old tarpaulin before making his way up to the farm house. He knocked on the door and almost immediately saw his aunt's cheerful face appear at the open kitchen window.

"Tom!" she cried. "What are you doing here...? Come in."

Before Tom had a chance to step inside, his vivacious aunt, with her curly auburn hair in disarray, was at the door hugging him.

"What a lovely surprise," she said, leading him into the kitchen.

"Now, sit down and I'll get you a drink, my darling... you look so hot... How did you get here...? You must be famished."

Aunt Kate, more interested in preparing some refreshment for her nephew than hearing his answer, fluttered around in the kitchen. It gave Tom some breathing space, for he knew he would eventually have to provide reasons for his sudden appearance.

"Why don't you pop over to the tractor shed and ask your uncle to come home for a cup of tea, he'll be delighted to see you," said Kate, as Tom began biting into a cheese scone she had hastily buttered for him. He quickly finished the scone, washing it down with a gulp of orange juice, and ran to find his uncle.

A welcoming bark from Sam the sheep dog made Bill look up from the work bench, just as Tom appeared at the large aluminium doors of the shed. "Good gracious, Tom, you're a sight for sore eyes, what brings you here, not school holidays already, is it?

"Aunt Kate wants to know if you'd like some afternoon tea," said Tom, evading the question.

Bill wiped away the beads of sweat that had accumulated on his partly bald head, rose from the bench, his round, shiny face beaming with pleasure, and ruffled his nephew's hair. "Hope you're here for a while, Tom, my boy, I could do with another man's help around here." Tom grinned, his uncle always made him feel important. Tom was pleased and relieved by the warm reception he had received from his aunt and uncle and it restored his belief in their obvious affection for him. Even Sam kept joyously barking up at him, until a gruff command from Bill silenced him.

For Tom, coming to the farm always felt like coming home.

It was only after Bill had finished his second cup of tea that Kate broached the subject of Tom's unexpected appearance. Tom, noncommittal at first, eventually told them all his reasons for leaving home and that he was determined not to return. He stopped short of telling them about the stolen bike, as he dreaded their disapproval, so when asked, he said he had walked to the farm after being dropped by coach on the main highway.

Bill and Kate had known of their nephew's growing unhappiness since the death of his father, Bill's younger brother. His situation at home with his stepmother had deteriorated, but they felt powerless to intervene.

"But what about school, Tom? You have to go to school," said aunt Kate, in a concerned voice.

"I'll go to Fliss's school," countered Tom.

Kate, with her large and expressive brown eyes, looked over at her stocky husband for inspiration. "Look, Kate, there's only another week or so before they break for summer term, so maybe it's not that important."

Kate gave a slight shake of her head before breaking into a smile for her nephew. "Don't worry, Tom, we'll try to sort something out. Why don't you go upstairs, have a shower and change into other clothes? Your room is still as it was, so you'll find everything you need."

Tom, relieved to have got some of his worries off his chest, needed no further inducement and after another hug from his aunt, he bounded up the stairs. His room was a dormer built into the roof. Bill had it constructed when Tom stayed at the farm after his mother died. Before the dormer was built, the farmhouse

10

had just three bedrooms. At the time, Kate's mother was also staying there, recuperating after an operation, so Tom had to share Felicity's room.

It hadn't taken long for Kate to realise this sleeping arrangement was far from satisfactory, for the cousins spent most evenings chatting and teasing each other until quite late, despite Kate chiding them. Finally, after a few weeks, with both the children grumpy in the mornings, Kate persuaded her husband to have the dormer built.

Tom lay on the bed looking up at the sloping ceilings and the walls that still had the wallpaper with the cowboy pictures on them. He had always felt so comfortable and peaceful ensconced in this room as a little boy, and the feeling had never changed.

Without warning a picture of the cave appeared again in his mind. He rose from the bed and went over to the window. From here he could see beyond the top fields to the rocky outcrop that bordered the acres of undeveloped land. The place was known as Devil's Ridge. It was an area of rocky terrain impossible to cultivate. Uncle Bill couldn't even use it for grazing his sheep as the fencing on the perimeters of the ridge was almost non-existent due to the hard, rocky ground.

It was on Devil's Ridge that Tom and Felicity had stumbled upon the hidden cave.

CHAPTER 2

Being allowed to spend that Easter weekend on the farm was a wonderful surprise for Tom. Earlier, his stepmother had decided to prohibit him from spending his Easter break there, as a punishment for not coming home in time to mind the twins one evening. A few days before the long weekend, Cynthia had phoned Kate to say she had changed her mind, and asked if they could pick Tom up around 5pm on Thursday.

Kate couldn't understand her sister-in-law's change of heart, as the woman seemed to derive some strange satisfaction from denying them the chance to see Tom whenever she could. She would later discover the change of plans was due to the expected arrival of Cynthia's parents; their sudden decision to visit and stay over the Easter weekend meant Tom's bedroom was needed.

Uncle Bill and Felicity picked Tom up, and an hour later they were back at the farm. Tom, with his aunt fussing around him and his cousin vying for his attention, felt on top of the world and he relished the thought of being at Long Acre for the next four days.

It was Saturday morning before Tom and Felicity were able to spend time together. In her excitement at Tom's arrival, Felicity had neglected to do her homework on Thursday evening, and by the time she had finished it on Friday morning and done some chores for her mother, Tom had already gone with uncle Bill to mend some fencing around the farm. They arrived back just in time for dinner.

On Saturday morning Tom woke to a nudge and the sound of Felicity's voice. "Come on, sleepy head, it's after nine." Tom stirred sleepily. "Go away, Fliss," he said, turning over in the bed. He felt another nudge on his back. "Come on, you promised we'd get away early today and anyway, mum's making breakfast." At those last words Tom came to life; the delicious smell of fried bacon was wafting through the house. "Ok Fliss, tell auntie I'm coming down now."

Tom and Felicity left the house just after ten. Tom breathed in the fresh morning air with its myriad of delightful country smells while Sam scampered around them, happy to be released from his kennel.

"Let's go up to Devil's Ridge," suggested Tom.

"Let's," said Felicity enthusiastically.

"Race you to the hay barn, Fliss."

"Ok, but you have to give me a start," she pleaded, grinning at him.

The hay barn was about half a mile up a wide concrete track. A stand of oak trees close to the barn provided shelter for the beef cattle that would often gravitate there during feed-out or in bad weather.

"First one to touch the big tree," said Tom, indicating the one nearest the barn.

"Okay," said Felicity, immediately tearing off along the track, her pony-tail flying, with Sam the dog in noisy pursuit. Both cousins arrived almost at the same time, and Tom allowed Felicity to touch the tree first, much to her delight.

From the hay barn the track turned into a narrow gravel path, deeply rutted by tractor tyres. Ancient whitish-grey stone walls about four feet high lined the track on both sides. It began as a gentle rise a little way beyond the barn, gradually becoming steeper as it approached the upper reaches of the grazing land of the farm. At this topmost boundary the stone walls veered at right angles, separating the fields from the rugged terrain beyond.

Devil's Ridge was an ideal playground for the two youngsters, and only recently had they been given permission to go there, after strict instructions from aunt Kate that they stay within the boundary of the farm. They had plenty of scope as there were about thirty wild acres of craggy landscape to roam around. The other stipulation from aunt Kate was that Sam, the sheep dog, must accompany them at all times.

They wandered along for some time, with Fliss hiding now and then from her cousin, only to be found easily by a tail-wagging Sam. Tom decided to climb a tree to see more distant terrain and Fliss joined him. In the distance, a little beyond a clump of Acacia trees, they could see what appeared to be a sloping ridge that ran for a couple of hundred yards or so before eventually petering out into a rocky mound.

They set out for the area as it was somewhere they had yet to explore; within a few minutes they were standing at the foot of a fairly steep bank. Grass carpeted the ground and clumps of wild flowering bushes grew erratically on the uneven, rocky terrain.

Tom's first thought was to climb the twelve-foot bank. He then thought of Fliss and tried to persuade her to go along to where the incline was not as steep, for he had promised his aunt he would take good care of his younger cousin. But she would have none of it and insisted on accompanying him on the climb. After some reflection, he decided the safest solution would be to let his cousin climb ahead of him so he could cushion her fall should she slip. Sam, who had come up to investigate what was happening, suddenly took off in pursuit of a rabbit that had foolishly wandered into the open nearby.

Felicity made surprisingly good progress, with Tom following close behind. Near the summit she hesitated, for the top part of the bank was almost perpendicular. Tom put his hand under his cousin's right foot and helped push her up on the top of the bank. But doing this put extra pressure on his foot-hold and before he could climb another step, he felt the bank giving way under his feet. The next moment he was sliding down the bank with a deluge of stones and dried earth falling on top of him.

Felicity, looked down with some concern, but before she could speak, Tom rose from the rubble, looked up at his cousin and grinned sheepishly. Her look of consternation quickly changed to one of merriment and she couldn't help giggling at his disheveled appearance. Tom brushed himself down and immediately began climbing the bank again.

He had almost reached the top when he felt the stones underneath his feet give way again and he found himself sliding down to the ground amid another heavy fall of stones, earth and clumps of weed.

He stood up, dusted himself down again and looked angrily up at his giggling cousin. It was then he noticed the hole that had appeared in the bank; a head-high cavity of about ten inches in diameter. Tom pulled at a large stone that partially blocked the bottom of the cavity and he barely had time to jump clear as a further avalanche of stones fell in a dusty heap near his feet. He looked up again and found himself gazing at a much larger opening. Tom called up to Felicity, who had been lying on her stomach, watching.

"Fliss, come down and look at this."

"What is it?"

"There's a big hole in the bank, looks like a cave or something," he said, peering into the black void.

"I'm frightened of climbing down," she responded.

"Just run along the bank where it's not so high," said Tom, pointing to his left. "It's not far." This time, Felicity hurriedly did as she was bid and was soon standing alongside her cousin, who was still gazing into the opening.

"What are you going to do, Tom?"

"We'll clear these rocks from the ground and try to make the hole larger," he explained authoritatively.

It took some time to clear the rubble at their feet, and then Tom started pulling more stones away from the bank, causing fresh falls of debris. He then noticed the larger rocks that concealed much of the opening appeared to be mortared together. The top layer of smaller stones that had first given way under Tom's feet seemed bound together with a similar material. With some effort, Tom started pulling each large rock away from the substance that held it, pausing every so often to help Felicity clear the ground of rocks. Finally, they were facing a fully exposed, but narrow cave entrance. Tom glanced at Felicity, grinned, and then gingerly took a step into the murky interior. He felt a hand clasp his own as his cousin drew up beside him. They hadn't seen Sam playfully bounding up towards them, for if they had, they would have noticed him turning abruptly, hackles raised, and quickly slinking away from the cave.

A dank, musty smell permeated the interior, but it was the coldness and utter silence of the place that made Felicity tighten her grip on her cousin's hand. Tom peered into the darkness and took another cautious step, with his cousin shuffling close alongside him.

Felicity's murmur broke the awful silence.

"Let's go, Tom, I don't like it."

"Don't be silly, Fliss," he whispered, as his eyes tried to penetrate the gloom. The boy could now make out the vague features of uneven walls that stood directly ahead and to his right. An area to the left was enveloped in total darkness as if the cave extended a lot further in that direction.

"Please Tom, let's leave," urged Felicity, this time jerking on his hand.

"Shhh, I think I heard something," he whispered.

Felicity, quite petrified, listened.

Suddenly Tom let out a piercing scream, causing heart-stopping terror in the girl by his side. "Something's coming! Run, Fliss, run!" he yelled.

His cousin responded so fast, she almost tripped as she turned and sprinted out of the cave. She was about forty yards away when a peculiar noise suddenly stopped her in mid-flight. She looked back to see Tom doubled up with laughter outside the cave.

He was still shaking with uncontrollable mirth when Felicity reached him, and before Tom could react, his raging cousin had launched herself at him in a perfect rugby tackle, knocking him hard to the ground. Straddling him, she started pummeling him with her small fists. Tom, trying to ward off the blows raining down on him, became even more hysterical, with tears running down his face in unrestrained glee. After a minute or so, Felicity couldn't help but see the funny side of it and collapsed on top of her cousin, joining him in a fit of helpless laughter.

After they had recovered, Tom suggested they make a comfortable resting place just inside the cave entrance, for whenever they came up again. "We could have a picnic here, Fliss, and if we had something better to sit on, we could shelter here whenever it started raining," he said, trying to rouse his cousin, who clearly wasn't that keen on the idea. Eventually, she was persuaded to help and they started gathering twigs, bracken and clumps of grass for the task. It wasn't long before they had created a suitable seating area inside the entrance, where two could sit down in reasonable comfort.

Felicity, however, still uneasy about the cave, preferred to sit outside the entrance where it was warm and sunny, and eventually Tom joined her. As they sat there, they came up with all sorts of reasons for the cave's existence.

"I bet it's been the home to fierce wild animals," said Tom.

"Or cave men in years gone past," suggested Fliss.

But Tom couldn't help wondering why the cave appeared to have been sealed with some sort of mortar. After a while, Tom decided he would wander back into the cave, as he hadn't yet fully explored it. He was about to go when Felicity, glancing at her watch, let out a cry,

"Tom, it's almost four o'clock and we promised mum we'd be home by then."

Tom grimaced. "I suppose," he murmured.

"And I think I can hear dad's tractor... listen!"

Tom nodded. "You're right Fliss," he replied, without enthusiasm.

"Well, if we hurry we might get a lift home... come on," she said, leaving Tom to chase after her.

Sam, who had been lying a discreet distance away, was alert to the sudden activity and immediately took off in pursuit. He soon led the way back, barking happily as he went. Uncle Bill had come up to the top of the farm to repair the valve on the water trough. He had just finished when Sam bounded up to him, followed by two breathless children. "I was just about to whistle for the dog as you arrived," said Bill, looking at his daughter. Kate knew whenever her husband whistled for Sam while the dog was with the children it would bark in response but would stay with them.

"So what have you two rascals been up to?" said Bill, as they both mounted the back of the trailer.

"Just exploring," they replied in unison.

"Looks like you've been exploring underground caves or something by the state of you both," said Bill, starting to turn the tractor around to go down to the homestead. The children exchanged glances and grinned at each other for they'd made a pact to keep the cave's discovery a secret.

As Tom lay in bed that night, he could think of nothing but the cave. He was eager to visit it again, but he knew his aunt had made plans, at least for the next day. The strenuous activity up on Devil's Ridge had thoroughly exhausted Tom, and he finally succumbed to a deep but dream-filled sleep.

Easter Sunday was a traditional day for the Watson family. Tom knew they would be attending a church service in the morning, and then, after lunch, would visit Gary and Rachel Peterson on the neighbouring farm. The compulsion to visit the cave persisted and Tom tried to make an excuse to stay behind on the farm, but Kate would not hear of it. "Tom, it's Easter Sunday, it's a family day. You're part of our family and that's that!" she said, quite firmly.

The Petersons were old friends of the family and they had two children of their own. There was Colin, who was two years Tom's senior, and his sister Ruth, who was Felicity's closest friend and school companion. Usually Tom looked forward to the event, as he liked Colin's company, despite the age difference, and the two of them had always got on well together, but on this occasion, he resented having to go there, for the yearning to visit the cave was compelling and unremitting. Sunday came and went. The weather was fine and Tom thoroughly enjoyed his afternoon on the Peterson's farm after all. That evening, Tom and Felicity made plans to visit Devil's Ridge the following day.

On Monday morning Tom woke early. He opened the curtains and to his dismay he saw it was raining heavily. He knew his aunt would not permit them to wander any distance from the farmhouse if the rain persisted - and persist it did.

It was late afternoon when it was time for Tom to leave. There was an emotional, drawn-out goodbye hug from Kate, who had been dreading the moment all weekend long. Tom struggled to keep a brave face as his aunt embraced him once again before allowing him to get into the car. Bill, accompanied by Felicity, drove his nephew back to his stepmother in Macefield.

CHAPTER 3

It had been the sudden scream from the boy that had stirred
Merlin from his deep slumber. The noise shattered the heavy
silence that had endured in the cave for almost fifteen hundred
years. His waking was immediate, but confusion followed when
his body failed to respond to the commands of his brain. He could
open his eyelids, but only a fraction, allowing him to squint at the
space above and to the side of him. He tried to move, but
couldn't. In fact, he could not feel his body at all.

As he sensed the bitter chill and utter silence of his
surroundings, awareness started to seep into his brain. Slowly at
first, then like a torrent, events began flooding back into his
mind. Merlin remembered clearly now; he and Salina coming
into the cave. He'd discovered the cave as a youngster, during
one of his many hunting trips with Keetah, his falcon. Later, the
cave had become his and Salina's secret refuge, somewhere the
two of them could be together, away from the prying eyes of
Arthur's court and the townspeople.

They had lit the torch, poured oil into the ceramic bowl
that contained a mixture of tree resin and peat, then ignited it with
the flint he always carried. He had lodged it on the small shelf he
had carved into the wall. It provided just enough light for them to
see each other. He remembered holding her hands in the soft,
flickering glow while they talked of their plans for a future life
together.

Merlin pictured the scene more clearly now; the wine she
had poured for him while they talked, and then the slow
realisation something was wrong. He had felt an overwhelming
tiredness seeping through his body and, moments later, saw the
hazy vision of Salina standing over him with his precious staff
raised above her head. Then the shock of seeing Salina's features
slowly turning into the face of Niddrym. Soon came the sound he
would never forget; the awful shrieking and hysterical laughter of
a demented witch.

He could hear again the incantation, feel the utter
helplessness, as lying prostrate and barely able to move, he
listened to the dreadful words that would seal his fate. He knew,
only too well, the awful significance of the curse she was about to
lay upon him; he would be doomed to lie there, suspended in time

like a frozen corpse, unless somehow, he remembered hoping, she failed to weave into the spell that which could break it.

As morning fog rises from a dew covered meadow, so the memories of that night slowly materialised. He remembered now, his devastation at hearing the words: "to be woken only by the cry from an orphan child". The likelihood of such an event coming to pass was so utterly remote, she might as well have said, 'til all the heavens collide'. The amulet! Recollection arrived in a flash. He had felt Niddrym slipping it over his head and, in his helpless state, watched her throw it wildly up at the roof of the cave, cackling hysterically as she did so. She knew of the amulet's significance; unless it was worn the spell could never be broken completely. Merlin recalled his desperate effort to stay awake, resisting with all his power the growing urge to sleep. Then the horror and despair of sinking into darkness; into the black abyss that was waiting to embrace him.

But now he was fully awake; the boy's cry still ringing in his ears. He began to wonder how long he might have slept. It seemed no more than a full night, but could more time have elapsed? Was it days... weeks, surely not longer? The reality of his appalling situation was slowly dawning on him. Without the amulet he would remain conscious, forever aware of these dark, deathly surroundings. Much better, he thought, not to have woken; to have remained blissfully unaware of his terrible fate.

Laughter coming from somewhere. Shrieks of laughter! Voices! Children's voices! But what strange language! Had Niddrym transported him to some foreign land? He tried calling out, but nothing more than a soft, hoarse sigh issued forth from his motionless lips. He listened intently to the voices, trying to decipher the unfamiliar language. His prodigious brain noted the intonation of various words and he started to memorise the sounds. In a short time, Merlin had mastered much of the children's vocabulary, but too soon the voices disappeared and he was left once again to contemplate his awful fate.

He focused entirely on his predicament. He was determined to extricate himself from this tomb and he would - through the awesome power of his mind.

As a youngster, Merlin possessed the extraordinary gift of spiritual sight; the ability to observe happenings without being physically present. More amazing even was his unique capacity to make objects move through the power of his mind. Uncle Cedrin, his master and tutor, became aware of the boy's amazing power and nurtured it to the best of his ability. He reached full mastery of his powers during the long and arduous years with the High Priests of the Inner Circle, the most revered school within the Ancient Order of Druids. Their strict tutelage would enable him to spiritually transcend physical laws at will.

Merlin's concentration was now directed at the source from which the sounds had come. Slowly, the two children appeared as a hazy picture in his brain. There was a girl running and a boy following a little way behind. As the vision cleared, he noticed the strange clothing the children were wearing, unlike any garments he knew. In his mind's eye he could also see a dog running ahead of them. The rough, rock-strewn terrain they were travelling through was all too familiar, for he had wandered around the place with Keetah, his falcon, since his early youth, and he knew every nook and cranny of it.

He watched as the children ran out on to a wide track and then, without warning, a strange vista confronted him. He could see nothing but barren landscape; fields green and fallow as far as the eye could see. There were clumps of trees dotted here and there, but nothing more. Where were the forests? How could they just disappear! Even the forest he used to walk through in his uphill climb to Devil's Ridge had gone. Now there was nothing… nothing.

He forced his attention back to the two children, and watched as they ran up to a smiling, red-faced man standing by a trough. A few moments later he saw the man climb up on to an extraordinary contraption that had two huge black wheels at the back and two smaller ones in front. He caught sight of the two children as they jumped up on a large cart that sat behind the strange monster. Suddenly, the creature began to move, pulling the cart behind it. How could this be? Surely carts could only be pulled by oxen, yet here was this thing with wheels, moving of its own accord.

Merlin followed the group as the creature made its way down the track. They passed a large building that seemed to be clad with what appeared to be a strange, silvery substance. Further down the track the thing eventually slowed before turning and disappearing into another big building. The wizard was about to follow, when the man and the two children reappeared and crossed over to another building. It was one of the strangest dwellings the wizard had ever seen. Merlin accompanied them as they went inside, and he suddenly found himself in a most extraordinary room. The uninvited guest stood there, astounded and mystified at what he was seeing around him. Too soon, however, his mind, overwhelmed by what it had to take in over the last hour or so, could no longer muster the concentration needed for mind travel and Merlin found himself once more back in the dark, depressing cave.

His thoughts turned again to Salina. He realised now, it wasn't her hand he was holding during their climb through the forest to Devil's Ridge, it was Niddrym's. But how did it happen? What had the evil witch done to Salina? The image of his lover remained sharp and clear; a face that would light up his whole world when she smiled; her long, dark tresses, although restrained by an ivory clasp, still tumbled over her shoulders; the way she tilted her head to listen to a noise in the forest; her slender hands always searching his. He thought of their walks in the forest, their laughter and love-making ... and then in a single moment, his beautiful Salina had been taken from him. He realised now his loss was not a recent happening, the denuded landscape implied a vastly different time-scale; a frightening one. And yet his pain lingered.

Merlin forced his mind to settle on the present. The boy had gone, probably never to return. Was he doomed to lie here forever in the dark, deathly silence? Merlin brushed the thoughts aside. His telepathic powers would induce the boy to return. With the boy's help he would, once again, possess the amulet. With the boy's help he would extricate himself from this living hell.

The wizard began to plan his strategy. While waiting for the boy's return, he would remove himself from his morbid surroundings whenever he could through mind travel. These excursions would give him greater knowledge of these strange people and their extraordinary world. He would make it his business to understand their language and their habits. For short periods each day he would attempt to make telepathic contact with someone... anyone, in whatever world it was that existed out there.

Just as important was the need to develop feeling and movement in his throat muscles. To enunciate clearly was vital, for he would need to be ready to communicate with the boy when he returned.

And return he would!

CHAPTER 4

After the long cycle ride Tom was glad to shower and change into other clothes. He noticed with some satisfaction how his clothes and other belongings lay tidied but otherwise undisturbed in the drawers and shelves of his bedroom.

"We've phoned your stepmother, Tom," Kate said quietly, as he joined her in the kitchen. "I had to tell her you were here, but said you'd just arrived."

"What did she say?"

"She wasn't very happy and wanted to talk to you, but I said you were having a shower and could she call later. She said she was going to arrange for you to be picked up tomorrow by child welfare officers, unless we bring you back ourselves."

"I'm not going back, auntie," he said quietly.

"Let me have a talk with your uncle this evening and we'll try to sort something out. I will handle it when she calls, so try not to worry," said Kate, seeing how troubled her nephew was. "Felicity will be home soon and you can both play around the farm until tea time."

At that very moment, they heard the back door open. "Hi mum" Felicity called as she hurried up the stairs without breaking step. "Fliss, there's someone here to see you," called her mother.

"Who is it?" she asked, pausing on the stairs.

"Come down and see."

The girl retraced her steps and peered around the kitchen door.

"Tom!", she cried, rushing over and hugging him, "what are you doing here?"

"I'll explain later, Fliss," said her mother. "Now why don't you go up and change, do your homework, then spend time with your cousin before dinner."

"I've only a little homework to do. Can I do it tomorrow before I go to school, mum... pleeeze?"

"Okay, but make sure you get up in plenty of time." warned Kate.

"Sure, mum. See you in a minute, Tom!" Felicity rushed out of the kitchen and back up the stairs to change.

**   **   **

Kate had been itching to discuss Tom's dilemma with her husband all evening, but had to wait until the children had finally gone to bed.

"We're going to have to sort this out, Bill, one way or the other."

"I can't see what we can do, Kate, we've tried in the past, but that witch of a woman will not let us keep Tom, and as far as I can see she never will."

"But Cynthia might have a change of heart," reasoned Kate, "now he's actually run away from home."

"Not from what you told me about the discussion you had when she rang earlier."

Kate had to agree. She knew he loved his nephew as much as she did. Somehow, somewhere, there had to be an answer.

** ** **

Tom waited until he had finished breakfast and Felicity had gone to school, before asking his aunt if he could go up to Devil's Ridge. He had not talked about his plans with his younger cousin, knowing she'd be upset at being unable to go with him. Neither did he want to explain this strange compulsion to visit the cave on his own.

"Yes, you can," said Kate, "but don't forget to take your anorak in case it rains... and Tom, before you go, you'd better see if your uncle wants any help around the farm, then see if you can take the dog with you."

As he made his way to the front gate, Kate called out: "Oh Tom, don't forget those welfare people will be here at 1.30, so make sure you're back by then."

"I'm not going back, auntie," replied Tom, with quiet determination.

"I know you don't want to, darling, that's why your uncle and I need to have a good long talk with them. But we'll still need you to be around."

It was mid-July and Bill was busy culling some late lambs for the market when he saw his nephew approach. "Auntie wants to know if you need my help."

His uncle grinned down at the boy. 'Why, you got something more important to do?"

Tom nodded, without speaking. "You go off then and enjoy yourself, son, but you can't take Sam 'cos I'll need him for the rest of the morning." The boy thanked his uncle and raced away to the tractor shed. After picking up a torch and stowing it in his rucksack he started to make his way up to Devil's Ridge, and, before long, he found himself at the cave entrance. He hesitated at the threshold, wondering if animals had got inside. He called loudly, listened, but heard nothing. Reassured, he turned on the torch and took a couple of slow steps into the cave. Again, he stood and listened. The dank, musty odour had almost disappeared, but the oppressive silence still lay heavy within the cave.

Tom moved slowly forward as the torch light penetrated the darkness. Directing the beam along the back of the cave, he could see how the rear wall extended further along to the left corner, exposing the outline of a crude arched opening. The area beyond the arch remained in darkness and Tom moved closer so the torch light could penetrate the gloom beyond. It appeared to be the entrance to a short tunnel. He was afraid to venture further. Something about the place troubled him. He regretted not having Fliss with him, and thought how much braver he would have been had she been there. He was about to turn to make his way out of the cave when he froze.

It sounded like someone softly calling his name.

He paused, listening, but apart from the wild thumping of his heart, he heard nothing.

Tom looked back toward the outer entrance. The welcoming sunlight beckoned and he felt the overpowering urge to flee. He turned to leave, but there is was again, more clearly this time, someone calling his name. Tom stiffened and through sheer terror, dropped the torch. He stood, immobile as a statue, his heart thumping wildly as he waited in dreaded suspense. The voice came again, it seemed to be directly behind him.

"Tom, be not afraid. No harm will come to you."

The boy, transfixed, could do nothing but wait.

"Tom, I need your help. Remain calm and listen to what I say. Do you hear me?"

The boy nodded.

"Have no fear – let peace be within you."

Tom could feel the tension ease and the terror diminish. He waited, wondering when the voice would speak again. Out of the darkness came the words: "Pick up from the ground that what gives light." It took a moment or two for Tom to respond.

"Listen now. Go through the tunnel, do not be afraid." Slowly, the boy began moving forward. The short rocky passage dipped sharply downward and he walked carefully to avoid hitting his head on the occasional stony protrusion jutting down from the roof. The torch beam guided him out of the tunnel into another cave.

Directing the torch light upward, he saw that the roof appeared to be higher than in the outer cave. Conscious of the bleak silence, Tom waited, letting the torch shine on the damp, grey walls confronting him. Suddenly the voice came again, the sound emanating from below his right side. He swung the torch down to reveal the apparition of a bearded man laid out on a long stone ledge. The muddy-grey texture of the prostrate figure appeared to blend in with its surroundings, as if it were part of the cave itself.

Tom was again conscious of the rising feeling of dread. He dearly wanted to run, to escape from this macabre place, but, like a rabbit caught in the hypnotic gaze of a snake, he could only stand and wait. Clear, precise words then issued forth from the half-opened mouth of the prone figure.

"Tom, be not afraid, nothing shall harm you. Do you understand?"

The tension slowly evaporated again, leaving the boy with an almost serene calmness.

The voice spoke again. "Now my boy, shine the light high on the wall in front of you."

Tom obeyed.

"A little to the left now." The beam moved over.

"A little higher please."

The boy did as he was asked and almost at once he heard a low gasp.

"You see it, Tom ...you see it?" The voice gasped breathlessly.

Tom saw what appeared to be an object attached to a golden chain lodged high on a stone protrusion.

"Now boy, please fetch it for me."

Approaching the wall, Tom saw the object was hanging about twelve feet up, almost where the wall curved into the roof. The climb, he knew, would not be too difficult, as there were firm hand and footholds everywhere. Tom thought about where to put the torch as he knew he would need two hands to climb the wall. With little time to think he lodged it under his trouser belt, so the beam shone up along and beyond the front of his body, and then began to climb until the suspended object was within his reach.

The voice came again, almost pleading now.

"Please... hurry... the amulet."

Tom's right hand closed over the object, taking it from its ancient perch. He climbed down, retrieved the torch from his belt, aware its light was dying. He quickly took the amulet over to the prostrate figure.

"Now place it around my neck."

Tom hesitated.

"Now boy." the urgency in the voice was unmistakable.

Tom gently lifted the head high enough to ease the amulet down around the neck.

"Now lay the amulet over my chest."

In the fading torchlight, Tom could barely see as he adjusted the star-shaped medallion over the front of the grey body.

"Thank you boy... thank you!"

Tom heard the relief in the voice and wondered if he might soon be free to leave the fearful place.

As he waited, Tom noticed a low pulsating glow radiating from the medallion. He watched in growing amazement as the glow gradually grew brighter until it flood-lit the cave with a rhythmic, blinding intensity. The light then slowly started to wane, fading back to a luminous glimmer.

Tom's attention was now drawn to the grey face, as a pulsing light began emanating from the half-opened eyes. The glow, as with the amulet, gradually increased in brightness. Tom watched in hypnotic fascination as the eyes slowly opened wide, with the ever growing light reaching the same staggering radiance as before. The boy waited... rooted where he stood while gazing down at the strange apparition. Slowly, the light started to fade again and all that remained was a pulsating gleam, regular as a beating heart, in the figure's now wide open eyes.

Stunned, Tom waited. The voice came again, much stronger now, from the lips of the figure by his side. "You may leave, Tom, but do not depart from the cave."

With these words, Tom suddenly felt as if invisible restraints had been lifted from him and without a moment's hesitation he groped his way back through the tunnel towards the welcoming light at the cave entrance.

Tom's desire to flee was strong, but as he reached the entrance something, he knew not what, prevented him from going further. Several times he attempted to escape into the bright daylight, but each time, something in the recesses of his mind commanded him to stay. Finally Tom sat down on the soft bed of bracken, grass and ferns Felicity and he had put together some months ago. The feeling of calmness returned, with the conviction that the man, whoever he was, meant no harm. In the warmth of the early afternoon sun he began dozing off into a fitful sleep.

**   **   **

A gentle nudge on his foot startled Tom from his slumber. He gazed up at the tall figure of a man standing in front of him.

"Tom, it is I, the great Merlin, who kneels before you in gratitude." As he uttered these words, the figure knelt down, clasped Tom's right hand and kissed it. "You have delivered me from a living death, and for that I can never repay you."

The confused boy could only stare, dumbfounded, at the figure kneeling before him and realized that this man was indeed the same lifeless, sombre figure he had left lying in the inner cave. The grey hair and beard were now transformed into a texture as dark and as lustrous as a raven's wing, while glistening eyes as black as coal peered out under thick eyebrows. The aquiline nose, the wide mouth and prominent cheek bones, presented a striking countenance, and yet the facial expression seemed to exude an expression of profound gentleness.

Slowly Merlin rose to his feet, gently pulling Tom up to stand by him. He gazed down at the boy for a few seconds and then smiled. "Take your leave now, Tom, your aunt Kate will be expecting you. Go with the officials. I Merlin will be watching over you."

"But... but how could you know about aunt Kate and... and everything," he stuttered. The bearded figure chuckled. "When the time is right, you will know everything."

Merlin took hold of the boy's hand once more and led him outside. He released his hold on Tom, raised up his arms and gazed skyward. "Ahh, what glory this is!"

The wizard stood silent for some moments, his face and arms raised to the heavens. Then, lowering his arms, he turned again to Tom. "You have given me back my life, Tom, and for that I can never thank you enough. Now go, my boy. From this moment, good fortune will be with you."

Then, as if in an after-thought, the wizard spoke again: "Take heed, Tom. The bicycle you had borrowed will now be returned to its rightful place."

Tom could only stare open-mouthed at the stranger before turning and hurrying away. As he ran from the cave, his mind was reeling. Had the awesome events been nothing more than some hideous nightmare? Had he fallen asleep on the bedding by the cave's entrance and dreamed everything?

The boy glanced back at the cave before it was lost from view. The stony bank could still be seen in the distance and he couldn't help but notice the tall, cloaked figure standing motionless near the cave's entrance. Tom turned and continued his hasty retreat down to the farm. At that precise moment, had he looked skyward, he might just have caught a glimpse of Jamie Sheriden's bike as it flew swiftly in the direction of Macefield.

Merlin waited until Tom had disappeared from view before slowly drinking in the wonderful scene around him. He walked a little way from the cave and sat down on the ground, then lay on his back to gaze up at the white clouds as they scurried along under a breathtaking blue sky. He revelled in the warm embrace of the sun, the gentle summer breeze wafting over his body and the aroma of nature, a bouquet of delightful fragrances, in his nostrils. As he lay there spread-eagled, he thanked God for his deliverance, and offered eternal gratitude to Tom, this boy who had saved him.

However, Merlin's exuberance quickly faded when his thoughts again turned to Salina. Her smile, her touch and even the scent of her still lingered. He recalled the moment he'd asked for her hand in marriage and the joy and delight reflected in those liquid brown eyes as she accepted his proposal. They wanted to keep their relationship secret, for a while at least. Except from the king, for he would need to know. Merlin was more than King Arthur's trusted adviser, he was also his confidante and closest friend, and he knew how hurt Arthur would have been if his betrothal to Salina had been revealed by others. The king had been delighted by the news and, with a smile, asked the wizard why it had taken him this long to find a wife.

Then Merlin's thoughts turned to his stepsister. He was well aware of Niddrym's hatred of him, her deep envy of Salina and of their happiness. He also knew of her evil powers. Why didn't he - the great Merlin - see the danger? Why couldn't he have protected Salina? He found it difficult to grasp that many centuries had passed since she had been taken from him; her lovely face and loving arms nothing more than a glimpse into the distant past... the knowledge was almost too much to bear.

He lay there now, oblivious to the blue skies, oblivious to the tears of grief that tracked down his cheeks.

CHAPTER 5

It was 473AD – the year of Merlin's birth. The Romans had departed the shores of England sixty three years earlier.

The influence of their three hundred and ninety year reign was to be felt for centuries to come, but their departure left a vacuum, and lawlessness was now rife throughout the land. Invasions from the dominions across the sea were on the increase and landfall on the southern and eastern shores of England provoked little resistance from the Romano-Britons, encouraging more alien tribes to follow. Few areas were safe from the marauding bands of heathen warriors anxious to settle in this island haven.

The Saxons, the Angles, the Jutes, the Franks and the fearful Vikings had already over-run the Saxons Shore, including huge tracts of The Wash and East Anglia. The tribes of the more aggressive and ambitious warlords began to make their way into the interior, death and destruction in their wake. Kingdoms emerged with warlords having complete dominion over the defeated populations. The men would be cast into slavery, often shipped back to the big land and sold or exchanged for goods. Most of the women and young children would remain as slaves and chattels of the conquering tribes. Eventually the cities of York and Londinium would become vulnerable. These were troubled times.

**   **   **

Twelve years later…

The boy ran easily through the forest. His brown, lean frame naked, apart from a tattered grey loin cloth tied casually around his waist. He ran without breaking stride, weaving his way through the trees. The morning sun was already high enough to filter through the canopy, its rays, now and then, catching the moving figure, turning his skin to gold.

The youngster came to the edge of a clearing in the forest and made his way over to a large beech tree already exposed to the sun. He hesitated for a moment before leaping up to grasp a sturdy branch with both hands then hoisting himself up; all in one movement. With apelike agility he climbed higher until he reached a heavier limb that splayed out almost horizontally. He swiftly made his way along it with a few short steps then settled down.

The boy sat motionless, as the tree itself. A squirrel darted along the branch and froze for a few seconds, observing the scene, then, with its nose twitching, it leapt on to the youngster's shoulder. The creature began muzzling into his long black hair as its inquisitive nose probed the boy's neck and ear. Strange clicking noises issued from the boy's mouth, causing the squirrel to jerk its head towards the sound before responding in a similar fashion.

Two wood pigeons flew down and perched on a higher branch, disturbing the squirrel. The nervous animal darted away, its bushy tail jerking upward as it went. The pigeons echoed a throaty coo as they sidled along the branch towards the boy's head. The boy mimicked the sound perfectly and within minutes other birds arrived, perching close to him. Now and then one would settle on his shoulder, jostling for space with others attempting to do the same. After a while the boy ignored the activity around him. He sat still, looking at nothing in particular, until a sound from below interrupted his reverie, causing the birds to fly off in disarray.

"Merlin, come down at once, your uncle is angry." The boy gazed down at the woman then slowly and silently began climbing down from his perch.

"You cannot leave your lessons whenever you feel like it. Why do you keep doing it?" said his mother, as he jumped lightly to the ground. Merlin refused to answer as he followed her back towards the village.

**   **   **

"Gwindore, I am at a loss to know what to do with your son," said Cedrin as his sister passed him a mug of hot brew. "He has done this a number of times over the last month or so, despite my warnings and penalties."

"I'm at a loss also, my brother, but I think the new lessons you started him on a few weeks ago might have something to do with it."

"He has to start studying plants and their relationship to medicine, Gwindore. Even with your son's high intelligence it's going to take many years before he is knowledgeable enough to take much of the burden from me." Cedrin paused. "And that's what I have planned for him."

"But it seems such a lot of work he has to do each day. What with his physical exercises, his mental recall of the previous day's lesson, his writings, his calculations and spiritual studies and now medicine, he hardly has any time to himself," protested Gwindore.

"He has all day Sunday to pursue his interests."

"I know! It's why I won't burden him with work around the house, but I never see him all day. He goes off into the forest immediately after he has taken breakfast, and never returns until nightfall," she said, placing hot food bowls on the table.

"We might have to forbid these forest ventures of his." The healer paused, then added: "We don't want him going the same way as his father, do we?"

With that last remark, both remained in silent contemplation as they ate their evening meal.

It was Cedrin who, after wiping his mouth with a cloth, returned to the subject of Merlin: "About your son, have you any better suggestions, my dear sister?"

"I do have one idea, and I think it might work," responded Gwindore.

"And what is that?"

"Well, I was thinking about the falcon."

"What about it?"

"You know how fascinated Merlin is with that bird, I thought maybe you could use it as a way of controlling him."

"Your words are of interest, so please, let me hear more."

"It is true, is it not, that in the past you would take Keetah out every week to hunt up on the ridge. But two winters have come and gone since I've seen that happen. Now, many days will pass before you take the bird out for an evening hunt."

Cedrin nodded. "Yes, that is true, but it's the extra time I've been giving to Merlin with his schooling. What with my normal work, it tires me, and I find I have no desire to walk out on a cold evening with Keetah."

"But that's what I mean... it will do you both good," said Gwindore enthusiastically.

"Please explain yourself, sister."

"Well, why don't you let Merlin do it? He's been out with you often enough, and you know how much he loves that bird. Let him take Keetah out on his own, but only if he attends his lessons each day."

Cedrin hesitated for a few moments, and then smiled fondly at his younger sister. "Sometimes, Gwindore, I don't know what I would do without you."

"Also we are in need of fresh rabbit for the table," said Gwindore, smiling at the compliment. "And I am sure Keetah needs the exercise."

Cedrin nodded. "I cannot understand why I didn't think of it myself. Tomorrow evening we shall go out with Keetah and I will instruct Merlin as best I can. Although, I must confess, he seems to get a better response from that bird than I've ever done."

"It's not surprising," she said, "he seems to have a special way with any creature he meets."

**   **   **

"Can it really be mine, Sire?" asked Merlin excitedly as he took the falcon from the cage.

His uncle had made the proposition more attractive by offering Merlin ownership of the bird.

"Only on the understanding you fully attend your lessons, agreed?"

"Yes, but what if I fall sick?" Merlin responded cheekily.

"You've never had a day's sickness in your life. Now, have we an agreement?"

"Yes Sire, thank you very much," nodded the boy, as he caressed the falcon under its throat. Cedrin noticed the oversized leather glove on the boy's left hand. "Your mother will need to sew another glove to fit you, for Keetah's talons will not hold firmly to that of mine," he warned, as the large bird kept grasping and re-grasping the loose folds of leather.

"Tomorrow, Merlin, you will be free to spend some extra time with your new companion, for I have some ailments to attend to in Heran. I will be gone at sun up. You shall do your exercises, then, if your mother has no need of your services, you can be free for the day." Usually Merlin would have been keen to accompany his uncle to Heran, but on this occasion he could only think of one thing; the delightful prospect of hunting with the falcon.

"Can I take Keetah up on Devil's Ridge, uncle?"

Cedrin was well aware the wide open spaces on the ridge were ideal for Keetah as there was small game everywhere among the huge rocks and boulders in the area.

"You can, Merlin. But make sure you return in good time for your evening meal, otherwise you will not be allowed up there again."

"I will. Thank you uncle," Merlin cried, as he continued to caress the bird's neck with his forefinger.

CHAPTER 6

Tom ran all the way down from Devil's Ridge without stopping. His mind, fully occupied with the awesome events in the cave, failed to notice the strange car parked outside the farm house.

"Oh Tom, we were getting worried about you. We were expecting you almost an hour ago," said Kate, as Tom came into the living room.

"Sorry auntie, I forgot about the time," he said, looking at the two visitors standing up from the couch.

"That's ok, darling, you're here now."

Kate led him over to the couple. "These people are Child Welfare officials, Tom. Your uncle Bill and I have been telling them all about you."

The lady immediately shook Tom's hand. "Hello Tom, my name is Kathleen, but my friends call me Kathy," she said with a wide smile. Tom thought she was quite nice, nothing like he imagined a welfare officer to be.

"And this is Stan, my colleague," she added.

"Hi Tom, nice to meet you," said Stan, shaking the boy's hand.

Stan was tall and thin with greying hair. Tom knew instinctively Kathy was the one in charge, although she looked much younger.

"Tom, I'd like to point out that we work for the NSPCC and represent an organisation called SOCAR. It stands for Services for Older Children at Risk," said Kathy.

The woman paused as if to gauge the boy's response.

"Bit of a mouthful isn't it?" she said, smiling at the boy.

"Yes, it is a bit," he replied, returning the smile.

"It's a fairly new department, principally to give support to older children who might be at risk in one way or another. The Social Welfare or local councils will often refer cases to us and then we try to resolve problems a child might have. Does that make sense to you, Tom?"

"I think so," he said, nodding.

"We have already spoken with your aunt and uncle, so now we'll have a quick chat with you. Then, if you're willing, we'll escort you down to see your stepmother. We'll have a talk with her and see if we can help improve matters between you both. Is that okay with you?"

Tom looked across at his aunt, then back at the official. "Yes, that's okay," he said, mindful of what the man Merlin had said to him outside the cave.

For the next half hour, the two officials made small talk with Tom in the lounge, while aunt Kate busied herself with preparing refreshments for everyone. A little later, Kathy stood up and announced they should be on their way as they were running late.

"Is it possible to wait until Tom's cousin arrives back from school, she will be so upset if she misses him?" Kate asked.

"I'm sorry Mrs Watson, it's gone 2.30 pm and we should have left half an hour ago at the latest. We have to attend a meeting when we get back to head office and before that we have to try to settle Tom in with his stepmother, and we can't hurry that," explained Kathy.

**   **   **

Merlin laid there, his thoughts of Salina pushed aside. He relished the warmth of the sun's embrace. How good it felt to be alive again, to be part of nature's world once more. Suddenly a practical thought broke his reverie. He was free from Niddrym's curse, free from the dark, dismal cave, but where was he to sleep tonight? Who in this strange world could he turn to for shelter?

During those long weeks of lying fully conscious in the cave he had managed to make psychic contact with two people; the only receptors of his daily telepathic searching. After weeks of communication he had come to know something about them. There was Emile; his signals were by far the strongest, and there were the weaker signals from someone who named himself Andrew. There had been others, but their signals had been far too weak to decipher. During these bouts of thought transference both men were trying to understand and accept Merlin's extraordinary situation, but they were distant strangers, unsure of his messages, wondering whether it was all some sort of clever psychic hoax.

The wizard recalled the various images and the recurring sequence of numbers that arose whenever he focused on these spiritual exchanges. The strange numbers had always puzzled him. The digits had been logged in his brain, but what did they mean? It then dawned on the wizard they must be the key to whatever it was Emile and Andrew had been attempting to say.

The dilemma made him think again about Tom. At this moment there was not a soul in this strange world that could help, apart from the boy. If only he had asked Tom about the numbers while he had the chance, but his euphoria on being freed from the cave had denied him rational thought. He now had to think quickly. His plan to let Tom return to his stepmother would have to be aborted because, once again, Merlin desperately needed the boy's help.

The wizard began to bend his mind to finding Tom. Images were hazy at first, but soon he saw Tom standing by a car. Merlin had become familiar with these incredible fast-moving objects for he had travelled in the one owned by Tom's relatives a number of times during his spiritual excursions to the town of Saltridge.

Standing close to Tom, he recognized the boy's uncle and aunt, but there were two others nearby, a young woman and an older man, who, Merlin guessed, were the officials waiting to take Tom back to his stepmother. Merlin needed to act fast. The amulet gave him the power of transmutation, the ability to change into another substance at will. It allowed him to disappear and physically re-appear wherever his spirit decreed. The wizard stood up and with arms outstretched he began to focus all thought into one powerful beam of concentration.

The unseen visitor arrived to see Tom and his uncle playfully sparing with each other. He observed the woman he had got to know as Kate say something to the boy before embracing him. The young female official had already opened the back door of the car and after another goodbye wave to his relatives Tom climbed into the back seat. The wizard seized his chance. Moments later they were cruising slowly down the driveway of Long Acre Farm.

Tom sat silently and gazed out of the window at the passing scenery and replayed the events by the cave in his mind; the strange man kneeling in front of him and kissing his hand. The words 'I Merlin, will be watching over you' rang in his brain, giving Tom a strange, settled feeling.

The woman, Kathy, would occasionally turn in the front seat to chat with her young charge and Tom would respond cheerfully. He still regretted having to leave Long Acre farm, and he certainly wasn't looking forward to returning to his stepmother, but he seemed strangely unconcerned by the thought.

They were about twenty miles away from Macefield when Stan told Kathy they were getting very low on fuel.

"I thought you'd filled up yesterday afternoon."

"I did, and I checked the gauge when we left the farm. It was showing over three quarters full, and we've only done forty miles since then," he said, shaking his head in bewilderment.

"Well, we'd better not risk going much further. Is there a petrol station close by?"

"Yes, there's one in Meridale, a little further on. But I still don't understand it," continued Stan, shaking his head again. As they drew into the petrol station, Kathy turned and asked Tom if he would like to stretch his legs and buy an ice cream. The boy, for some unfathomable reason, shook his head, saying he preferred to stay in the car.

After filling the tank, Stan spoke to Kathy, who remained sitting in the car. "Well, that's weird; tank took only eighteen litres... must be a fault in the gauge."

"Better to be safe than sorry," answered Kathy, as she alighted from the car.

As Stan went off to pay for the fuel, Kathy turned once again to Tom. "Sure there's nothing you want, Tom?"

The boy shook his head. "No thanks," he murmured.

"Well, I have to duck to the ladies, I won't be long."

Tom watched Kathy disappear into the building. He continued to gaze out of the window when suddenly movements at his side made him turn in his seat. To his amazement he found Merlin sitting there.

"I need you to come with me, Tom," said Merlin, smiling at the boy, who could only stare open- mouthed at the cloaked figure.

"Come Tom, quickly now," said the wizard, opening the door that faced the main street. Without further hesitation, Tom grabbed his backpack and followed Merlin as he made his way out of the service station. The wizard glanced back briefly to make sure the boy was following, then turned quickly into the busy high street.

CHAPTER 7

Did you see that?" said Chrissie to her companion who had just slid back into the driver's seat.

"See what?" said Mark, passing her a ham and salad roll.

"A strange bearded guy in a grey cloak and a boy got out of that green car, the one at the number five pump.

"Strange things happen," replied Mark, munching on his giant hamburger unconcerned.

"Hmm, but it was the way he did it; looking around to see if the kid was following him," said Chrissie. "They weren't holding hands or anything, they just hurried away without waiting for the boy's parents to return. You have to admit that's a bit weird!"

Mark didn't answer.

"Anyway, it's only a hunch, but I want to see where they've gone," said the attractive, blonde reporter as she opened her door.

"You and your hunches, Chrissie! Look, it's been a hectic week and I'm looking forward to knocking off and 'aving a beer," protested Mark.

"Be a sweetie and wait for me, I won't be long," said Chrissie, throwing him a kiss before hurrying off.

As soon as Chrissie turned into the street, she realised how difficult it was going to be to find the pair. She knew they had turned left into the high street, but the thoroughfare was busy with people because it was market day in the town. She hurried down the street as fast as she could, but after a few minutes she gave up and headed back to the petrol station.

'Ah, well,' thought Chrissie, 'maybe just granddad taking the kid for some last-minute shopping.'

Arriving back, Chrissie immediately noticed the tall, thin frame of Mark as he stood talking to the worried looking young woman and the older man by her side. Mark introduced them to Chrissie, explaining they were child welfare officers.

"Please, did you see them?" implored Kathy, nervously brushing wayward strands of dark hair from her face.

"No, I'm afraid not," said Chrissie. "Incidentally, has Mark told you we work for the Saltridge Echo?"

"No, he hasn't" said Kathy, warily. The last thing she wanted right now were reporters breathing down her neck.

"I have to report this to my superior, so can you give me anything more than your colleague has given us?" continued Kathy. "Stan's on the phone trying to reach her right now."

Chrissie shook her head and glanced over at the male official talking rapidly on the phone.

She smelt a story.

"Who was the bearded man in the cloak?" asked Chrissie.

"Your friend has asked me that and I don't know of any bearded man."

"But he was in your car because we watched him getting out."

"I'm sorry, I don't know what you're talking about. There were only three of us in the car, Stan, my assistant, the boy Tom and myself."

"But I definitely saw… "

"Please," interrupted the woman, "I cannot discuss this until I've spoken with my boss."

"Have you contacted the police?" The reporter persisted.

"Head Office will be seeing to that after I've spoken to them," replied Kathy, just as Stan passed her the phone.

Mark broke into Chrissie's thoughts. "We have to go Chrissie; they want us to move the car."

"Well… find a parking spot nearby," retorted Chrissie, who was trying to eavesdrop on Kathy's conversation.

"Robbo is expecting your report with photos before five; he wants it in tomorrow's edition. You know how he is, Chrissie."

"I'll speak to Robbo. You just park the car, there's a darling."

Mark raised his eyes, shrugged his shoulders and walked towards the car. He loved working with Chrissie rather than any of the other reporters, but boy, she could be as stubborn as a mule when she wanted to be. He was also aware, as were the rest of the staff at Saltridge Echo, that she was an outstanding reporter and could twist the Editor-in-Chief around her little finger.

As soon as Kathy was off the phone Chrissie pounced. "Well, can you give us some background, Kathy?"

The welfare official looked resignedly at the reporter. "My boss says as you are on the scene already and witnessed everything, I should give you the basics. She says you'll get details from the police anyway, as they will want the boy's picture circulated in the papers as soon as possible."

"So no-one has any idea who the bearded man is?" questioned Chrissie.

"That's correct," said Kathy, making her way to the car.

"What's the boy's name, and who are his relatives?"

"The boy's name is Tom Watson and we were escorting him back to his stepmother in Macefield; that's all I can give you, Miss...?"

"It's Chrissie Flowers... but at least give me the name of his stepmother, if nothing else."

"Sorry, Miss Flowers, we need to see her before anyone interviews her... department policy." With that, Kathy climbed into the front seat, nodded to her partner, who immediately engaged gear and began driving away.

Chrissie quickly looked around for Mark and spotted him leaning against the bonnet of the car parked on a loading bay on the far side of the fuel station. She ran over to him.

"Mark, get your arse in gear and follow their car," she commanded while opening the door and throwing herself into the passenger seat.

The photographer, knowing it was useless to argue, quickly took his seat and drove out of the court.

"It's that green jobbie..."

"I know what the car looks like Chrissie... and it's not a jobbie, it's a Toyota Corolla."

"Whatever...but hurry."

Luckily, red traffic lights at a nearby intersection had held up the officials' car, giving Mark the chance to catch up with the Corolla sitting just three vehicles ahead.

"Why are we doing this, Chrissie? Just gimme a clue," said Mark, in an exasperated tone.

"Kathy said she was on her way to see the boy's stepmother in Macefield, and I want to find out where the woman lives."

"But this might take ages, Chrissie. Macefield's about an hour's drive from here."

"I know that, Mark, but we'll only stay to see Kathy visit the place, then we'll take off."

"It'll be well after five before we get back to the office, Chrissie, and Robbo will hopping mad," said Mark, who was more concerned about losing drinking time at his local.

"Don't worry your pretty little head about the boss, Mark. I'll sort it."

Smiling at her photographer, Chrissie got on to the phone to the editor-in-chief. She listened quietly for a few moments, raising exasperated eyes to the heavens.

The lights had now turned green and Mark was comfortably keeping tabs on the green Corolla just a little way ahead.

"Yes, boss," Chrissie replied, at last getting a word in. "I realise we won't be back 'til well after five, but it can't be helped. You've always said to me, if you stumble on to something, follow your gut instinct - and prioritize... remember?"

Mark glanced at the woman. Chrissie seemed to have a way of making Robbo agree to almost anything she put to him, he thought admiringly.

She briefly outlined the situation to her editor. Mark listened and realised Chrissie had talked him around when she said: "Ok boss, we'll see you tomorrow. Have a good evening."

Chrissie snapped her phone shut and winked at Mark. He returned her smile, gave a shrug and continued to follow the green vehicle just a little way ahead.

When they reached Macefield they parked up in a tree-lined street and watched Kathy approach a house they presumed was where Tom's stepmother lived.

Chrissie wrote down the name of the street and house number before giving Mark the okay to drive back to Saltridge.

"Mark, be a darling, as soon as we get back to town, drive me around to the police station. My man Ross is on duty. I'll only be about ten minutes at the most."

Mark frowned at the thought of having to spend yet more time away from his local.

"Can't you do that tomorrow, Chrissie?" implored Mark.

"Would love to, but Ross might be off duty then, and he's the only one I can rely on for all the right info."

Chrissie glanced at Mark, who remained silent. "Pleeeeze, sweetie pie, drinks are on me tonight and I'll organise half a day off for you with the boss... okay?"

Mark nodded and gave her a rueful smile. He had the feeling he'd probably walk over red hot coals if she asked him nicely enough.

CHAPTER 8

Merlin waited until Tom had caught up with him.

"Just walk a few paces behind me," murmured the wizard as he followed a group of pedestrians dressed in old-fashioned regalia. Today was the last Friday of the month when the weekly market day in Meridale had a Victorian theme. Shopkeepers and stallholders, along with many of the locals, embraced the Victorian image with enthusiasm. It all helped to improve trade. It was also of great benefit to Merlin for his cloaked figure drew nothing but amused comments from the passers-by.

The pair walked until they had left the outskirts of the town behind. The wizard suddenly turned into a country lane and stopped by a wooden gate, waiting for Tom to catch up.

He gazed over at the fields as he spoke. "Tom, I took you from the car and brought you here so we can talk without disturbance." He looked down at the boy for a moment and then began to explain about his psychic connection with Emile and Andrew, the vague messages he had received and the sequence of numbers that had continued to puzzle him.

"So you see, Tom, I desperately need to make contact with these people and I think these numbers might explain something. My only hope is you might have some knowledge of what they mean." Merlin recited the numbers out loud and Tom quickly realised they sounded very much like a telephone number. As he tried to explain this to the wizard, Merlin got even more confused until Tom enlightened him about telephones.

"Where can we find one of these telephones?"

"There might be one back there," said Tom, pointing back to Meridale.

"Is there nowhere else?" asked Merlin, not wishing to take Tom back to the town.

The boy thought for a moment. "Well, my aunt and uncle have a telephone at their house, but we're too far away from there now."

"Then we shall return, Tom, and you shall ask them if we can use their telephone. I will also need to explain to your relatives my reason for taking you from the authorities."

"But how are we going to get there?" asked Tom.

The wizard scanned the area until his gaze came to rest on a small stand of conifers in the field beyond the fence.

"I will show you. Come," he said, leaping over the gate.

Tom, totally bemused, followed the wizard as he made his way over to the copse.

As soon as they were among the trees, Merlin stopped. "We shall leave from here, Tom, away from curious eyes."

"But... but how?" questioned Tom, more perplexed than ever.

"You are about to find out. Now hold both my hands tightly and do not release your grip."

Tom firmly grasped the wizard's long fingers.

"Close your eyes, Tom, and keep them closed until I tell you to open them."

Tom did as instructed, wondering with trepidation what was about to happen.

Suddenly a strange feeling of pins and needles began coursing through his body. He began to tremble uncontrollably until every part of his being seemed to vibrate. Gradually the tremors faded to a state of complete stillness. Merlin's voice broke the silence: "You may open your eyes now, Tom."

Tom did so and could hardly believe what confronted him. They were back on Devil's Ridge! He looked beyond the tall figure of Merlin and saw, with astonishment, the cave a mere ten feet away.

"How did you do that?" exclaimed Tom, still looking around in wonderment.

Merlin ignored the question and beckoned Tom to sit next to him on a grassy bank nearby.

"Tom, my boy, I think you deserve to know why I came to be entombed in this cave."

The wizard began to tell him in his slow, deliberate manner about the lovely Salina and their plans to marry, about Niddrym and how she tricked him into believing she was the woman he loved. Tom listened attentively as Merlin described the events of that terrible evening, the spell Niddrym had cast upon him and the conditions that would break it.

Merlin smiled at Tom. "Many, many years were to pass before God intervened and brought you to me. It was your loud cry in the cave that awakened me. It was many weeks ago... do you remember?"

Tom nodded, remembering what had happened that Easter weekend.

"Well, the rest you know, Tom. If you had not arrived at the cave, retrieved the precious amulet and placed it around my neck, I would still be lying in that accursed place."

Merlin pointed to the cave. "Just to think I would have been lying there for eternity, fully awake, but unable to move a muscle. Can you imagine such a fate, Tom?" Tom shook his head, shuddering at the thought. The wizard's silent gaze continued to rest on the cave entrance for some moments, before turning to his young companion once more.

"Niddrym also took possession of my staff." He spoke slowly and softly, his voice tinged with sadness and remorse. "The staff was presented to me during my last visit to the New World. It was made clear to me that no other being should be allowed to possess it, for the staff gave protection to the holder. But I was guilty of entrusting another with its divine force."

Merlin hesitated again as if groping for the right words. "As I was sinking into oblivion, she said something about the staff, but I was fighting desperately to stay awake and could not understand what she was saying. It is all in the distant past now, but..." The wizard's words suddenly tailed off. It seemed as if he was in deep thought.

Tom wanted to say: "But what?' Instead, he said: "Where is the New World?"

"The New World!" Merlin exclaimed, almost forgetting he had mentioned it. "Arkatra! Now that is a world for you to see my boy. Apart from the High Priests of the Inner Circle, no other druid priest journeyed there more than once. I, Merlin, was permitted there on two occasions."

Merlin sat still, quietly surveying his surroundings. "If I ever return to Arkatra, Tom, you shall accompany me, I promise."

The wizard gazed at the sky and slowly spread his arms as if to embrace the heavens. He remained in this pose for some moments before turning back to his young companion.

"After you awakened me well over three months ago – one hundred and seven days ago, to be exact – I was fully conscious

49

but I could not move. I tried with every fibre of my being, but even the enormous will-power of Merlin was rendered useless. I felt no physical discomfort, no hunger; I could feel nothing although my brain was functioning perfectly. Do you understand what I am saying, Tom?"

"Yes, I think so," he replied.

"But this situation allowed me to concentrate completely on the transmission of thought, and my first duty was to make spiritual contact with you. It enabled me to instill in you the desire to return to the cave. Did you not see images of the cave many times in your mind since the day you first discovered me?"

Tom nodded, remembering a day hadn't passed without the image of the cave and the urge to return to it constantly intruding upon his thoughts.

"Lying there in that dismal cave, unable to move, the only tool at my disposal was the power of my mind. I used this power to acquire insight into your world through spiritual transmission and mind travel."

Merlin saw the puzzled expression on Tom's face. "Think of it, Tom, you can rise up from where you are sitting and walk down to the house of your relatives. People in your world can go anywhere they desire, not just by walking but by riding in these wonderful things I have got to know as cars, or by travelling through the air inside incredible flying machines, or by sailing across the great seas in ships of unimaginable size. Well, this can also be achieved in a spiritual sense. Merlin can use the incredible force of the mind to take him wherever he wishes to go. It was my ability to undertake these mind journeys, to extricate myself from the deathly atmosphere of the cave, that kept me sane during these past three long months."

Tom nodded. "Are these journeys you go on like being in a dream?"

"Not really, you see with mind travel you go to real places and witness real things."

The wizard plucked a leaf from a weed that grew close by. He studied it for some moments, turning it slowly in his slender fingers. He rubbed it between thumb and forefinger and let the residue fall to the ground. Putting the thumb and finger to his nose, he reveled in the scent, closing his eyes for a moment or two.

"When you left me earlier today," he resumed, "I laid myself down on the wonderful, warm, sweet smelling ground and let my mind and body revel in my freedom and in the wonders of nature surrounding me. I recited the druid's prayer of thankfulness to our Goddess and offered up my eternal gratitude for this gift of life; a gift that allowed me, once again, to become part of Mother Nature's world... But enough of that for now, for there are other things I wish to make clear to you. Have you ever wondered how I have become familiar with your world and your language?"

"Yes, a little," Tom replied, intrigued.

Merlin began to explain how, in spirit, he had spent time with Tom's aunt and uncle. He described in his slow, purposeful manner, the terrifying experience of travelling in their car as an unseen passenger. Of the vast multitude of cars speeding towards them like shiny, multi-coloured monsters with large round glassy eyes. "There were times," said Merlin, "when the sheer terror of it caused me to retreat back to the safety of the cave. But I gradually became accustomed to all these astonishing contraptions and all the many other strange and wonderful sights of your world.

"One day, while in the town, I accompanied your aunt into a large building, that was named a library; a place that stores a great number of books. From that moment I would spend much of my time there, looking at open books and newspapers or reading over someone's shoulder. Sometimes, when the place was free of people I would spend hours studying; such a joy!"

Merlin turned his attention to a clump of wild flowers nearby. He wandered over and stooped down to pluck a couple from the centre of the bunch. Returning to sit next to Tom, he inspected the plant.

"You must understand this, Tom, once the Romans had left our shores, the populace began again to speak in the Celtic tongue. But we of the Inner Circle continued to keep the Roman language alive. My fluency in this tongue has been of great benefit to me for many of your words are of Latin origin.

"I have been trained since early childhood to accurately memorize words. My uncle, who was a respected seer and a high druid, was my first tutor and he taught me well. It was his druidic belief that the brain should be taught to memorize information at the earliest age possible. He believed that the young mind was like a sponge, capable of high levels of concentration, and that stretching the mental capabilities of the young would result in greater brain development in the adult.

"I was but three years of age at the start of my tuition. My uncle would dictate just a few simple words at first, and I would then be required to repeat them accurately. Later, my first exercise of the day would be to repeat, word for word, a short lesson I had learnt the previous day. As time went on my uncle would add more words for me to memorize and then recite accurately the following day. By the time I was your age, Tom, I could recall volumes of information as easily as memorizing a single sentence, and this included the study of numbers or learning an alien tongue. It was the druid way. So you see it wasn't difficult for Merlin to quickly understand and speak your language.

"There are so many strange and incredible things in your world, so much to understand! I discovered the wonder of calculating time. I analysed dates shown on your calendars and was soon to learn the world I found myself in was of the 21st century. It was some time before I could accept the awful truth, that the last conscious day in my world was one thousand five hundred and twenty six years ago. Think of it, Tom, I've been incarcerated in that awful place for all that time!"

Merlin gazed skyward for a few moments before looking down again at his young saviour. "There is much about this strange world I find difficult to understand, but one thing is certain; you, my boy, have given me the gift of life, and for that I can never repay you."

The wizard's tone changed. "It is now my duty to accompany you down to your aunt and uncle for they will be worried about you. It is also my duty to explain to them who I am and why I have taken you from the officials."

They were about to start walking when Merlin hesitated. "Tom, I think I should change my appearance to something more suitable to your world. What do you think?"

Tom could only shrug, not really fully understanding the wizard's meaning.

"Wait here, my boy. Do not be concerned by what you see, and please remain silent until I speak to you again."

With those words the wizard walked a few paces away. He stood quite still for some moments and then slowly lifted his arms to a crucifix pose with palms facing upward.

Tom became aware of a misty vapour gradually enveloping the motionless body, then watched in awe as the figure of Merlin started to fracture into countless jagged pieces that vibrated rapidly before breaking into tinier fragments, finally dissolving into a nebulous mass. Spellbound, Tom watched as the pieces began to re-appear, jostling against one another before binding themselves together once more into a human form. Eventually the shimmering ceased and the boy began to detect movement within the maelstrom. Moments later a body emerged from the dissipating haze.

The figure was wearing a brown casual jacket with light beige twill trousers and on his feet were a pair of light brown shoes. The white, casual shirt emphasized the brown neck of the wearer and the gold chain holding the star-shaped amulet across his chest.

The man walked over to Tom: "Well, my boy, what do you think? I saw a picture of a man wearing clothes like these in a magazine. I thought this attire would sit well on me. What is your opinion, my boy?"

Tom could only stare dumbfounded at the figure standing before him. "But… but how did you do that?"

"Manipulation of matter with the power of the mind, my boy," said the man smiling down on Tom.

Merlin's thick dark hair was now swept back in a modern style to reveal a broad forehead. The face, previously hidden by a full dark beard, was exposed, showing high cheek bones, a strong chin and wide mouth while the slightly hooked nose gave the face a hawkish, magnetic appearance.

The familiar slow, resonant voice and the piercing dark eyes gazing out under thick eyebrows reassured the young observer that this was indeed the same Merlin.

"What do you think, Tom, do the garments look well on me?"

"Er, yes sir… they look…very well," stuttered Tom.

"That's good enough for me. Come, Tom, it is now time to see your relatives."

Tom led the way down to the farmhouse. The afternoon was still quite hot and the air was as humid as it had been for the past few days. Merlin, finding it too warm for comfort, took off his jacket and slung it across his shoulder. As they walked the wizard reveled in the beauty of everything around him. He breathed in the scents of the countryside, marveled at the blue sky and felt content. He was sure somehow, somewhere, someone was watching over him.

They were about three hundred yards from the farmhouse when Sam the dog spotted the two figures coming down the hill. With ears upright the dog stood quite still for a few seconds, until it recognised the familiar figure of Tom. It ran toward the boy, barking excitedly. The dog had almost reached the pair when it stopped in its tracks; its eagerness to reach Tom suddenly dissolved as it caught sight of the stranger walking a little way behind.

Sam started a low growl, as he always did at the sight of a stranger, and began to turn away, when Merlin called out to the dog with strange sounds. The dog stopped in its tracks, turned and looked at the wizard. Merlin crouched, repeating the strange sound two or three times. Sam, with tail slowly wagging, walked hesitantly up to the stooped figure as Merlin, still emitting the unusual noise, held out the back of his hand. Tom gazed in wonder at the sight of Sam licking the extended hand before slowly lying down on his back at the wizard's feet to have his belly rubbed.

"How did you do that?" asked Tom. "He hates strangers."

"Simply communicate in their language, my boy," replied Merlin, looking up at the incredulous youngster.

The wizard fondled the dog's ears for a moment then stood up. "Come Tom, go and see your people. I will wait close by."

CHAPTER 9

Gwindore got up from the table as Cedrin walked in. "You are so late, have you some troubles, Cedrin?"

"Some," replied Cedrin, seating himself down at the large table.

Gwindore passed him a tumbler of ale. "Drink and relax while I prepare your supper."

The healer drank readily being quite thirsty from the heat of the mid-July sun.

"Is Merlin abed?" he asked.

"He is. He has a black eye and cuts and abrasions all over him. I'm sure he's been in a fight, but he tells me he fell out of a tree."

Cedrin took another drink, relishing the broth and the cool interior of the stone-clad dwelling. "He was in a fight, Gwindore, but it was not of his making."

"Was it that Jonas and his gang?"

"It was, I'm afraid."

Cedrin poured more ale into the tumbler from the stoneware jug Gwindore had placed on the table.

"Why didn't he run into the forest as he's always done, he knows they will not follow him there."

"It was not possible this time, Gwindore, for they had surrounded him."

"You speak as if you were there, my brother?"

Cedrin sighed, knowing he would have to explain everything to his sister.

"Yes, I saw everything, but I kept myself hidden."

"But why didn't you stop them, Cedrin? They would have run like frightened deer if they had seen you."

"Gwindore, come and sit here." Cedrin patted the space beside him, before taking another drink from the tumbler. He took hold of his young sister's hand. "You remember the time when you saw Merlin with that bowl of hot gruel, and you swore to me you hadn't given it to him?"

"I will never forget... and when I told you he must have spirited the bowl from the window ledge on to his eating tray, you said I must have imagined it," said Gwindore accusatively.

"I know, but I thought it impossible that a three year old could have that sort of mental ability. The concentration required to levitate the bowl would have been beyond most adults' capacity, let alone directing it on to his eating tray. It must have been at least five paces from the window ledge to his seat, Gwindore, so you must forgive me for doubting you."

"I have always understood the reasons for your doubts, my brother," said Gwindore, rising from the table to fetch Cedrin's heated meal from the fire hob.

She returned to her seat before speaking again. "I have sometimes questioned myself about what really happened... had I placed the gruel on his tray without thinking? Yet even now, to this very day, I still believe I would not have broken the habit of putting the bowl on the high window ledge to cool."

"We know the boy has incredible powers, Gwindore, I have been witness to them on many occasions, but he has never demonstrated his ability to move objects..."

"But if you remember, the hot gruel burnt his mouth quite badly," interrupted his sister, "and I believe his subconscious told him it was punishment for doing what he did, and he's never attempted it since."

"You never let me finish, my dear. I was about to say, he has never proved to me he has the mental ability to move objects... until this afternoon."

Gwindore looked puzzled.

"It was the fight, my sister. I was on my way home after attending to old Clem's hand injury, when I rounded a bend on the track and saw Merlin some fifty paces ahead. Big Jonas was saying something to the boy and prodding him with his finger. There were about five other boys who started to surround Merlin, and then they began pushing him against each other.

"I started to hurry toward them and was about twenty paces away when I saw Merlin go down from a punch by Jonas. It was as if it was a signal to the others, for they all started attacking him now. I was just about to shout out when everything happened so quickly.

"One of the boys was thrown up into the air and landed almost at my feet, a good twelve to fifteen paces away from the fight. Then another two were catapulted out, luckily both landing in nearby bushes. Another shot off like an arrow from an archer's bow and he landed on the lower branches of a tree, hitting his head quite badly. Almost at the same time I heard a scream and saw another boy roll away, scramble to his feet and run, holding what appeared to be a dislocated arm.

"By this time I had hidden myself behind a tree, as I was intrigued by what was happening and needed to observe Merlin undetected, while he was in this aggressive mood. But it was the way he dealt with Jonas; it was something to behold, I can assure you. I watched as your son sprung up from the ground and stood waiting for the big youth to get to his feet."

Cedrin took another sip of ale before continuing. "Jonas stood up and looked around as if wondering where all his friends had gone. He looked at Merlin with great fear and immediately began to run away. Your son pointed his finger at the running figure and Jonas instantly froze in his tracks. Merlin then strolled up to the statue-like figure, faced him and then with his forefinger, pushed poor Jonas to the ground. Jonas let out a scream as his unprotected head hit the ground. He lay there for a few moments sobbing and pleading with Merlin to let him go. He was allowed to get to his feet, and then took off again like a scared rabbit. But, as before, Merlin's outstretched arm and pointed finger froze the big youth in an instant. I watched as he casually strolled up to the sobbing Jonas, but before he could do anything more, I revealed myself and called out to them.

"My nephew looked in my direction and Jonas immediately came to life. He took off like a deer in flight, blubbing like a baby as he ran. As for Merlin, he just stared at me for a moment or two then disappeared into the forest without a word."

"Oh, those poor boys! How do they fare now?" said Gwindore.

"Two of them were, I believe, unharmed apart from minor bruises. I managed to help the boy who had landed in the tree, but he seemed disoriented, so I escorted him to his home and spoke with his mother. Then I called at Callan's farm to tend the boy with the dislocated arm. Luckily I had strappings in my bag so was able to attend to his ailments. I suspect the lad Marios, who ended up in the tree, may have a cracked rib, but time alone will heal that. As for Jonas, the way he ran from Merlin would indicate that nothing was amiss with him, apart from his hurt pride."

"I suppose now they will avoid Merlin, just when I hoped he might start making friends," said Gwindore. "He mixes with his animals in the forest, and Keetah of course, but I would feel pleased to see him make friends with one or two of the boys from the village."

She pointed to Cedrin's plate. "Eat your food, my brother, before it cools again."

Cedrin sampled his food and took another drink before speaking again.

"I don't agree, sister, I think there is a greater chance he will make some friends now he has humbled Jonas. Most of the boys disliked Jonas, but were frightened of him. His bullying presence discouraged them from becoming friends with Merlin.

"I noticed other boys gathering around after the fight, so the tale about how Jonas ran away from Merlin crying like a baby will spread around the village faster than a forest fire. From now on I think most of the lads will be more than keen to have Merlin as a friend. The trouble, I think, will be getting your son to accept them as readily as he does the creatures of the forest."

"I suppose time will tell," observed Gwindore.

Cedrin finished eating in silence. Then, pushing his plate away, he took hold of his sister's hand once more. "After seeing my nephew's unbelievable display of power, there is no doubt in my mind that he did indeed spirit that bowl of gruel from the window ledge to his tray and I would ask your forgiveness for having doubted you all these years."

"I forgive you with humility, my brother."

"But now, Gwindore, I have to re-think your son's training regime. The Saxons are attacking our towns and villages to the south, slaughtering many of our people, including our priests. They are burning our churches and forcing their heathen ways on our people. The worrying thing is, my dear, they are getting closer to our door."

"But how should this affect Merlin? He is but a child of fifteen years."

"He needs to know how to fight with the sword sooner rather than later. It is his wish also, Gwindore. I had planned to start his sword handling disciplines on his sixteenth birthday, but time is too short. I believe he is now physically capable of handling both the heavy broad sword and the short sword. I will visit Artor in Londinium to try and arrange the services of one of his retired swordsmen.

"I suppose this will mark the end of my son's childhood, will it not," said Gwindore quietly.

"I am afraid it will, my sister."

CHAPTER 10

"Oh Tom, we have been so worried about you. We've had all the news from your stepmother. What made you leave the car with this strange man?" said Kate, embracing her nephew at the door.

Bill came out of the lounge, meeting Tom in the short passageway to the kitchen.

"Hello Tom, you old scallywag, what have you been up to now?" he said, roughing the boy's hair.

Kate escorted her nephew into the kitchen and sat him down at the table before going to the fridge to pour him a lemon drink. She unwrapped some cheese scones and placed them on a plate in front of him. As usual, the first thing Kate concerned herself with was her nephew's stomach.

"You must be hungry, my darling, but dinner's not far away so don't eat too much. I can make more salad and there's ham, boiled eggs and quiche in the fridge."

"Where's Fliss?" said Tom, dismissing the thought of food.

"She's staying over at Ruth's place," Kate said, as she and her husband exchanged worried glances over the boy's head.

"Who is this bearded man in a cloak who was seen leaving with you at the petrol station?" queried Bill.

"His name is... is Merlin," said Tom, hesitantly.

"Merlin, is that his last name or what?"

"It's … it's just what he calls himself."

"Like the wizard?" Bill pursued.

"He…. he is the wizard," Tom muttered softly.

"That's poppycock, Tom."

"Bill, please!" admonished Kate. She placed an arm around her nephew's shoulders. "How did you meet him, Tom?"

The boy told them about the cave he and Fliss had discovered at Easter, and how he had re-visited the cave again only that morning. He then described the events in the cave and his meeting with the wizard.

"But that's preposterous," cried Bill, "there's no such thing as a wizard and Merlin is nothing more than a legend in the tales of King Arthur."

Kate, seeing her nephew was getting upset, frowned and shook her head at her husband. Tom sat there fingering his empty glass, not knowing what else to say.

Bill sat down and placed a comforting arm around his nephew's shoulder. "Come on Tom, it's not like you to carry on like this. So tell me, where's this Merlin person now?"

"He's... he's waiting outside," said Tom, looking down at his hands. Bill got up and went to the kitchen window that overlooked the drive. "You mean him?" he said, looking at the man leaning on the baler. "But he looks nothing like... like...Oh, I can't believe what I'm seeing!"

"What is it, Bill?" said Kate.

"It's Sam! He's lying down at that chap's feet. You know what he's like with strangers. I just can't believe it!"

Kate came over and peered out of the window. "Oh my God, that's amazing!"

Sam always avoided strangers like the plague. Even friends who stayed for a few days found it difficult to get close to the dog. Bill and Kate knew the reason. Sam was a pup when it happened. A man had come to the farm to see the old tractor Bill had advertised for sale. Bill was away at the time, so Kate showed the man the tractor, then left him to inspect it at his leisure.

It was Felicity who saw the man, about to get back into his truck, viciously kick out at the dog, hitting it hard in the stomach. The man drove off, never to be seen again, leaving a distraught young girl leaning over the puppy as it lay yelping in the driveway. The vet treated Sam, and within a few weeks the broken ribs healed, but the dog never ever forgot.

"They said you were seen leaving with a cloaked, bearded man. This guy doesn't look anything like that," said Bill, still observing the stranger.

"It's him, uncle, it's because he's... he's changed his clothes... and things."

"Well, if Sam can take to him that quick, Bill, he must be okay. Don't you think we should at least invite him in?" suggested Kate.

"Good idea! At least we might get some idea what this is all about."

"I think we'll see him in the lounge, its cooler there," said Kate.

Bill called out to Merlin from the front door, inviting him over. He watched as the stranger approached, closely followed by Sam, causing Bill to give a slight shake of his head in bemusement at the dog's unusual behaviour.

"Kate, this is er... Merlin," he said, on entering the lounge.

Kate took the proffered hand of the tall stranger, noting the firm handshake. "You seem to have a way with dogs, seeing how Sam has taken to you."

"I have an understanding with all creatures, Mrs Watson," said Merlin, with simple candor.

Kate couldn't help but be impressed by the man in front of her. He was strangely attractive and she guessed his age to be around fifty. But it was the gentleness that seemed to exude from him that drew her notice. Kate's first impressions of people had always been reliable and something told her this was a kind man. She remembered how she had taken an instant dislike to Cynthia when first introduced and her behaviour since becoming Tom's stepmother had confirmed her opinion.

Merlin gazed in awe around the room he had just entered, trying to take in everything from the chandelier on the ceiling to the patterned carpet. He had visited the Watson's lounge on a number of occasions during his mind travels, but then everything had appeared somewhat hazy, not nearly as clear and as sharply defined as now.

Kate invited the man to be seated.

"Now, who are you sir, and what is all this poppycock about?" said Bill abruptly as soon as the stranger was seated.

"I do not understand the word... poppycock," said Merlin in his slow, precise manner.

Kate and Bill exchanged glances.

"We understand you helped Tom abscond from the child welfare officials," said Kate, seating herself opposite the visitor.

"What does abscond mean?" The wizard asked again.

"That you encouraged Tom to leave the car and run away from the officials."

"That is correct," said Merlin.

"But it is against the law…don't you realise that?" prompted Bill.

"I am aware of that, Mr Watson."

"The boy is only twelve and he is under the guardianship of his stepmother. What you did is illegal and tantamount to kidnapping. Do you understand this?" said Bill, sternly.

"I understand your laws and I understand your concern for the boy. But should Tom be present while we discuss this?"

Bill looked over at his wife.

"Tom, would you mind going outside while we speak to this man?" said Kate.

"Ok auntie," said Tom, happy to get away from all the serious adult talk.

"Tell you what, Tom," said Bill, "if you need something to do, would you take Sam and bring the sheep into the field next to the pen. Make sure they are all there; there are thirty six of 'em."

"Ok uncle."

As soon as Tom had left the room, Bill turned once more to the visitor, who sat calmly waiting for their attention.

"Now what is all this nonsense Tom is saying, about finding you in a cave?"

"The boy speaks the truth."

"I cannot accept that, Mr... Mr... Merlin... or whoever you are. People aren't found in caves; especially caves that have been buried for hundreds of years."

"The boy speaks the truth," Merlin repeated quietly.

The wizard then gave a summary of everything that had happened, from the moment he had been awakened by Tom's cry months ago to the retrieval of the amulet earlier in the day.

Bill and Kate exchanged glances again.

"But this is preposterous!" exclaimed Bill.

"Please go on," said Kate, frowning at her husband.

Merlin began speaking about the unexpected psychic contact with a man called Emile while imprisoned in the cave, and the image of a sequence of numbers that had suddenly appeared in his brain.

"The numbers were a bother to me for I knew they were of some importance, but I was at a loss to understand what they meant. I realised they must have some connection with this strange new world, but I, Merlin, could not think of an answer. At that moment I realised I would need Tom's help again."

Merlin recounted the subsequent events; the transmutation process that allowed him to arrive unseen just as Tom was about to be taken back to his stepmother; how he had slipped into the back seat of the car and remained there until they stopped at the petrol station, where he encouraged Tom to leave the car and follow him. He also told them about how they arrived back at Devil's Ridge and the metamorphic process that changed his appearance.

For some strange reason both Bill and Kate listened to the visitor's account without further interruptions. The resonant, charismatic voice seemed to have some hypnotic hold over them, broken only when the visitor had finished speaking. Bill was the first to respond. "You make it sound as if all this really happened, yet you know as well as we do, it is not possible."

Merlin sighed. "In my world, Mr Watson, it is unwritten druid law that a wizard's powers should not be used as mere display, except where such display can assist in preventing harm or distress to others. Tom's future wellbeing depends on my ability to convince you that I am who I say I am, so I believe I am acting within these laws. Therefore I will give you right now a little proof of the powers I possess."

Merlin looked sombrely at the two people in front of him. "After being awakened by Tom I was left lying fully conscious in that cave without the ability to move a muscle. It was then I entered the psychic phase for mind travel. You see I desperately needed to discover what sort of world I had found myself in. These journeys also allowed me to escape from the depressing confines of the cave, thus preventing the curse of madness possessing me."

Merlin fixed his gaze upon Kate. "Mrs Watson, on occasions during these spiritual journeys I became an uninvited guest in your home. It was on one of those visits that I watched you searching for something in your bedroom one morning. You had fitted a small trinket to your ear and were searching for the other."

"My earring!" prompted Kate.

Merlin nodded. "You appeared to be agitated when you couldn't find it and you began looking on the floor. The bottom drawer of your bedside cabinet was slightly open and you opened it further and started looking though the contents; I had the

64

feeling that you were still searching for your ear trinket. It seemed the drawer contained personal mementos. You brought out a black book and rose petals fell on to the floor. You picked them up and then sat on your bed. You opened the book and remained there gazing at a certain page. I looked over your shoulder and saw what had been written there. The page marked the day of your marriage to your husband. I departed from your room soon after this."

Kate could only stare-open mouthed at the visitor. She then turned to her husband, her face pale with shock.

"Is this true, Kate... what he's saying?"

His wife could only nod. She then turned to Merlin. "How... but how could you know all this, even my husband was not aware I had that diary."

"It was one of many things I observed during my visitations to your home," Merlin answered softly. "I apologise for intruding," he added.

"And what about the lost earring, Kate, was he right about that?"

"Yes, he was," she said slowly, "and I still haven't found it."

They all sat quietly for some moments, until Bill broke the silence. "But you don't look anything like what the witness at the petrol station described, despite what Tom says about you changing your clothes."

Merlin got to his feet and studied them for few moments, before addressing them once more. "Please will you remain silent now, until I speak again."

Then with his arms outstretched and his palms turned upward he closed his eyes and remained still. He stayed in this pose for a few moments when suddenly two faint shafts of light came down from above, their beam directed on each open palm. The wizard's arms slowly came down to his side, and the process began. Bill and Kate could only stare in utter amazement at the extraordinary phenomenon unfolding before them. They watched, mesmerised, as the man before them dissolved into a nebulous mass of tiny fragments, out of which emerged the cloaked, bearded figure of the historic Merlin.

The wizard gazed down at the dumbfounded couple. "The Merlin of my world now stands before you."

It was a few moments before Bill and Kate could respond. Bill was the first to recover. "But this has to be some form of illusion... it can't be anything more."

"Then why don't you feel my garment? You are welcome to pull at my beard," said the wizard softly.

Bill shook his head. "I'm afraid I cannot believe what I see, there has to be some explanation."

"Every day I have witnessed the unbelievable in your world," said Merlin, casting a kindly look at Bill. "I have discovered this thing you name electricity. It gives instant light without flame, heat without the burning of wood or peat. What is electricity? Where does it come from? Where does it go? I, the great Merlin cannot comprehend such things... such magic. But believe I must.

"So many incredible and magical things... it is so hard to believe. There are objects that travel at unbelievable speed, faster than the swiftest chariot, faster than the red deer in flight. It is hard to imagine such speed! You name them cars... so many! Then there are those I have come to know as buses that carry many people. They all move at great speed! What power is it that enables them to travel so fast?"

Before Bill could think of an answer, the wizard continued. "You have that black box in the corner," said Merlin pointing at the television. "From somewhere inside that strange box, wondrous things happen. Real people and animals live inside this box for they miraculously appear out of nowhere. I have seen running streams, snow-topped mountains, great oceans, forests, deserts and much more; these are just a few of the magical visions that have passed before my eyes during my visitations to your home. These images... where do they come from? It is beyond my understanding, beyond my thinking, but believe I must.

"You can draw endless amounts of hot or cold water just by the mere turning of a lever. How is this done? I have seen Mrs Watson place slices of bread in a silver box. In moments they appear brown as if toasted on an open fire. How can that happen? I have seen a ring of blue flames appear like magic where Mrs Watson cooks her meals. Where do these flames come from? And colours; such colours! In your homes, on your cars... everywhere! So vivid, like those of the dragon fly or the humming bird.

"But the most magical of all is that small object you name a mobile phone. It is no bigger than the oak leaf, yet you use it to communicate with others of your world. How can a voice come through the air? How do words and images appear? Where do they come from? Where do they go? How is it all possible? There's that grey object you have in the room you name the office. It is known to me as a computer. I have looked over your shoulder and watched you create figures or words at the touch of buttons. Yet surely, these things I witness cannot be? Surely it is sorcery! Everywhere I venture in your world magical things are happening; wondrous things that I, the greatest wizard of my time, cannot begin to understand.

"But you, Mr Watson, would say I must believe; that what I see is no miracle; that I must accept all these incomprehensible things I witness in your world as the result of invention and industry that has taken place over a vast number of years. That would be your explanation, would it not, Mr Watson?"

Merlin paused, as he waited for Bill to respond.

"Yes, that would sum it up pretty well, but how can you rationally explain these... these actions of yours?"

"There are some things I cannot explain. Even as a child I had the ability to achieve physical action with the power of my mind. I believe in your world it is known as mind over matter. Only the Gods can explain why I was given such powers.

"But I can try and explain this to you. There are many parallel worlds and universes within this world we live in. We are conscious of a world of three dimensions, yet others exist. You might not be aware of them, Mr Watson, but they are there. Parallel worlds are all around us and with the power of the human mind they can be understood and utilised in so many ways."

Bill shook his head. "I have no idea what you are getting at, Mr...er... Merlin, but it doesn't alter the situation, even if you are who you say you are. We just want to know why you have taken our nephew from the authorities and brought him back here."

Just then the phone rang and Kate hurried to answer it. Bill listened to his wife as she answered mostly in monosyllables.

"Who was that, Kate?" he enquired as she put the phone down.

"It's a reporter. She wants to know if she can see us tomorrow to have a chat about Tom."

"What did you say?"

"I said she could – what else could I say? She'd probably have got suspicious if I'd refused her."

"I agree, my love, but when is she coming?"

"She asked if 2pm tomorrow would be okay for us, I said it was."

"Ok, we'll just have to make sure Merlin and Tom are not around."

Kate nodded then turned her attention back to the wizard.

"Merlin, you must understand, both my husband and I love Tom very much, but we cannot keep him. It's against the law and he must return to his stepmother."

The wizard addressed her in his slow, precise manner.

"Mrs Watson, I have no mind to oppose your wishes, if those wishes are truly from your heart. But your concern does not appear to be in your nephew's best interest, your concern is about how the authorities may react if Tom does not abide by your society's laws, not what is best for the boy."

Kate stood up and faced Merlin angrily. "I think that is a terribly unfair thing to say. We love Tom as if he were our own son. We have prayed for the chance to have him live with us. If you know anything about us at all, you must know that."

"I do," said Merlin kindly,

"But you know nothing about Tom," continued Kate, "about his past, about how we…"

"Mrs Watson," interrupted the wizard, "I know more about Tom than you realise. I know that he lost his mother around the age of three. She was named Angela and you and your husband were very fond of her. You had been caring for Tom during her illness and you then continued to care for the boy when his mother died and while his father went away to grieve his loss. Tom remained in your care for some considerable time, before returning to live with his father and his new wife. I know about the birth of the twins and the stepmother's lack of interest in your nephew. Then of his father's accidental death."

Merlin's mention of the death of Tom's father, Peter, brought everything sweeping back to Kate. It had been a bad time for Tom, but also for her and Bill. Peter had been a great friend and brother-in-law and a dear uncle to Felicity. It was over three years ago now, but to Kate it still seemed like yesterday.

The freak accident had happened a month before Tom's ninth birthday. Peter, a council building inspector, had called in to give an off-the-cuff appraisal on a partly derelict building one Friday evening. It was a favour to property developer Richard Bowen, an old school friend, who had recently purchased the building. Unbeknown to Richard, three tom jacks used to support a critical part of a load-bearing wall had mistakenly been removed that afternoon by one of the workmen to be used elsewhere in the building.

An ominous creak was the first and only warning Peter and the developer had. Before they could move, the structure caved in, burying both in an avalanche of bricks, timbers and rubble.

Peter died instantly. His friend Richard survived with spinal injuries that would leave him paralysed from the waist down.

After the funeral, Tom had stayed at the farm for three weeks while Cynthia went to her parents' home with the twins.

"I also know of your concerns about Tom," said Merlin. "You are worried over his constant absence from school and the lack of care and attention he receives from his stepmother. So you see, I know something of his past... and of the great attachment and love you both have for the boy."

Kate and Bill exchanged incredulous glances before focusing again on the awe-inspiring man standing before them.

Merlin spoke again. "You must understand that during those weeks when I was left lying in the cave, I spent much of my extrasensory time not just within your home but also in Tom's home and at his school. My sole interest then, as it is now, is your nephew's wellbeing. It is the only way of repaying him for saving me from what would have been a living death. So you see it is natural I should want only what's good for Tom, and not what suits others."

Merlin paused, gathering his thoughts. "I have been distressed to see how the boy has been treated by his stepmother. He was one of the few who walked to school, for his bike was locked up in a shed. And at the school there was much concern over Tom's continual absence, the boys he was mixing with and the lack of interest he was showing in his studies."

"That's exactly what the headmaster told me," said Kate.

Merlin nodded, shifting his gaze from one to the other.

"It was I who reminded your nephew of his meeting with the officials this afternoon. He came down of his own free will, for I had assured the boy I would watch over him. It was only after he had taken his leave that I realised I needed his help again."

Bill shook his head. "But what you did is tantamount to kidnapping, don't you understand?"

"I understand the meaning of your word kidnap, but surely that would mean taking someone away against their will?"

"As far as the law is concerned a child of twelve has no real understanding of what's best for them, so although Tom went with you willingly it would still be regarded as abduction in the eyes of the law."

"But should not your laws first consider the wellbeing of the child?" queried Merlin.

"Well, I think they do in some cases," said Kate cautiously, unsure of her facts.

"Tell me, how did you get back here from Meridale?" Bill queried.

Merlin slowly shifted his dark gaze from Kate to Bill. "I simply moved Tom and myself through the use of my own spiritual forces."

"I don't understand; how did you do that?"

"I have said before, there are other worlds around us. It was simply a matter of entering another dimension allowing us to leave one world and enter another."

Bill shook his head. "Sorry, but your explanation makes no sense."

"I regret I cannot be more helpful."

Bill, a practical man of basic convictions, could only shake his head again and look helplessly across at his wife, who was just as speechless.

"Mr and Mrs Watson, I cannot seek your forgiveness for taking your nephew away from the authorities for I believe I was right in preventing his return to his stepmother. It is now up to you both to decide your nephew's future. As he cannot remain here, you have two options, I believe. One, you can elect to send the boy back to his legal guardian, but I'm sure you believe as I do, his future would be bleak. Or you could allow Tom to accompany me, a complete stranger, but one who would care for this boy as if he were a son."

Kate looked briefly at her husband before turning her attention to Merlin: "But where would you take him? How would you look after him? What about his education?"

"I will care for your nephew as if my life depended on it, for his welfare matters more to me than anything else. Your third question was about his education. From what your nephew has told me, the school holidays will begin in a few days' time and he will not be required to attend school again for another six weeks. I would suggest to you it would be of little consequence if he misses his schooling this week and he could resume his education when your schools reopen."

"And where do you propose he will start his next term?" queried Kate.

"Why, somewhere near here, I believe," Merlin replied calmly, "for by then he should be returned legally into your care."

"And how do you propose to do that?" asked Bill.

"I will make a study of your legal system and look at cases similar to those of your nephew. I will then motivate those who have concern in such matters. I believe the boy's place is with you, and it is my duty to make this happen."

"Merlin, we both feel your intentions are honourable, but we still have reservations about all this. I hope you understand?" questioned Kate.

"I understand you well, Mrs Watson," said the wizard softly.

"But is it not time for Tom to be present?" continued Merlin. "Should not the boy have a chance to speak for himself?"

Kate looked at Bill, who was deep in thought.

"I think Kate and I should talk about this before we call Tom back," said Bill, standing up to address Merlin.

"Then I will leave your house now. I would like to look at this... this tractor I think you name it, if I can have your permission to do so, Mr Watson."

"Yes... if that's what you want then I'll show you where it is and leave you to it," said Bill as he rose to escort the wizard to the tractor shed.

CHAPTER 11

On his return, Bill found his wife back in the kitchen.

"You and I need to talk about this, Kate," said Bill, sitting back down at the table. "As far as I see it, Merlin is right, we only have two options. We let Tom go with him or we phone up Cynthia right now and tell her Tom is here. The second option is the lawful one, but you know what that would mean, Kate. Tom would continue in his old ways of truancy. His education would deteriorate even further. He might even get into trouble with the police. Worse still, he could get into drugs. All this could lead to him leaving home and taking to the streets. We see it every day in the papers, Kate."

"Well, why can't we apply through the courts for guardianship... or even adoption?"

"She already has legal guardianship over the boy. Our solicitor told us that when we looked into it some time ago, remember?"

Bill took hold of Kate's hand across the table.

"Even if we were to try for guardianship, Kate, how long do you think the process would take, just to bring it to court? Two months? Three? Four? And when it comes to court, what makes you believe our application would be successful? Why would the courts take Cynthia's legal guardianship away against her will? Her lawyers could prove she tends to Tom's material needs. He is well clothed and fed. He's got his own room and is not physically abused or maltreated, so what reason would they have to take the boy from her?"

"Cynthia has no love for Tom. He is emotionally neglected. You know that, Bill."

"We both know that, Kate, but try proving it to a court."

"What about the decline in his school work, his truancy and his general unhappiness? Surely they would take that into account?"

"Cynthia's solicitor would say his behaviour was due to the death of his father. She could quite easily convince a court she was doing her best under the circumstances, and that the boy's behaviour would be the same, no matter where he lived."

Bill hesitated, trying to find the right words. "I know how much you love the boy, Kate, but I just don't reckon the outcome of any legal battle would be in our favour. That's the way I see it."

"So you think it's best if Tom goes with this... this Merlin?"

"I didn't at first, but I do now. Just think of the consequences, Kate, if he's sent back. What would happen if he decided to run away again? I can't see him seeking sanctuary at Long Acre farm because he would naturally think we would automatically pass him over to the authorities again."

Kate gazed thoughtfully at her husband for a few moments. "Yes, I've thought about that too. I have a feeling his prospects would be far better with this man Merlin."

"So you are happy if he goes with him?"

"No, I'm not happy about it, but as you say, under the circumstances, it's the best option."

"He seems to like the man, so that's a comfort," Bill said, taking hold of his wife's hand. "Let's ask the boy," he said, rising to fetch him.

"Tom, we have been trying to decide what's best for you," said Kate, as soon as the boy had sat down. "As you well know, darling, we regard you as part of our family and your uncle Bill, Fliss and I would love nothing more than to have you stay with us always."

Kate put her arms around her nephew before continuing. "The trouble is, Tom, the authorities would not allow it. As you know, your stepmother is your legal guardian and we cannot have you live with us without her permission. I have spoken to her quite recently to try and get her to change her mind, but I'm afraid she made it quite clear she would not consider it."

Kate looked over at her husband for inspiration, but found none. "There are only two options we have, honey. You can return to your stepmother and try and make a go of it, or... or you could go with this gentleman who calls himself Merlin. Someone you and I know very little about."

"I would like to go with Merlin, aunt Kate," said Tom without hesitation.

"You need to be sure in your own mind about going with him, my darling." Kate looked appealingly at her husband.

"Tom, your aunt and I have given this a lot of thought. We believe this friend of yours seems genuine enough, but we find it almost impossible to take in everything that's happened tonight, and we are still a little concerned about letting you go with him."

"But I like him, uncle Bill. And he never hurt me when I was in the cave, did he."

"I suppose not... but... but I'm still not sure we should let you go."

Bill shook his head, turned to his wife and said: "Kate, this is all too much for me."

"You must admit, Bill, this man has done some astonishing things and you and I have seen them, so why shouldn't Tom's account be genuine? Also, I have a good feeling about him. Call it woman's intuition, or call it what you like, but I feel I can trust him."

"Well, you could be right, especially the way old Sam took to him. But if we allow it to happen, we're actually aiding and abetting his abduction. You realise that, Kate? So we've got to be sure it's what Tom definitely wants to do."

"It seems as if he's made up his mind about it ages ago," said Kate softly.

"It's almost tea time," she continued. "Shouldn't we at least invite the man in to have a meal with us. Hopefully, he'll help settle our minds once and for all."

It was a good ten minutes before Bill arrived back at the house with Merlin. She noticed he'd transformed himself into his modern image, much to her approval.

"I found him looking over the tractor engine, so I filled him in on what makes a diesel engine work," Bill said with a grin. It was obvious to Kate that the stranger's interest in Bill's beloved tractor had softened her husband's attitude towards the man even more.

Again, Merlin couldn't help but gaze with profound wonder at the room, from the large cream dresser that housed colourful cups, plates and dishes to the gleaming kitchen cupboards and the strange white and silver objects that stood on the long shiny workbench.

Kate's voice quickly brought his attention back to her.

"Would you like a cup of tea, or do you prefer coffee," she asked, beckoning the wizard over to the dining area and to a seat at the table.

"I would prefer a drink of water please," replied the wizard.

"You will stay and eat with us?" said Kate.

"Thank you, I would enjoy that very much," Merlin replied.

Sitting at the table the wizard looked over the food. Much of it was alien to his eye, but he refrained from saying so.

Kate invited everyone to eat.

Merlin realised he was quite hungry, but his appetite disappeared after just a small portion of salmon and some salad. "That's hardly enough to keep you alive, Merlin, are you sure you can't eat more?" questioned Kate.

"Thank you, but I have had sufficient. It will take some time, I think, before my stomach can take larger meals."

Bill and Kate exchanged glances over the table.

After the meal, Kate, responding to her nephew's request to go to his room, allowed him to leave the table. Bill poured the wine, offering a glass to Merlin. The wizard accepted and took a tentative sip before broaching a subject that was bothering him.

"There is a matter I need your help with," said Merlin. "I told you earlier about my contact with Emile and the numbers I received, which Tom believes to be a telephone number. If I gave you the numbers, would you give me your opinion?"

"Sure, only too pleased," said Bill.

"May I request a pen and paper in order to write the numbers down?"

"Of course you can," said Kate, going to a drawer. She placed a notepad and a ballpoint pen in front of Merlin and watched as he wrote down the digits.

Kate studied the numbers then showed them to her husband.

"Tom's right," Bill said, "certainly looks like a phone number, although I don't recognise the dialing code."

"Well, the only way to find out is to try it! Come on, Merlin, best if we go to the lounge to do this," said Kate, leading Merlin into the other room.

She gestured towards the sofa, inviting the wizard to sit before fetching the cordless phone. Merlin peered cautiously at the red object then turned to look appealingly at Kate.

"Come on, I will show you," she said, thinking how ludicrous it was that the simple act of using a phone could trouble a man of such amazing ability.

Merlin watched closely as Kate touched the digits shown on the notepad. She listened for a moment then passed the instrument to Merlin.

"Hurry, it's dialing,"

"What do I do now?" asked the wizard, holding the phone awkwardly.

Kate gently took the phone from Merlin and put it to her ear, and at that moment a male voice came on the line.

"Hello, my name is Kate, who am I speaking to?"

The man told her. "Please wait a second, I have someone who wishes to talk with you."

She turned to Merlin. "It's Andrew," she said, positioning the phone correctly in the wizard's hand and then guiding it to his cheek.

"Just speak into the mouthpiece as if talking normally."

The wizard did as instructed.

"Is that Andrew?" he said cautiously.

Kate decided to leave Merlin to talk in private, and left the room. Within minutes, the wizard was back in the kitchen. "Andrew wishes to talk to you," he said softly.

Kate took the phone and returned to the lounge.

"Andrew, this is Kate again."

It was some time before Kate returned to the kitchen and joined the others at the table. She then gave a full account of her telephone discussion with the man who'd had psychic contact with Merlin.

As soon as she'd finished, she spoke to her tall guest sitting opposite. "Merlin, on behalf of both of us, as I'm sure my husband will agree, we owe you an apology for doubting your story... you too, Tom," she added.

"I accept your apology Mrs Watson."

Kate nodded and smiled, then quickly changed the subject. "As I've said, Andrew is going to be at Edinburg station at 2pm tomorrow unless he hears otherwise. He's obviously studied the train schedule from Euston to Edinburg because he said you need to catch the train leaving from Euston at 7.40am and...."

"Mrs Watson," interrupted the wizard, "what is a train?"

Kate offered a fleeting expression of disbelief before turning to her husband, who explained as best he could, then turned his attention back to the train schedule. "It'll be an early rise tomorrow. It's about an hour and a half to get to Euston station from here, so we'll need to leave no later than 5.30am, in case of hold-ups." He turned to the wizard: "Is that alright with you, Merlin?"

"If you and your wife think well of it, then so do I."

"It's all settled then!" said Bill.

"Not quite!" said Kate. "I've just thought of something."

"What?"

She cast a look at the wizard. "You have no extra clothes with you, am I right?"

The wizard shrugged, grinned then spread his hands out resignedly. "What you see is what I have."

The hosts, flummoxed by his reply, could only smile and exchange glances. "I'll take Merlin into Saltridge. Bill, I need to get some shopping anyway."

"Can I come too, auntie?"

"No Tom, I'd like you to have a shower, then pack your clothes. Make sure you take plenty of underwear, T-shirts and socks," she said, before disappearing upstairs in her bedroom.

After readying herself for the outing, Kate instructed her husband to help their nephew find a suitable case for his things. She then beckoned to a perplexed Merlin and led him out to the car. Kate started the engine then secured her seat belt. She waited for her passenger to do the same, but he made no move to buckle up. She gestured towards the belt near his left shoulder, but all she got was a bemused look. She leaned over, pulled the belt across the wizard's body and secured it. After merging into the main road Kate glanced occasionally at her passenger, noting the fearful look on his face as he stared wide-eyed at the oncoming traffic, often closing his eyes tightly as the vehicles flew past.

She drove down the high street and into the large Saltridge mall parking area. It was Friday evening, and Kate knew the supermarket was going to be very busy. She hated crowds and always tried to shop at quieter periods, but today was an exception.

After parking up, she turned to her passenger.

"I thought I'd get a few things from the supermarket before buying your clothes. Do you want to stay in the car or come with me?"

"I will accompany you, if that is no bother." Kate smiled her acceptance, and together they approached the shopping area. On entering the supermarket, Kate picked up a basket and joined the other shoppers. Merlin, following her, was overwhelmed by the sheer number of people walking among seemingly endless shelves stacked with staggering quantities of unrecognizable objects in an infinite variety of shapes and colours. This, to the wizard, was a strange and frightening world.

He stayed close to Kate as she made her way through the throng. He watched as she stopped to inspect items, before placing them back on the shelf or in her basket. On a number of occasions he had to jump aside to avoid being hit by a shopper's trolley. He was enthralled yet intimidated by all the activity in the vast building; people coming and going in every direction, all intent on their urgent business.

Engrossed, Merlin had momentarily forgotten about Kate for she had now disappeared from sight. He looked in every direction then darted frantically between the shoppers. Where was she? Where had she gone? He ran from aisle to aisle, but nothing... no sign of the familiar figure...she had vanished.

The wizard began to get flustered. What was he to do? Which way should he go? He was utterly lost among the moving multitude. He stood now, rooted to the spot. Where could she be? He began to panic, needed to escape, to get out of the place and into the open air

It was only when Kate reached the fruit counter that she realised Merlin had not followed. She quickly returned to the aisle where she knew they'd been together. But he was nowhere to be seen. She looked down another aisle, and then another, but still no luck. She made her way along the central walkway, glancing down the aisles on each side. Suddenly there he was, just standing there, looking frantically in all directions. Kate came up from behind and tapped him on the shoulder. His response completely astounded her; the look of immense relief as he spontaneously grabbed her hand and kissed it. At that moment Kate was convinced this man had come from another time... another world.

From then on, Merlin stayed close to Kate, holding her sleeve as she strolled around the aisles. 'Like a frightened child,' she thought. At the checkout, Kate gave Merlin an occasional sideways glance. She noticed him watching with a concentrated frown as each article was passed over the sensor with a beep and as she placed her credit card in the machine to pay for her goods.

After returning to the car to drop off the shopping, the pair made their way back to the mall to visit the men's clothing store. The shop was on the next floor, which meant they had to use the escalator. Kate stepped on to the moving track, thinking her companion would follow. Half way up she looked back to see a bewildered Merlin waiting at the bottom. Seconds later, on reaching the top, she looked for him again, but to her utter astonishment he was at her side, smiling down at her. She returned his smile, thinking, 'how the hell did he do that?, knowing he could not possibly have reached her that fast by using the escalator.

Kate shrugged, grabbed Merlin's hand and made her way to the men's outfitters. The shop had recently been taken over by two men in their forties; both gay, thought Kate, while shopping there during their 'Opening Sale Week'. Merlin prompted her to take the initiative. She approached a man who was briskly sorting out clothing on a counter and asked: "Can you help?"

The man turned: "Of course!"

"My friend is a stranger to this country and would like a little help," she explained, waving a finger towards the wizard. She asked for a notepad and wrote down a list of garments Merlin would need. "Make sure you give him the right size underwear and I'd be grateful if you can persuade him to try on the shirts and trousers, is that alright?"

"Yes, of course. Leave everything to me, Madam," he said enthusiastically while eying the list which consisted of four changes of underwear and socks, three shirts, a belt, two pairs of jeans, and a pair of dress trousers. After a few minutes Kate, confident her friend was in good hands, decided to visit the W H Smith store to look for a present for Tom. She felt a little guilty at the way she and her husband had doubted much of what their nephew had told them, so she thought she'd buy him a gift to make up for it. Kate knew what he'd like; he was absolutely fascinated by dinosaurs. She soon found what she was looking for. It was a large book in the 'Nature' section by the lift. She scanned through the beautifully illustrated pages depicting these huge primeval animals in their habitat. Tom would love it. She then went to another store that sold luggage for she was aware her strange guest would be in need of a suitcase. With these purchases placed in the car, Kate hurried back to the men's outfitters just in time to see Merlin's new clothes being placed in two large plastic bags. "I should think this will be enough to keep you going," she said as they walked out of the shop.

"Thank you so much, Mrs Watson. I will repay you when I am able to earn some money," said Merlin.

"Taking good care of my lovely boy will be payment enough, and please, Merlin, call me Kate."

They were soon back in the car and driving towards Long Acre Farm. Once they had entered the house, Bill told his wife about the phone call he'd had during her absence. "It's someone called Miss Flowers, says she's a reporter with the Saltridge Echo. She must have been the same woman who called you earlier, Kate. Said she wanted to confirm the arranged time was still okay. Strange she should call again just for that."

"Maybe that's what they do these days"

"What is a reporter?" queried Merlin.

Kate hesitated, trying to take Merlin's remark seriously. "A reporter is someone who helps keep the public informed on things... news of interest and that sort of thing, and then they print the information in a newspaper."

"Yes, I know newspapers," said the wizard. "I saw them in the Saltridge library during my spiritual travels."

"Anyway," prompted Bill, "she's coming here tomorrow afternoon to talk about Tom's disappearance. She also asked if we can give her a suitable photo of him to publish in their paper. She said the police have already spoken to Tom's stepmother, and from their report it seems she doesn't have a photo of Tom anywhere."

"That tells you what she thinks of the boy!" said Kate.

Bill turned his attention to the wizard once more. "It seems we have no other choice but to let Tom go with you."

Merlin looked puzzled. "I thought that has already been agreed."

"Yes it has, Merlin," said Kate, deciding to change the subject. "But now we need to show you where you're going to sleep tonight."

"I will be comfortable sleeping in your barn or here on your floor."

"I won't hear of it. My husband will take you upstairs where you can shower and have a lovely night's sleep in our daughter's room."

Merlin thanked her, for in his world it was impolite to refuse what the host had to offer.

Kate then asked: "Where's Tom?"

"He's in the lounge on this Play-Station thingy of his," responded Bill. "I told him its getting late and he should be in bed seeing as we have an early rise tomorrow."

Kate took the Dinosaur book into the lounge and presented it to Tom. "It's a going-away present, my darling," she said, taking him in her arms.

"Cor, thanks auntie," he said, eying the large book over her embrace.

Kate kissed her nephew before returning to the kitchen. As she turned on the kettle to make tea, her husband whispered: "I think Merlin has a request to make." She eyed the tall frame of the wizard as he turned to face her.

"Mrs Watson, I need to do something. It is best if it is done now as we are leaving tomorrow."

"What is it?"

"I think I need... er an envelope?"

"An envelope! Of course, do you want it now?"

"Yes please."

After Kate returned with the envelope, he said: "May I ask for Tom to be here?"

Kate nodded. "Yes of course...Tom!" she cried.

"What is it auntie?" he asked as he walked into the kitchen.

"Merlin wants to see you."

The wizard took the boy's hand in his.

"Tom, my boy, could you please bring me some writing paper?" Tom looked at his aunt for a moment before leaving the room. Merlin turned to Bill.

"Mr Watson, could you please give me the name and address of a newspaper company?"

"Which one, there are quite a few of 'em?" said Bill.

"It must be one of great importance."

"Well, we have The Evening Mail, it's as good as any, I suppose."

"Would you know the address?"

"I think their details are somewhere in the first couple of pages, but what's this all about?"

"Mr Watson, would you find those details for me."

Bill was about to say something, thought better of it, shrugged and went to find the paper. Just then Tom returned. "I use this for writing and doing my homework," he said, handing an exercise book to the wizard. Merlin looked quickly through the lined pages. "This is good, thank you," he said, giving the book back to Tom.

"Now, my boy, listen carefully. I know why you want to leave your stepmother and live with your aunt and uncle. It is my wish that you write your reasons on paper, starting with why you left the official's car with me, your friend. Please start doing this now."

The wizard turned again to Kate. "Mrs Watson, you may help your nephew if you wish, but it is important he writes the letter as a boy would."

Although puzzled by these strange instructions, Kate decided to do what was asked of her. She grabbed a pen, led her nephew over to the desk under the window and sat with him. Moments later Tom, in deep concentration, began to write.

Bill returned and handed Merlin a sheet of paper. "I've been on the internet and found their email, postal address and post code. The best person to write to would be their Chief News Editor, a man called John Neilson. They'll obviously send it on to the right department if it's not correct."

"Would you now please write down on your paper, how you would address this person on an envelope?" Bill jotted down: 'To the Chief News Editor', followed by the address.

"Thank you, Mr Watson. We now wait until your nephew has written his letter."

"While we're waiting, maybe you and I could go outside," suggested Bill. "I'd like to see my dog's reaction when he sees you again."

It was a good fifteen minutes before the pair arrived back in the lounge.

"I've finished," said Tom, as he gave the exercise book to Merlin.

The wizard sat down on a chair and read:

Dear Sir, I'm sorry I left the car with my friend at the petrol station. But I don't want to live with my stepmother any more. I love my auntie and my uncle and my cousin Fliss and want to live with them because I know they love me as well. But I'm not allowed to. I'm going to stay with my friend until I'm old enough to do what I like. I hope you won't blame anybody because this is what I want to do.
Tom Watson.

After reading it, Merlin looked at the boy and thanked him. He then handed the envelope to Tom, asking him to copy the address his uncle had written on to the envelope. Bill and Kate could only look on with curious anticipation as the wizard carefully tore out the sheet with Tom's message and said to the boy: "Put this in the envelope, and seal it." Merlin then took the letter and placed it in the palm of his hand.

"Do you want a stamp?" said Kate, wondering why Merlin was staring at the envelope.

"What is a stamp?"

Kate gave a slight shake of her head, having to adjust once again to her guest's ignorance of the world. "It's a small piece of paper that is stuck onto the envelope."

"Do you have one?"

"No I'm afraid I don't."

"Then I shall proceed without it."

Merlin turned his attention back to the letter, his brow furrowed in concentration, his audience mystified. Suddenly the letter began to vibrate and to everyone's amazement the trembling article gradually became a blur, before disappearing altogether.

Bill was the first to respond: "But... but how did you do that?" he said, shaking his head in wonderment.

"I cannot explain, Mr Watson. Moving things is something I've done since I was a child."

They pondered his answer for a few moments until Kate, shaking her head in bewilderment, thought of more pressing things.

"Tom, you have an early rise tomorrow, so if you've packed your case and showered, then you should get to bed as it's getting late." She reminded him again of the clothes he needed, adding: "And don't forget your new dinosaur book."

"I won't. Thank you auntie."

"That's okay my darling," she said, going over and cuddling him. "We're going to miss you very much. You know that, don't you?"

She looked at the wizard. "We're entrusting him to your care, Merlin, please don't let us down."

"Have no fear, Mrs Watson; I will care for him as if he were my own son."

That night in bed, Kate spoke to her husband, describing Merlin's behaviour at the supermarket. "You should have been there, Bill, the man was utterly panic-stricken. It was no act. I know this might sound crazy, but I now believe this man is who he says he is." Bill shook his head and grinned. "It's crazy alright, Kate, but I have to agree with you!"

CHAPTER 12

Chrissie Flowers was not happy. She had sat listening to Mark's marital problems for almost an hour. She was very fond of him. He was a great photographer and some of his ways amused her, but she had heard it all many times before, and she was in no mood for more. She had already bought him two pints of Fosters, as promised, and was now ready to leave him to his own devices.

"Mark, I'm ready to go home. Can you drop me off or are you staying on?"

The photographer, preferring his own local to the pub they were in, drained his glass and stood up. "I'm at your service, Madame," he said with an exaggerated bow.

"I hope you're going to have a meal before you drink any more," admonished Chrissie, as they walked towards the car.

"Promise," said Mark as he searched for his keys.

"Make sure you do," she said.

Chrissie had often thought it odd how easily she'd fallen into the habit of treating Mark like a young brother. Even stranger was Mark's willingness to accept it. She supposed being thirty six and ten years his senior would have to be the reason, yet in her heart she knew there was another explanation. As a child, she had always yearned to have a younger brother. She remembered how disappointed she felt when her mother arrived back from the hospital with a baby girl. She loved her sister, but the feeling of wanting a brother in her life had never left her.

Chrissie got a fruit drink from the fridge as soon as she entered her kitchen. She took it out on to the wooden decking that passed for a patio. The two white ornamental chairs next to the small, round garden table were perfect for a relaxing drink. She kicked off her shoes and placed her petite frame on one and her feet on the other. The apartment block sheltered the decking from the late afternoon sun, and in the welcome coolness of the evening it was the best place to think - about something that had been nagging at her for some time.

It was the missing boy.

She cast her mind back to the interview she'd had with Ross at Saltridge police station. It had gone on longer than she'd intended, much to Mark's annoyance. The policeman told her they'd received a faxed report about the boy from the Child

Welfare Agency, but added, a little flippantly, no public reports had yet been received about any boy wandering around with a bloke dressed up like a wizard.

Chrissie, surprised and disappointed, asked Ross to call the local Macefield Constabulary to see if they had been in touch with Tom's stepmother. It was a positive; they'd visited the woman soon after receiving information about the missing boy. Ross then asked if they could fax over the report as soon as possible. The fax made interesting reading. The report said the stepmother had seemed more angry than upset over her stepson's disappearance, and when asked for a photograph of him she admitted having none to give them. She told the officers the boy's only blood relative was his uncle, William (Bill) Riley Watson, of Long Acre farm, St John's Road, Saltridge. The uncle was married with one child.

Then Ross came up trumps for the reporter. It seemed Barry, their desk clerk, had a smallholding on St John's Road. "I know this 'cos we all went out there for a barbecue last summer," Ross informed her. "It was his alternative lifestyle dream for his retirement, which is just two years away. They just run a couple of pigs and some chickens at the moment, but when Barry retires he says he'll get some sheep and maybe a horse."

"Can I see him?" She asked quickly.

"Sorry Chrissie, he knocked off about an hour ago, and anyway St John's Road is a pretty long road. Barry's place could be a good distance from the Watson farm."

"Well, can I phone him?"

"It's against departmental policy, Chrissie, you should know that."

"Well, darling Ross, do me this one favour and I'll be indebted to you for always."

"And how often have I heard that?"

She gave the curly-headed policeman the benefit of her most engaging smile and a pleading look in her appealing blue eyes.

"Then will you phone him for me... please," she asked. "You *are* allowed to do that, aren't you?"

The desk clerk had just arrived home when Ross phoned and was more than happy to talk to the reporter. Once again Chrissie found herself in luck. Barry actually knew the family; in fact, his smallholding was on the other side of the road from the Watson's property, and it was from Bill Watson that Barry had acquired much farming and livestock knowledge. The desk clerk gave Chrissie a good insight into the Watson family, including the special affection they seemed to have for their nephew, for he and his wife had occasionally spent an afternoon on their farm, and on two occasions had stayed for an evening meal. After the phone call, and with Ross's reluctant help, Chrissie was soon in possession of the Watson's phone number.

She poured herself another glass of fruit juice and then her journalistic brain began to itemize the facts.

(1) The boy Tom had left the car with a strange, bearded and cloaked individual. He had left without putting up any obvious resistance and it seemed Chrissie was the only one who had witnessed the event.

(2) From the stepmother's report, the boy had no other relatives apart from his aunt and uncle.

(3) The boy had run away from his stepmother's home the day before and had gone to his aunt and uncle, who lived near Saltridge, almost fifty miles away.

(4) It was Kate Watson, the report said, who had phoned the stepmother to say their nephew had arrived at the farm.

(5) From the police report, it seemed the stepmother didn't have much affection for the boy, and this was confirmed when she admitted having no photos of Tom in the house.

(6) From what Barry the desk clerk said, the Watsons have great affection for the boy.

Yet there was something bothering her. While Mark was driving back from the pub she had phoned the Watson's number and spoken to Kate, the boy's aunt. The woman, Chrissie thought, didn't appear to be too distraught about her missing nephew. Why? And when she asked Kate if she'd heard anything from her nephew, there was a slight hesitation. A mere second, no more. Yet it was enough!

Chrissie suddenly sprang into action; she swallowed the remains of her juice, put her shoes back on, grabbed her car keys from the kitchen table, and, with one brief look around, she was off. It took Chrissie less than twenty minutes to find St John's Road, and remembering Ross's information on the location of Barry's property, she soon found herself at the driveway of Long

Acre farm. Chrissie coasted a short way up the drive until, in the distance, the homestead came into view. She pulled the car partly off the tree-lined drive, turned off the engine and waited.

She sat there, wondering why she had bothered to drive out here in the first place. She already had an appointment to see these people the following day, so why do this now? Intuition - she'd learned to trust it. A hunch often followed by a correct analysis of the facts. She smiled and gave a disparaging shake of her head. She'd wait 'til it started to get dark, another hour or so at the most. If she'd seen nothing untoward by then, she'd go home, have a refreshing shower and forget all about the missing boy.

She thought again about Barry, the desk clerk's comment about the Watson's 'special affection' for their nephew. The comment niggled. What if the boy had returned once more to the farm, to seek refuge with his only relatives? If so, would they have reported it for a second time? Chrissie doubted it, and she for one wouldn't have blamed them.

It was a dog's bark that roused her. A glance at her watch told her she'd been dozing for at least twenty minutes. She immediately noticed a tall dark-haired man come out of the house and walk down the path towards the gate with a shorter, stocky man beside him. She watched the dog, its tail wagging furiously as it followed the men into the large aluminium shed on the opposite side of the drive. Their features, from that distance, were hard to make out, but the tall man, she noticed, appeared to have a loping kind of walk.

As the evening wore on nothing else happened apart from the shorter man returning to the house on his own. She waited a little longer, but her hopes of seeing the boy or some bearded man appear evaporated along with the fading light. As darkness descended, she started the engine, reversed down the drive and made her way home. After a stimulating shower she put on her old, blue bathrobe and headed for the drinks cabinet. She took down the unopened bottle of cognac, the one she had been given by her boss as a birthday present two months ago, and placed it on the kitchen bench.

Suddenly, on impulse, she decided to phone the Watson's once more. Her excuse for the call: to confirm her 2pm appointment tomorrow was still convenient. It was the uncle who answered, and once again she couldn't help feeling the man's response was not that of someone truly worried about the whereabouts of a beloved nephew.

She replaced the receiver and took the bottle and a glass outside into the warm night air. She poured a good measure of the rich liquid into the glass and took a couple of sips before swallowing the rest. Then she poured herself another.

CHAPTER 13

"I have word the Saxons are on the move and getting closer. It's only a matter of weeks, it could even be sooner, so both of you must make ready for a speedy departure," Cedrin had said recently at the evening meal.

"But where shall we go and what about your equipment, your medicines, your potions and everything? You cannot leave your life's work to be destroyed by these brutes," protested Gwindore.

"Merlin and I have already stored much in the under-floor cellar. When the heavy timbers are put back and the mats also, it might never be discovered. Over the next few days we will store all we can, but we shall need to take a good supply with us down to Londinium, for I will need to carry on with my practice down there, when the time comes."

"As you say, my brother," replied Gwindore, eyes brimming with tears.

The Romans had already removed their garrisons from Hadrian's Wall in order to quell the troublesome uprisings in Gaul. Even before their departure, heathen tribes had been arriving on the southern and eastern shores of the island, for the occupying force had ceased its vigil over the Saxons Shore, a series of defensive bastions stretching from the Isle of Wight to the Wash, years ago. These deserted outposts allowed the Angle and Saxon forces to attack and dominate vulnerable coastal settlements with impunity. For many years these tribes had been happy to settle where they were, creating new communities up and down the coastal fringes. However, other tribes were to follow, their warlords more ambitious, more brutish than their predecessors. It was these tribes that had begun travelling inland from the coast, causing panic and suffering wherever they went.

Over the last few months, word had been getting through about two Saxons tribes joining with one warlord and making their way into the heartland of the country. The news had become more serious and depressing of late as refugees were passing through Heranium, heading for safer areas. Some had injuries or illnesses through accident or privation and would seek out Cedrin, for his healing powers were known throughout the region and beyond.

The Heranium region covered an area of around forty square miles of undulating farmland and forest. The River Weer flowed through the region, winding its way southward. At the far end of Heranium, the river disappeared altogether into thick forest, marking the southern boundary of the region. There were eight villages strung out along the river valley, and some isolated settlements further away.

Cedrin's home was on the outskirts of the village of Weerby, the second furthest village from the main town of Heran. It was a pretty place sited on higher ground, a little distance from, but overlooking the Weer. It was once established further downstream on lower ground, but after some bad floods it was abandoned in favour of the present site. The big forest lay just behind the village, giving protection from the cold northerly and north-easterly winter winds. Cedrin's home was only thirty paces from the forest edge.

        **   **   **

Cedrin shook Merlin awake. The youth sat up, rubbed his eyes and looked with puzzlement at his uncle.

"Quickly, my boy, we have to leave. The Saxons are coming."

Merlin's acute hearing detected the fading sound of horse hoofs galloping away. He glanced out through his open window at the grey and cold early morning sky then quickly began to dress. The first weak rays of a liquid sun reached the village as Cedrin hitched the spare horse to the back of the wagon. "Come, Gwindore, we have done all we can. We must leave now."

Cedrin climbed up on to the driver's seat. It had been raised to allow for better allround vision, as vigilance on the road was crucial. "Come, Merlin, where are you?"

Merlin emerged carrying the caged Keetah.

"Londinium is no place for a falcon, my boy."

"But uncle, I cannot leave him; it will not survive here without me."

"Then free him, Merlin, he will be miserable in Londinium"

"Please uncle, please let me take him."

Cedrin had never known his nephew plead with him for anything, even as a child. It unsettled Cedrin and he felt a deep sympathy for the youth. "Alright, my boy, if you can find room in the back for your feathered friend you may take him, but be warned, it may be difficult to give him the exercise and the freedom he enjoyed here in Weerby."

Gwindore stepped up on to the padded seat next to Cedrin. She had been crying profusely, but now, apart from the odd sniffle, she was calm and even managed to smile bravely at her brother. Merlin was now seated on the back-to-back seat facing the rear of the wagon.

"You have your weapons, Merlin?"

"They are with me, Sire."

"With his great sword fighting skills, Gwindore, your son could ward off a dozen robbers."

Cedrin knew the youth always felt uncomfortable receiving any sort of direct compliment, so by speaking to his mother in his presence, he could give his nephew a little praise without subjecting the young man to embarrassment.

"But with the other powers at your disposal, we may not even need to show them the sword, eh Merlin?"

Merlin couldn't help but smile at his uncle's attempts to make light of their situation.

"Are we clear at the back, Merlin?"

"Yes, Sire," he said, jerking the rope of the trailing horse. With that the healer urged the horses forward.

CHAPTER 14

Bill tried to console his wife as he drove back to the farm. She was, as always, terribly upset at Tom's departure and this time was no different.

She had watched the two of them walk down the platform, Tom pulling on Merlin's hand as if to hurry him up. The wizard seemed reluctant to respond to the boy's entreaties and could only stare at the train and carriages as if they were from another world - and, thought Kate, to him they were.

"The boy will be okay, I can assure you Kate. Did you see the grin on his face as he waved us goodbye from the window? He was never like that when we returned him to his stepmother."

Her husband was right, she had to admit it. Her precious nephew looked so happy and relaxed, and she knew, deep down in her heart, Merlin would care for him.

"He certainly looked happier despite his fair hair," observed Kate.

"Sure did! Cripes, I could hardly believe how different he looked."

It had been Bill's idea to have Tom's hair dyed. He reminded his wife that Tom's photo might be plastered over all the newspapers and if that were to happen, eventually someone would recognise him. Tom objected at first, but when Merlin agreed, saying a change to his hair colour made sense, he decided to go along with it. Kate had no hair dyes herself and was about to phone her friend, Rachel Peterson, on the neighbouring farm, when Merlin said he could do it quite easily.

Kate and Bill had been astonished when Tom appeared at the breakfast table next morning. His hair, usually brown and straight, had now become fair and curly, a change that altered his appearance completely.

Merlin, who had joined them at the table, had asked: "Tell me, does the change in Tom's hair please you?" They both agreed it did.

"What about you, Tom, do you like it?" Kate had asked as her nephew ran a hand through his hair and shrugged. "No, not really, auntie, I look stupid!"

**   **   **

Tom sat opposite the wizard on their long train ride up to
Edinburg. Most of the time Merlin gazed out of the window,
mesmerized, calling to Tom now and again as strange sights flew
swiftly by. When the train sped past a station his fright was
obvious. Such odd behaviour from a grown man had others in the
compartment eying Merlin with suspicion, much to Tom's
amusement.

The wizard cast his mind back to the morning. He had
sensed for some time Kate and Bill's discomfort and guilt at
having to assist in the abduction of their nephew. It was when
they said they were worried about having to lie to the police on
their pending visit that Merlin decided to erase the memory of his
visit from their minds.

The opportunity arose when Tom left the breakfast table,
leaving him sitting opposite the two of them. "Please," he said in
a low, commanding voice, "look at me and listen carefully." They
immediately became silent. "When you return from London later
today and enter your home, the door will close behind you and all
memory of my visit with Tom will disappear." Both Kate and
Bill continued staring for a few moments, blinked and then
carried on talking as if nothing had happened.

The metallic rhythm of train wheels on track brought
Merlin out of his reverie, but he dozed off once more and another
world emerged before his sleepy mind's eye; a stately world of
courtiers, ambassadors and ladies-in-waiting; officials always on
hand to serve His Majesty, King Arthur and his lovely wife,
Queen Guinevere. But it was the image of the queen's favorite
lady-in-waiting standing to her left that caught Merlin's eye. It
was his betrothed, the beautiful Salina.

A prod to his arm brought the wizard out of his day-
dream. Tom whispered urgently, "Wake up Merlin, we're coming
into Edinburg Station." Soon both were hurrying along the
platform, each carrying a suitcase, and with Tom's help Merlin
managed to negotiate the exit gates. The wizard, with his keen
eyesight, immediately spotted someone answering the description
Andrew had given him over the phone. The man was standing a
little to the left of the exit gates, as arranged, with a newspaper in
his hand.

"Are you Andrew?" asked Merlin, as he approached him.

The man smiled. "Yes, that's me. And you are Merlin, I presume? "

"Yes, that is I."

The neatly dressed sandy-haired man looked up at Merlin, his grey eyes taking in the wizard's appearance. "I must say, you don't look anything like I imagined."

The wizard looked down at the clothes he was wearing. "I have changed my appearance to suit your world. I will change into the Merlin of my world whenever the time is right to do so."

"I can't wait!" said Andrew, with a grin. He extended his hand. "Welcome to Scotland, Merlin." They clasped hands.

"And this young man, I presume, is Tom," he said, looking down at the boy.

Tom, not knowing what to say, gave a slight grin and nodded.

Andrew shook the boy's hand. "I'm pleased to meet you, Tom."

"Pleased to meet you, sir."

"Have you eaten anything?" Andrew asked, looking at Tom.

"Just some sandwiches auntie did for us."

"Okay, we'll find somewhere to have a late lunch before heading back, as it's quite a long drive."

It was almost 4pm before they left the small cafeteria. As they began to drive out of the city, Andrew received a call on his mobile. It was Geraldine, one of his daughters. She was staying in digs in Musselburgh with her sister for they both attended the Queen Margaret University. She needed money and wondered if her father could send her some.

"I'm in Edinburgh now, honey, so I'll come by and give you some." The Scotsman raised his eyes at Merlin, "Kids, who'd have 'em!"

Andrew found an ATM machine, drew out some cash and visited his exuberant daughter, introducing her to Merlin and Tom. By the time they began driving out of the suburbs of the city it was almost 6.30pm

"We have about a three hour journey to my village, so sleep if you wish," said Andrew glancing over his shoulder at Tom, sitting in the back.

It wasn't long before Merlin, in response to Andrew's questions, began to tell the story of Niddrym's curse and his deliverance from the deathly bed in the cave by Tom.

Andrew, who displayed no skepticism at Merlin's extraordinary tale, drove in silent contemplation for a few minutes afterwards.

"Did you not wonder why I was willing to believe you might actually be who you said you were?" he asked at length.

"Yes of course! I found it difficult to believe my extraordinary circumstances, so why wouldn't others?"

Andrew glanced in the mirror at Tom, who had fallen asleep. "There are three very good reasons why I gave credence to your situation. First, a great friend of mine phoned to say he received a telepathic image showing what appeared to be the interior of a cave. Within the cave he saw a clear image of a bearded man lying there. Only hours later I received almost the same image."

"Who is this man you speak of?" enquired Merlin.

"His name is Emile Bernard. He is a Frenchman and one of the world's great psychics."

"Yes, I recall it well because his name was the first to enter my mind, but after my response, there was nothing… until yesterday."

"He probably would have been using his psychic powers elsewhere. You see, much of Emile's time is taken up by police investigative work. His unique gift places him in great demand around the world, so he's often away from home, months at a time."

"I do not understand. What is police investigative work?" asked Merlin.

"That's out law enforcers searching for information about people involved with crime. You see, sometimes they become so desperate for more information on a case they are working on - can be anything; murder, kidnapping, missing person, you name it – that they will call in a psychic like Emile, who's probably the best in the business. His work is not widely known to the public, because the police are loathe to publicize the fact they've been assisted by spiritual means. Clairvoyance they call it! Mumbo-jumbo to some! Nevertheless, it's because of his success rate that Emile is so much in demand by these people.

"Anyway, he was on his way to Chicago, in Illinois," continued Andrew, "that's in the United States. He phoned me soon after to say he'd received contact from you, but would need to ignore any further signals as he was about to be briefed by the Chicago police department on a kidnapping case, and he couldn't allow anything to intrude. That was when he asked me to enter a receptive state to see if I could pick up your signal.

"But you will meet him soon, for he's here in Craigemere to attend our annual convention. Oh, I haven't told you about that! For the last fifty years or more we've been holding an annual get-together for our members. It's held in one country or another. This year it happens to be here in Scotland. Your visit is fortuitous, for our convention started yesterday.

"We wanted Emile to stay at our place, but he preferred to stay at the Rambler's Rest, the village hotel. These police investigation cases can be quite harrowing for him at times, and he finds he needs his own space. He was resting on his bed yesterday when the image of a bearded man leaving the cave with a young boy suddenly came into his consciousness. He told me afterwards he could sense the euphoria, the immense feeling of freedom emanating from you."

"I am looking forward to meeting this man."

"Yes, I'm sure you will like him. He is a giant of a man, physically and intellectually. Lives in a chateau in Brittany, less than twenty miles from the village where he grew up. He comes from a long line of 'psychic intelligentsia', as he often calls it.

"Anyway, he phoned me immediately after his experience. Of course, we had no idea where you were, but we knew we had to try to regain spiritual contact in an attempt to meet with you. We knew of your exceptional receptive capability. We also thought the boy might assist you somehow, but in truth, both Emile and I were unsure you'd know what to do, now you were out of the cave."

"I knew more than you realised, Andrew, for each time you thought of me, I was able to reach into your mind. Your thoughts became my thoughts. I tried to make you aware of this, but you were never in a truly receptive state."

"I must admit," conceded Andrew, "things were coming through to me, but often I couldn't make sense of them."

"When your friend Emile made contact with me outside the cave, he sent me a series of digits. They were a puzzle to me. Tom later told me the digits might be a phone number, but it was only after visiting the home of his aunt and uncle that I really understood. It was Kate, Tom's aunt, who showed me how to use this incredible object you name a phone so I could speak with you."

Both concentrated on the road ahead for a while.

"I believe there were other reasons that made you think I might be genuine?" said Merlin.

"That's true," said Andrew. "Since the start of the convention, a number of our people have mentioned receiving images of a dark cave and a bearded man. Most of our members have psychic capacity to a greater or lesser degree. The extrasensory signals you gave out must have been very powerful for it seems these images appeared simultaneously in each of the receptors, and almost at the same time Emile received them."

Andrew threw a glance at the man sitting at his side. "There was another reason that made us give serious thought to this predicament of yours. It was the overriding justification for trying to keep in spiritual contact with you," he said, then paused. "It has to do with the ancient writings."

"Ancient writings?" asked Merlin.

"Yes, there is much to tell about these manuscripts, written by druid scribes. They have been preserved down the ages and translated from Latin to medieval English and subsequently to modern-day English. Only those accepted into the fraternity are privy to this information. It's always been that way. However, Emile and I talked about it before I left for Edinburgh, and we both agreed there would be no harm in you knowing a few crucial things about the manuscripts and about our village.

Andrew glanced in the rear view mirror and adjusted it slightly before carrying on. "You see these manuscripts have played an important part in our culture. They have, since ancient times, been the foundation of Craigemere's existence.

"Crucially, the early manuscripts suggest Merlin - actually, they use your Celtic name, Myrddin - will one day, reappear on this earth. There are probably some literary inaccuracies due to the translation process, but the meanings are unmistakable. One such statement from a druid scribe reads: 'As one season follows another, so Myrddin the great wizard, will one day appear among you'.

"So you see this sudden spiritual manifestation of you, this Myrddin we've been half-expecting, is not greeted with outrageous disbelief, but rather with cautious skepticism bordering on hope."

Andrew glanced at his passenger, who continued to sit in silence, listening.

"These ancient documents," he continued, "trace the existence of our village back to the seventh century and possibly earlier. From these records, it seems Craigemere then was a druid settlement.

"The manuscripts have been the basis of our way of life throughout the ages. I suppose you could call it our bible. Our ceremonies and practices have always been conducted in privacy, away from the prying eyes of the general public, and we continue to observe them to this day, although in a much more conservative way."

The driver concentrated on the road for a few moments. "Much of what I am about to tell you comes from our study of the manuscripts and our own intensive research. To explain, I need to go back in time. Many believe feudalism – the granting of land and status by lords to their vassals - began in 1066 with King William; in fact, a type of feudal system was well under way long before then. From the records we have, it seems a similar system had been in place since the demise of King Arthur. In fact, it appears King Arthur himself began the system by granting each of his loyal knights a part of Britain to preside over. And that's when trouble began for the druids."

"I know King Arthur," Merlin cut in. "I also know of the druids, for I am of that order. But I wish you to continue for your words interest me greatly," he added.

"Of course! I should have realized, I'm sorry…" cried Andrew.

"No, please, I wish you to continue for you speak of things after my time," responded Merlin.

"Well, these presiding lords began to resent the druids because of their elevated status within the community," continued Andrew. "As you know, the druids were the aristocracy of their time. They were the judges, the teachers, the administrators; in fact, any high post in the land was usually occupied by a druid.

"But over the years campaigns were devised against them, their beliefs and practices. First, laws were imposed, restricting their activities. But that was only the beginning. Eventually, anyone who had a druid connection would be punished. And the druids were not the only ones being persecuted; seers, shamans, healers, preachers, anyone who appeared to have too much influence over the populace became a threat to be dealt with, and trumped up charges were made to be rid of them. They would usually be accused of engaging in satanic activity or witchcraft. That was a certain way of causing resentment against them; it is obvious from the records we have that superstition was rife in medieval times."

"Yes, the druids were also persecuted during the time the Romans controlled our land," said Merlin. "Cedrin, my uncle, taught me much of the history of Britain during the years of Roman occupation. I learned that when Rome converted to Christianity, they started hounding the druids mercilessly."

"I can imagine. Of course, in medieval times," Andrew resumed, "laws differed from district to district, depending entirely on the whim of the local lord. If a person was accused by another of witchcraft in one region, the law might require two or three people willing to come forward to refute the accusation. In another it might take five to establish someone's innocence. And if there was more than one informant citing witchcraft against an individual, there would have to be six or maybe ten to claim the person's innocence.

"As you know, druids were, in the main, highly intelligent, and it didn't take them long to realise, given such unjust laws, there had to be safety in numbers. So they created settlements for their people. Then, if one was accused of some sort of heresy, they would have the whole village come out in his or her defense.

"As time went on, these settlements would become sizeable villages. The inhabitants had no option but to observe their beliefs and conduct their practices and ceremonies in the strictest secrecy, for druidism had become unlawful. Craigemere is such a village. To the outside world, our people would appear as ordinary folk going about their business, and we have lived this way ever since."

"So there are other villages like Craigemere?" asked Merlin.

"There have been, through the ages. The scribes made occasional references to other spiritual villages but, to our knowledge, ours is one of just three in existence to this day. From the records we have it would seem these druids possessed psychic powers far beyond anything we in the modern world can imagine, and many in Craigemere have inherited these spiritual abilities, but to a lesser degree."

"You speak with truth about the druids, Andrew. But in my time, they would never put their thoughts to the pen. All knowledge was retained in the brain. It was the acquired ability to learn and memorise that gave the druids superior control over the mind and with it great spiritual power."

"Yes, we are well aware of this, but there must have been druid scribes around in those days for these manuscripts to exist," said Andrew.

"This is true. During the Roman occupation of Britain, many druids were forced to become scribes for the ruling powers; even the military hierarchy had private scribes on hand to record events that would be of interest to Rome."

"So it is possible then," quizzed Andrew, "after almost four hundred years of Roman rule, druid culture might have changed in that respect?"

"Yes, but the method of teaching remained the same and all knowledge continued to be confined to memory. I should know for I, as a young man, was also a druid student. We were taught how to read and write at a much younger age, for these were essential skills and you could not be accepted into the druid schools without them, but their philosophy on learning remained the same it had always been... Listen, memorise and retain."

Andrew glanced in his rear view mirror. "Anyway, another village like ours lies on the English and Welsh border near Montgomery and the other is in Brittany. These are the only remaining villages we know of which still have a strong link with our spiritual past.

"Andrew, you said your village is mostly made up of people with the same spiritual interest. Your words seem to suggest there are some who do not have the same beliefs?"

"Yes, that's correct. Before the First World War... Oh I forgot, you wouldn't know about our wars, would you?"

"I know a little about your war that ended in 1945 for I read much about it during my mind travels to the Saltridge library, but I would be interested to know more."

"Well, there was another war before that; it started in 1914 and ended in 1918. It was called the Great War. Everyone thought it would be a war to end all wars, but then, about twenty years later, the Second World War began, and that's the one you've read about.

"Before 1914, most villages in Britain were virtually as they had been for hundreds of years. Strangers would rarely visit, for there was little in the way of transport for the common man, apart from the horse or bullock and cart. Only the well-off could afford cars in those days, and anyway, roads to many outlying villages were not conducive to this form of transport. These villages remained relatively untouched; so much so, any visiting stranger would have been regarded as a foreigner and treated with suspicion.

"Up until that time, our village was the same, except we were of a different culture and had very different beliefs. In those days druid philosophy was taught in the village school. It was part of the curriculum. We started to learn about it from the age of ten. The lesson, called Spiritual Awareness, was always the first of the day. After the first year we were allowed to experiment with thought transference. We'd take turns in going to the front of the class and attempt to read the thoughts of one of the kids. We'd write on the blackboard what came into our thoughts. The results, I remember, were pretty spectacular at times.

"Later, at the age of eighteen, every boy and girl would undergo a ceremony inviting them into the psycho-physical fraternity. The final part of the ceremony was the most crucial. It was the pledge of secrecy - a commitment they would honour for the rest of their lives.

"At that time, every adult was involved in the psycho-physical activity of the village, each to a greater or lesser degree, depending on their psychic abilities and interest. But the start of the First World War disrupted our way of life as many of the young men were conscripted into service for their country.

"We continued with our ceremonies during and after the war, but it wasn't the same. Then, when the second war came along, it was the beginning of the end. We eventually stopped holding the swearing in ceremony, hoping to start again when the war was over. After the war, it was conducted every so often, but in 1963 it was stopped altogether. You see, there weren't enough young people in the village. I was lucky to have been one of the last to go through.

"At about that time the very first new resident arrived in the village. The man was a retired solicitor. He bought two adjoining farmhouses and had them renovated. He lived in one and his daughter and son-in-law arrived later to live in the other one with their two kids.

"As you can imagine, the children presented a problem. They were around the age of ten or eleven and were immediately enrolled at the village school. The school committee therefore, had to make a decision about the Spiritual Awareness lesson and they quickly removed it from the curriculum altogether. Maintaining secrecy was crucial and the over-riding factor in their decision."

"I find it hard to believe this pledge of secrecy would have been kept by everyone throughout the years," Merlin retorted.

"You are quite right, but surprisingly, our activities have been disclosed very rarely. It was hardly an issue in the old days because villages were isolated. Any outside scrutiny never amounted to much because, as always, the villagers would just close ranks and any suspicions would fade away.

"We had a situation as recent as five or six years ago, when an investigative journalist and a photographer came to the village, enquiring about psychic activity and devil worship rumoured to be going on around the place. My wife and I were away at the time, but we heard all about it when we returned. Apparently, after about a week of fruitless interviewing and questioning, they finally disappeared. A few weeks later, an article appeared in their magazine, I've forgotten which. Anyway, the piece was entitled 'Everyday life in a remote Scottish village' or something like that. It described the simple way of life we villagers have, compared to urban dwellers. It didn't mention anything about psychic activity or so-called devil worship."

Andrew negotiated the people carrier through the narrow streets of a quiet town. He waited until he was on the open highway again, before speaking once more: "As I've said, it's not the same these days. Our village is suffering the same fate as most villages in Britain. Youngsters opting for more exciting careers have been leaving the villages for decades now. They began to realise there was more to life than ploughing fields or feeding stock; there was a big world out there, and opportunities for different careers were springing up everywhere. With sons not willing to follow in the footsteps of their fathers, farms were subdivided and sold, families broke up. I was one of those for my heart was set on becoming an airline pilot, and to achieve my ambitions I had to leave the village.

"In the last twenty years or so, townsfolk with money have been slowly buying up cheap rural properties, even barns and suchlike, and re-developing them. Over the years a number of people have settled in and around our village, as they have in other villages in Britain."

Andrew sighed and stayed silent for a while.

"Ah well, I suppose that's life," he said, with a rueful smile.

"But most of the older generations in our village hold on to their beliefs, and we come together regularly. We still celebrate the summer and winter solstice and the onset of the seasons, spring being the most important of all. The newcomers know nothing about this, of course, and neither do our children these days. That's why I had to be sure Tom was asleep before talking about it," said Andrew, glancing in his rear mirror at the sleeping boy.

"Since my enforced retirement from flying, I have turned my attention once again to the study of psychic phenomena. Many of our members live in, or have originated from, Craigemere. Others come from the Welsh spiritual village of Kingsvale. Most of our French people hail from Emile's village, Lametsoing, in Brittany. At our conventions we have talks and discussions on the power of the spiritual mind and its effects above and beyond physical law. Some members give amazing demonstrations of their psychic powers."

"But I do not understand, why do you still need to maintain secrecy?" asked Merlin, "Surely the authorities do not punish you for observing these doctrines today?"

"That is correct, but old habits die hard, as they say. There is also the fear of publicity, which, in itself is a form of persecution.

"As I have already mentioned, a lot of young people began leaving the villages many years ago. Some have risen to prominence in different fields, including politics, the military and the police force. In fact, 60 per cent of our fraternity members are career people. So, you see, there are good reasons why the vow of secrecy is still observed and honoured."

Suddenly, a cow appeared on the road, forcing Andrew to hit the brakes hard. After driving slowly around the animal, which had refused to budge, he remained silent, content to concentrate on his driving.

After a while, Merlin broached the subject of Tom and his problems.

"Yes, Tom's aunt explained the situation to my wife yesterday," said Andrew. "There was a similar situation here in Scotland only a few months back. A boy was prohibited from staying with his father whom he adored. He finally ran away from his mother and her new boyfriend and hasn't been seen since."

"Yes, I believe this could easily have happened with Tom," said Merlin. "I owe the boy too much to risk leaving him there."

The wizard told Andrew more of the boy's life, the death of his mother and father, and the current situation at his home and school.

Andrew gave a slight shake of his head. "It sounds as if he's had a rough deal during his young life. But I'm sure he will be happy with us during his stay. Monica will want to spoil him for she misses our own children, who have now grown up. Our two girls are at university and our boy, Rob, he's our youngest, is travelling around the world. We believe he's in Thailand at the moment, but we're not sure because he rarely makes contact with us, much to his mother's anguish."

About half an hour later they approached a cluster of dim lights, signalling the presence of a sleeping village.

"This is Craigemere, but this is only one part of it," said Andrew, as they drove past a straggling clutch of cottages and then an assortment of small shops on either side of the road. "The older section lies about a third of a mile over that way," he said, pointing to his left, where, in the moonlight, the vague outline of a leafy road could be seen as it emerged beyond the fringe of outlying cottages and disappeared into a copse of trees.

A little further on, they drove over a concrete bridge before turning left on to the same narrow road leading into the woods.

Minutes later they drew up into the grounds of an old but impressive house. Although the building was visibly beyond its best, it retained an appearance of restrained elegance; evidence that it had been a residence of some importance in the distant past.

Andrew's wife met them in the passage. Monica Robbins was a small, buxom woman with a ready smile and sparkling blue eyes.

After being introduced to the visitors she immediately took Tom by the hand.

"Look at this poor darling, he looks asleep on his feet," she said in a lilting Scottish brogue. "I will take him to his room, and you, my bonny man, can attend to our guest."

Andrew did most of the talking once Monica returned. He gave her an account of almost everything he had learned about Merlin on the drive up from Edinburgh. The wizard refused the offer of wine, but asked for water instead.

Not long afterwards, Monica realised their adult guest was also ready for bed.

"Come on, Merlin, let me show you to your room," said Andrew, after getting a hint from his wife. He led the wizard up the wide sweeping staircase, talking as he went. "The house is really too big now for Monica and I, but it's nice to have the extra rooms for the girls and their friends when they're back home from Uni"

Andrew opened the door and turned on the light before stepping aside to let Merlin enter the room belonging to his daughter. Merlin had been just as astonished the previous night when Bill had taken him to his daughter's room. He had shown

Merlin the bedside lights, the bathroom, shower and toilet, and how to use them, before leaving his guest to care for himself.

In awe he looked around the room before his eyes alighted on the double bed. The previous night he had slept in a single bed with cream sheets. But this was different. The sheets here were whiter than any white he had ever seen. Andrew watched silently as Merlin gently pushed the pillows with his hand, then caressed the silk counterpane with the back of his fingers.

"Come, I will show you the bathroom." The host opened the door to the ensuite and motioned with his hand for his guest to enter. Once again, the wizard could only gaze in awe at his surroundings.

"This is the shower," said Andrew, but before he could say more, Merlin quietly said: "Andrew, I think I understand. Mr Watson showed me everything last night."

"Oh yes, of course… I didn't think." He bade Merlin good night, adding: **"I** will be away early in the morning, so just sleep in if you wish. Monica will be happy to cook you some breakfast once you're up."

CHAPTER 15

Christine Flowers knocked on the door of the Watson farmhouse. The door was opened by a stocky, ruddy-faced man Chrissie assumed to be the husband.

"Mr Watson?"

"That's me. You are the reporter, I suppose?"

Chrissie introduced herself and was shown into the lounge.

"My wife is just boiling the kettle. Would you like a cup of tea or do you prefer coffee?"

"Coffee, if you wouldn't mind, no sugar or milk please."

She looked casually around the room, taking in the photographs on the wall and the free-standing ones on the old mahogany sideboard near the television. There were a few photos showing a boy and girl in various stages of growing up. Chrissie presumed the girl was their daughter and the boy was Tom. She looked down at the coffee table and suddenly noticed what appeared to be a phone number jotted down on a notepad. She sat down on the settee close by and took out her own leather-bound notebook. But before she could write down the number, a woman came in carrying a tray, followed by Mr Watson.

Chrissie quickly stood up as he introduced his wife.

"Just call me Kate if you wish, and my husband is Bill," said Kate.

"Thank you and I'm Chrissie."

Chrissie still had the notepad in her hand.

"Do you mind if I take notes while we talk, Kate?"

"You will need to, I suppose."

This gave Chrissie the chance to jot down each digit from the number on the pad while talking to her host.

She took a sip of her coffee. It was just what she needed after going through almost half a bottle of cognac last night. She hoped the black liquid would ease her hangover, but doubted it.

"I suppose you haven't seen or heard from Tom, have you?"

Kate looked up to her husband then quickly shook her head.

"No, we haven't, I'm afraid." said Bill.

"Ahh, then you both must be desperately worried?"

"We are, you see we love him dearly, like our own son," said Bill.

"By the way, I was the person who saw your nephew leave the car with the strange bearded man at the petrol station. You see, Mark, he's my photographer, and I, were sitting in our car near the shop, because we wanted something to eat. That's when I saw was this man with the beard jump out of the car, followed by the boy. They both disappeared up the road. Mark didn't notice, he was looking at something else. I thought it was strange, so after a few seconds I jumped out of my car and tried to follow them, but they had simply disappeared in the crowd."

The reporter looked at Kate then smiled sympathetically. "There's no-one you know who would answer the man's description, is there?"

"No, of course not," answered Kate, almost indignantly. "If we knew someone like that, we'd know where to look for him, wouldn't we. If only we'd refused to let him go back, none of this would have happened. He would be with us… people who love him."

Bill put his arm around Kate. "I'm sorry, but my wife is terribly upset."

Chrissie nodded. "I understand. Have the police been around to see you yet?"

"No, but they have phoned," said Bill. "I believe they are coming today or tomorrow."

On her way back to the office, an hour and a half later, Chrissie tried shaking off the nagging thought that they might not have given her the full story about their missing nephew. Outwardly they appeared very concerned, they even sounded genuine when they said they hadn't seen or heard from Tom since saying goodbye to him earlier that afternoon. And yet some voice in the back of her mind told her something different.

But despite her suspicions, one thing was certain, they both cared very much for their nephew. It was there in the way they spoke about him, the way the woman got glassy-eyed when showing Chrissie photos of the boy. She then heard all of Tom's history from the time his mother died to his present-day problems with his schooling and his stepmother. She had, at the very least, obtained two good photographs of the boy… and the phone number, if that's what it was!

CHAPTER 16

Artor Karalios entered the large timber-clad hall that overlooked the Thame River and strode towards the seven members of the Londinium War Council seated around a large rectangular oak table in the middle of the room. Even in this big hall, almost fifteen paces long and ten paces wide, the Commander was an impressive figure. The typical Roman military tunic covered his huge solid frame, exposing the tanned muscular arms and legs.

The fighting skills of the great Artor were well known throughout the land. A man of Roman/Greek descent who, like many Romano-Britons, dearly wished for the return of the Romans and the order and discipline they had imposed on the country during their 400-year reign. But Artor Karalios was also a thorn in the side of many in the military hierarchy, for he steadfastly adhered to the old military methods of the Romans. There were a few tribunes and die-hard commanders who embraced the old Roman army traditions, but Artor in particular followed Roman military procedures to the letter. His strategic intelligence, his own high standard of performance and his strict discipline with his officers and troops, made his regiment the most feared by the enemy and the most respected by his allies.

It was known that Artor's great-great-grandfather was none other than Karalios the Greek, the great warrior captured in battle by the Romans near Thessalonika and taken back to Rome. His awesome strength, his fighting ability and his final heroic stand had so impressed his captors, they decided to spare his life, on the condition that he entered the gladiatorial circuit.

His success in the fighting arena, combined with his good humour, keen intelligence and compassion for his victims, made Karalios a favourite with the populace. Three years were to pass before the Greek was badly wounded in a gladiator fight against two African tribesmen. On the insistence of a senator's daughter who had fallen in love with Karalios and had been seeing him secretly, he was to be granted the right to become a free man should he recover from his wounds. Karalios did recover and eventually the Senate agreed to bestow on him the status of free citizen, though he was denied full Roman citizenship.

Due to his popularity, favours were extended to the former gladiator, and having a shrewd business brain, he soon became a successful promoter of gladiatorial contests in the provinces. He married Orphalia, the senator's daughter, in Rome less than a year after he had become a free man.

The great-great-grandson of Karalios the Greek now looked down at the seven individuals seated at the table. "I believe you wish to see me about a coming invasion?" Artor said, to no-one in particular.

"We do, Artor Karalios," answered a pale, dark-haired man at the end of the table. "You have been chosen for this mission because of your reputation. This war council meeting is to discuss with you the strategy of your campaign and to establish what likely costs the Londinium Council will incur in order to bring about the total destruction of these Saxons heathens."

Paulinus, the spokesman, introduced the council members and himself to the Commander.

"We have had news that the Saxon warlord, Aktar, has invaded the region known as Heranium. Do you know the area, Artor?" he asked.

"I know little of it, apart from the village of Weerby, where I had once visited a dear friend at his home.

"Do you know anything about this invasion, Artor?" questioned Paulinus.

"I have only the information given to me by your messenger some days ago. Before that, rumours and nothing but rumours was to be heard from Londinium."

"Well, the situation is now critical," said Paulinus, ignoring the jibe. "The Saxons have completely overrun the region, including the town of Heran. If they become established there, the Roman road will be open to them. It would mean, sooner or later, our city will be vulnerable to attack. We need your military experience to be rid of these pagans, once and for all."

Roman road builders had, in the distant past, built a first-class road heading south-west from Londinium. After some thirty odd miles the road met the Weer River. Due to the forested terrain, it had been necessary at this point to continue building the road on the other side of the river. A wide, sturdy wooden bridge was installed, allowing the road to advance southward, but less

112

than six miles further on, it petered out altogether. It was as if the road builders had suddenly dropped tools; for what reason, no-one knew.

It was around this bridge that a settlement developed. The new road had given the surrounding region some strategic importance, enabling trade with the big city. Quickly, the settlement became a village and eventually grew into the bustling town the Romans named Heran, and the surrounding region became known as Heranium.

"I understand your fears about the Roman road, but it could also work in our favour," contended Artor.

Paulinus nodded: "That maybe so, but the purpose of this meeting is to find out how you intend to go about this mission and what the cost is likely to be for Londinium."

"Before I can answer either of those questions, I need to know much more about the Heranium situation; for instance, how many Saxons are we likely to face?"

The group looked at each other for some moments before Paulinus responded. "We're not sure, we've heard varying accounts, possibly seven or eight hundred, maybe more."

"Is there more than one tribe to deal with, and where are they now?"

"We have been told about a gathering of two tribes. We're not sure exactly how much of Heranium has been taken, but we believe the town of Heran and parts of the surrounding area are already under their control," answered the spokesman.

"Have there been many refugees arriving from the region?"

"Yes, there have been many. They are becoming a nuisance as they have nothing apart from personal belongings. Few have money, many are destitute and…"

The Commander cut in: "Are they safely housed and cared for, and have you questioned any?"

The councillors once again exchanged glances. They had not expected the meeting to go this way. They had thought to dictate their requirements to this man, not the other way around.

"We are not sure of where they are in the city, but we believe many have taken sanctuary in the churches," ventured Paulinus.

"And have you not questioned *any* of these people?"

113

"No, why should we?" said the spokesman, a little impatiently.

"Why should you… why should you?" Artor raised his voice for the first time. "Do you not realise the refugees are the best source of information about the region and the invaders?"

"We didn't think the…" began the spokesman.

Artor interrupted harshly: "Do you mean you have brought me here to present you with a campaign plan and an estimate of the cost of the operation, yet you have no idea of how many of the enemy my men have to face? No idea where their main camp is situated or what buildings they have commandeered! No idea what weapons they carry! What about the terrain around Heran? Is there much marshland in the area? Will our chariots be of use? Do these Saxons possess horses? " Artor leant his big frame over the table and said quietly: "Can't you give me any answers at all?"

"We didn't think…"

"No, you didn't think. But that's what you were elected to do, isn't it?"

"We are not familiar with your military requirements, why should we be?" This time the comment came from a man sitting to the right of the spokesman. His first name, Artor recalled, was Collain. Artor sized the man up; dark hair sleeked back into a pony-tail exposing a spotty, round face on top of a rotund body. 'No doubt a Thane,' thought the Commander. Plenty of property in his possession, but how much of it gained by honest means, he wondered.

"If Vortigern were alive, it would have been left to him," continued Collain. "He would have handled this situation without fuss."

"Vortigern!" exclaimed Artor. "The self-proclaimed King of all Britannia! It is he who has brought our country to its knees."

The council members exchanged quick hooded glances. To talk of Vortigern this way almost bordered on heresy.

"It was our esteemed leader who allowed these alien heathens to settle on our coastal fringes. He said in return they promised to guard our shores and repel other invaders. We in the military knew what the outcome would be. We wanted to run the alien savages back into the sea, every last one of them, but Vortigern would not listen."

Artor hesitated, gratified with the signs of confusion among some members of the council.

"You should all know your history, but in case your memory is a little hazy, let me remind you," said the Commander, in a quiet but meaningful voice. "It was the troubles in Gaul that caused the depletion of the Roman forces in Britain during their last fifty or so years of occupation. Detachments from Britain were sent over to bolster Rome's position there, so the Romans began to conscript many young Britons into their depleted ranks. As more divisions departed, compulsory recruitment of all youths on attaining the age of sixteen was put in force.

"Their military service was for five years. Those who wished to leave at the end of their term were free to do so. But the promise of land grants for long service encouraged many to stay on. As you all know, an effective army of Britons trained and controlled by Roman officers was created. If that recruitment had continued, we could have repelled these alien savages easily as soon as they arrived on our shores. But once the Romans had finally left our soil, what did your illustrious Vortigern do? Within four years he dissolved all compulsory military service. His reason, he said, was that the young men were needed on the land. But his real reason, as we in the military knew, was money. He did not see the need to pay for a large conscripted army when he could obtain the cheap services of Saxon renegades.

"From then on, his policy was to rely on volunteers to keep the armies going, and to appease the heathens now overrunning our country. That's what the great Vortigern has done for our people."

The Commander cast a dark glance over the small assembly. "And I should not need to remind you, but it was the policy of Vortigern that eventually caused the death of Ambrosius Aurelianus, our most fearless warrior."

Paulinus, quickly brushing aside the slur on their past king, said: "We have been discussing the possibility with York of resuming compulsory military service for all youths."

"I wouldn't bother, Paulinus," retorted Artor. "It's too late to close the stable door… the horse has already bolted."

The Commander looked down at the table, purposefully changing the subject. "As members of this war council, should you not become familiar with our military requirements?" For a few moments, silence reigned.

"Can I ask that you list everything you require from the war council? Then, once we have worked through that list, we could set a date for another meeting."

Artor regarded the speaker with favour. The man spoke sense. He was a big man with partly balding reddish hair and a freckled complexion to match. Artor noticed the big hands which looked as if they had done more work than all the others put together.

"I agree entirely… Marius, isn't it?"

"That is correct. Named after the great Roman General," said Marius, with a look of amusement in the expressive blue eyes. The Commander nodded his approval.

"If you are all in favour of this suggestion, I can list for you now what is required of you," said Artor. The council murmured their consent.

"First then," said Artor, "I need you to secure a suitable building where the refugees can be gathered, sheltered, fed, watered… and then questioned."

"I think I might help there," said Marius. "I have been waiting for one of my ships to arrive from Greece with cargo, but it has been overdue for many weeks and I believe by now it must have foundered. I am left with two partially empty warehouses. I can store all my goods in the one and leave you to use the other."

"Thank you for that, Marius," replied Artor.

"Second, I need the services of a competent artist at my disposal, for I will need maps and diagrams of Heranium, based on the information we hope to gain from the refugees.

"Third, I need you to make contact with York Council and request the transfer of at least a cohort of their troops from their coastal defenses or from Hadrian's Wall, I don't care which. The southern positions along the Thame River need to be well defended. I will be taking a cohort of my best fighters from there, and they need to be replaced."

"We have tried to talk to York in the past, Artor, they will not listen," Paulinus explained. "They say the northern incursions from the Picts and the Scots are increasing, and the Vikings have made further raids into the north/eastern regions close to their city, so they need all the military might available."

"You realise then that while my forces are away from their posts, much of the bastions and ramparts along the Thame will be undermanned. That will leave Londinium vulnerable."

"It is a risk we are prepared to take, Artor. We have no choice," said Paulinus.

Artor paused for a moment, contemplating the councillor's words, then he went on. "Fourth, I need you to arrange an early meeting with my supply officer, for he will need to issue you with an inventory of everything we need for this campaign. Which one of you will he be able to contact tomorrow? I need to know where and when, so he has no trouble finding you."

"Might as well be me, Artor," said Marius. "I'll be around my warehouses for the next few days, as I need to tidy them up a bit for the refugees. My premises are close to the quay side just downstream from Herculan Bridge. Ask anyone there, and they'll tell you where to find me."

"Thank you again, Marius," said the Commander.

"Finally, I want council members to find a dear friend of mine. His name is Cedrin, a well-known healer. It is likely he has left his village in Heranium with his sister and Merlin, his nephew. If that is so he will be living somewhere here in Londinium. Find out from the refugees, for some of them might know of their whereabouts."

"I know of them, Artor, for a cousin of mine has had treatment from Cedrin," said Paulinus. "As for Merlin, his nephew," he continued, "we have had word from our messengers, who say people in the region of Heranium believe he is a wizard of great power."

"I know of the lad, but only of his combat skills with the sword," Artor replied. "I have no knowledge of his wizardry, but I need you to make the matter of locating them a priority."

Council members managed to locate Cedrin on the second day, and that evening, the Commander stopped by to spend a little time with the man who had saved his life over ten years ago. At the time, Artor had lain critically injured in his quarters on Hadrian's Wall. It had been one of the medical auxiliaries who had told Gaius Theonis, a senior commander, about a great healer named Cedrin, who lived in the south. It had taken eight days for them to locate Cedrin and accompany him back to the northern border. It took another eight days for Cedrin to bring Artor back from the brink. The healer nursed the Commander for a further ten days before he was fully satisfied his patient was out of danger and healing well. On the morning of the 19th day, Artor awoke to find his saviour had vanished. None of the medical staff or his officers had seen the healer depart.

Four years ago Artor had an opportunity to call on Cedrin at his home in Weerby. An additional division of troops had been sent to the Thame defenses, allowing the Commander a few days respite; enough time to visit the man who had saved his life.

On this occasion the healer humbly apologised for the austere surroundings of his recently acquired refugee dwelling. Artor brushed the explanation away with a quick response. "Desperate times often mean desperate measures for us all Cedrin, so please do not demean yourself with apologies."

The visitor settled his huge frame in a chair and gazed around the tent. "So much has happened since the last time we met." said Cedrin. Artor nodded. After some small talk, the Commander enquired after his friend's nephew. "And how is Merlin?"

"He is well. But my nephew is more concerned about his falcon than with his own wellbeing. He will be out there now, on the common lands, giving the bird its exercise."

"I have heard about his sword skills."

"Yes, I believe he learned much from your two swordsmen."

"Athol is one of my best swordfighters. What he said about the lad impressed me."

"He certainly stretched my nephew to the limit," said Cedrin. "So I thank you, Artor, you are a true friend."

"Ahh, but nothing will compare with your devotion and skill in restoring me back to health those many years ago. Now about this nephew of yours, I am more than a little curious about him."

"Why should that be, Artor?"

"I will explain. My curiosity was first aroused when the first swordsman I sent you reported back less than six weeks later, to say he could no longer teach your nephew anything more. He admitted to the boy's superiority in every armed discipline. I found it hard to believe how anyone, let alone a mere lad of sixteen, could develop into an accomplished swordsman in such a short time. I needed to satisfy myself the words from my veteran soldier held some truth, and that's why I assigned one of my very best fighters to you."

"And you have already said he was duly impressed with my nephew."

"That is the least of it! Athol says the lad is more than a match for him also. It seems your nephew has the strength, the stamina and skill in either arm to compete with any in the land."

"It is good to hear these things about him, Artor, for there will be many troubled times ahead, and he will need to fend for himself."

"That is indeed true, but I also heard he can take care of himself without the use of the sword. Is that not correct?"

Cedrin hesitated, wondering how much to tell Artor. "He has had special gifts bestowed upon him that is certain."

"These 'gifts', as you call them, are well known among the refugees we have been questioning. Merlin is considered to be your apprentice, but to most he is referred to as the young wizard."

"Yes, I am aware of that, Artor. I can only hope I have given him the guidance to use his magical gifts with wisdom."

"I have no reason to disbelieve you, my friend. But I now need to place myself further in your debt and ask you once more to render me a service."

"If I can, I will, Artor. Just ask."

"I need both you and Merlin in my coming campaign. If you are in agreement, I would appreciate having your nephew as an escort to my scouting group. These legionaries will be leaving in pairs for Heranium within the next three days."

"He is not yet seventeen, Artor, and this scouting expedition will not be without dangers, will it?"

"I cannot deny that, my friend, but it is imperative my scouts be accompanied by locals of the region. We already have five suitable refugees who are familiar with different regions of Heranium. Each one will escort a pair of my scouting legionaries to a designated area. I have chosen two of my ablest legionaries to concentrate on locating the headquarters of the Saxons invaders in the town of Heran. It's probably somewhere near the eastern outskirts of the town, if the information we have received is correct. These men have instructions to seek out any location where Saxon groups might be found. It is a dangerous assignment, and my scouts will need someone to help them operate right under the nose of the Saxons. It is why I need your nephew to act as the main guide for this important assignment."

"He is little more than a boy, Artor, and his mother would not agree, I'm sure," protested Cedrin.

The Commander placed a hand on his friend's shoulder. "I have asked this because of the talk I have heard from the refugees. They say Merlin moves like a shadow, that he calms the most savage of dogs and knows the forest like the palm of his hand. Some even say they have seen him disappear in front of their eyes, and we know first-hand of his fighting capabilities, do we not?"

"I will need to discuss this with his mother, Artor. She is helping with the refugees this evening and I do not expect her back 'til late. Merlin will also need to agree."

"Merlin has already approached us, my friend. Once he'd heard about the need for scouting volunteers he made it known to my officers that he was able and willing to join them."

"I will still need to ask his mother, although if my nephew has his heart set on going, I can't see her words having much effect."

Artor raised himself slowly out of the chair. "It has been a pleasure meeting you again, my friend, but I must take my leave now as much has to be done tomorrow. Please take heed now of what I say. The outcome of this campaign may mean the difference between losing Heranium to the Saxon invaders and paganism forever, or ridding ourselves of these barbarians once and for all. Failure will mean the inevitable fall of Londinium, and the rest of our country would then capitulate to the many wolves waiting to join the fray. From what I've learned about this nephew of yours, he could help make the difference between success or failure."

"I understand what you are saying, Artor. I will give you an answer tomorrow after speaking to my sister."

"If we can call for your answer at noon tomorrow, my friend, I would be grateful. I also need your advice on a location for our campaign camp. My officers, after talking to the refugees, seem to think the camp needs to be somewhere in the region of Weerby. It's not the closest village to Heran, but we've been told it's completely deserted. It has good elevation, ideal for observation. More importantly, Merlin has informed me there is a clearing no more than half a league into the forest. It sounds as if it might be the ideal place to set up our campaign camp."

Cedrin nodded. "Yes, I know the place well, and Merlin of course knows it better."

"Our concern is there could be Saxon warriors holed up in the village. If that is so, our scouting party will need to inform us of this before the forward contingent arrives."

"I doubt you will find a Saxon warrior anywhere near Weerby village, Artor. It is too close to the forest for their liking." Artor knew the Saxons were almost as fearful of the forest as of the darkness. According to their heathen beliefs, the forest was where the spirits hid during the hours of daylight.

"Then my artist will need full details. He has just completed drawings of the layout of Heranium, showing the lie of the land, the village sites and so on. He will need to illustrate the approaches to Weerby and the location of the forest clearing if we are going to use it as our forward camp. If you could look at this with him tomorrow, my friend, I would be grateful.

"I will be pleased to give you what help I can, Artor." The Commander grinned. "That's all I can expect, my friend." Both men embraced before showing the palms of their hands in a farewell salute.

CHAPTER 17

The editor fingered the unopened envelope for a few moments, then pressed a button on the intercom. "Miss Carr, may I see you in my office please... right away"

Before the secretary had closed the door, the chief editor spoke again. "Miss Carr, er... Rosemary, what do you know about this?" he asked, tapping the envelope.

"Nothing sir, why?"

"Because this morning I came into my office and found this propped up against my pen stand." John Neilson once again tapped the offending envelope.

"I don't understand it, sir. All the mail comes through me, as you know. I certainly wouldn't leave a single letter like that on your desk. All your mail is sorted in order of what I think is important, and then it is all placed on your blotting pad."

"I know, I know, but then, how did it get here? It has no stamp or post mark, so someone must have brought it here by hand."

"I can't see how, sir," said the secretary, getting flustered. "None of the news room staff are allowed in your office without you being present."

"What about the cleaners, it must have been one of them?"

"We only have one cleaner doing this office sir, and Mrs Berenson has been with us for well over fifteen years. She just wouldn't do it. Not only that sir, but the CCTV camera automatically comes on whenever you are out of the office. It's directed every few seconds from the filing cabinet to your desk," she said, waving a manicured finger at the camera high up in the opposite corner of the room.

"Yes of course, but someone *must* have placed this letter on my desk. It couldn't get here by itself. Maybe it was here yesterday afternoon and I didn't notice it," he mused out loud.

"I would have noticed it, sir, when I was tidying up your desk after you'd left for the day. But sir...," the secretary hesitated.

"What is it?"

"Well sir, why don't you let me open the letter anyway."

John Neilson looked again at the envelope. "Looks like a kid's writing! No, I'm quite capable of opening it, Rosemary. But if this is some sort of joke, I'll have someone's guts for garters."

"Yes sir," said the secretary, wondering who would want to have a joke with someone as serious as her boss.

The editor held the envelope with forefinger and thumb while slitting it open with an ornate paper knife. He gingerly withdrew a folded page that had been torn out of an exercise book. He studied the contents of the page for a few seconds and then turned to his secretary again. "Rosemary, would you get Paul Mac' up here pronto."

John Nielson waited until his chief reporter was comfortably seated before passing the page over to him. "Paul, what do you make of this? Oh, and try not to handle it too much, the police might need it fingerprinted." Paul Mac'Veer read the note and looked at the envelope while his boss explained how he had come by it.

"What do you think, Paul?"

"Not sure, John, it's certainly weird how it got here. Why don't you go through the CCTV tape? You never know, that might throw some light on it."

"Didn't think o' that Paul, I'll get someone onto it, but what do you think about the letter? Worth a look at, don't you think?"

"Certainly is! It's either a hoax or it's genuine. If it's genuine then it's got the makings of a story," concluded the reporter. "Will get onto it right away," he added, getting up from the chair.

"Yes, I'd appreciate that. Come back to me if you find anything," said the editor.

It was after mid-morning before Paul Mac'Veer contacted his boss again. "Got something on that Tom Watson note, John," he said, over the phone. "An article in the Saltridge Echo. Do you want to see it?"

Five minutes later, Paul sat waiting while his boss read the article he had brought up to show him.

"Hmm, very interesting," mused John Nielson. "Who's the editor there?"

"It's at the top of the page. Robert somebody-or-other. Calls 'imself 'editor in chief'"

The editor scanned the heading.

"Hmm, Robert Maitland, eh? Well, well, well!"

"Why ... do you know him?"

"Yes, I certainly do. Dear old Robbo! He was my boss years ago, when we both worked for the Argus, a local paper down on the south coast. His wife wanted to move back to where her ailing mother lived, and I was promoted into the vacancy when he left. Last time we spoke was at his farewell party. What a small world!"

John Nielson pressed a button on his intercom.

"Miss Carr, would you please look up the phone number of the Saltridge Echo. I want to speak to the Editor-in-Chief, a Mr Robert Maitland. Thank you."

"Robbo, is that you?" said the editor, when the voice came on the line. "It's Johnnie here. John Nielson..." The newspaper men had some catching up to do, but after a while John Nielson brought up the subject of Tom Watson. "Robbo, I've just been reading this article of yours on a missing lad called Tom Watson... An interesting story... That bit about the bearded guy with a long cloak who coaxed the lad out of the car? Seems a bit dramatic! How reliable is the source? I see... That's a bit of a coincidence, your own reporter? You say she's one of your best..."

John Nielson glanced at Paul Mac'Veer at the last statement, but carried on talking.

"From the article, it's obvious she's interviewed both parties... I see. What about Child Welfare? SOCAR! At the time...I see..." The editor once again glanced at Paul.

"Robbo, can I send someone over to meet up with this Christine Flowers, either this afternoon or tomorrow? I see. How long is she away for? I see. Well, that's ok we'll probably meet up with her when she gets back... No Robbo, there's no urgency... just heard about the case on the police grapevine that's all." After a little more small talk with his past boss, John Nielson offered his thanks and put down the phone. He then turned to Paul Mac'Veer.

"Apparently his own reporter, a woman called Christine Flowers, was the only witness to the abduction. Even the photographer sitting next to her didn't see it."

"If it *was* abduction?" queried Paul.

"The lad's note would indicate he went of his own free will, but he could easily have been coerced into writing it. No, Paul, we'll report this as abduction unless we hear otherwise."

"I notice you didn't mention the kid's letter, John?"

"Didn't think I should. If Robbo knew about it, the Saltridge Echo might well steal our thunder."

"Cut-throat business, 'aint it!" quipped the chief reporter.

"Anyway, this Christine woman is away on annual leave for a month, so it leaves us to do our own research. We'll start with the police, then child welfare, then the two affected parties, the step-mother and the aunt and uncle. And Paul, I'd like you to handle it. It might not lead to anything, but the letter intrigues me and makes me think there's more to this than meets the eye."

"Trouble is, John, I've a deadline on that drug bust in Soho, and I've also got the football hooligan case on the go at present."

"Look, I'll get Regan to take care of the drug case; you're almost there with that one, aren't you?" suggested the Chief Editor

"Yep, just a chat with the pub proprietor needed."

"Ok, brief me on it before you leave, and I'll arrange for Mat to pick it up. As for the football hooligans, hasn't Emily been tagging along with you on that one?"

"She has, and I must say she's ok, considering she's only been with us for six weeks."

"Alright, then let her finish it off. It'll give her some confidence."

"I'm happy with that, John. She's itching to get into it anyway."

"Oh, by the way, Paul, get Miss Carr to make a copy of this for your use," said the editor, holding out the letter. "Tell her to handle it as little as possible, in case the police want their forensic people to look it over - the same with the envelope. Then get her to put a dated 'Received' stamp on both, you know what the Bill are like for detail."

As the reporter went to the door, the editor called to him: "Paul, I have a strange feeling on this one, so give it your best."

CHAPTER 18

The late July sun was sinking low on the horizon as a mounted officer and four legionaries led the forward campaign detachment out of Londinium. Behind them, Cedrin, with Gwindore at his side, drove his medical supply wagon ahead of a troop of sixty auxiliaries and a further two mounted officers. Artor had assigned Cedrin as the official medical officer of the detachment.

Seated behind Cedrin and Gwindore was a skinny, pimply youth called Dorian, who was one of the boys involved in the fight when Merlin had humbled Jonas, the village bully. Dorian had met Merlin again in the refugee hall on the first day, and they had become the best of friends. On the boy's lap was a cage containing Keetah, the golden falcon.

Merlin had persuaded his uncle and mother to take Dorian with them. "After all," he had argued, "who else but Dorian could I trust to care for Keetah while I am away?"

Behind Cedrin's wagon were eight supply wagons, four carrying sacks of grain, salted meat and other provision for the coming campaign, the other four containing leather tents, ropes, pegs, spades and additional equipment and tools for setting up the campaign camp. It would shelter and feed the body of legionaries following behind. About thirty able-bodied male and female refugee volunteers brought up the rear.

The six pairs of scouting legionaries had left for Heranium with their guides two days before. They were dressed in peasant tunics and were equipped with dagger and short sword, the weapons hidden under their tunics in specially made leather slings. They had their instructions; they were to report to the campaign camp within seven days from the time of their departure. To expedite their assignment, the twelve legionnaire scouts and Merlin, together with the five refugee escorts, were assigned two transport wagons. Two auxiliaries accompanied the group, each driving one of the wagons.

At a safe distance from the beleaguered town of Heran, the scouting party split up into pairs, and walked into Heranium with their guides. The two auxiliary drivers took the transport wagons into the nearby forest, which lay on the northern side of the road. There, hidden from view, they would await the arrival of the forward camp detachment.

Soon after his talk with Artor, Cedrin advised the artist on the drawing-up of several maps of Weerby and the surrounding area, which were given to the centurions, auxiliary officers and the scouting legionaries.

The campaign's camp site had been established and all officers briefed on its whereabouts. The officers in charge of the auxiliary forward detachment were instructed to have two guards placed at the forest entrance on arrival to mark the route for other military units to follow.

It was common knowledge the Saxon pagans feared the dark; it was their belief that evil spirits were abroad during the night. Artor therefore arranged that the forward detachment and the main division of the 36th would travel during the hours of darkness.

"We will take advantage by travelling the Roman road at night," Artor had said at the final meeting with the Londinium War Council. "It will make our march much easier."

Two days after the departure of the forward camp contingent, the main body of troops under the command of Artor Karalios was on the move.

The Commander, mounted on his favourite grey horse, was at the head of the seven hundred-strong formations, flanked on the left by Gaius Theonis, his divisional commander, and on the right by Julius Medinas, his third-in-command. Behind them came a single legionnaire officer marching five paces ahead of the first one hundred legionaries, flanked by a mounted centurion. Fifteen paces behind marched the next bracket of a hundred troops and so on. Bringing up the rear were eighty bowmen and twenty supply auxiliaries. In this formation, the army made its way out of Londinium and on to the road leading to Heranium, just as the sun was going down.

Early dawn saw the 36th regiment finally arrive at their destination. The forward camp detachment was already buzzing with activity. All the tents had been pitched and the smell of cooked food was in the air.

It was another three days before the scouting pairs and their guides began to arrive at the camp. By the end of the day, four pairs had returned, but Merlin was not among them. The Commander with his two senior officers, seven centurions and Cedrin, questioned each party soon after their arrival, while their memories were still fresh. The following morning saw the arrival of the fifth pair. Later that morning, Artor Karalios was about to start questioning the last pair of scouts when a commotion in the camp caught everyone's attention. Merlin had just emerged out of the forest. He and a legionnaire scout were carrying their wounded comrade between them. Gwindore was fussing behind them as they made their way to the sick tent, delighted to see her son back unharmed.

Artor ordered Merlin and the fit legionnaire to join them immediately. They were questioned for some considerable time, the interrogators pausing now and then to allow Cedrin to record significant details on parchment. Satisfied he had gleaned all he could from the pair, Artor dismissed the scout, but requested Merlin's presence at the conference table. The Commander turned to Cedrin. "I have asked your nephew to be present at this meeting because your combined knowledge of Heran will be invaluable."

Artor looked around at his officers. "The information we have gathered about the enemy is this. There are, we are told, around twelve hundred Saxon warriors in the region. All but around fifty of them are in or around Heran town. They have turned three large villa halls into their strongholds. These halls are within two hundred paces of each other. It is thought around six hundred Saxons return there each evening to eat, drink and sleep. Their leader, Cissa, and some of the hierarchy, are quartered in one of the villas attached to the halls.

"It appears these buildings are located on the outskirts of the town, away from the poorer districts. The surrounding area is partially cleared of forest, so there's a good opportunity to mount a full-scale attack, leaving no chance for the pagans to escape.

"Another sixty or more have taken over a community hall on the other side of the old Roman Bridge to guard the road and river, and to prevent townspeople from leaving. The Londinium road has been barricaded at the edge of town. There are about forty Saxons guarding around three hundred or more Heran men in a livestock pen on a nearby cattle farm. They're probably meant to be taken back to the Saxon's homeland to be used as slaves or sold elsewhere.

"But Merlin brings us the most worrying news. As you have just heard from him, many of the Saxons have taken over houses in the Heran Township, capturing or killing the males and then having the females tend to them. There are about four hundred or more of the enemy living this way.

"The roaming band of fifty Saxons is holed up in a big hay barn near the village of Chewle. It lies about three leagues south of here. During the day they roam the territory in groups of around ten, terrorizing other settlements and villages, looting what they can carry to take back to the barn before it gets dark."

Artor looked around the table. "Are there any questions?"

"Can you tell us what our individual duties might be?" Theonis asked.

"We are already in agreement we attack the main body at early sun-up. The fifty Saxons quartered in the hay barn near Chewle will be taken care of by Medinas and sixty legionnaires. The group of Saxons housed on the other side of the bridge will be attacked immediately after the main assault."

Artor looked at his first officer. "Theonis, this will be your responsibility. We will discuss this further during the march down to Heran. The Saxons guarding the young Heran men will be taken care of by a small detachment of our best legionaries, but we will arrange this operation once we have arrived at our destination."

The Commander now rested his gaze on both Cedrin and Merlin. "Cedrin, you have tended many of the people of Heran, and I presume you have often had Merlin accompany you?"

Cedrin nodded. "That is so, Artor."

"Then have you any suggestions on how we can get our hands on these barbarians holed up in houses within the town?"

Silence followed while Cedrin considered this.

Finally he spoke. "There is a way, Artor, but unfortunately Merlin will need to be involved for it to work. However, my sister, Gwindore will be deeply hurt if he leaves again so soon."

"Then say to her, Cedrin, I have commandeered the lad to act for his country, and you have no say in the matter."

"I will explain it to her, but she will grieve nevertheless."

Artor Karalios grinned. "It's a woman's place to grieve, Cedrin."

The healer gave a wry smile and nodded.

"That's settled then, my friend," said the Commander. "Now please tell us the plan you have in mind."

CHAPTER 19

Robert Maitland, Robbo as he was affectionately called by his staff, had not been happy with the sudden request from his star reporter, Chrissie Flowers, for a month's immediate leave.

"I am already short-staffed, Chrissie. Two other reporters are off, one of them on sick leave. I know you have annual leave due, but can't you at least wait until Jerry gets back?"

Chrissie was not swayed. "I'm sorry, boss, my annual leave is not due, it's overdue. You promised when I filled in over Christmas as a favour, I could take my annuals whenever I wanted. Anyway, I need to get away. I just need a break! Do you realise I've had no proper time off now for well over fourteen months?"

Robbo sighed. He knew he couldn't dissuade her. He never could, not once she had made her mind up about something.

"Is the Tom Watson story wrapped up, Chrissie?"

"Yes, of course, completed yesterday."

"Well, if you've tidied up all the other bits and pieces, I suppose I'd better let you go."

Chrissie was in no hurry. She had promised herself a holiday from the relentless deadline stress, and a holiday is what she was going to have. She had told her parents she'd visit and stay for maybe two or three days before heading up to Scotland. Chrissie owed them that, for it was well over a year since her last visit. She was determined to find out about Tom, her instincts told her there could be a big story there, but her first priority had to be her parents.

Two days later Chrissie drove out of Woodford, where her parents lived, and headed for the M1. She would have stayed another day, but her mother's dedication to tidiness and cleanliness irritated and hurt her. It always had done. Even as a little child when they lived near Salisbury, in Wiltshire, she remembered being smacked just for letting a small piece of a pear she was eating drop on the floor.

Her father also got on her nerves, because he had never stood up for himself or his children. All he ever did was try to pacify his wife. He never seemed to have a mind of his own. Chrissie had pulled him aside in the garden on her first day and said: "Dad, why do you always ingratiate yourself to her? Why don't you tell her where to get off sometimes? You never know, you might get into the habit. You also know she bloody well deserves it."

"It's ok for you to have a go at your mother, Chrissie, but you don't have to live with her," reasoned her father.

"Neither do you, dad. You can always come and stay with me."

Her father appeared shocked at the suggestion.

"What are you saying, Chrissie, that I should leave your mother?"

"If you're unhappy, yes," Chrissie retorted. "My mother might get such a shock you've actually left her, she might start being more considerate. You both might end up having a happier marriage."

"Who says I'm unhappy?"

"Tell you what, dad, look me in the eyes and tell me you're happy with mum, and I'll never mention it again."

Her father looked at his daughter for no more than a second before letting his eyes drop. He turned on his heels and slowly went back into the house.

Chrissie had realised long ago that her need for a strong minded-man in her life had contributed to her two failed relationships. Both had been with men who eventually let Chrissie make decisions about almost everything. Both would say 'sorry' for any reason, even when Chrissie knew they were not at fault. It tended to make her complain unduly at any opportunity, just to get a 'sorry' out of them. She finished with both men in the same way - quickly, and without a fuss. She just didn't want to end up like her mother.

The last word she'd had from each of them was "sorry".

Chrissie drove off the M25 and took the A1 to Scotland. It felt good to get away from the office for a while. It was the phone number she had copied at the Watson house that had made up her mind. Good old Ross had once again come up trumps. She had come away from the police station with the name of a village, even a house name. The strange thing was, the village was the one she had visited some years ago. She'd been working freelance for a magazine to gain experience – and extra money. She was instructed to investigate a rumour about witchcraft being practiced in the village. But she found nothing to substantiate the rumours and finally came away with a story on the friendliness of the villagers and their relaxed way of life. This new development, however, could not be a mere coincidence.

It was late afternoon when Chrissie unexpectedly came upon Craigemere village. She had been so enthralled by the beauty of the countryside during the last part of her journey that time seemed to have flown past. She already recognised some landmarks as she approached the village. Sited on the hill to her right were the neat cemetery and the small church beyond with its impressive entrance. A little further on to her left was the stud farm, with beautiful race horses grazing in an adjacent field. Immediately after the stud farm came the quaint thatched cottages. Here, two or three narrow streets branched off from the road, lined with cute, white-fenced gardens and whitewashed cottages. In another, she caught a glimpse of thatched roofs overhanging the narrow bricked pavement.

Soon she was driving past the butcher's shop and the post office where she had posted a card to her parents all those years ago. There were other shops that were vaguely familiar; as if nothing had changed since her last visit. And of course, nothing had.

Chrissie passed quickly through the tiny village centre, keeping an eye out for the old pub where she stayed during her last visit. It was a little way out from the village, she knew that, but couldn't quite remember how far. She suddenly spotted the building as it came into view with its high, red-tiled roof and the tall, neatly cut privet hedge partly surrounding the building.

The reporter pulled into the wide driveway and parked below the 'Rambler's Rest' sign. A slight, dark-haired woman Chrissie didn't recognise greeted her at the reception window.

"Yes, we do have a free room, but it's at the top, if you don't mind the climb?"

"No, I don't mind. I'll take the room," said Chrissie, anxious to get out of her clothes and into a refreshing shower.

As she reached the first floor with her suitcase and was about to take the narrower staircase up to her room, a huge man with an untidy mane of dark hair came out of a nearby room.

"May I assist with ze case, please?" asked the man.

French, thought Chrissie, detecting the distinctive accent. "No, I can manage, but thank you… Er, merci beaucoup!" She said, happy to experiment with her rusty school-girl French. "Tres bien, d'accord, Madame," he said, and then, with surprisingly light footsteps, he descended the stairs.

CHAPTER 20

"Cedrin, your plan's merit lies in its simplicity," said Artor. "Merlin will go before sun-up. I will also heed your advice on the importance of the full moon tomorrow night. We will have the men rested tomorrow, but prepared to move soon after midnight. If, as you say, the Saxon savages celebrate the night of the full moon, it will make our job that much easier."

The morning light was not welcomed by Merlin, for he preferred the comfort of darkness. But it was necessary to visit the widow Marian in daylight. To make a clandestine night-time visit might have risked a scream from the old woman, and noise had to be avoided at all costs.

Merlin found the house quite easily for he had accompanied his uncle on past visits to the widow to administer treatment. The building consisted of two smallish rooms. The young wizard was certain the back room with the faded blue curtain over the window was the widow's bedroom. He started tapping on the small window pane with a pebble, paused, and just as he was about to start again, the curtain moved, exposing the frowning face of Marian Cutter. Her expression changed to one of delight as she recognised Cedrin's young helper.

"And how be your uncle?" asked the widow, as she quietly ushered Merlin inside.

"He is well and sends his best wishes," Merlin replied.

The widow nodded. "It was so good to see your face at the window, Merlin, for you know, things are not good here, and all our young men have been taken away."

"That's why I have come to see you, Widow Marian."

The young wizard then told her about the army and the coming battle. The widow could hardly contain her excitement at the news, and only when Merlin spoke about the Saxons who were holed up in many of the houses around the town, did she become serious.

"They are cruel, dirty savages, the lot of them," she said with venom.

"We will be rid of them soon, Widow Marian, but we'll need your help."

"I will willingly die to be rid of these vermin. What do you wish of me, Merlin?"

"My uncle says you might still be buying white sail cloth from Londinium for the dying and making of work tunics and the like?"

"Yes, I did, until these brutes arrived, but now… nothing."

"But you still have white sail cloth?"

"Of course, why?"

Merlin then outlined his uncle's plan.

"Yes, that can be done, and I have many old but eager friends to help me."

"What about the young boys?"

"We have more than enough willing hands to act as guides for the soldiers," said the widow.

**   **   **

At the prescribed hour, the 36th legion moved single file out of its camp. The full moon shone brightly, showing them the way. Once out of the forest, they walked two abreast in the direction of Heran. Scouts had gone ahead to guide the leading marchers and to make sure no there were no nasty surprises waiting for the soldiers.

The Commander arranged for ten auxiliary troops, together with Cedrin's medical team and the refugee volunteers, to mind the camp.

With the fifty extra auxiliaries drawn from the camp, the total number of fighting troops under Artor's command now stood at seven hundred and fifty. Of these, one hundred and fifty were auxiliary troops, eighty of them being skilled bowmen.

Silence was essential, so talking was forbidden as the soldiers advanced. The wheels of the supply wagon that followed had been wrapped with layers of cloth, as had the horses' hooves.

At the river, a detachment of eighty men under the command of Julius Medinas were diverted toward Chewle to attack the Saxon warriors quartered at the barn. They were expected to get there at about the same time Artor's division would arrive at Heran - the dark early hours when the Saxons would be at their most vulnerable.

The main body of men veered to the left and continued their march along a well-worn cart track. Soon they were silently

135

marching on the unfinished Roman road which wended its way towards the town of Heran.

**   **   **

Julius Medinas had been serving under Artor Karalios since joining the 36th legion at Hadrian's Wall as a junior officer of seventeen. He looked very different form his commander for he was of slim build and olive complexion, but his hatred of the Saxons matched that of his senior officer. As a boy of sixteen he had seen his father, the commander of a southern garrison, cut down by a horde of Saxons. Later, after managing to escape through a secret tunnel in the fort, he had heard from fleeing refugees that both his mother and young sister had been publicly executed.

Julius, his officers and a legionnaire from the scouting mission led the men across a ploughed field towards the back of the barn. The Saxons had lit torches at the front of the building, and even though morning was approaching, raucous laughter and shouting could still be heard from inside. The officer looked up at the full moon low in the south-eastern sky. He was thankful his Commander had acted on the advice from the healer, to take advantage of the full moon and the Saxon celebrations.

Medinas now had to judge the appropriate time to make his move. He was sure their attack would be successful, but his main concern was to minimise the risk of injury to his men. Time was important, though, as Artor was expecting his senior officer and his troops to be on hand for the initial onslaught on Heran.

Julius whispered an order to the two officers standing close by. Quietly, they divided the troops into four groups of twenty. At a hand signal from an officer, two groups filed out from the barn in opposite directions, then, after ten paces, they stopped. On another signal they fanned out until they had completely surrounded the barn.

Then Julius and one of his officers led the remaining two groups along the sides of the barn. Staying close to its stone walls, both parties stopped at the open end of the barn. The soldiers quietly drew their short swords, the only effective weapon in close-quarter combat, and waited for the order from their commander.

Julius was about to give the signal when he froze. Three Saxons emerged from the barn. They stopped within the circle lit by the burning torches to urinate. Knowing they were unlikely to venture out into the darkness, Julius waited. As the last of the Saxons had disappeared back inside the barn, he counted to twenty before his 'call to arms' went out. His main aim was total surprise, giving those inside little time to draw their weapons.

The soldiers stormed the barn in pairs. With short swords raised, the first to enter ran to the back of the barn to prevent the Saxons furthest away from going for their weapons. The tactic also allowed full access to the troops following on behind.

A small number of Saxons had been able to get at their weapons. One had his forearm completely severed in his hurried attempt to defend himself; another had his throat sliced so deeply, his head fell backward, exposing shattered vertebrae. A third had his right hand dismembered while attempting to raise his sword. Two managed to meet the soldiers' short swords with their own, but one was cut down from behind, the blade cutting deep into the side of the neck. The other Saxon caught one legionnaire in the shoulder, but he was struck by another British blade, and then another, before collapsing to the ground in a bloody heap.

It was all over very quickly. Some lay where they fell, hands clasped, crying out in their strange tongue as they pleaded for mercy. The soldiers knew their orders; no Saxons to be left alive. The short swords were used mercilessly; any Saxon who moved was killed quickly.

Julius Medinas had his troops form up for inspection. The bleeding from the casualty's deep shoulder wound had been staunched as well as possible and Julius decided to send the wounded man, together with an escort, back to the camp for medical attention. Once both men had reluctantly taken their leave, Julius sent two scouts ahead to inform Artor the mission had been successful and his troops were on the move. The centurion then headed his men in marching order towards the beleaguered town, where Artor was waiting.

Heran was asleep when the 36th regiment came to an orderly standstill outside the town. Then it was down to Merlin to lead

137

the troops around the outskirts of the town towards a large stand of trees that would conceal them from the Saxon's stronghold. They were within three hundred paces of one of the villa halls the Saxons had made their headquarters. The men were stood at ease and then allowed to rest within the shelter of the trees.

Artor requested Merlin's presence again. It was time to implement the strategy for dealing with the Saxons domiciled in the Heran households.

The twelve legionaries waited in the dawn gloom while Merlin tapped cautiously on widow Marian's door. It was opened almost immediately, for Marian was awake and expecting him. Six scruffy young boys filed out and stood looking up expectantly at Merlin.

"They know what to do, Merlin. Each boy will lead the soldiers to a part of the town they are familiar with."

The old woman then took hold of Merlin's sleeve to pull him closer. "Many of the vermin are staying over there tonight," she whispered, jerking a gnarled thumb in the general direction of the Saxon's stronghold. "They've had a wild party, full moon celebrations is what we've heard. I could hear their evil shenanigans from here. It should make your job a lot easier."

"How many of them are here in the houses do you think, Widow Marian?"

"Two hundred at most, I'd say. We've been busy removing the signs from the homes that are clear of the vermin tonight."

It had been arranged for a piece of white sail cloth to be pinned on houses containing Saxons. Women and children inside would be awake, expecting the soldiers' arrival.

The twelve legionaries Merlin had brought with him split up in pairs and took one of the young guides to lead them to their sleeping targets.

"Merlin, a torch will be alight in each house, for these monsters hate sleeping in the dark," whispered the widow.

The silent massacre began. One by one each targeted house was quietly entered by a pair of legionaries. With his broad sword raised, one would approach the sleeping Saxon, while the other stayed by the door. With two deft strokes the victim would be left dead or dying. Now and then the legionaries would enter a house where a Saxon was awake, but such was their speed of execution, he was cut down before he could reach for his weapon. The process was repeated again and again, until all resident Saxons had been accounted for.

In the meantime, Gaius Theonis had dispatched a further thirty legionaries and an officer to eliminate the Saxons guarding the Heran men who had been taken prisoner. Led by a guide, the soldiers silently and expertly slaughtered the sleepy guards at the entrance to their captives' enclosure.

The legionnaire officer had been instructed not to rouse the prisoners, but a few had been awake already and witnessed the slaughter. From then on, the legionaries had the difficult task of maintaining silence among the three hundred or so excited men, who were beginning to realise liberation was at hand.

Now, with the approaching dawn, two scouts were dispatched to reconnoitre the three halls and report back. Within fifteen minutes they returned to inform the Commander of the presence of guards at only two of the villa hall entrances, and they appeared sleepy and inattentive. It was pleasing news. Gaius suspected the guards, too, had been involved in the full moon celebrations.

Gaius Theonis selected four of his best close-combat legionnaires to return with the scouts and quietly dispatch the Saxons guards. Not long after that, a message was relayed to Artor Karalios of the arrival of the two scouts Julius Medinas had sent on ahead. After speaking with them, the Commander was ready to put his battle strategy into action. Julius Medinas, he knew, would arrive shortly; he would then have his full complement of troops and officers for the coming battle.

Once word came that the six Saxons guarding the villa halls had been successfully dispatched, Artor gave instructions to Gaius Theonis, his Divisional Commander, who sent two centurions and their troops to guard the town side of each of the three buildings. The two hundred legionnaires quietly spread out until they stood, a wall of shiny steel breastplates and helmets, spears and shields, facing the villa halls that housed the Saxons. Artor hoped the formidable sight would deter panicking Saxons from retreating into the town.

The first glimmer of daylight was emerging from the eastern horizon when Julius Medinas arrived with his march-weary troops. All officers knew Artor's battle strategy, and the necessity for daylight. If they attacked before sun-up, it was thought many Saxons might try to escape under cover of darkness.

Gaius Theonis ordered the eighty bowmen out into the open field, where they lined up three hundred and fifty paces from the villa halls. Here, in full view of the Saxons headquarters, they checked once again the tautness of their bows and tightened the waist straps holding the quiver of arrows securely to their back.

A centurion then led out eighty legionnaires to line up in single file, each kneeling in front of a bowman, hidden behind his upright shield, making it appear the eighty bowmen were the only soldiers facing the enemy. Gaius then ordered another two hundred legionnaires to stand in battle-ready formation, but out of sight, on the right hand side of the villas.

The remaining two hundred legionnaires were to conceal themselves in the forest that lay close to the third villa hall. This building was a little further away, on the left of the other two halls. The seventy remaining auxiliaries stood out of sight and to the left of the line of bowmen where Artor and his auxiliary officers were stationed.

The Commander then ordered his senior officers to their posts - Julius Medinas to the two hundred legionaries stationed behind the trees concealing them from the furthest villa hall, and Gaius Theonis to the two hundred troops on the right side of the nearest villa. The entrance to the main villa hall was facing the line of bowmen and the hidden legionnaires.

Many of the Heran townspeople were now gathered and watching proceedings from a safe distance, for word had quickly spread of the arrival of Artor's army and the battle that was about to begin. With the sun now caressing the tree tops in the east, Artor decided to start the attack. Ten bowmen with torched arrows fired at the two ventilation openings high up on each of the two nearest villa halls. Four reached their targets, immediately causing chaos within. A moment later the large hall doors were flung open and Saxon warriors poured out of both buildings. The commotion soon roused the Saxons housed in the hall furthest away, for within seconds the hall doors burst open and the occupants rushed out to join their cronies.

Panic reigned as they beheld the row of motionless bowmen ahead. Suddenly the horde became silent as a gap opened among them to reveal a huge bearded man striding out into the front. The man, Artor Karalios guessed, was Cissa, their leader, who stood with his warriors as they gazed out at the distant bowmen.

The throng of Saxons was already an ideal target for the bowmen, but they remained quietly at attention while the Saxon chiefs were loudly addressing their men and pointing occasionally to the line of bowmen, with Cissa pacing in front of them, constantly glaring at the thin line of troops standing like statues in the distance.

Artor Karalios waited as he watched proceedings from his position in the fringe of trees. Suddenly a bellow from the huge Saxon warrior spurred his men into action. Brandishing their swords, they started to rush across the field towards the bowmen, as Artor hoped they would.

The Commander waited until most of them were halfway across the open field before giving the order to sound the trumpet to set things in motion.

Artor immediately led his seventy auxiliary troops and ten legionnaires behind the double rank of bowmen and legionnaires, who were now standing with spears held high. At the same time, the two hundred legionnaires stationed on the town side of the villas stepped in front of the building where, only minutes before, the Saxons had been gathered. They were now immediately to the rear of the Saxons horde.

At the sound of the trumpet, the bowmen had taken two paces forward to stand in front of the legionaries, and were directing their arrows at the leading warriors, now less than a hundred paces away. The rushing vanguard was mowed down by a rain of arrows, causing those behind to trip on the fallen bodies. A bellow from somewhere in their midst stopped the Saxons' headlong rush. Now they stood, looking at the formidable sight of two ranks of the 36th regiment in full armour standing behind the bowmen, and the two legions who had closed in on them from behind. Another line of a hundred legionnaires had emerged from the trees, and was now standing, battle-ready, to the left of the Saxons.

The only escape route the desperate Saxons could espy was to their right, and when some began to flee, others followed. Commander Gaius was prepared for this and was already moving his two hundred troops at the double to head the Saxons off. Seeing this, the fleeing men turned quickly to rejoin the main body of bewildered Saxons in the centre of the field.

The trumpet sounded again – the signal for the two detachments headed by Julius Medinas and Gaius Theonis, to start marching forward abreast towards the Saxon fighters. Another trumpet sound and the 36th regiment came to a standstill. The four hundred or so Saxon warriors were now completely surrounded.

At a sharp order from an auxiliary officer, the bowmen moved a few paces to the rear of their formation, allowing the legionaries to cast a rain of spears into the midst of the helpless Saxons. Fifteen minutes of carnage followed before the trumpet to cease action was sounded. Twenty Saxons were left alive; among them was Cissa, his huge frame lying on the ground, hiding under his own shield.

Gaius was now given his orders to take a detachment to the bridge, where the Saxons had their remaining stronghold. He took a hundred legionaries and twenty bowmen for he needed to get the battle over quickly. On their way up to the bridge, his soldiers were surrounded by ecstatic crowds, some of them chanting and cheering as they danced ahead of the marching troops. On reaching the bridge, Gaius was annoyed to see a great throng of people, many with crude weapons, jeering at the Saxons who were guarding the other end of the bridge. Most were men who had been held captive and some were brandishing Saxon swords taken from their dead guards.

Gaius barked an order for his soldiers to push through the throng, but before they could reach the gate, about seventy of the former captives rushed over towards the Saxons. It left the commander with no option but to cross the bridge in their wake. The soldiers dealt death blows to five Saxons who had been over-run and lay wounded on the ground. The remainder, to the commander's annoyance, had retreated back into the community hall.

Gaius ordered his men to clear the crowds away from the hall, and only after they brandished their swords did the throng quieten down and start to edge back. Suddenly smoke appeared at the far end of the hall. Fierce flames soon enveloped the area, for the wattle and daub structure was old and dry. All Gaius could do now was to order his troops to push the crowds away from the burning building to the river bank.

An expectant hush came over the crowd as they waited for the Saxons to come out of the burning hall. Moments later they emerged, some rubbing their eyes, others with hands over their heads. Gaius was about to issue an order when they were engulfed, once again, by the vengeful crowd. He ordered his men to try clearing them away, but to no avail; as some were pulled away, others barged in to fill their place. Gaius realised his position was hopeless and ordered his officers to have the soldiers form up on the far side of the bridge.

As they marched away, they heard the screams of the Saxons warriors. The commander looked back at the frantic mob with distaste. He had spent most of his life as a military man. He had always killed knowing he was defending himself or his fellow soldier against a foe, who would, given the chance, gladly do the same to him. Kill or be killed was the fighting soldier's motto; it was the only maxim Gaius understood.

In marching formation they made their way down to the main assembly of Artor's troops.

The Commander nodded when Gaius told him what had happened up on the bridge. "Gaius, it's been difficult enough keeping the crowd at bay from these heathen wretches, even with over seven hundred soldiers at my disposal. You would have had no chance, so do not concern yourself. Anyway, you can understand these people, for they have suffered greatly under these animals."

"That is true, sir," acknowledged Gaius.

Artor grinned at his first-in-command, then said: "Bring Julius to me, for I need to speak with both of you."

When his senior officers were at attention before him, Artor ordered them to stand easy and thanked them for the vital part they played in the battle. "We've still got some work ahead of us clearing up this mess, but we've enough hands to make light of it. Get those remaining Saxons to help with the digging, but keep the crowd from getting their hands on them."

Artor broke out in another grin. "Those Saxon savages will make handy slaves for our regiment, don't you think?"

"That's true, sir," answered Gaius, "there's much labouring work they can do; work that would otherwise keep our men from their soldiering duties."

"But what about Londinium," said Julius, "was it not their wish to have every Saxon put to the sword, apart from Cissa, their warlord?"

"Leave it to me, Julius. The Londinium Council owes us many favours, do they not?" said the Commander, still grinning.

CHAPTER 21

"What have you three been up to today?" asked Andrew, as they sat down for their evening meal.

"Merlin wanted to see our beautiful countryside, so we've given him the tour of our beauty spots," said Monica enthusiastically.

"Since my release from the cave, one of my greatest joys is experiencing the beauty of nature; the trees, the hedges, the wild flowers, the animals grazing in the fields, the clouds, the blue skies, the far off hills…" Merlin's voice trailed off as he remembered the dank cave in which he been entombed.

"So much to see," he said, almost to himself.

"Even our young man enjoyed it, didn't you, Tom?" said Monica.

Tom nodded enthusiastically.

"Especially the ice cream, eh Tom," she said.

Tom grinned. "I thought Merlin's face looked so funny when he tasted it."

"It seemed unfamiliar on the tongue, but it was an enjoyable taste," said Merlin.

Monica turned to her husband, her blue eyes reflecting merriment. "He must have liked it, because the next time we stopped, Merlin had an ice cream all to himself."

Andrew laughed. "It will not be long, Merlin, before you become used to the decadent lifestyle of our age."

After Tom had gone to bed, the three adults retired to the lounge. Over a glass of wine, Andrew told them about the day's events at the psychic convention. Finally, he turned to his guest: "Tomorrow was to be the final day of the convention. It's always the most hectic day of all and Emile will be addressing us during the last session.

"I would enjoy listening to him," said Merlin.

"I'm sure you would, but I'd prefer it if you didn't. You see I made an announcement to the fraternity about the coming of a very special guest. Only the committee and Emile knew who I was referring to, although I imagine others who experienced images of you in the cave might have some idea who the mysterious guest might be. As you might have guessed, Merlin, that special person is you! Anyway, I asked for a show of hands to see who would wish to stay on for another day, and the response was overwhelming."

Andrew hesitated for a moment. "Of course, now the question is, are you willing and able to address the fraternity the day after tomorrow?"

"I would regard it as an honour, Andrew."

"I was hoping you'd say that, because I've already booked the hall for another day," said Andrew with a grin.

"What do you wish me to do and what should I say?" enquired the wizard.

"It's up to you, Merlin. It'll just be a gathering of very curious fraternity members. Tell them how you came to be here and about your past life. You may wish to demonstrate some of your powers, for there will be much scepticism, even among the most enlightened of our members."

"I see… and how many will be at this gathering?"

"Around ninety to a hundred, I should think. We used to have over four hundred members attending these annual events, but that was thirty, forty years ago, before our young people were enticed away from the villages. The numbers have been dwindling ever since."

Andrew was about to say something else when the doorbell rang.

"I'll get it," said Monica from the kitchen.

Moments later a huge man appeared in the doorway.

"Emile, come in! Let me introduce you to Merlin," said Andrew.

Merlin could only recall one man with the same immense stature as the tussled, dark-haired man standing in front of him. That was Artor Karalios.

"You do not look like zis …er great Merlin we 'ave read about in ze Chronicles," said Emile, in a slight French accent, "nor like ze image I 'ad of you outside da cave."

Andrew answered for his guest. "He underwent a transmutation process, Emile."

"Tom's aunt and uncle have seen it," added Monica, who had just entered with a tray. "Kate told me on the phone, she and her husband saw Merlin change his image in front of them. Tom said he has also seen it happen."

"I will also be 'appy to watch zis 'appen," said Emile, staring at the wizard.

"Will you stay for supper, Emile?" asked Monica.

"Zank you, Madame, but I must get back to ze hotel, I am expecting a call from my girlfriend in Paris. I only came over to see zis man, zis Merlin, for I was 'curious like ze cat', as you say in English."

As he reached the door, Emile looked back at the wizard. "Merlin, I look forward very much to your address."

CHAPTER 22

Gwindore answered the knock on the door.

"Goodness! It's you, Julius Medinas. It is so good to see you after all this time. Please enter and accept our hospitality."

"Thank you, Gwindore. I came to see Cedrin. Is he about?"

"He returned just a little while ago. I think he will be with Merlin in the store room, I will fetch him."

In moments Cedrin appeared, with Merlin close behind.

"Julius, welcome to our home. It gives us much pleasure to have you with us."

"I too am delighted to see you all again," said Julius.

How long has it been, Julius? Two years at least since your victory over the Saxons, is it not?"

"Something like that, Cedrin... But I come with bad tidings."

"Not another invasion coming?"

"No, not in these parts anyway... It's Artor, I am sad to have to report to you our great Commander is dead."

Both Cedrin and Merlin recoiled at the words. "I cannot believe... How... How did it happen?" asked the shocked Cedrin.

"A patrol! Our Commander, and two of our officers, decided to go on a patrol with a squad of legionaries. News had reached us over a month ago that a tribe of Jutes, about five hundred strong, had captured Dover and had been moving north toward the Thame. We thought they would be coming by boat around the foreland and into the Thame estuary, so we had much of our military resources focused on the first reaches of the river. About twelve days ago, we heard news of refugees arriving in Londinium, saying their villages had been destroyed. We soon realised the Jutes were coming overland and heading our way.

"Our patrol was passing through what appeared to be a deserted village when they were ambushed and set upon by around two hundred of these savages. Our men managed to inflict much damage to the enemy before they retreated, but our Commander went down with a spear to the head. It was a mortal wound. The surviving officer said he died within a few minutes. We also lost another officer and twelve of our best legionaries."

"Oh, Julius. We shall be grieving the loss of a great man, and one who has been a great friend to me and my family," said Cedrin.

It had suddenly occurred to the healer that Julius had remained at attention, with his helmet held across his body since his arrival.

"Come and relax, sit down, my friend, eat and drink with us," implored Cedrin.

"I cannot at this moment, for I have other tidings to impart."

"What else do you wish to say, my friend?"

"Our Commander left a will, sir. Gaius Theonis and I were each given a copy, with instructions to break the seal in the event of his death. He has laid down the will in his own hand. There are four requests. One: We continue to command the 36th as he would have done. He has appointed Gaius Theonis as his successor, and myself as Gaius's Divisional Commander, but these appointments have yet to be approved by the military hierarchy.

"Two: His funeral to be conducted not in Londinium, but at the headquarters of the 36th with all his men in attendance.

"Three: His burial place to be in York, at the cemetery of the Church of Peace, and his body to be laid at rest alongside that of his beloved wife, Auvilia."

Julius hesitated, as if unsure how to explain the last of the Commander's wishes.

"Sir, did you know about Artor's son?"

"Artor told me his wife had died in labour," said Cedrin, "but that was years ago. I regret to say, since that time he has not mentioned anything to me, and I had not thought of asking him if the child had survived. Artor and I did not see each other often."

"Let me tell you that the child lives," said Julius. "The boy is twelve years of age now. Artor brought the boy down to Londinium from York two years ago, where he was given education at an institute. The boy always hated it there, and one time he escaped and made his way to the regimental barracks on the Thame. The men were highly amused and impressed, for the journey had taken him three days. The Commander, however, didn't see the funny side of it. He promptly took his boy back to the school by chariot."

"But what of the fourth request?" prompted Cedrin.

"My Commander's last request was for you to adopt the boy, educate him further and rear him in your family, as if he was your own. And that Merlin should befriend the boy and teach him the art of sword combat when he comes of age. He has allotted annual funds to accommodate this service."

"This is all entirely unexpected, Julius, but we would be more than happy to agree to his wish, without payment."

"We wish to follow our great Commander's dictum to the letter, Sir, therefore the funds must be allocated to you."

"As you wish, Julius. We will be honoured to make a home for Artor Karalios' child."

"Thank you, sir. I am sure your kind deed will not go unnoticed by our good lord."

"Never mind that, Julius. Bring the boy to us whenever it's possible to do so."

"I can bring him right now, sir, for he is outside sitting in the chariot."

"Well, you old fox, Julius" said Cedrin laughing. "You'd better bring him in."

"I will, sir, right away."

"By the way, what is the boy's name?"

"It is Arthur, sir."

CHAPTER 23

Chrissie Flowers showered and unpacked before venturing downstairs, where she then spent a valuable half hour chatting with the slim lady at the hotel reception, whose name she discovered was Yvonne. Chrissie soon realised, to her delight, Yvonne was quite a chatter-box, and with discreet questioning, the reporter gleaned much about what was going on in the village of Craigemere.

She gave Yvonne the impression she was an avid hiker, and she had worn her shorts, denim top, and trainers to prove it.

Yvonne was the proprietress and had only been in the area a little over two years. There was not enough income from the hotel to support her and her husband, so he had found work as a mechanic cum odd job man for a squire who owned a large estate, a few miles from the village.

"It is barely worth keeping it open in the winter months, I can tell you. If it wasn't for a few hardy hikers dropping in for a meal and a bed now and then, we'd probably close off the accommodation in the winter. We are lucky, though, since we took over, visits from hikers and rambling clubs in the summer have increased quite a lot; although at the moment we've only two ramblers in the house, apart from yourself, that is," said Yvonne, hardly stopping for breath.

Yvonne told her about the current hotel guests. "We've had full occupancy all this week. All eight rooms! That's why I had to put you in the top room. You don't mind, do you?"

Chrissie shook her head. "No, not at all."

"There's a convention being held in Colkean. It's a pretty town about fifteen miles or so from here. A number of our guests have been attending it, not that I know what it's all about. I tried asking about it when they came back on the first day, but they wouldn't say anything, just kept changing the subject. It's all pretty secretive if you ask me."

'Phew, can this woman talk!' thought Chrissie, relieved to know she hadn't revealed any personal details about herself to this loquacious woman.

After listening to another ten minutes of Yvonne's ramblings, about the village shops and what you could and couldn't buy there, Chrissie finally ventured to ask about the property called Brae'mar House, the name Ross, the policeman, had given her.

"Oh Brae'mar? It's a lovely elegant house, I believe, not that I've seen the inside of it, mind.

It belongs to a couple by the name of Robbins. His name is Andrew. He was an airline pilot, but had to retire because of his eyesight. They've eaten here now and then, him and his wife. She's lovely! They had a meal only the other evening with that big Frenchman, Emile Bernard, who's staying here. He's psychic, you know. Best psychic in the world, I've been told, not that I know much about that sort of thing. A bit strange if you ask me. Anyway, Mr Robbins is also going to the convention. I know because he picks up these people in the morning and drops them off in the evening."

"How interesting," said Chrissie, wondering if all guests got the same verbal rundown.

"That place of theirs is very old," continued Yvonne. "Once belonged to a Duke who had been exiled from England. Didn't get on very well with the Scottish locals, I've been told, and after a few years he moved over to France and then got himself guillotined during the French Revolution, can you believe?"

"Yes, I had heard something about that," Chrissie lied, "it's why I would like to see the place, and maybe take some photos."

Armed with a rough map of the village Yvonne had gone to the trouble of sketching out for her, Chrissie set out to take a first look at Brae'mar House.

It didn't take her long to find the ancient building. The sign 'Brae'mar House' was embedded in the high flint stone arch spanning the entrance to the driveway. Driving slowly past, she glimpsed the ivy-covered house a discreet distance away from the narrow, leafy road. Chrissie stopped the car and eased the vehicle off the road, parking a little distance from the driveway. She took a road map from the glove-box. If anyone approached, she could give the impression she was lost.

She had been waiting almost two hours when a vehicle coming towards her suddenly slowed down before turning into the driveway. It caught Chrissie by surprise, but she had enough time to catch a glimpse of the occupants of the car as it turned in.

The driver appeared to be a middle-aged woman. The man seemed familiar, but she couldn't place him. The brief glance at the boy told her little, except he looked similar to the boy she'd seen getting out of the car in the service station, apart from his mop of fair hair.

Chrissie decided to drive away. She didn't want someone coming out to enquire about her reason for parking there. She decided to return the following day on foot and try to find a hiding place in one of the large bushes close to the drive, from where she could watch the house undetected.

At dinner that evening, Chrissie, at her request, was placed at a small table by a latticed window to eat alone. She didn't want to listen to idle chatter from strangers. It would also give her the chance to observe other dinner guests without distraction. She immediately noticed the two middle-aged women seated at the next table. They caught her eye, then smiled and nodded in a knowing sort of way. Yvonne, she thought, would have told them about the rambling aspirations of her latest guest.

Her eyes wandered over to the other table. The big Frenchman was seated with the other two couples. They were conversing in a decidedly fervent manner, but in hushed tones. Chrissie would have loved to have been a fly on the wall near the group. She thought Andrew Robbins had to be connected in some way to Tom's disappearance, as it was his phone number she'd found at the home of Tom's relatives. He was well acquainted with Emile Bernard, that was obvious. This meant the big Frenchman might also be involved in Tom's disappearance, along with the group having dinner with him.

Chrissie's thoughts turned to the convention being held at Colkean. Emile Bernard was a psychic of great renown, Yvonne had said, so maybe this convention was also about psychic matters.

**   **   **

The early morning sun filtered through the fine, yellow curtains, flooding the room with a soft radiance. Chrissie glanced at her watch and rose from a surprisingly comfortable bed. It was 8.45am; time to shower, do her hair, apply a little make-up and get down to breakfast before it finished at 10am.

After spending another illuminating but frustrating five minutes listening to the hotel proprietor, Chrissie entered a deserted dining room. She helped herself to a glass of orange juice and a bowl of muesli, idly musing about the other guests. She had been told the two female ramblers had left very early. She didn't think she could ever become a dedicated rambler if it meant getting up in the early hours. She loved her bed too much.

The Frenchman and the others had been picked up about an hour ago, according to Yvonne. Chrissie also learned today was the last day of the convention, and the two couples had already checked out, but had left their luggage in reception to pick up later in the day. As for the big Frenchman, he was staying on for another two days.

After breakfast, Chrissie returned to her room to tidy herself again, then hurried downstairs, quickly passing Yvonne with a cheery wave as she headed for the door. The last thing she wanted was to be held up with another monologue on parochial goings-on from the voluble proprietress.

She walked briskly along the highway towards the village and eventually reached the road that forked off in the direction of Brae'mar House. It wasn't long before she found herself walking towards the driveway. She wandered past, glancing up the drive as she did so. The car was still in the car-port, so the people must still be in the house, she thought. She walked back again to the bushy area on the other side of the flint wall, and, crouching down, managed to work her way in amongst the fern and bracken until she found the ideal place to sit and watch the house unobserved.

Chrissie had only seen Tom once, when he had left the car with the bearded man at the petrol station. Her memory for detail was excellent, it was one of the things that made her an outstanding reporter, and the boy's profile was etched in her memory. The photographs in the Watson's lounge had fleshed out the picture, yet her recent sighting had not been good enough to be certain it was the same boy.

This time she didn't have to wait long. Within ten minutes of settling into her hideaway, the door of the big house opened. The boy appeared carrying a football. He started kicking it against the thick granite walls of the house. Chrissie was almost certain this was Tom… but was it? She had time now to study him more closely, especially when the ball rebounded off the wall and rolled towards the bushes she was hiding in. Yes! This was the boy. His hair was different, but that had probably been dyed... for obvious reasons.

She quickly took the camera out of her rucksack, but before she could open the lens, the boy, in answer to a call, had scooped up the ball and disappeared back inside the house.

"Damn!" said Chrissie, under her breath. "When will I learn to have my camera always at the ready?"

Half an hour later she noticed movement by the car. She saw what she thought might be the same lady who had been driving the car the previous day, get into the vehicle, and then saw the boy scramble in beside her. She swore a second time, realising they must have come out of a back door.

She waited to get a snap of the boy as the vehicle drove by, but now found the bushes that had been useful as camouflage obstructing her view of the moving vehicle. In desperation she clicked away rapidly as the car went past, hoping maybe some of the shots might show a clear picture of the boy.

Chrissie arrived back at the 'Rambler's Rest' in time for lunch. She wasn't in the mood for food. She was hot and frustrated, so she went out to the small beer garden at the back and sat sipping from a bottle of lemon juice she'd bought in the village. It had been a wasted morning... almost. She now had to re-think her plans for the rest of the day. The sun on her face soon lightened her mood, and it wasn't long before she decided her next move.

It took her twenty minutes of careful driving along the country roads to reach the town of Colkean, and then another ten to find the hall where the convention was being held. The function hall was a recent addition to the only hotel in the town. Chrissie went into the building and checked out the entrance to the conference room. An easel placed to the left of the varnished double doors held a sign saying 'Private Function' and standing by it was a uniformed security guard.

Chrissie decided a brazen approach was required.

"Excuse me sir, I'm running awfully late. The traffic out of Edinburgh this morning was appalling. Can you let me in please?"

The security guard's face instantly lit up at the sight of the appealing blue eyes and the vaguely seductive smile of the woman.

"Certainly M'am, may I see your membership card please?"

"My membership card?" said Christine with a puzzled expression. "Oh yes, of course, it's in my handbag."

Chrissie gave the impression of rummaging through her purse.

"Oh, bother! I must have left it back at my flat, I'm so sorry," she said, this time putting on her 'woman in distress' look.

"Sorry M'am, I'm not allowed to let anyone in without a membership card. Orders, I'm afraid"

"Won't you bend the rules for me, please… just this once … pleeeze," pleaded Chrissie

"Sorry M'am can't do that, strict instructions. Anyway they're finishing early today. They'll be out in another hour."

A frustrated Christine Flowers drove back to the 'Rambler's Rest'. She needed a shower and a stiff drink, but not necessarily in that order.

CHAPTER 24

A hush gathered in the hall as Andrew appeared on the stage, silencing the buzz of speculation as to who the mysterious guest speaker might be.

"Dear members, I am very pleased to see so many of you decided to stay for another day. I can assure you that after our guest speaker has finished, you will be very glad you stayed. Without further ado, I would like to welcome none other than the great Merlin to speak to you - and when I say Merlin, I really do mean 'Merlin of the dark ages'."

At once, a fresh hiss of whispers arose amongst the incredulous audience, and their skepticism grew as Merlin came up on to the stage in his modern attire.

Andrew shook the wizard's hand and placed the microphone stand in front of him, but Merlin moved it to one side, smiled and nodded to his host before casting his eyes on the expectant assembly.

"I have spoken to much larger crowds in the past without the use of this... this object," Merlin said, pointing to the microphone.

He hesitated, waiting for the murmurs to die down. "There will be doubt in most minds that I am who I say I am", he began. "When I was roused from my slumber, I too, found it difficult to believe I had been asleep for more than one and a half thousand years. Therefore my first task must be to try and eliminate the doubt from the minds of all those gathered before me."

Merlin's elegant appearance, his assured manner and his strangely resonant voice immediately had the audience spellbound. "Many of you will also doubt that Merlin ever existed at all and think the stories you have heard are just legend. Even those who do believe may wonder what Merlin looked like... I will show you."

He paused for a few moments for his words to sink in, before saying: "Please, there must be no sound during the transmutation process."

He then began the same procedure as witnessed by Tom and his relatives. The assembly gazed in awe as the man on stage gradually disintegrated into a vibrating mass of particles and eventually the cloaked figure of Merlin emerged out of a shimmering mass. There was no sound from the audience, not a clap, not even a murmur. As if in a trance, they sat frozen to their seats, their gaze fixed on the tall, bearded figure now standing before them.

His amazed audience listened intently as he began to reminisce about his boyhood, his mother, his education under his uncle Cedrin, about Keetah, the golden falcon his uncle had given him, and recounted some of the most wondrous experiences he had with the creatures of the forest.

In dulcet tones, the wizard went on to talk about the troubles of those times. He spoke of the invasions by the Franks and the Jutes, who established settlements on the southern and eastern coast of England, and of the persistent incursions by Saxons and Angles, who penetrated into the heart of the country. He described the Saxon invasion of Heranium, where he lived, and how they were finally expunged by the Romano-British army led by Artor Karalios.

With rapt attention the assembly heard him speak of the young Arthur Karalios, who, after the death of his father, was sent to Merlin's home to be brought up under his uncle Cedrin's tutelage. He spoke of Arthur's early teenage years and the close relationship he had with the boy; of the youth's intelligence and how, after two years of sword combat training, the student became a match for his master.

The wizard told the enthralled audience of Arthur's craving to become a soldier, and how, at the age of seventeen he was conscripted into his father's 36th regiment. Merlin described Arthur's rapid rise through the ranks, from legionnaire to centurion in three years. By the age of twenty seven, he had risen to centurion commander, and at the age of thirty, due to the retirement of Julius Medinas, he was made commander of the regiment.

Merlin, by this time, had kept his audience engrossed for over an hour – by what was probably the most exciting history lesson any of them had ever had – and yet there was no sign of restlessness among them. He went on to describe the country's chaotic situation in some detail - the constant battles, over power and territory, among the tyrannical warlords who ruled the forty separate kingdoms in existence in Britain at that time, and of the desperate need for one ruler to bring peace and harmony to the troubled land. He told of how, through his and his uncle Cedrin's efforts, and eventually those of the Londinium and York councils, Arthur was nominated to become the sovereign of the land.

A challenge went out to all the warlords, he said, to participate in a contest of armed combat that would decide who should become the rightful King of all Britain. A huge festival was held to mark the occasion, and the combatants fought each other in pairs until only two remained, a huge Kentish warlord, who had taken on the name of Brutus, and Arthur, who carried a most powerful weapon - Excalibur.

The wizard revealed to the hushed audience how the legendary sword was forged. He explained how the druid priests of the Inner Circle had brought in a mysterious druid from Gaul to work the steel - heating, hammering, heating, hammering it... again and again, which lent the layered steel enormous tensile strength. The cooling of the sword was controlled, he told them, by covering it with a special form of clay. Then, as the clay hardened, the sword was immersed in water to cool.

The breaking of the clay took place at a secret ceremony within the hallowed halls of the Inner Circle, and in the presence of the Grand Priest. "It was here at the ceremony," he added, "that the sword received sanctification." The weapon was also endowed with a strange power of its own, he said, and then, at the final blessing, was given its name... Excalibur. The sword was presented to Arthur on the day before the final combat.

The wizard went on to describe the great battle between Arthur and Brutus, which was watched by thousands of people in the arena, and how finally, after two long hours, Arthur emerged as victor.

He told of Arthur's coronation, and how he, Merlin, was appointed personal adviser to his long-time friend, the newly crowned King of all Britain. Peace finally came, he said, with the appointment of fifteen of Arthur's most able and trusted men from his regiment as guardians of law and order throughout the land. He described the knighthood ceremonies, where each of the fifteen swore allegiance to the king before they were knighted.

Merlin expounded on the peaceful years that followed, but also describe how his own peace was destroyed by a new woman who had come into Arthur's life. He told his captivated audience how he discovered she was his half-sister, a woman he had never met, and an evil sorceress. Her name was Niddrym - Myrddin, the Celtic word for Merlin, spelled backwards.

The wizard explained the difficult task he faced in exposing her wicked ambitions to his king, who had come to love her, but eventually had no choice but to banish her from his court. He then told his audience of the hatred Niddrym had for him, her half-brother, for betraying her, and how she vowed one day she would have her revenge.

But he also spoke of love – that of King Arthur for Guinevere, the new fair lady of Viking heritage who had come into his life and who became a fitting and popular queen, and his own for the beautiful Salina, who lived near the lake, and whom he had pledged to marry. The hurt in his voice was palpable when he spoke of their last few weeks together, and then of that final evening in the cave.

The wizard spoke of his anguish at being rendered powerless as he had to watch his beloved Salina being transformed into his evil half-sister Niddrym. He told them of the spell she had cast over him, and his desperate fight to stay awake before sinking into the black abyss of a timeless sleep.

He concluded his tale with an account of his unlikely deliverance by Tom, the orphan boy, and his awakening in the twenty first century. At this point, he took the amulet from around his neck and held it aloft to display the golden star-shaped medallion and expressed his undying gratitude to the courageous 12-year-old who had set him free.

After Merlin finished speaking, the audience remained silent at first, then two or three people started to clap before the rest of the assembly erupted into spontaneous applause, rising from their seats for a standing ovation.

After the noise had finally died down, Merlin spoke again. "I hope I have managed to set your minds at rest. However, if any of you have questions, please speak now."

At the back of the hall, a woman stood up. "Merlin, you spoke about one incident in your childhood, when at the age of three you spirited a bowl of hot gruel from the window to your feeding tray."

Merlin nodded. "Yes, that is so, but I don't remember the incident myself. It is my mother who has often told me about it. Why do you ask?"

"I was wondering," said the woman, "if you still have the ability to do this sort of thing, and if so, could you demonstrate it to us now."

Merlin smiled at the woman, but remained silent for a few moments.

"It is in my power to do what you ask of me, but I am afraid I must deny your request. From the time of my youth with Cedrin, my uncle, through to the days of my manhood with the priests of the Inner Circle of the Ancient Order of Druids, it has been instilled into me that the powers I have been gifted with should be used with restraint. I cannot display any mystical or magical act for the sake of mere display, or self-seeking motives. It would be, as you would say, unethical. My powers are to be used only when it is necessary to use them - to assist those in need, to prevent wrongdoing and to right that which is wrong."

"But you displayed your power when you transformed yourself at the beginning of your speech," retorted the woman.

"This is true, but the transformation was not done entirely for display. It was done to help give some credence to my talk with you this morning. I am sure you would all have found it more difficult to accept the account of my history had I delivered it in modern garb."

Merlin realised that, to many, his authenticity would still remain in doubt because of his refusal to show his magical powers, but that was something he knew he would have to accept.

"If any of you have any further questions you would like ask, please do so, and I will try to answer them."

The man's words were greeted with a murmur of approval from the assembly. But before anyone could say anything, Andrew interceded to announce lunch was about to be brought in. Many looked at their watches in disbelief. They suddenly realised with amazement they had given undivided attention to the wizard, for nearly three and a half hours.

CHAPTER 25

The editor looked across at Paul Mac'Veer.

"You say the police had some response from the Saltridge Echo article, Paul?"

"From what Jim Nayler, my contact, said in the pub last night, yes. Apparently two people, both women, said they'd seen a tall bearded man walking along the high street and remembered a young lad walking close behind. He said both reports were independent of each other and that the time of the sightings corroborated the reporter's story."

"Well," said the chief, "that confirms the authenticity of the original report, we'll now wait and see what our article brings up. Reproducing the boy's actual handwritten note under the photograph is bound to stir up public interest. By the way, have the police got anything on it?"

"Yes, they've established that it's the boy's writing as they've been to his school and compared it with some of his work. Nothing out of Forensics yet; Jim would have told me if there was. However, he did say they were looking at the saliva trace on the envelope, but that it didn't look promising."

"The clever things they can do these days, eh Paul. Do they think the aunt and uncle have anything to do with it? After all, it seems they would desperately like to have the boy live with them?"

"No, I wouldn't think so. After all, it was the boy's aunt who phoned the stepmother to tell her the lad had arrived in the first place. The police said they couldn't imagine the pair would then try to arrange the boy's abduction. Not only that, but Jim said they just didn't seem the type.

"Anyway, when I saw them they were pretty distraught, as you'd expect. She obviously dotes on the boy. The uncle didn't say much, except to say the kid loved nothing more than helping him around the farm. I also had a word with the boy's cousin, a girl called Felicity, and it was obvious she was very close to the him, 'cos she started getting teary when I told her we'd had no word on his whereabouts."

"What about the police, have they been around?"

"Yes, a couple of days ago. They took away a couple more photos of the kid, some of his clothing and a comb the aunt had found in the bathroom. That was all, I believe."

"What about the stepmother?"

Paul made a face. "Didn't think much of the lady, neither did the Bill, from what Jim tells me. She doesn't like the Watson couple much, that was obvious. Didn't seem to be too distressed about the boy either, although she kept saying she was. The police took things away from there also, but Jim didn't say what."

"How did you get on with the Child Welfare people?"

"Ok, I saw the couple who had been escorting the kid. They had already been interviewed by the police. They were obviously upset, but couldn't give me any more information than we already have. However, they had this Mrs Roper in the room with them - a senior executive, probably there to make sure they didn't say anything to further embarrass SOCAR.

"This Mrs Roper did say one thing, though. Apparently the stepmother had told Social Welfare some weeks before that she was thinking of putting the boy into care if he didn't mend his ways. She said that was why SOCAR got involved. I phoned the stepmother again to confirm that, but she denied ever saying anything about putting the boy into care."

"Well, she would say that, wouldn't she? Anyway, it's all good stuff, Paul. Try and get an early press release from the police on what they've got. Tie it up with the info you have, and let's have a look at it when it's complete."

"There's something else, John"

"I'm listening, Paul."

"Well, the Bill seemed to be looking at both angles. They are naturally going on the assumption the kid's being held somewhere against his will, but they're also thinking the note might be genuine. Perhaps the boy is hiding out somewhere and being cared for by this weirdo with a beard, and is just waiting for someone to say it's legally okay for him to live with the Watson couple."

John Nielson squeezed his chin in thought. "That's interesting, Paul, but if it's true, and we certainly can't rule it out, the lad could be in for a long wait. Even if there was a good case for the Watson couple to become his new guardians, there'd have to be some long-winded judicial process to bring it about.

"Yes, that's what this Mrs Roper told the Bill during their interview."

"Did she tell you too?"

"No, Jim mentioned it to me yesterday."

"Ok, then here's what I want you to do, Paul. Go and see this woman ASAP, and ask her what the likelihood is for her department to pursue this matter in the light of the boy's note. Don't let her off the hook too easily. Get some sort of commitment from her. You could also gently insinuate, in your own inimitable style, that the public expects some sort of positive action from the department, seeing as the boy was in their care when he was abducted."

"Yes, I think I know how to handle it," said Paul Mac'Veer, a little sarcastically.

"But tell me, John," he continued, "why are you taking so much interest? Normally, you'd just let me get on with it."

"Can't fully explain it, Paul, "said John Nielson, in a circumspect tone, "maybe it's the way the letter landed on my desk, but whatever the reason, the boy's name keeps coming into my head, and I can't help wanting to follow up on the story. Oh, and by the way, we went through the CCTV footage. It was really strange; one minute there was no sign of any letter, then ten seconds later when the camera panned back to the desk, there it was. We re-ran sections of footage a dozen or more times. Really weird, I can tell you."

CHAPTER 26

The evening meal was wonderful. Chrissie had decided on venison simply because she had never had it before. The meat was surprisingly tasty and the minted new potatoes and fresh vegetables complemented it perfectly. Two glasses of a delectable Australian Shiraz rounded off the evening meal wonderfully.

The frustration of driving all the way to Colkean town and the humiliation of being refused entry into the hotel's conference hall by that good-looking security guard had really been too much. But now Chrissie Flowers felt decidedly better. Over the meal, she decided she would take a break from pursuing the story tomorrow and do a spot of sightseeing instead.

On her way out of the dining room, she stopped to look at some of the brochures displayed on a wall cabinet in the hallway when she heard the front door opening and two people moving past her to approach the reception. She was all attention when she heard a man's voice mention the name Emile Bernard. At a sideways glance, she thought one of the two, a tall, dark-haired man, was familiar. She was certain it was the same man she'd seen on the Watson's drive that evening, and the one she'd caught a glimpse of just recently.

"Yes, he is expecting us," said the other man.

"Well, I will still need to call him," retorted the proprietress.

"Yes, I understand. Tell him it's Andrew Robbins and his friend."

"Of course Mr Robbins. You and your lovely lady have dined here occasionally. How is she?"

"She is well, thank you. She has people staying, keeps her busy."

"Oh it would, but it's so beautiful, your home. I've heard so much about Brae'mar House. I bet it keeps both of you busy looking after it."

"It does, Madam, but it's a labour of love, I can assure you. Now would you be so kind."

"Oh yes, I'm so sorry," said Yvonne. "I will call him now."

Chrissie watched out of the corner of her eye as the two made their way up the stairs. She picked up a couple of brochures and then headed for her own room.

"'E's a stranger, that tall one. Never set eyes on him before," said Yvonne, stopping Chrissie in her tracks.

"Oh, really?" said Chrissie casually.

"Must be a foreigner…looks foreign to me," observed the proprietress.

"Yes, you might be right, but please excuse me, Yvonne, I need to go to the bathroom," said Chrissie and started to make her way up the stairs.

She went into her room and sat on the bed. It was then that she realised Emile Bernard's room was directly below hers. She would give anything, she thought, to hear what was being said, just a few feet below.

Then, conscious of the creaking floor boards under her feet, she had another thought. 'What if one was loose? After all, they certainly creaked quite a bit.' Chrissie knelt down to have a closer look, but they all seemed to be securely fastened. She was about to get up when she noticed a worn rug covering the floor underneath the bed. She rolled part of the carpet away and saw the boards were unvarnished and quite short. She tapped one and to her delight it rattled. She got up and rummaged around her handbag until she found what she was looking for. It was a large stainless steel Swiss army knife her father had given her as a present. It had come in handy many times.

Chrissie prised open the big blade and then returned to the loose floorboards. She chose a short one close to the edge of bed and deftly levered it out, and then it was a small matter of lifting adjacent boards out by hand. Soon she had exposed a sizeable part of the ceiling of the room below. And then she noticed it, a hole the size of her finger. It appeared to have been a light fitting once for she could make out indentations surrounding the hole, as if oversized screws had broken through the plaster from below.

Putting her ear as close as possible to the hole, Chrissie could hear the sound of male voices, but couldn't quite pick up what was being said. She sat back upon the bed, frustrated at the results of her efforts, when suddenly her eyes lit up - the eavesdropper! She jumped to her feet, grabbed her car keys from her bag and ran down the stairs.

The eavesdropper was a gadget often used by undercover police, but at times also by investigative journalists. Chrissie had borrowed it from stores a few weeks ago and she was almost certain it was still in her car. It was powerful and could detect sound through walls and other solid barriers, like a doctor's stethoscope. The sounding piece, which looked like a small black rubber funnel, had a compact, battery-powered unit housing an integral digital enhancer. Small dials controlled the volume and two ten inch tubes with ear fittings extended from the top.

It was hardly ever used at the Saltridge Echo, but Chrissie had needed it recently to investigate corruption claims involving a local councillor. She had meant to check the eavesdropper back into store afterwards, but kept forgetting. She faintly remembered seeing the box somewhere when cleaning out the car before her trip. She looked high and low inside the car, but nothing. Finally she found it in the boot, tucked away in a corner.

Back in her bedroom, Chrissie immediately switched it on and breathed a sigh of relief - the gauge was responding. Getting down on the floor, she put the ear pieces on and placed the sounding funnel over the hole. "Eureka!" she said to herself, realising she could now hear every word coming from the room below.

Almost immediately, she realised they were talking about Tom, so, lying flat on her stomach, she settled down to listen.

"...Merlin," said Emile Bernard, "I must meet zis boy of yours, zis Tom. From what you 'ave told us, he must be a little hero, yes?"

"He is what you say, and I will be forever indebted to him," said the wizard.

"Yes, and Monica seems to have taken a real shine to the lad," said Andrew. "He goes everywhere with her. She'll certainly miss him when he's gone."

Andrew changed the subject. "There is something about our fraternity you should be aware of, Merlin, now that you've been accepted as a member. It's about the Chronicles."

"Yes, you mentioned these before."

"Well, let me tell you about their origin," said Andrew. "I'm not sure if I told you that our village was founded around the seventh century when people seeking refuge from persecution began to unite and form a settlement?

167

At first these were mostly druids, the very people who had acted as scribes for the Romans and later, continued to chronicle events for the powerful and wealthy of the land until they were persecuted for fear of their influence with the populace. As you told me, this also happened in Roman times, when the empire converted to Christianity.

"Yes," said Merlin, briefly glancing up at the ceiling, "but during my time - I was born 60 years after the Romans departed our shores - the druids had returned, and, as you say, had become prominent citizens once more. Among them were scribes who continued to record matters of importance throughout the land, as had been the practice during the Roman occupation.

"These were people of ancient Celtic blood, but they were revered for their intelligence and mystic powers. It was the druids who had always forecast the downfall of the Romans and their departure from British soil. Artor Karalios used their services in recording the battle at Heranium, for example, and I was regularly summoned to record King Arthur's dictum."

Chrissie listened to the charismatic voice of the speaker. She knew the words came from the tall man she had seen at reception, but she was puzzled at their inference. What did he mean when he said he was born sixty years after the end of the Roman occupation of Britain? Chrissie could only vaguely remember her history lessons at school, but she knew it must be well over a thousand years since it happened. She shook her head – and why were they calling him Merlin?

She tuned back into the conversation below.

"…we can only assume the first druids seeking sanctuary in this settlement must have brought old scriptures with them," said Andrew, "for we have written material stretching back to 500 AD. Yet, as I said, from the Chronicles it appears this village of ours emerged some time in the seventh or eighth century AD, when the purges against the druids were at their height.

"Anyway, from what we can gather, whenever a new spiritual leader was appointed, the scriptures would be handed over in a ritual known as the 'Pass-down ceremony'. A crucial part of the ceremony was the Vow of Secrecy, for it was vital the existence of these records did not become known to anyone outside the village.

"What we have found difficult to understand is how those early records would have stood up to the passage of time. Our damp climate is not the best for the preservation of parchment or paper, so we can only assume they must have been re-copied over the years. These records were to grow in size as subsequent generations added their writings to it."

Again Andrew noticed Merlin's eyes wander to the ceiling.

"Because of the growing amount of material, the writings were eventually re-bound into two separate books. The last re-copying and re-binding was dated 1927, and we refer to the two separate volumes as The Chronicles."

Emile nodded and turned to Merlin: "It iz what makes Craigemere so important. You see, Merlin, I come from a village in Brittany. It iz much like Craigemere, for it also began life as a settlement of refuge for ze psychic intelligentsia. For in France also, innocent people like zese were accused of 'eretic activities and were 'ounded by ze auzorities of ze time. 'Owever, we only 'ave preserved records dating back to ze early tentz century, whereas Craigemere records date back almost to your own century."

"Emile is right," said Andrew. "Your name appears in many of the old transcripts, but in the earliest writings, we find the name of Myrddin is always used."

"Anyway, in 1927 an extra edition of The Chronicles was produced for Emile's village in Brittany."

"But 'ave you not yet shown zem to Merlin?" questioned Emile.

"I was going to this evening, but we ran out of time. The members were bombarding Merlin with so many questions and invitations we found it difficult to get away. After we dropped you off, we only had time to shower, eat and return here to meet with you as arranged."

"Ah yes, I understand," smiled Emile. "But now, Merlin, zis transmutation, it is somezing I 'ave 'eard about but never before witnessed. I was… er, 'ow do you say…spellbound. Your speech also was incredibly fascinating, and from what I've 'eard, you 'ave found yourself many new believers. So, my friend, whenever you find ze time, please be my guest at my chateau in

169

Brittany and give me ze benefit of your company. I 'ope to learn from ze prodigious psychic powers you 'ave wizin you."

"I appreciate your comments and your invitation, Emile. When the time is right, I will look forward to staying with you," said Merlin, studying the ceiling once more.

Chrissie shifted her position slightly to ease the pressure of a floor joist on her forearm.

".... is somezing Andrew has yet to tell you, Merlin, for zese manuscripts where your name is mentioned not only refer to your sudden disappearance but also contain prophesies zat one day you will appear again on Earz. Zis is why, when we received zose early telepazic messages from you, we did not dismiss zem."

"Yes," Andrew added, "but we have also come across a number of other prophecies in the Chronicles which have turned out to be unbelievably accurate. One is the Norman invasion. It even mentioned it would happen during the 11th century! There is something else many in the fraternity have been curious about. In the early manuscripts the occasional mention is made of a place called Arkatra and it's often referred to as the New World. It also says the only way to 'look upon this land' was by a passage through the Humming Tree. Have you ever heard of this, Merlin?"

The wizard hesitated, frowning at the ceiling.

"Yes, I know of it," he said at last, "but in my world, no-one, apart from those chosen by the spiritual leader of the Inner Circle would have had knowledge of its existence."

"Were you one of ze chosen, Merlin?" said Emile.

"I had that honour, yes."

"Can you tell us more, Merlin? Zis world you speak of, did you also go zere?" prompted the Frenchman.

"I did, Emile. I had the greatest honour bestowed upon me, for I was twice chosen to visit Arkatra."

"But what sort of a place was it?" questioned Emile eagerly. "And ze Humming Tree, what does it mean when zey say it was ze passage to zis New World?"

Merlin smiled at the Frenchman. "Firstly, let me explain something of importance to you. You will recall my comments about the druids at the convention today?" Emile nodded. "Then you will remember little was said about my association with them. You see, my druid beliefs and activities became a large and important part of my life from my early manhood, but I felt it was not the right time or place to share my beliefs with your members. To give you a satisfactory explanation of 'Arkatra' , I need to tell you a little more about the druids and my association with them."

The wizard turned his attention once more to the ceiling, before addressing his two companions.

"My uncle was also a druid of high repute and when I reached the age of twenty he enrolled me into their 'School of Learning' within the monastery of the Ancient Order of Druids. Although druids were never regarded as Christians, we fervently believed in the Creator of the Universe, and the Creator was the most central being in our studies and our worship. I was to spend five years at their monastery before returning to my home in the village of Weerby.

"According to the Romans, who had become Christianised, we druids were pagans. We worshipped the sun and all the life-giving things it embodied. The beginning of each season was an occasion for worship and festivity, but the most important was the coming of spring. This marked the beginning of life and it was the occasion for the greatest festivity of the year. We also worshipped the rain, for it was as essential to life as the nourishment from the sun.

"One day, after I had been at the monastery for almost three years, I was invited into the presence of the Grand Priest. He was standing in the middle of this very large unlit room, and he silently beckoned me to sit in an ornate chair placed in front of him. As my eyes became accustomed to the gloom, I saw there were other priests in the room. They appeared to surround myself and the Grand Priest in a complete circle. It was to be my induction ceremony.

"It was my first meeting with the druids of the Inner Circle. I had, on rare occasions, heard them mentioned, in hushed voices, by my fellow druids, so I knew of their existence, and of their enormous spiritual power. As I sat listening to the incantation of the Grand Priest, a wonderful feeling of inner peace came over me. I then realised that the chair I was sitting in was rising up in the air. The next thing I remember was seeing this golden amulet appear out of the darkness and move toward

171

me, nestling into the palm of my hand. My fingers closed around the star-shaped medallion that was to be my amulet."

Merlin suddenly stopped, slowly raising his eyes to the ceiling again. But then he smiled and continued to talk.

"During the ceremony, the amulet was placed around my neck by the Grand Priest, and I wore it always - until Niddrym tore it away from me in the cave.

"At day break the following morning I was asked to accompany the Grand Priest on a journey. We set off at quite a brisk pace. This surprised me for the Grand Priest was thought to be over a hundred years of age. We headed deep into the great forest; it took us hours. Eventually we reached the edge of a clearing. He bade me come closer, and there, in the centre of the clearing, stood this enormous oak tree. It was much larger than any tree I had ever seen. The Grand Priest then took hold of my right hand and together we walked up to the tree and embraced it. The trunk was so big, we could reach less than half way round with our outstretched arms.

"Suddenly, I found myself being absorbed into the tree. I will not go into detail about this incredible experience. I lost all sense of time until the tree released me – and I found myself in a world of incredible beauty. All around us were trees yet larger than the oak by which we had entered this world. There were countless birds, of every colour imaginable, I had never before set eyes upon and I could hear the chattering of monkeys as they scampered about in the trees above. This place was not of our world, yet where it was in the immeasurable cosmos, no-one seemed to know.

Merlin's last comment was met by silence as Andrew and Emile struggled to digest what they had just heard.

"Well, tell us more, Merlin. What else did you see? Where did you live? Was it like Earth?" demanded Emile, who was finding it difficult to contain his excitement.

"There is much to tell, Emile, but it might be best if I speak of it another time."

"You said zere were monkeys, but were zere any ozer animals?" Emile persisted, ignoring Merlin's comment.

Merlin looked up at the ceiling again, shook his head slightly and turned his attention once more to the big Frenchman.

"There were animals of huge proportion, creatures defying the imagination. Yet while I have been staying with you, Andrew, I have had the opportunity of seeing images of these strange animals again."

"What do you mean?" queried Andrew.

"Many of the animals I saw in the New World appear in a book Tom has with him."

"What book is that?"

"The book is called The World of Dinosaurs."

Emile and Andrew looked at each other.

"But that's impossible," said Andrew. "They became extinct on Earth millions of years ago."

"It is what Tom told me. Nevertheless, the creatures I saw in his book closely resemble the ones I saw on the grazing plains of Arkatra."

Once again, silence followed the wizard's revelations.

"But... but some of zese creatures..., ze predators, zey would have been very dangerous, yes?" said Emile.

"Yes, it is what Gregor said also."

"Who's Gregor?" asked Andrew.

"He was the keeper of the druid's village retreat in Arkatra."

Merlin once again gazed up toward the ceiling, while his associates remained deep in thought.

"But zis world you speak of, does it still exist?" Emile asked.

"Does not this world of ours still exist? Are there not planets still orbiting our sun? Are not the stars still in the heavens? Arkatra is as eternal as the great cosmos itself," replied the wizard.

"If what you say is true, zen possibly zis New World you speak of could be reached at zis present time, couldn't it?"

"It is possible, Emile."

"If it is possible, what would prevent you from taking us zere?" he asked eagerly.

"It is not that simple, Emile. The only way to reach this world is through the Humming Tree. It possibly no longer exists, and if that were so, Arkatra would be as unreachable as the most distant planet of our universe."

173

"But what if ze tree does exist? What if we were to search for ze tree and find it, would you be willing to take us to zis world you speak of?" Emile persisted.

"If the tree has survived and can be found, I would be willing to see if it would accept us, but there is unease within me."

"Can we ask what your concerns might be?" questioned the Frenchman.

"My visits to Arkatra were sanctioned by the druids of the Inner Circle. I am aware that fifteen centuries have passed, so many things will have changed, but if the druids have survived through the ages, I would not be willing to reveal their secret."

"Unfortunately," responded Andrews, druids do not exist today as you remember them. There is a small minority of people who are part of a movement trying to revive druidism in the modern world. They worship at Stonehenge now and again, but to my knowledge they have no monastery or permanent place to perform their ceremonies."

"The words you speak fill my heart with sadness, for they were the most revered people in my society."

He stood in silence, mourning again the loss of his world.

"What is Stonehenge?" he asked suddenly.

Andrew explained, at some length, everything he knew of the ancient monument.

"Ah, then I will tell you something," said Merlin. "I know of this Stonehenge you speak of. Did you know it was built by the magical powers of the druid priests of the Inner Circle, long before the birth of Christ? There was also a great temple there. It was the largest building in Britain before the arrival of the Romans.

"It was Cedrin, my wise uncle, who gave me knowledge of this. He told me of the great circle of buildings that once surrounded the sacred stones. There were many small dwellings in the great circle, each exactly one thousand paces from the stones. Every alternate dwelling housed a druid scholar and the others were for those of the populace wishing for sustenance of the spirit. These buildings were of simple construction, with walls of wattle and daub. This sacred centre area was then known as Callishra.

174

"Its location was known throughout the land, and even the druids of Gaul, Ireland and Wales knew of it. Many would make pilgrimages to Callishra, for it was a revered place of worship; a place to celebrate life; a place to remember the souls of the past.

"The Romans despised it. To them it was a symbol of paganism, and therefore it had to be destroyed. They razed the monastery and burned the wooden dwellings to the ground. They even dug up the foundations for they wanted no vestige of the monastery to remain. The ruined stones were left as a constant reminder of the might of Rome and of Christianity.

"My uncle also acquainted me with the great druid retreat during the latter part of the Roman occupation. Most of them retreated deep into the West Country and into Wales, where it remained free from Roman rule. The Ancient Order of Druids, the order I studied under, left the shores of Britain altogether, taking their followers with them to Brittany."

"Yes," said Emile, "many of the druids in Gaul came from Britain around that time."

Merlin again glanced briefly up to the ceiling.

"But about zis new world, my friend," continued Emile a little impatiently, "if the Ancient Order of Druids no longer exists, what uzer reasons would you 'ave for not searching for zis tree, zis 'Umming Oak you speak of?"

"If the druids no longer exist, I have no reason. I am sure Andrew speaks the truth; I have no reason to doubt his words. I have already made a promise to Tom, that should I ever visit Arkatra, he would accompany me. Whenever the time is right, I would be happy to have you join us if that is your wish."

"But the boy is only twelve, would it not be a risk to take him?" said Andrew. "After all, there must be some danger with these pre-historic predators. That's what I have read anyway."

"I understand your concern, but the promise has been made. I have spoken of this world to Tom while we were looking through his book on dinosaurs. The boy has much knowledge about these creatures and I could detect a great eagerness in his eyes and his voice as he questioned me. You must understand, I owe Tom everything, for without him, I would not exist. If we ever do reach Arkatra, he will be in my care, and the powers I possess will protect him from harm."

"Understood, Merlin." Andrew nodded. "I still find it difficult to believe this tree, or this world of yours actually exists, but I would like to volunteer with Emile and help with the search, if that's alright with you."

"If you are serious about joining us, Andrew, I will be happy for you to do so."

"But do you have any idea where zis tree, zis 'Umming Tree, might be?" asked the big Frenchman.

"If I can locate the druid monastery I attended, it would not be too difficult to calculate with some accuracy the position of the forest, but this would not be a simple task. You see the world you live in is so different from mine. Where there were forests, you now have fields for grazing your livestock and growing your crops. Where there were rivers and tracks, you now have big roads. You have large towns and cities that have spread and enveloped much of what was once open ground or forest."

"Can you recall any geographical feature close to the monastery, such as a hill, a lake or a river?" questioned Andrew. "It might help us to locate the site of the monastery, roughly, and then the forest, if it still exists."

"I know the monastery was sited on a hill, and this Stonehenge you speak of was a half day's walk in a south-easterly direction. I know this because we walked there a number of times each year to worship and to celebrate the start of a new season. The forest was about five to six hours' walk and southeast from the stones, if I remember correctly."

"I don't know the area too well," said Andrew, "but it sounds like the New Forest; I think it's the only woodland in that vicinity. Given your excellent memory, Merlin, I am sure between us we can find the site of this monastery of yours.

"What is it…?" asked Andrew as he saw Merlin's gaze wander up to the ceiling again.

"Would either of you have a pen and paper?" the wizard asked.

"Yes, I 'ave a pen, and you can use a page from my notebook on ze table", said Emile, reaching over to get it. Merlin wrote a few lines and returned the notebook to the Frenchman.

Emile read the note then passed it to Andrew. It read: 'Keep talking as if nothing is amiss. Speak as if I am still with you.' Merlin then tiptoed over to the door and silently slipped out of the room.

CHAPTER 27

Graham Marshall, area manager of the child welfare agency, SOCAR, speared his desk pad with a pencil, slid his fingers down its length, turned it and repeated the process… It was a habit Ann Roper found most irritating, especially as he seemed to do it only while she was talking.

"Yes, I have seen the article from the Mail, Ann, and I agree that this Watson boy's disappearance is embarrassing for the agency, but we are doing everything we can to publicise the case. It's been given considerable television exposure, so all we can do now is to maintain continued dialogue with the police and the media, then simply wait to see if there's any response from the public."

"But this reporter, Mr Mac'Veer, is suggesting the note from the boy might be genuine, and that possibly, he is really being cared for until such time as he can live with his aunt and uncle. The police, I believe, are also considering this possibility."

"Yes, you have already mentioned that, Ann. What's your point?"

Ann Roper sometimes wondered how a person as naïve as her boss could possibly have attained the lofty position of department head.

"Well, seeing as the boy absconded while he was in the care of two of our field officers, we have a greater responsibility, as the department involved. We must be seen to be doing our utmost to resolve this situation, by exploring every possible avenue."

"But I still don't understand where you are going with this."

Ann Roper sighed inwardly, and watched as Graham Marshall started to tap the pad again with his pencil.

"Would it not be possible for us to instigate a court hearing for this truly unique case, with a view to having Tom Watson reunited with his uncle and aunt? Mr Mac'Veer suggested if we could expedite this, they would display a prominent notice, with the details of the court hearing, in their paper, in the hope the boy or his carer or carers may see it."

"Ann, we have thousands of cases to deal with each year. We have a backlog of family law cases that Social Welfare have

178

involved us with. We are desperately trying to clear these; many of which are more serious than the Tom Watson case. No, I'm afraid this will have to go through the normal channels. If the aunt and uncle feel they can provide a better home for the boy, let them seek legal advice on how best to go about it."

"But sir, it will take weeks, probably months before the case would reach the family court," Ann protested.

"Mrs Roper, I gave full consideration to the e-mail you sent me about this matter, but I still cannot see how this warrants more attention than the hundreds of other children at risk cases we have on file. I would give consent for a field officer to visit the relatives of the boy and advise them on procedures to apply for guardianship and on their legal rights, but that's as far as I'm prepared to go."

He paused. "If you have no other matters you wish to discuss with me, then I think we should conclude this meeting, as we both have more urgent matters to attend to."

Ann Roper flipped down the sun visor of the car, to check her make-up. Her boss always had the same effect on her, she always came away from meetings with him feeling hot, sweaty and irritated. She decided there was no need for any cosmetic adjustments, so after a quick disapproving look at the grey streaks in her light-brown, page boy style hair, she started the engine and headed back to her office in Crawley.

She was furious at the outcome of the interview with her boss. She had been through many contentious issues with Graham Marshall in the past, and usually she would just shrug her shoulders and get on with it. Yet on this occasion she felt rebellious and angry at his obstinate, narrow-minded attitude but was as determined now as she was when she stormed out of his office, not to let the matter rest.

By the time she had reached Crawley, Ann Roper had decided her next move.

She had remembered the party to celebrate the creation of SOCAR, the Court Advisory Services for Older Children at Risk, in 2002. She had been excited about the new concepts, the restructuring of the over-burdened child welfare system; optimism felt by everyone else at the party. And it was at this party that that she had bumped into a woman who had introduced herself as Emma. There had been instant rapport between them and both were exactly on the same wave length when it came to child welfare issues.

A day or two later, one of her colleagues informed her the woman she had spent so much time talking to at the party was none other than Lady Woodford, the chairwoman of the select committee which had been instrumental in setting up the new child support service.

The first thing Ann Roper did back in her office was to ask her secretary to bring her a much needed cup of strong coffee – and the phone number of Lady Emma Woodford.

CHAPTER 28

Chrissie couldn't fully comprehend the conversation she was hearing. There wasn't much that could throw her these days, but this talk she was hearing of a new world called Arkatra, and dinosaurs and everything, was too much for her pragmatic journalistic sensibilities. This was like the plot of a Sci-Fi novel, she thought. She could well understand the Frenchman getting excited about this sort of thing; after all, he was regarded as something of a world expert in psychic phenomena and all that stuff. As for Andrew Robbins, he was a retired airline pilot and appeared to be quite an ordinary, sane, intelligent man, yet he seemed as keen and credulous as the Frenchman.

But this strange, tall man they called Merlin. Who was he? What was he? She was still certain he was the one she had seen at the Long Acre farm that evening. As the reporter lay prone on her stomach listening to the talk in the room below, she failed to hear the door to her room open and the silent footsteps approaching the bed.

Merlin looked down for a few seconds at the female form lying there, with her head and shoulders under the bed. He then gently touched the sole of the woman's shoe with his toe.

"What the…!" exclaimed Chrissie. With her heart beating wildly she squirmed her way out from under the bed and turned to see a tall man smiling down at her.

"What… what are you doing in my room?" she blustered, trying to hide her embarrassment.

"Have you lost something?" he enquired, ignoring her question.

She thought she detected humour in the innocent tone of the man's voice.

"…um…yes, I seem to have lost my… my earring," she said, rising up quickly from the floor. As she spoke, Chrissie could feel her face getting hot and red.

"I see. Well, would you mind explaining what it is you have in your ears?" With a mixture of horror and humiliation, she realised the eavesdropper was still attached to her ears. It was no use trying to lie her way out of the situation. Instead she decided to go on the offensive.

"I want to know what you think you are doing, coming into my room like this," she demanded, taking the earpieces out and flinging the eavesdropper on to the bed.

"And I should like to know why you have been listening to a private conversation," responded the wizard calmly.

"I have not… Well, yes I have, but… but it's none of your business," she blustered.

"Well, I think it is our business, and I would like you now to accompany me down to my friend's room and explain why you have been doing this," Merlin said, quietly.

"I shall do no such thing," said Chrissie, brazenly.

"I think you will."

She now found herself caught in the man's intense gaze. She tried tearing her eyes from his, but couldn't.

"Now follow me," the wizard ordered. He then turned and slowly disappeared from the room.

Chrissie shook her head. "No, I will not," she said out loud, but found herself following in the footsteps of the man ahead of her. As she reluctantly descended the stairs, she kept thinking 'Why am I doing this? Why can't I just turn around and go back?'

"I would like to introduce you to my friends, but I do not know your name," said Merlin, as Chrissie hesitantly followed him into Emile's room.

"It's Christine… Christine Flowers."

"Now Miss Flowers, would you mind explaining to my friends why I have brought you here?"

Chrissie could feel herself reddening again under the scrutiny of the three men.

"Well, if you must know, I've been listening to your conversation," she blurted out, deciding the best policy was to tell them the truth. "I am a reporter for the Saltridge Echo, and I am investigating the disappearance of a boy named Tom Watson." Emile turned his attention from the woman to Merlin: "So zis was why you kept looking up at ze ceiling while we were talking," he said in an incredulous tone.

Merlin smiled and turned to Chrissie again: "So you have come all the way to Scotland to find this boy?" he quizzed.

"Yes, I believe he is somewhere in this village. In fact, I know he is," she said, almost belligerently as she looked up at the tall wizard.

"And you think we are involved with his disappearance?" asked Merlin.

"Yes I do. Well, I know you are."

"You certainly get around, Miss Flowers."

The wizard once again held her in his compelling gaze and in a soft resonant voice asked her to tell them everything she knew about Tom and all she had discovered about Craigemere village.

Chrissie felt her lips moving, involuntarily uttering words almost without thinking. She told them everything she had done since she saw Tom following the bearded man out of the car at the service station right up to the moment Merlin entered her room. As soon as she had finished, the strong compulsion to speak gradually disappeared.

Merlin was the first to respond once Chrissie had fallen silent.

"I believe my companions will agree, you are a very resourceful young lady, and yes, you are right, Miss Flowers, I did take the boy with me to this village. I was also the bearded man you saw at the service station. It was the boy's own wish to come with me, and at this moment he is being cared for in a loving environment. Would you prefer to see him taken back to his stepmother?"

"No, not really, not if he is unhappy there, but it's against the law to abduct a child."

"I understand your laws, but is it right to obey that law if it's against the wishes and the wellbeing of the child?"

"Maybe not, but it is still a crime in the eyes of the law."

"So what do you wish to do now, Miss Flowers?" Merlin enquired.

"Well, I would like to see Tom and talk to him privately, just to reassure myself he is happy where he is."

Merlin turned to Andrew: "Would Monica mind if Miss Flowers called tomorrow to see Tom?"

"I can't see why. I will arrange it. By the way, are you thinking of reporting this to the authorities, Miss Flowers?" asked Andrew.

"No,… well, I don't want to, but I don't want to be accused of being an accessory either, and that's what will happen if I ignore this."

"There need be no quandary for you, Miss Flowers," said the wizard, smiling down at her, "for if you wish, I can obliterate from your mind all recent memories involving Tom and the village of Craigemere."

For some reason, Chrissie found this tall, dark man they called Merlin quite attractive. She hadn't yet fathomed why, but one thing was certain, somehow he seemed to put her at ease. Even when he had walked into her room, she had not felt the least bit threatened by him.

"No thank you. I would prefer it if you leave my memory alone," Chrissie retorted.

"Then I will not invade the sanctity of your mind, unless it becomes necessary to do so, Miss Flowers."

"Can I ask you something?" said Chrissie, waving his comment from her mind, mainly because it sounded a little like a veiled threat. "Why do they call you Merlin?"

"Because it is who I am."

"You don't mean the Merlin in the King Arthur stories?"

"My name was obviously used to create the legend. This King Arthur was also once a real figure. I should know for he came to my family as a boy after his father, Artor Karalios, had died in battle."

"But… but you can't be. You would be over a thousand years old."

"One thousand, five hundred and thirty three years altogether, Miss Flowers, although all but forty eight of those years have been spent in a death-like coma."

Chrissie looked at the big Frenchman, then at Andrew, as if wanting some sign of denial from them.

"Merlin speaks the truth, Miss Flowers," said Andrew. "Many extraordinary things have happened and are still happening in our world. Things alien to our narrow three dimensional perspective. As for the survival of life, it has been discovered life can exist under the most hostile conditions, in the totally sulphuric environment of volcanic activity under the oceans or in the frozen wastes of the Arctic."

"It is correct what Andrew says, Miss Flowers," added Emile. "Do you know zere 'ave been er… how do you say in English?… auzenticated cases where lake beds dried out for countless years 'ave suddenly been replenished due to abnormal flooding and fish 'ave miraculously appeared? Zese creatures or zeir eggs 'ave lain dormant in ze dried earz wizout any sustenance for ages. If zey can lay dormant for five, ten, twenty years, why shouldn't zey be able to remain in zat state for a 'undred or a zousand years?"

It took Chrissie a few moments to digest what the big Frenchman had said. She then turned to Merlin. "I'm afraid this is so hard for me to take in. In my profession we only deal with facts. So please forgive my scepticism."

"When you see Tom tomorrow, will you ask him to explain how he discovered me, Miss Flowers? Only then will you begin to believe what happened, really did happen."

"So that's how the boy is involved? Yes, I certainly will ask him. I'm sure it'll be interesting, if not believable," said Chrissie with a wry smile.

"By the way," she continued, "I heard you mention Stonehenge. I was brought up near there, so I know the area pretty well. There *is* an old ruin up on a hill. As kids we used to play up there. We thought it must have been an old castle. There was this boy, Henry, who one day found a metal object that looked like a broach among the ruins. His parents sent it off somewhere and sometime later the place was cordoned off and we used to see a group of people digging around. Much later we heard, to our disappointment, it wasn't a castle after all, but just the ruin of an old monastery."

"Is that right? Sounds interesting, don't you think Merlin?" said Andrew.

"It does, but there would have been many other monasteries built over the years, and all buildings of importance were usually sited on high ground due to constant threats of invasion."

"Yes, but it would be werz investigating, wouldn't it?" said Emile.

"There's also a forest not too far away," Chrissie said. "It's all part of the New Forest area. My parents used to take my sister and me there on picnics during the summer and sometimes we'd drive there in the winter to collect pine cones for the fire."

Merlin gazed at her with interest. "Christine, do you think you could find the ruins again?"

"Possibly, why?"

"I would like to visit the area, if possible."

Merlin turned to Andrew and Emile. "This place interests me greatly. It might be helpful if we could find it."

"Well, maybe we can, that's if Miss Flowers can give us a more precise location," suggested Andrew.

"Merlin, may I ask why you are so interested?" asked Emile.

The wizard thought for a moment before answering. "Gentlemen," he said, "I do not wish to discuss my reasons while Miss Flowers is present."

"In heaven's name, why not?" exclaimed Chrissie. "I've given you some good information and yet you don't want to tell me why you need it."

"You know too much already," said Merlin, "and we're still not sure if, sooner or later, you are going to report your findings to your newspaper or to the police."

"I've already told you, if Tom's happy there's no reason for me to report anything. I'll give you my word on it. Anyway, if everything you say is true about this new world of yours, then I might want to come along." There was momentary silence as the three men exchanged glances.

"Miss Flowers," said Merlin, slowly and deliberately, "we admire your resourcefulness and spirit, but that would be out of the question."

Chrissie stared up at the dark, fathomless eyes of the wizard, her blue eyes gleaming in defiance. "Surely, those qualities you say I have would be essential in any expedition. Also, if Tom is going, he might need a woman around; after all, the boy is only twelve."

Merlin smiled down at her. "You certainly are a resolute young lady. You remind me very much of a woman I once knew. I will need to discuss your proposition with my two friends tomorrow, for now it is getting late. It might be best if we wait until you have seen Tom and reassured yourself he is in good hands before we discuss this business again."

"That's fair enough, but if you decide against me coming along, then I don't see why I should give you more information about the ruins." Chrissie saw the wizard's features change in response to her words. His eyes sparkled with mirth and a broad grin, showing even white teeth, creased his swarthy, handsome face.

"I think, Miss Flowers, it would be wise to wait until tomorrow before deciding your intentions, don't you?" said Merlin, still grinning down at her.

He then turned to the two men. "Can we discuss this in the morning, gentlemen? If Miss Flowers meets us here at two o'clock tomorrow afternoon, we can inform her of our decision." Both Andrew and Emile readily agreed.

Merlin then went to open the door for Chrissie and, still smiling, said: "We'll expect you here at two o'clock, Miss Flowers. Oh, and you will not be offended if you return to your room unescorted, will you?"

Chrissie felt indignant that this man found her so amusing. She bade goodnight to Andrew and Emile, and as she walked past the wizard she retorted: "I'm sure I won't be offended, sir, and I will be even more pleased if you'll promise to stay out of my room in future."

She glanced back as she turned to climb the stairs to her room. The door to Emile's room was slowly closing and she couldn't help but notice the broad grin on the disappearing countenance of the tall stranger.

**   **   **

Merlin was the first to stand as Chrissie entered the room. "So, Miss Flowers, you have spoken to Tom, I presume?"

"Yes, and you were right, he is ok." She then turned to Andrew. "Your wife Monica is a lovely lady, and she's really making Tom feel at home."

"I'm pleased you think so. However, she's going over to Edinburg to spend time with our daughters tomorrow, so the boy will have to put up with us men for a while."

"It sounds as if I'm not to be invited to come down with you?" said Chrissie, quickly interpreting Andrew's words.

"It is not so, Miss Flowers," said Merlin. "We have decided you can contribute to our search for this ruin you speak of, and we also agreed you were right about Tom, it would be better for a woman to be with him while we search for the Humming Tree, which may or may not have survived. If we do find it, we cannot take the risk of having you with us. You must

187

understand Miss Flowers, I cannot let its location or the method of transport to the New World be exposed to the public."

"Let me get this clear," said Chrissie, her blue eyes flashing. "You want me to show you the monastery ruins and look after Tom while you three men look for this tree. Then, if you are successful in finding it, you'll wave me goodbye and take Tom with you to this… this Arkatra world. Is that it?"

Merlin looked down at the reporter, a smile once again hovering around his mouth.

"It sounds as if you're not entirely happy with this arrangement, Miss Flowers, but it is a decision that was reached after a great deal of thought and discussion."

"Obviously, but you haven't thought of how I might react to your decision," she retorted. "I will be quite happy to look after Tom, seeing as Monica is going to visit her daughters, but I will not accompany you down to Hampshire to find the ruins."

"I am sure you realise, Miss Flowers, should it be necessary, I could quite easily persuade you to accompany us. However, it would be preferable if you would change your mind and come with us of your own free will," said the wizard, a little sternly.

Chrissie well understood the meaning behind the words, for she remembered how she'd unwillingly followed the tall man down the stairs, and was somehow compelled to divulge all she knew regarding Tom and the village.

"When are you thinking of going?" she asked resignedly.

"It is convenient for Andrew if we leave as soon as possible while his wife is away. It would suit Emile also, as he has no requests for his services at this time. So we have decided to leave early tomorrow morning. Emile has already given notice to the landlady that he will no longer need his room from tomorrow, I suggest you do the same."

Chrissie's normal reaction would have been to argue her case with a mixture of reason and feminine wiles, but she was beginning to realise the power this man had over people, over her. He had a positive mind, but she knew there must be other reasons why she found him so attractive.

Her best plan, she knew, would be to go along with the arrangements they had made, and look for any opportunity to reason with them.

CHAPTER 29

The drive down to Hampshire in Andrew's car was enjoyable for Chrissie. She sat in the back with Tom and Merlin, while Emile, because of his huge frame, sat in the front passenger seat.

She noticed how this fascinating man sitting next to her responded to Tom's questioning. He spoke as he would to an adult, encouraging the boy to respond likewise. She found the resonance in his voice captivating and was happy to sit back with her eyes half closed listening to him.

She was well aware of his extraordinary powers, but still found it hard to accept he was actually Merlin, the wizard of Arthurian legend. Chrissie wondered how she could ever report what she'd seen and heard. Robbo would probably laugh her out of his office.

'Oh yes, and this man, this Merlin, who by the way, is over fifteen hundred years old, hypnotised me into doing things against my will. I then went down to Stonehenge with him and two of his psychic friends … Oh, and Tom, the missing boy, came with us. We were all going to search for a special oak tree that has the ability to transport people to another world; a world full of dinosaurs!' Chrissie shook her head slightly as if to rid herself of the ludicrous dialogue.

"Miss Flowers." Chrissie sat up at the mention of her name. "Miss Flowers, sorry if I woke you, but do you not find interest in the beautiful countryside?" Merlin asked.

"I …I wasn't sleeping…just relaxing, that's all. Yes, I love the countryside. It's just that I didn't sleep well last night," stammered Chrissie, feeling a little embarrassed.

"I see," said the wizard, smiling. "I apologise for disturbing your sleep. I will leave you to return to your slumber."

"I told you, I… I wasn't sleeping," Chrissie insisted, conscious of the heat rising to her cheeks. 'What was it about this man', she thought, 'that makes me blush like a stupid teenager?'

It was well after 3pm before they finally stopped at the 'The Forest Inn'. Andrew had booked it through the internet the previous afternoon. Like many other hotels in the region, it boasted close proximity to the New Forest. As it had been a long drive down, Andrew suggested everyone should relax for the rest of the day.

"I do not feel like relaxing," said Emile, "for I 'ave relaxed enough in ze car. I will look around for ze carte, or … 'ow you say it, ze map of ze area."

"If we can rely on you to get the map, Emile, then perhaps Miss Flowers might try to show us the location of the ruins she has spoken of," said the wizard.

"Yes, I would be happy to do that," said Chrissie. "The trouble is, it was such a long time ago, and sometimes childhood memories can play tricks on you."

"I think we all understand that, Miss Flowers," said Andrew. "By the way, can we address you by anything other than your surname?"

"Of course! I was going to suggest you call me Christine … or Chrissie, as that's what I've been tagged with since I was a kid."

"Ok, Chrissie it is then!" said Andrew.

"I would prefer to call you Christine, if it meets with your approval," said Merlin.

Chrissie cast a quick glance at the wizard. "Certainly, if it's what you wish."

**   **   **

It was mid-morning of the following day when Andrew turned into a quiet street in the town of Benidale, a few miles from Salisbury.

"Yes, this is the house I used to live in as a kid," said Chrissie , excitedly pointing to a semi-detached on the other side of the road. "It's number eighteen; nothing seems to have changed much, though the garden is not as nice as dad used to keep it!"

Andrew stopped the car and everyone waited patiently while Chrissie aired her nostalgic memories.

The previous evening she had found it difficult to locate the ruins on the map Emile had bought. So in the morning they made enquiries at the nearest Visitor Centre, to see if the ruins were noted on any of the copious literature on Stonehenge and surrounding area, but there seemed to be no reference to such a place. Even the two assistants were of no help. Chrissie suggested they find the house she used to live in. From there, she thought she might have a better idea where the ruins were.

"If we go along this street and turn right, we should see the hills and the woods where we used to play as kids. It was all national park area so, hopefully, it should still be untouched."

Sure enough, as soon as they turned the corner, they could see the hills over the roofs of the houses ahead.

"If you turn right at the next street and drive slowly, I might be able to see the alleyway we used to go down to get out on to the fields."

Andrew turned as directed and drove at a snail's pace down the street.

"I think you'd better stop here," said Chrissie. "I can't see much with all the parked cars."

Andrew stopped the car and Chrissie got out. They watched as she walked along the pavement. Suddenly she stopped and waved for them to follow. Andrew parked the car, and minutes later they all emerged from the alleyway on to open land. "That's the hill we used to climb up, where all those trees are," said Chrissie, pointing over to her right.

On arriving at the edge of the woods, she had to stop and think. She remembered a fence had been erected to protect some saplings, and that's where she and her friends used to venture into the wood. It wasn't long before she found what she was looking for. Most of the fence was lying half hidden under bracken. A few half-rotten posts poking up from the undergrowth had caught her eye. She skirted the posts and moved cautiously into the woods, closely followed by Tom and the others.

Chrissie walked slowly, trying to remember the direction they had taken as children. After walking around for about ten minutes, she suddenly let out a squeal of delight. She pointed at something through the trees and rushed over to the spot. The others found her standing, hands on her hips, a satisfied smile on her face. "There! Not bad after twenty odd years, is it?"

She was standing by the remains of a flint wall about eighteen inches high. It was the highest part of the ruin. Vestiges of wall could be seen here and there, marking the contour of the ancient foundations. Bracken concealed much of the perimeter and even trees had grown within its confines. Merlin went to take a closer look, followed by Tom. He would stop now and then to look at lines that marked out rooms, halls and passages. He disappeared among the trees as he surveyed the extreme boundaries of the ruin, while Andrew, Emile and Christine stood around talking in hushed tones.

It was some time before Merlin had finished surveying the ruins. He approached the threesome in a thoughtful mood.

"I believe it is the remains of the druid monastery I attended all those years ago," said Merlin, quietly.

"Well, that's marvellous!" exclaimed Chrissie.

"It is. But it fills me with sadness. In real time, it is over fifteen hundred years since I last saw this place, but in my consciousness, it is no more than twenty-two years since I was here as a student."

They all looked at him as he stood there, as if lost in time. Emile finally broke the silence. "So, Merlin, you would 'ave set out from 'ere, from zis monastery, to find zer tree of yours, no?"

"Yes, Emile. We would walk from here in a south-easterly direction to reach the tree."

"But how did you know you were walking in the right direction?" asked Andrew.

"We knew where we were any time of the day because we were guided by the passage of the sun. Even when hidden by heavy cloud, we still knew its position in the heavens, regardless of the seasons."

"We have long lost this skill, Merlin."

"There was also a defined path through the forest," said the wizard, as he watched Chrissie walk away to join Tom, who had disappeared into the trees. "But the terrain I see today is so different. The landscape has become unrecognisable. Now there is nothing but open countryside, buildings and roads, where once there was forest."

"I understand, but do you still remember how long it took to walk from the monastery to the tree?" persisted Andrew.

"I accompanied the Grand Priest on two occasions and each time we set out, the sun was at its height and cast no shadow. On reaching the tree, dusk was upon us, so eight would have passed since waving farewell to our brother druids."

"Why do you wish to know zis, Andrew, I do not understand?" Emile queried.

"Well, just think, Emile. If we knew the distance they walked to get there, we'd have a fairly accurate idea of the tree's position."

"Ah, yes! I see. But surely you'd need to know za speed zey walked to have some idea of distance?"

Andrew turned to his tall friend. "Merlin, do you have any idea of the distance you walked?"

"In my world, distance was measured in leagues; it was an ancient Celtic measure. The Romans adopted it during their occupation of our land."

"Yes, I remember reading about it as a student," said Emile. "A league was adjusted by ze Romans to measure ze distance a soldier could walk in an 'our and it was t'ought to be zree miles."

"That's excellent!" Andrew exclaimed. He then turned to the wizard. "So Merlin, if it took eight hours for you and the Grand Priest to walk from the monastery to the tree, then we're looking at a distance of around twenty four miles – assuming you walked at the same pace as a Roman soldier!"

"It might be so," agreed the wizard, "we tended to walk at a good pace."

"I've been thinking," said Andrew. "Let's assume your tree still exists. Would it be possible to identify it from the air?"

The wizard gave Andrew a quizzical look.

"I mean finding the tree from an aeroplane," said Andrew, smiling at his friend. "My idea is to hire a small aircraft, maybe a Cessna, because I'm familiar with it. We could cover a lot of ground in a short time, and have three or four sets of eyes looking out for the tree. What do you think?"

"I keep forgetting about these wonderful inventions of your world. It would of course be faster and easier to seek out the tree that way. If the Humming Tree still exists, it will be larger than all its neighbours and will be standing alone, in a small clearing,"

"When could you get this flying machine of yours?" he asked.

"I still have my pilot's license for light aircraft and there are two or three air-bases near here. There's one I know called Highdown Airfield. It's not too far from here. I know the base is still active, because a colleague of mine used it last year."

It wasn't long before the group was back in the car and heading for the air base.

CHAPTER 30

Ann Roper was quite taken aback by Lady Woodford's response to her telephone call. The woman not only remembered her from the conversation they'd had three years previously, but she also recalled her name and knew about her role in the department. What was even more surprising was Lady Emma's spontaneous approval of her request for a private interview.

She had made the phone call two days ago, and now here she was, seated in a comfortable cane lounger, in a lovely conservatory looking out over the South Downs and being waited on by the tall, flamboyantly dressed lady herself.

"I hope this Australian chardonnay is to your liking, Ann, it's my favourite wine, and sometimes I think I drink too much of it," said Emma Woodford, as she placed the two glasses of wine on the glass-topped white cane table.

"It will be lovely, I'm sure," said Ann, as she watched her hostess pull up the other cane chair and sit down.

After a little small talk, during which Lady Emma insisted Ann address her by her Christian name, the hostess said: "Now Ann, I believe you have something you wish to say about the Tom Watson case. I have read the agency report and am aware of the press and TV coverage about the missing boy. It is a unique case and your comments on the phone intrigued me. May I just say that anything you tell me will be entirely confidential, just between the two of us." Ann smiled and thanked her for her kind words.

"Well, it's something a reporter, a Mr Mac'Veer, said to me the other day. He said the police were keeping an open mind on the situation. Apparently they are still treating it as abduction, but are not discounting the possibility the boy might actually have gone willingly and be somewhere safe; that his message might be a genuine call for him to be allowed to live with his uncle and aunt. Mr Mac'Veer said his paper held the same view and wanted to know whether we, as the department whose care the boy was in at the time of his disappearance, would consider taking some sort of official action to encourage a possible response from the boy."

"I understand what you're saying, Ann, but in what way do we bring about such action?"

"Well, first of all, I think you should know I have discussed this whole thing with Mr Marshall. I thought you should be aware of that, just in case you want to discuss it with him."

"I don't think that will be necessary at this point, but thanks for letting me know."

"It's just that he doesn't agree with my view on what action we should take on this case. Normally I would accept his decision and that would be the end of it, but this time I feel convinced we should take some positive action to help resolve the matter, and hopefully reunite the boy with his relatives."

"I must say it is quite clear from the case history, the boy was very much attached to his relatives, and they to him, but his stepmother has legal guardianship, has she not?" questioned the hostess.

"That's correct."

"Then tell me, Ann, how do you propose we should bring about this reconciliation?"

"Well, would it be possible for the department to expedite a court hearing in order for the relatives to apply for legal guardianship? If they were successful in getting it, we could publicise the decision in the press and on TV, in the hope Tom might then return of his own volition."

"I suppose Mr Marshall told you about the enormous backlog of family court cases involving minors?"

"Yes, he did, but he wasn't telling me anything new. It's just that this is an unprecedented case, what with the way the boy absconded, and then the note in his own handwriting ending up on an editor's desk at Fleet Street. I feel we should respond to the boy's note, on the off chance the message might be genuine."

"Umm, I see," said Lady Woodford. The hostess sat in silent contemplation for some time. She then took a sip of wine and said: "I definitely agree with you Ann. We should make an effort to bring this one to court as early as possible, but there are some stumbling blocks. In this case, as in most others nowadays, the wishes of the child will be taken into account along with other material from interested parties. It is quite likely the magistrate or county court judge will refuse to preside over any family court hearing with a guardianship issue, without the boy being present."

"Yes, I suppose you're right," responded Ann, "but couldn't we still press ahead with an early hearing, then publicise the date of the hearing with an appeal for the boy to attend?"

"If we go on the premise the boy is out there somewhere because he wants nothing more than to leave his stepmother and be reunited with these relatives of his and that he'll reappear when he sees a notice to that effect, then I agree we should act accordingly, but Ann, it's a most unlikely premise."

"I know it is, but surely it is better to consider it than to ignore it and do nothing."

"I think you're right. At the very least it would show we are making an effort to do something positive. I will see what strings I can pull with the judiciary. As for Mr Marshall, I'll explain I've had some personal concerns about the case. If I know Graham, I will have him believing it was his idea in the first place." The hostess proffered the wine bottle to her guest.

"Just a half glass, thank you, Emma. I'm driving."

"It could still take a few weeks before the case comes before the courts, Ann," said Emma Woodford as she finished pouring the wine. "In the meantime the two interested parties will need to be advised of their rights, but I am sure you know all about that."

Ann Roper nodded. "Yes, I will see to it, and thank you for spending the time with me, Lady ... I mean Emma, I'm really grateful."

"Think nothing of it. Oh, and about that reporter, Mr McVie, or whatever his name is, it might be best if you don't divulge anything until such time as we have a definite date for the hearing. In fact, it might be better if I speak to the press and the police department once we know dates and things."

Ann Roper drove away from Lady Emma's country estate, satisfied she'd done all she could to bring the Tom Watson case to the fore, but there was still a nagging thought going round her head. Why was this case so important to her?

CHAPTER 31

A little after ten o'clock the following morning, Andrew Robbins taxied the small plane to the end of the concrete runway. Minutes later the yellow, four-seater Cessna 172 was flying over the ancient woodlands of the Black Heath forest. Merlin sat next to the pilot, with Chrissie and Tom behind them.

Emile had opted not to go. Flying in jumbo jets was bad enough, he had said, but flying in something as small as this was 'utter madness!'

It had taken Merlin a few minutes to recover from the shock of take-off, but he was now beginning to enjoy the experience thoroughly.

"We'll approach the forest from the direction of the old monastery ruin," said Andrew loudly, trying to make himself heard above the engine noise. "I'll keep the ground speed down then to under a hundred and ten miles an hour. Means we should arrive at the tree site in around fifteen minutes. If we can't spot it, we'll fly on for another five minutes then return on a slightly different track. We'll repeat the procedure until we're satisfied we've fully checked the area. What do you think, Merlin?"

Andrew shouted more words for the benefit of the two sitting behind him: "Keep your eyes peeled for any tree that appears to stand alone in a clearing. If you see anything, we'll go down for a closer look." They had been in the air for almost thirty minutes when Tom called out. He thought he saw what looked like a large tree in a clearing far away to his right. Merlin looked over to the spot Tom was pointing to, his keen eyesight quickly spotting what the boy had seen. "There is something, but it's too far away to be certain. Can you fly over there?" he asked.

"There are binoculars above your head," said Andrew as he banked the plane to starboard. It took a while for Merlin, with Andrew's instructions, to get a handle on the device, but he was soon zoning in on the forest below.

"We're just about over the area now," said Andrew, bringing the speed of the aircraft down to just above stalling. Chrissie now saw the clearing Tom had referred to. She touched Merlin's shoulder and pointed. As the clearing came into full view, the wizard took a sharp intake of breath. "Yes, I am sure this is it! I won't be certain until I approach the tree on foot, but I have the strangest feeling…" Merlin broke off suddenly, a wistful look in his eyes.

"Are we ready then to return to base?" asked Andrew.

Merlin nodded. "I think so."

"I have a GPS fix so it shouldn't be too much trouble locating it from the ground," said Andrew, who then spent the next few minutes explaining to Merlin how, with the help of satellites, a global position can be obtained from wherever you happen to be in the world. The wizard was still shaking his head in wonder at it all as the wheels of the plane gently touched the runway.

Emile was waiting near the main hangar with the car. They drove back to the hotel to plan and prepare for the next day.

After lunch Chrissie thought she might go on one of the forest walks she had seen displayed on a notice board in the parking area. Tom responded with enthusiasm when she asked him if he would like to accompany her. Chrissie found Tom to be enjoyable company. Previously, she had questioned him in depth about Merlin, for she hadn't quite believed what he had been telling her. But Tom confirmed Merlin's story and she was certain the boy was speaking the truth, for he'd need to have been a little genius, she thought, to make it all up. However, she had still found it difficult to get her head around some of the incredible things he had told her.

On this occasion, she asked Tom about his home life and about his deceased parents. As they walked, Tom talked about his cherished memories of his father, and of the vague memory of a dark-haired lady reading him a story when he was very young. He spoke about his unhappiness living with his stepmother and his desire to live with his aunt and uncle, who seemed to care for him.

The boy had lost a lot in his young life, Chrissie thought, yet he seemed devoid of self-pity. She was beginning to understand why Merlin took the boy away, but she wondered how it was all going to end. They arrived back at the hotel fairly late. The walk had taken longer than anticipated. By the time she had showered and seen to Tom, it was dinner time.

During the evening meal, Chrissie listened to everything the group had arranged for the following day. Merlin had organised an early breakfast to allow them to begin the walk no later than 9am. Andrew reminded everyone to bring water and adequate clothing. He said he'd arranged with the proprietor to supply a lunch pack of cold meat, cheese, sandwiches and fruit. The hotel landlord had also agreed to let them leave the car in their carpark and to drive them to the forest himself for a fee Andrew and Emile thought was quite reasonable.

Emile had told the proprietor, his group were on an investigative mission, searching for a rare species of an ancient tree that was thought to grow somewhere in the Black Heath section of the New Forest. He had added "we might be away for some time". Laughing, Emile said it was as close to the truth as he dared go.

Chrissie, however, was perturbed that no mention was made during the meal of her role in the coming expedition. If they expected her to wait in the hotel for days on end while they trekked around in the forest, they could think again! She knew she had good persuasive powers, she also knew she performed at her best when confronted with what she perceived to be unfair or unreasonable behaviour towards her, and this she thought was such an occasion. If there *was* such a thing as a world with pre-historic monsters and everything, she wanted to see it for herself, although the practical part of her brain was telling her no such place existed.

She decided not to bring the matter up at the dinner table. She'd wait until Tom was in bed and then confront Merlin, for she knew if she could persuade him, the others would go along with it. Later that evening she knocked on Merlin's door. He opened it, invited her in and showed her to the only seat in the room and sat himself on the edge of the bed.

"Can I ask why you have given me the pleasure of your company this evening?" he said, a familiar smile lurking around his mouth.

"I think you know why," said Chrissie, a little haughtily. "I would like to know where I fit in with all these… these plans you are making for tomorrow."

"What are you trying to tell me?" enquired the wizard, appearing a little perplexed.

"I want to know if I'm to be included in your activities tomorrow?"

"You have been on a long forest walk with Tom today, is that not sufficient?"

'Why do I think this man is deliberately playing with me?' thought Chrissie.

"You know what I mean," she said, glaring across at him. "To search for the tree we saw from the air this morning."

"Oh yes, the tree, hopefully it will be the Humming Tree. What about it?"

"Am I going with you is what I want to know," said Chrissie, realising this was not the way she had planned to tackle the situation.

"Yes, of course, if it's what you wish. I spoke with Emile and Andrew this evening after the meal, and we agreed you should join us. We thought it would be better for Tom to have you along."

"Then why didn't someone tell me this evening?" she asked, annoyance reflected in her tone.

"I believe Andrew was going to call on you…"

At that moment, there was a knock on the door. Merlin opened it to find Andrew standing there.

"I have been to her room, but she doesn't appear to be there," said the Scotsman.

"The lady is here. She wanted to know about tomorrow, Andrew. Please come in."

"Sorry Chrissie, I was calling to tell you… but anyway, now you know."

"Yes, she knows," said Merlin, "although I feel she was a little disappointed, for I think she wanted to make a fight of it."

The wizard looked at her, a wide grin spreading across his face.

"Not true," she said, a little indignantly, knowing his comment wasn't too far from the truth.

Chrissie was in high spirits when she climbed into bed, so much so, she found it difficult to sleep. Yet the thought of what tomorrow might bring troubled her as much as it excited her.

CHAPTER 32

The walk through the forest was relatively easy at first. They managed to take one of the defined public walkways that led in the general direction of the 'fix' Andrew had put into the hand-held GPS. But eventually they were forced to go off the track into the heart of the forest. The going was much slower, and after a few minutes Merlin asked Andrew to point in the direction of the GPS fix.

The wizard then took the lead. Merlin seemed to glide through the trees with ease and the others were finding it hard to keep up with him. Tom managed to keep pace with the wizard for some distance, but even he started to tire. Chrissie was determined not to lag behind because the last thing she wanted was to have them rest because of her.

It was Emile who finally requested a rest. His large frame and general unfitness made it more difficult for him to keep up. On hearing Andrew's call, Merlin retraced his steps to the group, who had seated themselves on a tree trunk to rest.

"I hope I have not been walking too fast. It's just that we still have a long way to go."

"Probably about another ten miles to reach the spot, from what the GPS tells me," said Andrew, who was deeply impressed by Merlin's uncanny ability to stay on the bearing he had given him.

"We will rest here for fifteen minutes and then walk for another hour or more before stopping for lunch, if that suits everyone," Merlin said. Chrissie had the feeling Merlin was eager to carry on, for instead of sitting down, he continued moving around. He drank from a water bottle he took from a small rucksack Andrew had given him. She discreetly observed the wizard as he bent down to inspect the forest floor, and on two or three occasions she saw him tasting a leaf or a berry from a ground plant.

She was a little concerned about Emile, for he had been breathing quite heavily some time before the stop. She wondered whether she should say something to Merlin, but then thought better of it. Soon they were on their way again, with Merlin leading. Tom was close on Merlin's heels, with Andrew, Chrissie and Emile following in single file. They continued like this for some time until Chrissie noticed Emile was lagging further and further behind. She waited for the big Frenchman to catch up with her, then made him take off his backpack and drink from his water bottle. As they walked on, she decided to keep an eye on him.

By now Andrew had disappeared from view and there was no-one ahead to follow. Soon both Emile and Chrissie became disoriented. She told Emile to stop walking so they could listen for sounds made by their companions, but nothing. Chrissie started shouting. The faint noise made Merlin stop in his tracks. He turned back to look beyond Tom, who had been walking close behind. He saw Andrew following, but there was no sign of the other two.

"I don't know when they dropped behind. Maybe five, ten minutes ago, I'm not sure," said a worried Andrew to the approaching wizard.

"Quiet, Andrew…listen," commanded Merlin. Andrew watched as Merlin stood still, eyes half closed in concentration. Tom approached the wizard to say something, but Merlin showed him his open palm as a sign to be silent.

"There! Did you hear it?" said Merlin quietly.

Both Andrew and Tom had to admit they couldn't hear anything except for the rustle of leaves and occasional bird sounds.

"Wait here. Do not move until I return," ordered Merlin.

The wizard was about to move off when Andrew stopped him.

"Let me try to get Emile on the phone first, Merlin."

Andrew reached for his mobile phone and saw there was no signal. He tried twice to phone, but both calls were aborted.

"So much for your wonderful inventions," said Merlin, with a little smile. He then quickly disappeared into the forest.

"Emile, all we can do is stay right here and keep shouting" said Chrissie, in answer to the Frenchman's wish to keep going. "If we carry on walking, we could be going further away from them. Let's take turns shouting. Hopefully one of them will hear us."

Emile brushed his thick curly hair away from his sweating forehead and started yelling.

Merlin ran through the forest, stopping now and again to listen. Each time the cries became a little clearer until eventually, minutes later, he came upon the couple just as Chrissie was about to shout once more. "Oh, thank goodness!" she exclaimed, as she saw Merlin emerge from the trees. She quickly went to him and threw her arms around him in an impulsive gesture and felt his strong fingers clasp her waist. She quickly disengaged herself from the wizard, cursing her momentary weakness.

"We are sorry to 'ave caused you so much trouble, Merlin, but it is good to see you," said the big Frenchman.

"No, it is I who should apologise, Emile, for I should have been more aware of you all. In the forest I seem to enter a world of my own. It has always been like this for as long as I can remember. From now on, Andrew can lead with my guidance."

Both Tom and Andrew were relieved to see the wizard reappear with Emile and Chrissie.

"I think we should stop now and eat," said Merlin. "When we continue, we will go at a more leisurely pace."

Merlin suggested they walk another two hours before resting again. The journey was now more enjoyable, allowing occasional chatter between them. "We have only another three miles to go," announced Andrew as the group settled down once more to rest.

Chrissie felt energized by the walk, but kept berating herself for putting her arms around Merlin. She was thoroughly embarrassed, but what concerned her most was the undeniable feeling of pleasure she experienced when he had his hands around her waist.

They had been walking again for about an hour and a half when they suddenly broke into the clearing they had seen from the air... and there it was - the majestic oak tree standing right in the centre. Slowly, Merlin walked up to the giant and placed his ear against the massive trunk. Then he stood back and began to scrutinise the ground around it, widening his search to take in the whole clearing and the forest's edge. It was some minutes before he returned to the waiting group.

"We have found the Humming Tree! I have the feeling no-one has visited this place for many, many years." The group remained silent, digesting the news.

"What do you want us to do now?" asked Andrew, quietly.

"It will be necessary, from this moment on, for you all to do as I ask."

The wizard approached the tree once more, turned and bade the group come closer.

"I would like Tom to stand on my right and Andrew to stand on Tom's right. Christine, I want you to stand on my left and Emile to stand next to you."

Once they had arranged themselves, Merlin asked them all to join hands. "Now stretch out as far as you can, for it is best if we can completely encircle the tree."

This was done when Emile's left hand found Andrew's right.

"Are we all joined as one?" asked Merlin.

Emile and Andrew answered "yes" in unison.

"Now, move as close to the tree as possible and with your hands still joined, embrace it."

"Is everyone ready?"

There was a murmur of assent.

"I am hoping that once my thoughts are concentrated on the task in front of me, the tree will begin to accept us. Please make sure you have a firm grip of the hands you are holding, and now, completely clear your mind of everything but the tree."

Chrissie gripped the hands of Merlin and Emile tightly, and with her heart beating rapidly, and eyes tightly closed, she waited in silence for what might happen. The first thing she became aware of was a low humming, similar to the noise her radio made when not quite on the proper channel. She noticed the hardness against the side of her face had softened and a silky sensation began to envelop her. Gradually, the humming became louder and she felt as if she was being drawn into the tree, causing her to step forward to retain her balance. She expected to bump her knee on the trunk, but found no resistance whatsoever. Instead she felt a spongy softness as first one leg then the other stepped hesitantly forward. Then came the awesome realisation that she had actually been absorbed into the tree itself. Chrissie forced herself to open her eyes and was confronted with a misty greyness as if in the midst of the densest fog.

The humming sound grew into a roar, then a high-pitched whine as it increased in intensity, and the thick mist disappeared into darkness. A feeling of buoyancy, as if floating in mid-air, came over her. She became light-headed and breathless, yet strangely comfortable.

Chrissie had no awareness of time or those who were with her. The strange sound now seemed to engulf her whole being. It was as if she was suspended in some sort of tube, wrapped in some incredible space warp. Whatever it was, she felt as if she could stay in this comfortable womb forever. Soon, the high-pitched whine began to diminish until it finally softened to a familiar hum. She felt gravity taking hold again and then, as if being released from some restraint, she felt herself stepping backward - out of the tree and into another world.

CHAPTER 33

As a dazed Chrissie looked about herself, she saw her
companions bathed in a pink glow that reminded her of the way
the world looked through a pair of sunglasses she once owned.
There they stood around the same tree, in the same clearing – but
beyond… myriads of colours and sounds swamped their senses as
birds and exotic creatures of every description busied themselves
among an explosion of unfamiliar greenery.

"Please remain here until I return," said Merlin, bursting
the bubble. "Stay by the Humming Oak, and I will return as soon
as it is possible to do so."

"But what about those… those dinosaurs you spoke of?"
said Chrissie.

"You need not be afraid. There are no dinosaurs in this
part of Arkatra. I would not leave you if there were. I will explain
later."

Before anyone had a chance to respond, Merlin had
turned, and, breaking into a loping run, disappeared through an
opening in the trees.

The group was so enthralled by the world they'd entered
they could do nothing more than stand and stare. Tom was the
first to notice activity in the heavy-leafed canopy and soon all
were gazing up into the verdant tangle that supported a vast array
of chattering and screaming monkeys of different hues, shapes
and sizes.

"We can now continue toward our destination," said
Merlin, whose silent return among them had gone unnoticed.
"Please follow me, and soon you will be able to rest."

Merlin realised he needed to travel at a much slower pace
with his distracted companions for they would frequently bump
into one another while gazing entranced at their exotic
surroundings..

Eventually Merlin led them out of the forest into open
terrain. Here they paused to gaze at a delightful scene. A broad
valley cloaked in a carpet of grass, horsetail fern and flowering
shrubs lay before them. Beyond the valley, groves of heavily
foliaged, unfamiliar trees, gave emphasis to the splendour of the
countryside. In the distance, amber-coloured hills rose gently,
disappearing into a fringe of dense forest, before emerging higher

up in a steep tussock-clad incline that ended abruptly in a flat plateau. It appeared to drop away sharply to the right into an almost perpendicular cliff face, which gradually merged into a gentle downward slope, finally flattening out into a meadow, where they could just make out a little village. Snow-tipped purple mountains, their far-off peaks almost surreal against the red-tinted glow of the Arkatra sky, formed the stunning backdrop to the scene.

At Merlin's bidding, the group walked on in silence, totally immersed in the panorama..

They followed Merlin through a gate and into a field that lay fallow. He then led them into the garden of the first of the cottages. As they neared the cottage, the door suddenly opened and a short man in a faded blue work shirt, grey tunic and sandals appeared on the threshold. The man had ridiculously short but muscular legs, tanned by constant exposure to the elements. His brown arms, too, were very short in relation to his torso and also very powerful. A broad hunched back emphasized the man's squat, stocky frame.

Merlin conversed with the man in a strange language for some time before the wizard turned to the group. "This man is named Gregor, and you may call him that. I address him as Brother Gregor for that is our way. He is of the Ancient Order of Druids, my order, and keeper of the druid village in Arkatra. He will not be able to communicate with you for he speaks in the tongue of our time, Latin. It was Brother Gregor who met me on my last two visits to this world. There is much more to tell, but Brother Gregor would... "

Merlin stopped in mid-sentence for Brother Gregor was worriedly scanning the sky. The wizard looked up and spoke rapidly to the keeper. Gregor answered, but his eyes remained fixed on the heavens. By now, all had their eyes cast upward at the ominous dark clouds that were building up at great speed above their heads. Suddenly, out of the darkening maelstrom, came a clap of thunder so loud, everyone instinctively covered their ears and cowered down.

Lightening followed, almost rending the ever-darkening skies apart. Somewhere in the heavens deep ominous rumblings were heard, the reverberations shaking the ground beneath the fearful onlookers. The unbearable noise climaxed in another clap of thunder, louder and longer than the last. For some moments, there was utter silence. Then, without warning, a voice so powerful, so awesome, even Merlin flinched, spoke thus:

"MERLIN... AT LAST YOU APPEAR BEFORE US... IT WAS OUR WILL YOU WOULD DO SO... WE BESTOWED UPON YOU A STAFF OF OMNIPOTENT POWER....YOU HAVE UNWITTINGLY RENDERED THAT STAFF INTO EVIL HANDS... WORST OF ALL, IT GAVE THE EVIL ONE ACCESS TO OUR WORLD. WE SEE THAT YOU HAVE BROUGHT OTHERS WITH YOU... IT WILL BE CONDONED, FOR WE BELIEVE YOU WILL NEED THEIR AID IN RIDDING OUR WORLD OF THIS EVIL SORCERESS."

The group was stunned into silence. No one moved.

"...AS FOR THE BOY, HE ALONE WILL BREAK THE CURSE THAT GIVES HER THE POWER OF THE STAFF. HE ALONE WILL BE UNDER OUR PROTECTION. BEWARE, MERLIN... SHE CANNOT BE DESTROYED WHILE SHE POSSESSES THE STAFF, FOR SHE WILL TAKE ITS POWER WITH HER TO THE SPIRIT WORLD. THIS MUST NOT HAPPEN... FOR IT WILL PREVENT HER BEING JUDGED FOR HER SINS.
"GO MERLIN, ONLY WHEN THIS DEED IS DONE, WILL YOUR ACTIONS BE PLACED BEFORE US AND JUDGEMENT MADE."

Silence now reigned again in the heavens. The clouds dispersed as quickly as they had gathered, and the warm rays of the large orange sun once again embraced the land. For some time the stunned companions stood there speechless. Merlin turned to Brother Gregor. "I did not realise..."

"There is much you need to know, Brother Merlin, but in good time. I thought it best to welcome you all to my home and feed and rest you, before revealing all. We have not had the pleasure of greeting another human soul in our home for an immeasurable number of years. Now that time is upon us, I want it to be a special occasion."

The wizard then turned to his overawed friends. "I realise you had no understanding of what was said, for it was spoken in the language of my world. But you have a right to hear the message for it is of grave importance. I will explain everything to you this evening, after I have spoken with Brother Gregor."

Merlin turned to Gregor. "I gather from the way you speak, Brother Gregor, that you are not alone?"

"Ahh yes, there is another big surprise to come, Brother Merlin, but I think you'll find it far more pleasant than the one you have just received from the heavens."

"I am waiting to hear what good tidings await me, Brother Gregor, for I need some cheer after hearing those words."

Brother Gregor grinned. "It is my pleasure to tell you that Brother Alexinus will be arriving shortly."

"Alexinus…surely not! But how…," blurted the wizard.

"It is another long story to be told later this evening, but what I must disclose to you at this present moment is this; when Brother Alexinus arrives you will not recognise him, for he has been transformed into a bird, a very large bird."

"But how…?"

"It was Niddrym's doing," said Gregor, anticipating the wizard's question, for his attention was focused on movement in the direction of the plateau. "But let us speak of it later, my brother, for I believe it is he who is flying towards us."

Merlin cast his eyes in the same direction and immediately saw a monstrous flying creature gliding down towards them.

CHAPTER 34

John Nielson picked up the phone and pressed line 2 on the intercom in response to the flashing light.

"Paul, thanks for coming back to me. I'd like a chat with you about this Tom Watson boy, something of interest has come up." It wasn't long before Paul Mac'Veer was seated at the desk, opposite his long-time friend and boss.

"Just had a phone call from Emma Woodford. It seems she's got more than a little interest in the Tom Watson case."

"You mean the late Lord Woodford's wife?"

"The very same," informed the editor. "I didn't know she was a bigwig in the new child welfare agency, SOCAR, but apparently she is."

"Has this come about from my chinwag with Ann Roper?"

"Well, I wouldn't be surprised. Her name came into the conversation a number of times. Lady Woodford seems to think highly of her. Anyway, she was enquiring about the Tom Watson story, and whether we'd had any further response from the article. I told her that apart from the two women who'd reported seeing the bearded man with the boy that day, we received nothing more, and nothing from recent police press releases either."

"I see, but I bet it wasn't the only reason for the interview," said Paul.

"No, in fact, I think it was just an excuse for her to question me, and put forward her own agenda. She said an early hearing for the case has already been arranged. I suspect she's been using some personal clout to expedite this one."

"How long?"

"Just over five weeks."

"I suppose she's worried about the adverse public reaction, due to the boy being abducted while in their care. I did stress the point with Mrs Roper."

"I'm sure she is, Paul. Anyway, she has requested we run an article showing the photo of the lad, together with the letter he presumably wrote, at least once a week. She also said she wants to see it have front page exposure each time. I've told her we would need new angles, fresh sightings of the kid or new witnesses to his abduction before we could give the story that sort of treatment. She has also requested we run it on seven consecutive days immediately prior to the court hearing. I've agreed to this, subject to the boss's approval."

"She's certainly keen for a result, John."

"That's not all. She has also provided me with material she would like to see included in the article."

The editor pushed a medium-sized brown envelope over to the chief reporter. "Go through this stuff, Paul, and use your own discretion."

"Are you saying I'm not obliged to use any of it?"

"Of course not, she just said these were suggestions we might like to consider." The editor paused a moment. "I must tell you that although Lord Woodford is no longer with us, no longer chairman of the board, his shares in the paper went to Lady Woodford, making her a major shareholder of the company. So I think it would be prudent on our part if we at least give the appearance of co-operating with her."

"I get the picture, John. Just leave it with me."

Tom saw the bird almost at the same time as Merlin. "Look everyone, it's a Pterosaur!" he shouted, as he watched the gigantic creature glide towards them. Hearing the boy's cry, Chrissie, Andrew and Emile joined Merlin and Brother Gregor as they stood watching the approaching colossus.

"I hope you're sure this is Alexinus, Brother Gregor, otherwise we might be sitting targets for this monster," said Merlin, a little tensely. Gregor just kept grinning as the massive bird's shadow darkened the ground beneath them. Strangely silent in its approach, it circled the village once before coming in to land a few feet away from where they were standing. Tom could only stare in amazement at the huge creature, whose image he had seen so many times in his books on dinosaurs. On spindly pink legs that looked like they had recently been plucked of feathers, the bulky bird jump- hopped in a rather ungainly manner towards Gregor and Merlin.

"Is it truly my great friend Merlin who stands before me?" The words emanated from the long, sand-coloured beak.

"It is I. And am I to believe it truly is Alexinus who towers over me?"

"Indeed it is so, Merlin. Your evil half-sister used her powers to transform me into this flying caricature of a bird. You will be eager to discover why, but I think it will be appropriate to explain later, once you and your friends have settled in and rested."

"Yes, I have much to ask of both you and Brother Gregor, for my head is filled with so many questions," said Merlin.

"I understand, my friend," responded Alexinus. "Before the night is out, Brother Gregor and I will have satisfied your hunger for knowledge."

The others listened in awe to the strange unintelligible discourse between the extraordinary trio. Merlin, engrossed in talking with Alexinus and Gregor, had given little thought to his friends. He now turned and introduced each of them to the astonishing talking bird. Then, after a brief exchange of words with Gregor, he said. "Brother Gregor would be pleased if you would enter his home and enjoy the comforts he has to offer."

Gregor followed his guests into the cottage. Tom, however, stayed where he was, completely oblivious to everything except the bird. He watched with continued amazement as it settled on the ground by the cottage wall, then placed its long head in the open aperture that served as a window.

Inside, Andrew turned to Merlin. "Did we actually hear that bird speak?"

"Yes, it spoke in the language of my world."

"I thought that, but how… but how can that be?"

"Alexinus was once a great and loyal friend of mine, a brother druid, a man of great intelligence and spiritual power. He was transformed into this flying creature by Niddrym, my evil half-sister, many, many years ago. I heard this terrible news from Gregor, just before Alexinus arrived.

"I have a feeling there are many more revelations to come; only then can I give full explanation to you, my friends. You will all need to be patient. I will disclose everything I know once I have spoken further with Brother Gregor and Alexinus."

"Can I say something to him, Merlin?" asked Tom, who had just entered the room, but was still unable to take his eyes off the enormous winged creature.

"You can try, but he will not understand, not yet anyway." Merlin spoke to Alexinus in his Latin tongue then stood behind Tom, placing his hands on the boy's shoulders. "Alexinus, this is my great friend and saviour, for without him I would not be here today."

Then Merlin said softly to Tom: "Say hello to Alexinus." Tom pronounced the words clearly. His eyes widened and a huge grin appeared on his face as he heard the bird respond with: "Hello Tom."

Brother Gregor showed much delight in playing host to his visitors. They were all invited to be seated at a large table that took up half the space in the bare room. He smiled at each in turn as he ceremoniously placed ceramic tumblers in front of them. He then left the room and returned with two stone jugs, one of red wine and another of water, and a smaller elaborately painted jug, which he placed in front of Tom.

The wine was light and delectable, and Chrissie saw Tom, too, seemed to be enjoying his drink. She asked him what it was, but he said: "I have no idea, but it tastes great!"

In the meantime, Merlin and Gregor were wrapped in an intense exchange. Now and again, Merlin would translate something for the benefit of the group or join in their conversation, but whenever Alexinus uttered a word, foreign though it was, all eyes would be riveted upon him.

After some time, Gregor began preparing food for his guests. First, he brought in a huge pot of steaming vegetable soup. Taking his seat at the foot of the table, he clasped his wide hands together, closed his eyes and, joined by Merlin and Alexinus, softly gave thanks for their meal. After the prayer, the keeper invited everyone to start eating.. The thick brew was delightful to the taste, and all but Chrissie accepted Gregor's offer of a second helping. After the soup, he reappeared laden with two huge bowls of hot vegetables and an iron platter with roasted meat.

Before helping himself to the food in front of him, Tom asked Merlin if Alexinus was going to eat something. Having had the question relayed to him by Merlin, Alexinus laughed. The wizard continued to translate as he replied: "I, my friend, eat nothing but fish. It is the diet I need to keep trim and light, otherwise I would be unable to fly the great distances I do."

"But doesn't he get fed up with just eating raw fish?" asked Tom.

"Alexinus says his kind eat only when they are hungry", said Merlin. "They do not taste as we do. Fish are simply caught by the teeth and thrown down the gullet. When the gut feels empty after a day or so, they return to the sea and repeat the process."

Everyone wanted to compliment the cook on the meal, especially the meat.

"Would you ask Gregor what the meat was?" said Chrissie. "It was so succulent and tender. It tasted a bit like the venison I had recently, but the flavour wasn't as strong."

"Well, I can tell you what it was," replied Merlin, "because it was standard fare when I came here those many centuries ago. It is dhuka. Looks like a rabbit, but it is twice the size and lacks a tail."

Merlin turned and spoke to Gregor, who smiled and bowed towards Chrissie. "It is the druid way of thanking you for your compliment about his cooking, Christine."

After the main meal, Gregor carried in two huge bowls overflowing with a colourful array of fruit, most of which his visitors had never seen before. Black grape-like berries mingled with yellow tubular fruits, which turned out to be similar to bananas only in their skin texture. They recognised the apples, but even these were much larger in size and of a uniform golden colour. There were vivid blue pear-shaped fruits alongside knobbly, orange coloured specimen, large brown raisins and a huge variety of nuts, which crowned the abundant display.

Once the meal was over, Gregor replenished the water and the wine on the table before Merlin told his companions: "Brother Gregor, Alexinus and I are going into the garden to talk, for we have much to discuss. My friend has asked you to help yourself to the wine and treat his house as if it were your home. I will disclose all tidings to you upon my return." Merlin then followed the keeper out of the house.

Emile poured drinks for everyone. "What kind of flying creature is zis Alexinus, Tom?" he asked.

"From the pictures I've seen of it, I'm sure it's an Ornithocheirus," said Tom. "It says in my book they're supposed to be the biggest Pterosaurs ever."

Chrissie brought the subject around to the wizard. "I thought Merlin appeared very worried when he was listening to that loud voice from above."

"The word 'Merlin' was the only one I recognised, couldn't make head or tail of the rest," said Andrew.

"I was taught Latin at school," said Emile, "and yet I also 'ad difficulty understanding what was said. Some words I recognized, like 'ze evil one' and ozer words zat meant 'forgiven' and 'justice'. Ze voice seemed angry at Merlin for some reason."

"I think it was God speaking," said a wide-eyed Tom.

Chrissie smiled at Tom's simple and direct statement. But it wasn't too far, she thought, from what she and the others were thinking.

"Obviously some omnipotent power presides over this world," suggested Andrew.

"Did I hear Merlin say Gregor was here when he last visited this place?" asked Chrissie. "If so, that would make him over fifteen hundred years old, like Merlin."

"Zat goes for Alexinus also," said Emile.

"Yes, I thought about that too, but I'm sure Merlin will explain everything on his return," said Andrew.

CHAPTER 36

As Merlin and Gregor joined them at the table a little later, Chrissie happened to glance through the window. "Goodness, it's only six thirty and its gone dark already!" she exclaimed.

"There is no twilight in this world. It changes from daylight to darkness of night in just a few minutes." Merlin explained. "And do not be guided by your watch, Christine, for your earthly time bears no relation to time on Arkatra.

"Then how do you measure time here?" she asked.

"Time is measured by the position of the sun as on Earth. For greater accuracy reference is made to a sun dial in the centre of Gregor's garden. There is no need to measure time at night, for that is the time for sleep, but it would be easy enough to study the relative positions of the two moons, if it were necessary."

"Two moons!" exclaimed Tom.

"Yes, you will see them later tonight. One moon is a lot smaller than the other," said Merlin. "A month is measured by the phases of the two moons. There is a very different way of calculating a year too. A large celestial body passes by this planet every fourteen months and this event has always marked the start of a new year. This comet, for I believe that is what it's called on Earth, is very spectacular. Its tail spans the horizon from east to west, and it lights up the night sky in a splendid fashion. I have never seen it, for my visits to Arkatra were of short duration, but Brother Gregor says it is a wonderful but frightening sight to behold."

"How does time 'ere compare wiz time on Earz?" asked Emile.

"For every year in your world, fourteen months will have passed in Arkatra," explained Merlin

"So if we were here for thirty years, thirty five years would have gone by on Earth?" said Andrew.

"What we'd like to know," said Andrew, changing the subject, "is why Gregor and Alexinus haven't aged? It seems they've been around for about as long as you have."

"There is quite a different reason for their ageless condition, but I will come to that later, for now I think it is time to explain everything. It is such an unbelievable story even I, the believer of the unbelievable, found it difficult to accept what has been revealed to me this evening."

Merlin, who had seated himself at the head of the table, shifted his penetrating gaze from one member of the group to another, as if wondering where to start. "I will begin by relating something of my past that is unknown to you.

"Before I was born, my father, who was also named Myrddin, was heralded as the greatest wizard of his time. Myrddin is the ancient Celtic word for Merlin. It was my mother who latinised my name when she left home to live with her brother, Cedrin, in the village of Weerby.

My father was held in great esteem by all, for his magic and his healing powers had helped to raise many from their death-bed. He was drawn to the secrets of the forest. He spent much time there searching for certain plants with special healing properties. These he would grind and mix to make his healing potions. My mother said about a year after I was born, my father started acting strangely. She couldn't understand the change in him for he had always been of a bright and cheerful nature; but over time he became withdrawn and sullen. Once she visited him unexpectedly in the room where he prepared his potions, and saw him chewing on one of the root plants. That's when she started to suspect this might the reason for his behaviour. My mother and father had words and then my father struck my mother before running off into the forest.

"Nobody saw him for some time. Then one day, mother said, he appeared at our door thin and dishevelled. He demanded my mother hand me over to him, as I was needed for the ultimate sacrifice in order to appease the Gods that had been tormenting him. My mother refused him entry to the house. There was a desperate struggle before he ran back to the forest screaming revenge. My mother was scared of what he might do next, so she left our home and travelled down south to the district of Heranium where she knew her older brother lived. It was here, in my uncle Cedrin's house, where I was nurtured and educated.

"One evening, I overheard my uncle say to my mother my father had another child. They said he had fathered the child by casting a spell over a woman in the village, but I could not hear more for then the door was closed.

"It was many years later, after Arthur had become King of all Britain and I had been appointed as his special advisor, that a woman called Niddrym came to be at his court. King Arthur had met her while out hunting and had taken an instant liking to the woman. I did not know at the time she was my half-sister. She was a very attractive woman and King Arthur fell in love with her. However, for some strange reason, I did not like or trust her.

"Some weeks later my uncle came to visit and he recognised the name Niddrym as that of the girl-child born to my father. He used his influence to find out more about her. A few days later he called again to say the woman Niddrym was certainly my half-sister. He said her name was the ancient Celtic word for Merlin spelt backwards. Soon I was to realise she had entered our lives in order to destroy me."

Merlin sighed and looked down at his hands, deeply troubled. "Andrew and Emile, you both know the rest, for I spoke of it at the APD convention. For the benefit of Christine and Tom I think I must speak of it again." He then explained how he had finally convinced his king that Niddrym was a sorceress of evil repute, and if he married her she would eventually destroy all he held dear. He spoke of her banishment from King Arthur's court, and of her fierce hatred of him for betraying her.

"I have explained to you how Niddrym used her powers to possess the image of my love, Salina," continued the wizard. "I had thought this transmutation process had occurred during her last visit to the cave, but it appears I was mistaken."

Merlin remained silent for some moments. It was as if he himself could not, or would not believe what was now becoming obvious. "It seems she may have transformed herself into the image of Salina long before the event in the cave. In my exuberance of love for the woman I thought was Salina, I did not think it strange at the time that she should suddenly take a greater interest in my psychic powers or my druid beliefs. At her insistence, I told her about the staff I always kept with me and of the great magical powers I had been endowed with through its use.

"I should have been curious about her constant requests for information on such things as the druid's Inner Circle. On one occasion I remember making mention of this planet, and, like a love-smitten fool, I told her about the Humming Oak and its purpose. I remember once taking her to see the tree, as she kept asking to see it." Merlin shook his head slightly, as if in disbelief at his own stupidity.

"What happened to the real Salina?" Chrissie enquired, softly.

"Niddrym would have killed her after the transmutation had taken place,"

The group waited as the wizard sat quietly for a few moments.

"As a druid it was sacrilege to reveal anything about the Inner Circle of the Ancient Order, or the New World, to a living soul. I broke the fundamental law, for I spoke of it to the one I thought was my betrothed. I realise now, with much sadness and anger, it was not my loved one who shared my secret knowledge, but Niddrym." Merlin sat studying the empty tumbler in front of him, his mind filled with memories of his beloved Salina.

"I sink we should all take another sample of Gregor's delicious wine, is zat not so Merlin?" said Emile, trying to lighten the situation.

Merlin smiled, then turned and spoke to the druid keeper. Brother Gregor beamed at the compliment Merlin had translated to him, and made a comment directed at the Frenchman.

"Brother Gregor says he feels honoured a Frenchman should value his wine so highly," translated Merlin, "for he remembers the old days when brother druids would arrive from Gaul with the most delectable of wines."

"Ah, zo Brother Gregor is a wine connoisseur?" said Emile, with a wide grin.

"He also said he would be happy for you to pour more wine, Emile."

After the wine was poured Merlin continued: "Once Niddrym had accomplished her evil ambition and placed me under her curse, she must have cast her insidious influence over some unfortunate peasants and ordered them to seal off the cave with mortar and stone. With my precious staff now in her possession, she went to the Humming Oak and was transported to Arkatra. That's how Brother Gregor first encountered her, for he was still the keeper of the retreat."

He sighed. "It is because of her the Gods are angry."

"You see I had told her everything about Arkatra, including the village retreat, so when she met Brother Gregor, she was able to supply false details without arousing suspicion. She lied to him, saying she was from another druid sect and had permission to visit the New World. He had no reason to doubt her story for although no woman had ever set foot on this planet before, they were regarded as equals in druid society. Her demeanour allayed any suspicions Gregor might have had, and he allowed her to stay at the retreat.

"She took her leave after a few days and Brother Gregor did not see her again for some weeks. The next time she came she brought with her a group of people she said were from her druid sect. On this occasion there were three other druids staying at the village retreat. They confronted Niddrym, for they doubted she was genuine. In the end, all any of them could remember was waking up from a deep sleep to find Niddrym and her group had disappeared.

"Brother Gregor said he had no knowledge of where she might have gone. But weeks later he caught sight of her leading a few people across the grazing plains towards a migration trail that led westward to the Draigoor Mountains."

"But wouldn't that have been dangerous, because of the dinosaurs I mean?" queried Chrissie.

"You must remember this evil woman now had possession of the Sacred Staff. It would have given her great powers, and she would have been quite able to protect herself and her followers from the largest of predators."

The wizard sipped from his tumbler before continuing: "Some time after my disappearance, King Arthur called on the services of a druid named Alexinus, for the king needed some explanation as to why I should have deserted him in such a way.

"Alexinus had once visited the castle to see me, for we had studied together at the Monastery of the Ancient Order and had taken a great liking to each other. You may remember me saying I had been invited to visit the New World on two occasions; well, it was Alexinus who accompanied me on my last visit and over the years that followed we remained great friends."

Merlin looked across at the window. "Alexinus," he said in Latin. "I am telling them about our visit to the New World when we were both druid priests at the monastery." All eyes turned to the large head of the bird protruding into the room.

"Ah yes, I remember it well, though countless years have passed," said Alexinus.

Merlin turned back to the group. "I had introduced Alexinus to the king and to his newly betrothed, the Lady Guinevere. She came from a notable family that had settled near York many generations ago. Her fair skin and striking beauty was a vision to behold, but it was her intelligence and kind nature that had enraptured the king and his people."

"The king and his future queen were impressed by the manner and the wisdom of their guest, so they asked Alexinus to find out what had happened to me. King Arthur had also been concerned over reports he'd had about the disappearance of people from nearby towns and villages; most were artisans - masons, carpenters and hewers of wood."

"Weeks later, Alexinus returned to the castle to report back to the king. This is when he became aware of a change in character of the beautiful Guinevere

"Alexinus suspected that, during his absence, Niddrym may have transformed herself into Guinevere, but he remained uncertain. For the deception to be carried out successfully, she would have had to end Guinevere's life, just as she had done with Salina. She was now in possession of my staff and this would have given her even greater powers to commit her evil deeds.

"The new Guinevere was in fear of Alexinus, for not only was he renowned for his great wisdom and prophesies, but she also knew of his psychic skills and his ability to read minds; therefore she made every excuse to avoid him during his regular visits to the king's court."

Gregor interrupted and spoke to Merlin in the ancient language before leaving the cottage.

"My friend has gone to prepare places for you all to sleep. I have explained to him that Tom should sleep in a room with you, Christine. Is that to your liking?"

"Yes, that's fine by me," she replied.

"Would you wish to sleep now, Tom, for you must be tired?" Merlin asked.

"No, I don't feel tired, honestly," said Tom, who was eager to stay and listen to all the exciting things he was hearing.

"He probably won't sleep while this is going on, so maybe it is better if he waits for me," said Chrissie.

"If that's what you wish, then I will continue," said the wizard.

"As I have just explained, Guinevere feared Alexinus, and during his visits she would take leave from the court whenever possible. On the rare occasions she was in his company, she would avoid all eye contact with him.

"However, he had no definite proof of what was amiss, so he could not warn the king of his suspicions. Then, one summer's day, not long after the summer solstice celebrations, Alexinus also disappeared from the king's court, never to return. I will tell you more about this later."

"What about all these people who had gone missing? Was she also behind that?" enquired Chrissie.

"Yes, of course. From what Brother Gregor has told me she must have been searching for an ideal location to build her dream castle during her early visits to Arkatra, although he wasn't aware of it at the time. It seems she had gathered a hundred or more workmen from Earth, bringing a few of them up on each visit, sometimes under the cover of darkness while Gregor was sleeping. Under her powerful influence they were working like slaves until the castle was completed."

"But how long had this been going on, building the castle, I mean?" she asked.

"Her periodic visits to this world probably spanned a period of about five years. It is probable she also acquired, through her sorcery, the services of Gorbarin, the Welsh castle builder, for he also mysteriously disappeared during his last visit to the king's court. The man was renowned throughout the land for the design and construction of many castles, including Camelot."

"But what of the king… King Arthur?" enquired Tom.

"It is believed her final journey to the New World, to Arkatra, was in the company of King Arthur and three of his knights."

"But the king would not have gone willingly, surely?" said Chrissie.

"No, of course not. In those days druids still regularly visited the retreat and they told Brother Gregor about King

Arthur's disappearance, for it was such a momentous happening. It would seem Niddrym, in the guise of Guinevere, had accompanied Arthur and three of his knights on one of his hunting trips. They never returned. It was thought by many they must have met with a terrible accident, and there was great mourning in the land. Instead, we think my half-sister must have transported King Arthur and his three resident knights to this world. King Arthur must have been under the woman's evil power, for he would never have deserted his people."

He was silent for a while, lost in memories of his friend, the king. "But I must tell you more about the druids and their association with Arkatra," he resumed.

"Long, long ago there was a very wise man roaming the Earth. His name was said to be Drerwyd. Loosely translated from the Celtic tongue, it means 'one who has great knowledge of trees'. He was from a nomadic Celtic tribe, who were mainly wood craftsmen and plant gatherers.

"Drerwyd was of a gentle nature and he revered all of the Earth's natural bounty. He was also endowed with great courage and would often confront the chiefs of the many warring tribes in an attempt to get them to live in harmony with each other. It is said that one day he aroused the anger of the chief of one tribe and they knocked him to the ground and tied him to a tree. It was the sport of those days to do this to their captured enemies. The tribe would mark out a line fifty paces or so from the tied captive, then, starting with the chief, they would take turns casting a spear at the human target.

"As the chief was about to throw his spear at Drerwyd, another man is said to have appeared seemingly out of nowhere. The man was dressed in a pure white robe and his white hair reached down to his waist. The chief threw the spear at the visitor, for the man was now standing in front of Drerwyd. The spear hit the man, but then dropped harmlessly to the ground. It is said the thongs holding Drerwyd to the tree then just fell away, and the tribe watched in awe as the man in white took Drerwyd by the hand and disappeared with him into the forest. On order from the chief, two of the tribesmen followed them. It is said the two men saw Drerwyd and the man with the beard being 'swallowed up' by an oak tree of massive proportions. The two tribesmen cautiously approached the tree, and placing their ears to the enormous trunk, they heard a strange humming sound. In the tribe's ancient Celtic tongue, the great oak would become known as the Humming Oak.

"It is believed Drerwyd was taken up to the New World on that day. Some time later, he returned to Earth, to the tribe he had escaped from. This time the chief listened to what the seer had to say and he soon became a devout follower of Drerwyd's philosophy. Over time, the tribe became known as the tribe of Drerwyd.

"It is said, a little while later, he took some of the tribe to the New World to help build the village. Once the work was finished, the chief, with Drerwyd's approval, appointed his eldest son as the first keeper of the village. Since then, there has always been a keeper there. The rest of the tribe then returned to Earth and they became known as the Druids. That is how the druid way of life was born. Druid priests kept visiting Arkatra, of course. They would bring tools and materials, and give of their labour to help the keeper maintain and improve the village.

"But you were also wondering why Brother Gregor is still alive, for as you know, he was keeper of this retreat when I was first visited Arkatra."

"Yes, it did cross our minds," Andrew replied.

"Well, let me explain." said Merlin. "Being keeper of the village remained an honourable position and only the most deserving of druids would have the opportunity to serve their fellow druids in this way. The keeper could request to be relieved of his duties at any time, to be succeeded by another. Sometimes keepers served for twenty years or so, sometimes much longer. Former keepers would be allowed to live out their days in a cottage close to the monastery back on Earth.

"Not so Brother Gregor. Because he was in charge of the retreat at the time of Niddrym's arrival, anger from the Gods has been directed at him also. It was his responsibility, in their eyes, to prevent the woman from coming here and desecrating the Creator's realm. So he was ordered to remain as keeper for as long as it takes to be rid of her.

"But... but how can that happen, what stops him from ageing?" asked Chrissie.

"It is the water from an artesian spring. It is known to all druids as 'Vita Sacrum'. It is the 'Sacred Spring of Eternal Life'.

The spring lies somewhere within the grounds of this retreat, but its location is known only to the keeper. There is one other we know of which contains this extraordinary element in its water and it is located somewhere in the foothills of the Draigoor mountains, and only the keeper would know of its whereabouts. The water from these two springs must draw from the same deep underground reservoir and drinking from it each day appears to arrest the normal onset of aging."

"So I gather Niddrym has found the other well?" suggested Andrew.

"Yes, it is what Brother Gregor thinks. He believes she would have got that information from him through her sorcery during her second visit."

"I wonder if Brother Gregor would reveal it's whereabouts to me if I was extra nice to him?" said Chrissie, offering Merlin a cheeky smile.

"I do not think he would appreciate your comment, Christine," said the wizard with a serious tone, but Chrissie couldn't help but notice the smile hovering around his lips.

"You talk about 'the Gods' as if there is more than one presiding over this world," quizzed Andrew.

"We believe there are many worlds in the universe that support life; worlds that need Gods to preside over them. The ancient druids believed only one God reigned over a single world, but that all Gods are subordinate to the one true Almighty God, Creator of the Universe."

"But if this God is so powerful, why has it not destroyed this woman?" queried Chrissie.

"Ahh that is the question I put to Brother Gregor this evening. He told me he also received a message from the heavens, not long after Alexinus and his party's fateful journey. More of that later. The Gods told Brother Gregor of their displeasure over the evil one's arrival in their world and that she could not be destroyed until the sacred staff had been taken from her. It was feared the woman, should she die, might use its enormous powers in the spirit world. It was foretold that one day I would return to repossess the staff and destroy the evil one, and until that day, Gregor must remain as keeper of the village."

There was silence among the group, as they absorbed what they had just heard. Emile, who had been listening intently, poured out more wine. "I ave a strong feeling you ave somezing more serious to say to us," he said at last.

Merlin looked long and hard at the big Frenchman. He had given little thought to Emile's own powerful psychic abilities, but now realised his friend had become attuned to his own innermost thoughts.

"You are right Emile, there are indeed more serious issues on my mind. First of all, I need to reveal to you all, the message you heard from the heavens today."

His translation of the portentous words were followed by a stony silence.

Emile was the first to speak. "It is obvious zis God expects us to 'elp you find zis evil woman, and I for one will be ready to assist, my friend, but somezing in my zoughts tells me you are of a different mind."

Merlin nodded. "Tomorrow I intend to escort all of you back to the Humming Oak and back to your world. My work is here. I have to make amends to the Gods by destroying Niddrym once and for all. There is much danger in what I am about to do and I cannot allow you, my friends, to become part of it."

"But if what you have told us is correct, Tom is the only one who can break the hold Niddrym has on your staff, so obviously you intend to take him along?" Chrissie cut in.

"Yes, if he is agreeable, for he is the key," explained the wizard. "Also the Gods have vowed to protect him.

"Since waking from that cursed sleep, I have been taxing my brain to make sense of those final words Niddrym uttered before I sunk into oblivion. It was Alexinus who has, just this evening, made the meaning of those final words clear to me. It is this: Once she looks upon the orphan child who released me from my bonds, she will have to relinquish the staff. To her, the chance of such an event occurring would have been too remote to take seriously."

"But how would Alexinus have known about the spell? I thought you were alone in the cave with Salina or... or Niddrym?" said Chrissie.

"That is correct, Christine. Alexinus knew nothing of my fate until he confronted Niddrym many months later. It was to be his misfortune." Merlin looked over at his friend, who was still looking in through the window opening.

"I told you about the suspicion Alexinus had of King Arthur's betrothed. One day she asked the king to give her leave from his court to visit her sick father. Alexinus secretly followed Guinevere as she rode to a nearby village, whence she emerged accompanied by a small group of trade's people. He followed her as she made her way into the forest. To his consternation, he soon realised she was leading the group to the Humming Oak.

"To his knowledge, none but the druids of the Ancient Order knew of the tree's existence. Now Alexinus was convinced this woman was not the real Guinevere. He waited until they had all merged into the Humming Oak before returning to the monastery to seek an audience with the Grand Priest."

"But why didn't Alexinus report back to the king and tell him what he had seen, before going to the Grand Priest?" Chrissie wanted to know.

"The first responsibility for Alexinus would have been to report such a grave transgression to his druid master, for only he could decide what should be done. He was then given leave to call on the king. Arthur, however, was absent from court and was not expected back for some days. Alexinus wrote a personal note and gave it to a senior courtier, advising him of the gravity of the message. However, he believes the message never reached the king, probably because the courtier would have been too frightened to relay such scurrilous news about the future queen.

"Alexinus was given permission, by the Grand Priest, to return to Arkatra, with six of the most skilled druid priests from the Inner Circle. Their duty was to track this woman down, destroy her, and then accompany all those who had been taken to the New World back to Earth and rid their minds of all knowledge of the Humming Oak and of Arkatra.

"Days later, they set off. At the druid village, Gregor gave them directions to the Draigoor hills and told them where, within those hills, they would find the false Guinevere.

"Although Gregor had warned them about the dinosaurs, they were not deterred from their quest, for the seven priests had incredible powers of their own. They were prepared to face whatever dangers there might be, but were pitifully unaware of the terrible power my half-sister possessed.

"Towards the evening of their second day of travel, they were set upon by a creature of mammoth proportions. Alexinus and two of the group managed to escape, but the other four priests were killed in a single nightmarish attack.

"The three carried on with their journey, constantly in fear of their lives. Towards the end of the third day, after climbing for some hours in the foot hills of the Draigoor Mountains, they caught sight of a band of horse riders galloping towards them. Alexinus said their appearance was alarming for they were dressed completely in black. The only colour he remembered seeing was the red dragon crest emblazoned on their chests and the red eyes of their black steeds. Alexinus recognised the crest as that worn by King Arthur's knights, but he had little time to dwell on the matter, for the horsemen were charging towards them with their swords raised. The three priests rushed madly down a hillside to escape the black riders, when suddenly they espied the castle some distance away. On approaching the castle walls, they were surrounded by a group of armed men. When Alexinus looked back, he saw no sign of the black knights. It was as if they had disappeared into thin air.

"They were then taken to the castle grounds by their captors to await the arrival of the woman they had been sent to destroy. Before too long, a beautiful woman appeared on a balcony above them, holding my staff. She ordered the guards to leave and then gazed in silence upon the three druid priests. Suddenly she pointed to Alexinus and shrieked with laughter; she had recognised him.

"Niddrym ordered the other two druids to stand apart. Then, Alexinus had to watch as the unfortunate priests were transformed into two small prehistoric reptiles, which scurried away into a crack in the wall, accompanied by her manic laughter.

"She prolonged Alexinus's ordeal for she wanted to boast about how she had overpowered the Merlin, the greatest wizard in the land. She told him how she had entombed me in a cave. Alexinus then bravely spoke out. He prophesied one day Merlin would return to reclaim the Sacred Staff and would then destroy her.

"His courageous words goaded Niddrym into revealing the key to the spell she believed would never be broken – she would have to cast her eyes on the orphan child that had freed Merlin for him to repossess the staff. 'But that, my dear Alexinus, will never happen,' she shrieked.

"At that moment a huge creature flew overhead. Niddrym pointed the staff at the gigantic bird, stopping it in mid-flight. She then turned the staff towards Alexinus and with a few potent words consigned his physical being into that of the bird.

"Alexinus remembers suddenly seeing two enormous wings stretched out on either side of him, as he merged into this strange body gliding through the air..."

Merlin gazed in compassion at the bird outside the window. "That is Alexinus's tale. He has lived the life of this flying creature ever since."

The group sat in stunned silence as they tried to absorb the wizard's extraordinary story.

"But how is it that Alexinus has been able to live as long as he has?" Andrew asked at last.

"In one way, Alexinus was fortunate," said Merlin. "You see, Niddrym had not transformed his mind, just his body. Perhaps, in her euphoria, she simply forgot to complete the spell. Whatever the reason, my good friend found he could still think and reason as Alexinus, the highly intelligent druid he was, and still is. He immediately flew back to the druid retreat and met with Gregor. After his initial astonishment, Gregor invited him to make the retreat his home.

"Not long after that, Gregor received the message from the heavens I spoke of earlier, which confirmed Alexinus's strong belief that one day I would return to seek the Sacred Staff and destroy the one who had taken it from me. Gregor, now bound to dwell as keeper in Arkatra until this should come to pass this, invited his friend to join him in drinking daily from the Sacred Spring, so however long it took for me to return, they would both be there, ready to assist me."

Merlin then turned to Tom who had been quietly listening to what the wizard had been saying. "Tom, have you fully understood what has been said this evening?"

"Most of it, I think, but when will we see the dinosaurs?"

"Ahh yes, the dinosaurs!" exclaimed Merlin with a smile. "Tomorrow morning Brother Gregor will escort us up on to the plateau. From there, you will have a panoramic view of some of the creatures you have shown me in your book. What do you say to that?"

"That'll be great! But why haven't we seen any yet?"

"That question will also be answered when we reach the plateau tomorrow."

"Merlin, can I say something?" Andrew asked quietly. "It's a thought that has nagged me since your remark about these dinosaurs of yours."

"Of course, please say what is on your mind."

"Well, if, as you say, they closely resemble the ones in Tom's book, could it be that this new world you call Arkatra might not be what you think it is?"

"I'm not sure I understand you."

"I was wondering if, instead of standing on some planet out in the cosmos, we might actually be standing on planet Earth as it was seventy million years or so. In other words, the Humming Tree has literally taken us back in time."

The group, including Merlin, sat quietly, digesting Andrew's words.

"But what about the two moons? We've only got one on Earth," said Tom.

"Yes, I've thought about that also, Tom. Did you know that our moon on Earth is moving away from our planet by three centimetres or more each year? So the smaller moon we see could well have disappeared over a vast space of time."

They all sat still reflecting on Andrew's compelling idea.

More questions were thrown at the wizard, and as many answers returned until Gregor appeared again.

"Brother Gregor has told me your sleeping arrangements have been made ready and he would like to show you to your beds. He says tomorrow will be a tiring day, for the climb to the plateau requires much effort. He thinks it would be advisable for all of you to retire early."

With consent all round, the keeper escorted them to their respective cottages. Torches in clay bowls lit the entrance to each cottage, which had one bedroom containing two single beds, a wooden water pump over a large ceramic wash bowl on a wooden plinth, and a solitary wooden chair.

Chrissie and Tom were shown to the cottage immediately behind Gregor's own, while Emile and Andrew were settled into a dwelling a little further away. Merlin was to sleep in the spare bed prepared for him in Gregor's cottage.

The visitors were woken at the first light of dawn by a crowing cock and reassembled in Gregor's cottage for a delicious breakfast of thick porridge coated with honey, and boiled eggs on leavened bread.

Everyone apart from Chrissie, who had woken early with thoughts racing through her mind, had slept like babies on the paillasses, which, Merlin told them, were covered with sheep's skin.

"The softness comes from having the sheep's wool on the topside. The blankets are of woven sheep's wool. It is similar to the bedding we would have used in my world," explained Merlin.

"But if Gregor has been the only one living here, apart from Alexinus, where would he have got the extra bedding from at such short notice?" wondered Andrew.

"He had been informed we were coming," said Merlin.

"But he could have known that only yesterday when you left us at the Humming Oak," Andrew persisted.

"Not quite, Andrew. Alexinus warned Brother Gregor of our coming some days ago. He is highly skilled in all psychic disciplines, including extra-sensory perception."

"Do you mean he actually sensed we were coming?"

"Alexinus sensed my awakening many weeks ago, when I was making mental contact with you. His spiritual efforts to reach me always met with failure. I do recall seeing vague images of a large flying creature, but I disregarded them. However, he had clear visions of me lying in the cave and also of me walking from it with a boy. To answer your question, Andrew, yes, he had a strong premonition I would visit, and that I would be with company. It gave Gregor time to prepare."

"He must have worked so hard," said Chrissie with admiration.

"Brother Gregor has only one way to work, and that is fast and furious" said the wizard with a smile.

"I noticed a wooden cubicle in the back garden. There was a metal contraption that looked like a shower head, and what appeared to be a water tank above. It wouldn't be a shower, would it?" said Chrissie, hopefully.

"It is as you say, Christine, a shower, but not quite the same as you would be used to," said Merlin.

"I don't care. When can I use it?"

"I will ask Gregor if he can arrange it for you when we arrive back later today."

"Thank you! That would be lovely," said Chrissie, smiling at the wizard.

CHAPTER 37

After breakfast, the group prepared for the climb to the plateau. They gathered at Gregor's cottage. Alexinus was already there, his head resting on the window sill as he talked with his fellow druids.

Merlin addressed his friends: "Alexinus cannot fly to the plateau at this time, for it is too early. He says the sun has to warm up the ground, so the rising warm air can help him become airborne."

"When will he be able to fly?" asked Tom.

"He says he will make his attempt in about two to three hours."

"How long do you sink it will take us to climb to ze plateau?" asked Emile, who feared he might not be fit enough for the climb.

"About the same time, I should think," said Merlin.

All except Tom had been deeply sceptical about the prospect of seeing dinosaurs. After all, they reasoned, how could pre-historic creatures that have been extinct for millions years on Earth now be living on this planet? But ever since they met Alexinus, there had been an undercurrent of excitement, a feeling that maybe it was a possibility after all.

Gregor led the group towards the rear of the cottages, then out through a gate into open ground covered in coarse grass, rag-tail fern and ground-hugging flowering shrubs. A large herd of goats, similar to those on Earth, were busily grazing everywhere. Now and then a goat would look up and gaze at the human procession passing by. Soon the terrain began to rise and it became difficult for the visitors to keep up with Gregor's forthright pace. Massive conifer trees and other giants of unknown origin appeared a little distance ahead, obstructing the view of the plateau.

At the edge of the forest, Gregor paused and spoke to Merlin. The wizard turned to his companions and asked them to stay in single file while in the forest. Gregor then moved on at a slower, more cautious pace, while Merlin brought up the rear. Once inside the forest they were enthralled by the variety of creatures surrounding them. They would look upward every so often at the activity in the canopy high above. There were apes and monkeys everywhere, screaming, whistling and whooping as they moved effortlessly through the leafy highways of their lofty domain. They could see countless birds darting between the branches, adding their calls to the great cacophony of sound that enveloped the walkers.

The forest floor continued its upward gradient and eventually the trees began to thin out until only stumpy trees and tangled foliage surrounded them. These gradually gave way to sporadic tussock grass amid rocky terrain, which became yet steeper as it rose towards the plateau. All except Merlin and Tom struggled to keep up with the squat figure of Gregor, who was oblivious to the discomfort of those behind him.

Emile had been lagging behind for some time and Merlin, still at the back, finally called out to his brother druid, suggesting they rest awhile. Gregor waited for everyone to catch up and then produced a goat skin bag of fresh water for everyone to drink their fill.

The climb took longer than expected, and they were forced to rest once more before the final push to the plateau. Once on top, they followed Gregor through sand-coloured tussocks of grass, broken by dark green clumps of spiky fern. Suddenly they heard Gregor call out and wave. Looking ahead, they caught sight of the huge bird waiting for their arrival.

Tom eagerly ran on ahead, for he could see the edge of the plateau behind Alexinus. Within ten paces from the edge, Tom stopped, gazing open-mouthed at the spectacular scene below. He was hardly aware of the rest of the group as they approached to stand quietly beside him.

"Are these your dinosaurs, Tom?" asked Merlin.

"Yes sir. Look!" Tom pointed to a group of huge creatures feeding from the top-most branches of a grove of cycad trees. "They look like iguanodons. See, they have that beak for biting off hard stuff. But it's hard to tell properly 'cos they're too far away. Look! Those smaller ones grazing this side of them, the ones with the dark green body and black stripes down the side, I think they are Camptosaurus."

"What are those massive creatures around those water holes?" asked Andrew, acknowledging Tom's expertise.

Tom looked to where Andrew was pointing. "They look like Apatosaurus. They used to be known as Brontosaurus, you know the same as in 'The Flintstones'. They are supposed to have died out at the end of the Jurassic period. The trouble is, a lot of the giant sauropods look the same."

Merlin translated some of Tom's information to the two druids. Alexinus, the Pterosaur, looked down at Merlin. "These are just the first of many," he said, nodding with his long beak at the grazing animals, "for this is the time of year when the great migrations start. Soon these southern plains that stretch for hundreds of miles will be a moving mass of all sorts of creatures."

The rest of the group couldn't take their eyes off the vista of unbelievable grandeur before them. A vast plain stretched into the distance, a blue-grey mist concealing its furthest extent. Above the mist, green and purple rolling hills could be seen rising into the orange-tinted horizon. Merlin pointed left towards a distant range of snow-capped mountains.

"We call those the Southern Alps, and beyond them lies the Great Southern ocean, where Alexinus spends much of his time hunting fish."

From the foothills of the mountain range nearer to them, thick forest had crept like a dark carpet over much of the countryside. It petered out in a breathtaking spectacle as a fast flowing river emerged from a cleft in the forest, then disappeared as it plunged into what appeared to be a huge tree-rimmed ravine. The plummeting water created in its wake a curtain of mist that floated high into the air. From where they stood, the vapor appeared like a huge umbrella spanning a great expanse of ground around the ravine. This constant dampness had created a micro-climate where massive tree ferns, flowering cycads and thick groves of swamp cypresses grew in profusion amidst lush vegetation. Here also, gigantic boulders, ten metres high or more, could be seen around the primordial fissure, as if thrown there by the hands of giants.

"There must be a huge waterfall for us to hear the sound from up here," said Andrew, listening to the constant rumble.

"There is," said Merlin. "The river falls away into the ravine, and then into a subterranean river."

The group's attention shifted to the right, where a herd of khaki-coloured animals with large horns were grazing alongside two-legged striped creatures with short forearms.

"What are those striped ones called, Tom?" Chrissie asked.

"I'm not sure, they look something like Maiasaura, by the shape of their bodies and their faces, but the pictures in my book don't show them having stripes."

"And what about those feeding near them?"

"They look like Centrosaurus going by the large horn and bony frill at the back of their heads. And see, their mouths are shaped like beaks. They reckon sometimes different species support each other if they get attacked, that's why they graze close together," explained Tom.

"How do you mean?" asked Andrew, who had been listening to what the boy had been saying.

"Well, some species of plant-eaters have been found close together, and palaeontologists think it might be because they had ways of protecting each other. Like, maybe, one species was good at giving early warning signs that a predator was coming, and another, more heavily armed kind would then protect the herd by circling it, or something like that."

Chrissie looked intently at the boy standing next to her. "Tom, how is it you know so much about these creatures?"

"It was my dad, really," Tom replied, his attention still fixed on the creatures in the distance. "He bought me a book on dinosaurs for my birthday and he told me all about them, about how they had been on Earth for millions of years and then how they suddenly died out."

"So the book you had up in Scotland was the one your dad had given you?"

"No, that was the one my aunt Kate gave me. My dad's book is in my room at the farm. But I have read a lot more books about them. My stepmother has a library card. I used to take it out of her handbag and get books from the library."

"You must be so thrilled to actually seeing these creatures?"

"Yes I am." Tom turned to look at Chrissie and grinned: "I think I am the luckiest boy in the world."

She spontaneously took Tom's hand in hers, and felt the boy tighten his grip on her fingers.

Suddenly Gregor took everyone's attention. He was pointing to the grove of swamp cypresses close to the ravine.

237

"Over there! Do you see it, Brother?" The keeper turned and looked up at Alexinus.

Alexinus, whose eyes were able to detect ground movement from high up in the Arkatra skies, peered in the direction Gregor was pointing.

"Yes, it is definitely what you think it is," he said at length.

Merlin called across to Tom. "Gregor has seen the terrible hunter. Tom, can you see it?"

The boy scanned the area where Gregor was pointing. Then, out of the mist he saw a huge dark shape moving into the open. It turned its massive head towards the grazing herds then, just as quickly disappeared again into the trees. It was quite a distance away, but it was unmistakable.

"A Tyrannosaur! A Tyrannosaurus Rex!" exclaimed Tom. "Did you see it Chrissie, did you see it?"

Chrissie shook her head. "Where?"

"You must watch. It will appear now and then to see if any of the plant eaters get close, 'cos it doesn't like to run too far before it attacks," explained a wide-eyed Tom.

They all watched and waited for the creature to reappear.

After a few minutes, Merlin said: "Tom, you wondered why you have not seen any dinosaurs in the area around the cottages."

He pointed to what appeared to be a long, wide ribbon crossing the terrain far below. "That is a river, my friends. It completely surrounds us, like a moat around a castle. It is what you would call a canal, I suppose."

"Do you mean it completely separates the area like… like an island," said Tom, astounded by what the wizard was saying.

"That is exactly it. We are on an island separated from the main land. It is what prevents these creatures from reaching us."

"But how do you get on to the land where those dinosaurs are?" Tom asked.

"There is a footbridge the druids have used since ancient times. It is maintained regularly by the keeper."

"But surely some of the smaller dinosaurs could cross?" reasoned Tom.

"Gregor follows an ancient procedure for entering or leaving the bridge. It makes it almost impossible for any creature to cross, apart from the smaller reptiles."

"Couldn't some of them swim across?" queried Andrew.

"The water is too fast flowing. The druids believe the waters from the ravine flow into the channel through subterranean caves and are carried away through a lower watercourse. This causes much turbulence and discourages animals from approaching it. These waters eventually re-emerge in another big river lying to the east," explained the wizard pointing in the opposite direction. "Alexinus says the river eventually veers to the south, continuing through the mountains before spilling out into the Great Southern Ocean."

As the group were once again scanning the grove of swamp cypresses, hoping to catch a glimpse of the mighty tyrannosaur, Gregor turned to Merlin. "While your friends are preoccupied with those creatures, Brother Merlin, we would like to know what plans you have to overcome the sorceress."

"I have given much thought to what the Gods have said and what I must do to bring about the destruction of this evil woman," Merlin replied. "I plan to take the boy with me, if he is agreeable, for no matter how much I regret having to involve him, it seems only he can break her hold on the staff."

"He will have the protection from the Gods, but what about the rest of your party?" asked Gregor.

"I intend to escort them back to the Humming Oak tomorrow and return with them to Earth."

"But the Gods said you might need their aid," said Gregor.

"I cannot put them at risk, Gregor. Andrew and Emile have been so kind to me. I regard them both as dear friends, and I cannot expose them to the dangers I know I will soon have to face."

"What about the woman?" asked Alexinus, who had been quietly listening.

"She helped us find the Humming Oak and was invited to accompany us for the boy's benefit."

"Is that the only reason, my friend?"

"What other reason should there be, Alexinus?"

"It is just the way she looks and speaks to you."

"Her ways are of no interest to me, but I know she has a great fondness for Tom, and he for her."

"But what if they wish to accompany you, despite the dangers?" probed Gregor.

"I will make it clear to them they will impede my progress. You both may have forgotten, but I still possess the ability to travel through the air. I will have the boy with me and we shall reach the castle in hours instead of days."

"I do not think it would be wise to travel that way, Merlin, my friend," said Alexinus. "You would be at great risk of being attacked by Perodors."

"The name would imply they are merely troublesome, if the word derives from perodiosus," countered the wizard.

"They are more than that, my friend, they are extremely dangerous. It is why there are few other flying creatures in this area. Even the large carrion eaters have to be watchful of them. In your situation they could be deadly. I have had some close encounters with them, so please, my good friend, take heed of what I say."

"But if you can escape them, why would I not be able to do the same?"

"There are a number of reasons," said Alexinus. "Firstly, Niddrym may have put a spell upon these creatures, for they seem to attack anything that approaches the castle. I have flown over her domain a number of times. Each time I get close, those flying savages attack in numbers. The first time it happened, they almost brought me down. It was only intelligent thinking and good up-draughts that saved me, for I soared as high as these wings would allow, and was surprised at the extreme lift I achieved. The Perodors began to drop away, for you see, they are not equipped to fly to great heights. I was badly damaged by them, and the wounds took many weeks to heal."

"That is grave news indeed, Alexinus, but I would need to hear other reasons before I can be convinced of the danger."

"As you wish my friend. Most importantly, you will be encumbered by the boy, which makes you vulnerable to Perodor attacks, for they approach at great speed from below. Remember also, your aim is to gain access to the castle or its domain, which means you will be compelled to fly into areas of danger, whereas whenever I was threatened, I would merely fly away. Also, the

Perodors patrol a very wide area. I once came under attack flying over the Samean caves, and they are a considerable distance from Niddrym's domain. They have poor air to ground vision, but they have excellent flying vision, so it is likely you would be easily detected from a great distance. If they are under the control of Niddrym, as I suspect, she would be made aware of your movements throughout your flight, and you might be at her mercy for much of the time."

"But surely there is as much danger on the ground. Did not some of your comrades die having been attacked by some monster?"

"Yes, it is true, but we three who escaped didn't see the monster or the attack," said Alexinus quietly. "It was getting quite dark at the time. Our four comrades who were taken had dropped some distance behind; maybe it was tiredness, for we had been walking for many hours. Suddenly we heard this great commotion. We saw nothing, just heard this terrible sound as if something monstrous was smashing through the thick foliage. Then came an unimaginable high-pitched shriek that made the blood run cold - and then nothing. No sound from our friends, no sound from whatever it was that had attacked. There was nothing but deathly silence.

"We then started to run, for we were terrified. In am not sure how long we had been running, but eventually we found a small cave, just big enough for us to crawl into. We lay there, huddled together until daylight. Only then did we venture out and continue our journey."

"Then surely there is as great a danger travelling by land?" Merlin said.

"It may appear to be so, Merlin," admitted Alexinus, "yet travelling by land would give you a greater chance to maintain secrecy, especially as there are but two of you. There were six of us and there was no-one to warn us of the dangers beforehand. There's something else that might interest you too."

"And what might that be my friend?"

"By transforming me into this flying freak, Niddrym has provided me with excellent eyesight. I can detect a medium size fish swimming below the surface of the sea from a great height. Imagine the help I can be in your quest, my friend! With such incredible vision, I can not only warn you of approaching dangers on the ground but also guide you to the castle by the least hazardous route."

"Alexinus, my dear friend, you bring great comfort to me. I will think carefully about your words before deciding what to do."

"When are you planning on going, Brother Merlin?" enquired Gregor.

"As soon as I return from delivering my friends back to Earth."

"I would advise you delay your departure for twelve days at least," warned Alexinus.

"Why wait so long?"

"Because of the carnivores. There is much danger at this time, for many of them have not yet arrived from their territories. As I have already explained, the next few days will see the arrival of great numbers of herbivores, as the huge migrations from the north begin."

"Yes, I remember seeing countless creatures grazing this land on my last visit. But what is the significance of having so many creatures grazing here?"

"Well you see, my friend," explained Gregor, "when there are lots of herbivores in the same area, the meat eaters will leave their usual haunts and come down to the plains to hunt and feed. There will be fewer territorial disputes, for there will be more than enough meat for everyone. Then and only then, will it be safe for you to take to the higher ground."

"It is well you are both here. What would I do without your guidance? I will give serious thought to all I have heard, and by sun-up tomorrow I will have made my plans."

Gregor turned to look towards the visitors. "I think it is time for us to return to the village, Brother Merlin."

**   **   **

Chrissie was lying on her bed. She felt hot and sweaty and wondered if Merlin had said something to Gregor about the shower. At that moment there was a soft knock on her door. When she opened it, she found the squat keeper beaming up at her and beckoning for her to follow. He led her outside to the shower cubicle and started pumping a carved wooden lever that

242

was attached to the pipework near the big tank. Chrissie heard water rushing into the overhead container and after a minute or two, Gregor stopped pumping and still beaming, went over to the cubicle and gestured with his hand, as if to say 'please use'. Chrissie needed no further invitation.

By the time they were seated for the evening meal, everyone, including Tom, had made use of Gregor's shower.

The following morning after breakfast, Merlin addressed his companions. He told them about his deliberations with his fellow druids. "So you see, many hazards may lie ahead, but with the help from Alexinus and our God, my quest to rid this world of my evil half-sister will come to pass."

The wizard paused, and then said resolutely: "Tom will need to accompany me, but I believe it is best for the rest of you to return to Earth as soon as possible. We will start our journey twelve days from today."

"If Tom goes, then I want to be with him," said Chrissie.

"I cannot allow you to come, Christine, for I cannot guarantee your safety. There are things out there that even I have no knowledge of, therefore I may not have the power to keep you from harm."

"I still want to come," persisted Chrissie, glaring at him obstinately.

"I want her to come as well," said Tom.

Merlin sighed, cast his dark eyes first on Tom, then Chrissie. "If I cannot persuade you against joining us, then so be it," said the wizard, a little angered by her stubbornness.

He turned his attention to Emile. "Now I have agreed to allow Christine to join us, it is only fair you and Andrew should also have the opportunity. So Emile, what do you wish to do, my good friend? "

"When would I 'ave another opportunity as wonderful as zis!" exclaimed Emile, "I 'ave no close relatives, I 'ave a beautiful girlfriend, but we 'ave little free time to be togezer, because of our business commitments. If anything 'appened, she would miss me, yes, but she 'as too much in her life to mourn for long. I 'ave no children, my friends are few, so not many tears will be shed over my deas, should zat 'appen. Also, I 'ave no police business at zis moment, so my answer is yes. I would not miss zis adventure for anysing, despite zese 'azards you speak of."

"And what about you, Andrew?" asked the wizard, turning to him. "You have a wife who loves you dearly. You have three children, who are no doubt very proud of you. I think it would be folly of you to be of the same mind as Christine and Emile."

"Yes, you are right, Merlin. Although I would dearly love to join you, it would not be fair on my family to do so. As it is, I will need to return within the next three or four days as Monica is expecting me back. It doesn't stop me from being a little envious, though, for it will be the adventure of a lifetime."

"It is nevertheless a very dangerous adventure, Andrew, and I agree entirely with your decision.

"If you all have made your minds up," he continued, "then I will tell you what our strategy will be. We have twelve days to go before we start on our journey. We will use these to improve our fitness, for it could mean the difference between life and death. Starting from sun-up tomorrow, we will run a certain distance. Those who cannot run may walk at a fast pace instead. The aim will be to improve your performance every day. After breakfast you will rest for a short time, before climbing the plateau. Gregor will accompany you, and he will expect to see you reach the plateau a little faster each day."

Merlin looked at the three intrepid adventurers. "This is a dangerous mission, so if you have a change of heart, I will not think any the less of you." Chrissie noticed the hint of humour in the wizard's eyes.

"I still want to come!" exclaimed Tom.

"Me too!" said Chrissie.

All eyes were now on Emile. The big Frenchman brushed his unruly hair from his brow before answering: "I am not looking forward to zis… zis exercise, for I 'ave not ze fitness I should 'ave. But nozing will stop me from 'aving zis adventure. "

"All the more reason for the training regime, Emile," said Merlin.

Emile responded with a weak smile.

"Now, during training hours, I will spend time with Alexinus, for he has spoken of his desire to speak in this strange language of yours."

"But, surely, Alexinus cannot be taught much in twelve days," queried Chrissie.

"Ahh but Christine, you do not realise, Alexinus was a druid of the Inner Circle. To attain such a position is a rare achievement and only those with high intelligence and a prodigious memory reach this ultimate level. You will also have noticed that Alexinus has been listening to us talking together, so he will already be familiar with many of your common words."

**   **   **

Not to feel completely excluded from the forthcoming adventure, Andrew decided to join his companions in their daily exercise regime.

On the third day, Gregor began the trek to the plateau much earlier than usual. They reached the summit before noon and walked to the western edge of the table mountain to find Merlin and Alexinus waiting for them. "Today you may rest a little before returning to the village", Merlin told them. "As you know, Andrew will be leaving us tomorrow to return to Earth. Alexinus has kindly offered to take him on a ride to show him a little more of Arkatra, then on to the Great Southern Ocean to find fish."

Tom gasped. "Cor, can he take me too?"

"You will have the opportunity later, Tom, as will Christine and Emile."

Andrew cast a worried glance at Alexinus, then at the wizard. "I'm… I'm not so sure about this, Merlin. What if I happen to slip off his back?"

"It is not possible, Andrew," said Merlin, stooping to pick up a loose tangle of leather straps from the ground. "Gregor often goes on fishing excursions with Alexinus and has devised this harness that keeps him secure."

"You should have warned me earlier, Merlin. If I had known about this yesterday, I could have psyched myself up for it," protested Andrew.

"It is more likely you would have worried all day and all night," said the wizard smiling.

"I … I'm still not sure I want to do this," muttered Andrew.

The huge flying creature turned his long beak towards Andrew as Gregor was busy with the harness. "I... will... not... let... you.. fall, Andrew," he said.

Andrew couldn't help but shake his head in amazement at hearing the creature speak his own language, and after a moment of hesitation, he smiled at the bird and said: "Alright Alexinus, let's do it!"

When Gregor had secured Andrew in the harness, Alexinus arose and, with Andrew holding tightly to his collar, he hopped towards the edge of the plateau.

"Are... you... ready, Andrew?"

"As ready as I'll ever be," said Andrew

"Wait! Wait!" shouted Merlin, just as the huge bird was about to spread its wings.

"You have forgotten the fish bag."

Gregor ran forward and threw Andrew a leather bag.

"It's for the fish he catches," explained Merlin. "Gregor says he'll swallow some, the others you'll need to take from him and put in the bag."

"But how will I know which ones to take from him?"

"You will find out very soon, my friend." Merlin said with a chuckle, slapping the big bird on its hip.

This time the Pterosaur opened up its enormous wings, which spanned twelve metres, and the warm, rising currents carried them up into the air.

"Wave... to... your... friends... Andrew," shouted Alexinus, gliding around in a full circle. Andrew looked down at the group below, and was amazed at the height the Pterosaur had attained in just a few seconds.

He raised his left arm in salute before he was swept away on the giant's back southward towards the mountains and the Great Southern Ocean. Gliding along smoothly and silently, Andrew felt his trepidations evaporate. The giant bird had not flapped its wings once, and the former airline pilot marvelled at the incredible aerodynamics the creature possessed. He began to take in the breathtaking scenery below, and he laughed to himself, wondering what his old airline colleagues would think if they could see him now.

They were already over the forest, then, minutes later, a huge mountain range loomed ahead. The bird carried them over a lower mountain range, rather than the higher ones Andrew had first seen. He gazed in awe at black jagged peaks below and the majestic, snow-capped heights in front. Then, before he had time to think, he sensed a change in the Pterosaur's flight angle as the huge bird began swooping down faster and faster.

Looking ahead, he saw the sparkling waters of the ocean.

   **   **   **

That evening they dined on freshly caught fish and were entertained by Andrew's tale of his flying adventure with Alexinus.

Gregor had made his departure soon after he had finished eating, for his boundless energy was such that he preferred to busy himself, rather than sit listening to words in a tongue he was not privy to.

Andrew's eyes glistened with excitement as he told of the great shoals of fish they found and how the Pterosaur glided at speed just inches from the waves, occasionally dipping its long beak into the water to catch a writhing fish in its sharp teeth, causing a stream of sea spray to wash over them both.

"It was all over in about thirty minutes," said Andrew. "By then, Alexinus must have swallowed at least twenty fish, before allowing me to bag those we have eaten this evening."

Andrew went on to describe how, on their return, Alexinus would swoop down over plains and valleys, just metres above all sorts of strange and exotic creatures. "I wish you'd been there Tom, you could have named many of them for me."

Tom, who couldn't hear enough of the adventure, began bombarding Andrew with questions.

Then Merlin addressed Alexinus, who had been lying in his usual position by the window. "Alexinus, I hope your new passenger was no trouble?" Merlin enquired in English.

"What... is... 'passenger'?" asked Alexinus hesitantly.
Merlin explained.

Slowly, Alexinus replied: "Andrew... was... good... No... trouble."

Now the group wanted to ask him all sorts of questions, but Merlin stopped them. "It would be best if we continue speaking among ourselves, and allow Alexinus to absorb all he hears," he advised. "He will talk to us when he feels ready to do so."

After the meal they all raised their tumblers and drank to Andrew's health as it was his last evening among them. "I think I should also drink to yours," said Andrew, with a wry smile.

**   **   **

Late afternoon the following day, everyone said their goodbyes to Andrew as he and Merlin prepared to make their way to the Humming Oak.

"My thoughts will be with you all, and my prayers also," said Andrew to the melancholy group.

"We will be seeing you sooner zan you sink my friend," said Emile, enveloping his friend in a huge bear hug. Andrew took his leave of the others and kissed the Pterosaur on the beak. "Take great care of them Alexinus. Hopefully one day we'll meet again." On reaching the tree, Andrew checked Earth time by glancing at his watch once more. "Hopefully we'll be back on Earth by around mid-morning," he said to Merlin. But it was almost mid-day before they found themselves back in the New Forrest. The wizard escorted Andrew much of the way toward the edge of the forest before they parted under an overcast sky. Andrew embraced the wizard and wished him well in his quest before he set off back to civilization and Benidale.

Merlin arrived back in Arkatra just as the sun was going down.

CHAPTER 38

The big Frenchman had been sorely tested by the exercise regime Merlin had organised for them. But Emile had persevered without complaint, much to Gregor's admiration, and now, on the eleventh day, he felt for the first time that the early morning run and climb were getting easier. It was to be the last day of their customary physical grind, and also the day of Chrissie's long-awaited excursion with Alexinus.

Tom had experienced the wonder of flying on the back of Alexinus two days after Andrew's flight as the Pterosaur was in need of more fish. They had returned from their five-hour flight in the late afternoon and Tom was so enthralled by his adventure, he could barely stop talking about it, and spent much of the evening chatting with Alexinus, whose English was improving by the day.

Two days later it was Emile's turn, but at the last minute the big Frenchman chickened out. He told them about his acrophobia, which had him panic even on the top floor of a tall building, and yet he could fly in a plane without any trouble. "But flying on ze back of zis bird fills me wiz dread, so I'm sorry but I cannot accept your invitation." But the Pterosaur needed fish, so it took to the skies unaccompanied.

Now it was Chrissie's turn, and her heart skipped a beat when she saw the huge bird, already harnessed, waiting at the plateau's edge. She approached with the intention of calling the whole thing off, but one look at Merlin's amused expression made her decide to go through with it. She gritted her teeth and let them hoist her on to the Pterosaur's back. Chrissie lay with her eyes closed while someone strapped her in. Opening her eyes on an impulse, she found she was looking into the dark eyes of the wizard. He handed her the fish bag, laid his hand on her arm and said: "Once you are up in the air, Christine, open your eyes and be captivated by all the beauty you will see around you."

Chrissie was struck by the lovely words and the gentleness of the wizard's tone. She could only nod, for she was too terrified to speak. As the Pterosaur spread its wings and rose into the air, she felt the heady euphoria she had once experienced when riding on a roller coaster with a boyfriend.

Soon the creature began to glide on an even path high above the ground, its wings hardly moving. It didn't take long for her nervousness to vanish and, holding the collar around the neck of the Pterosaur, she pushed herself up to gaze over its wings at the incredible scenes below.

But Alexinus had decided on a different route for his female passenger, so suddenly, from a height of many thousand feet, he began to glide downwards. He chose an area devoid of up-draught to increase his speed, and Chrissie felt as if they were falling from the sky, such was the velocity. All at once they were cruising at low altitude over large herds of strange creatures grazing placidly on the grassy plains.

The bird glided along serenely until it approached a grove of cycad trees. As they got closer, Chrissie spotted some massive creatures grazing among the tree tops. But Alexinus gave his passenger little time to dwell on the scene as, with an almost imperceptible movement of the edge of its frontal wings, he soared upward and over the grove to glide on towards the mountains.

The Pterosaur moved silently through the mountain passes, buoyed by the thermals. Chrissie saw the foothills give way to another vast area of open land holding more dinosaur herds until, all at once, they were flying high above the surf line and heading out over the limitless reaches of the great ocean.

The bird flew into the wind allowing it to maintain its height, for there were no up-draughts above the water. The Pterosaur was looking for tell-tale signs, such as the gathering of sea birds, which usually meant a shoal of fish was close to the surface. They had cruised for almost an hour, when Chrissie noticed a sudden change in their flight path. Alexinus was now flying at a steep angle towards the ocean and was soon cruising two or three feet above the surface, on an invisible cushion of air. With his beak slightly open, he readied himself for his first catch of the day.

**   **   **

It was approaching evening when the large bird glided in to land in the field close to Gregor's cottage. A very wet woman managed, with some difficulty, to unbuckle herself from its back and, holding on tightly to her bag of fish, she walked proudly towards Gregor's cottage, with Alexinus waddling close behind.

During the meal, consisting of a delightful fish pie and vegetables, Chrissie's blue eyes lit up as she spoke excitedly about her day's experience. Alexinus interrupted her on one occasion, saying: "Every time I... caught a fish...sea spray came over and... each time... she screamed."

"It is her right, Alexinus, after all she is a woman!" retorted the wizard.

Chrissie felt herself blushing and becoming angry, all at the same time. 'Who does he think he is, making such a condescending remark,' she thought.

Shortly after the meal, while everyone was still at the table, Merlin stood to address his companions. "As you all know, today was the last day of your training. Although your fitness was uppermost in my mind, there were other important aspects to consider. Your flying expeditions have not been arranged purely for your enjoyment, they were planned so you would become familiar with riding on the back of Alexinus. In the event of any of us becoming separated or if you need to escape, for whatever reason, he will be close by. Your ability to quickly mount and ride with him might be key to your survival. Instructing him in the use of your language was done for the same reason; good communication between yourselves and our flying friend might be vital. Tomorrow we will get ready for the journey. Gregor has been at work these last ten days, preparing supplies for us. We will climb once again to the plateau, for it is from there our journey will begin."

"But, Merlin, my friend, 'ow can we start from zere?" questioned the Frenchman.

"Let me answer that question tomorrow, when we are up on the plateau, Emile."

The wizard then turned to Alexinus.

"Do you have anything to say, my friend?"

Alexinus hesitated for a moment or two, gathering his thoughts in the new tongue.

"I wish to say my... my thoughts go with you. ...I will be...watching from above... With our God's help, we will... destroy this evil witch."

"But how can Alexinus communicate with us when he is high up in the air?" asked Chrissie.

"He can only make contact with me," said Merlin. "We have redeveloped our telepathic skills over the last few days, and I am confident I will understand his thought messages, and he, I am sure will understand mine."

"Your words are… not wrong, Merlin," said Alexinus, "for you and I are of the same… mind."

The wizard cast his eyes toward Chrissie and Emile. "Once again, I wish to offer both of you the chance to withdraw from this hazardous journey. It could be fraught with unknown dangers from which I cannot protect you. If you decide not to join me, no-one will think any the less of you, for this is my fight, not yours, so you could stay here and enjoy Gregor's hospitality until my return.

Both Chrissie and Emile gave their answer. Their minds had not changed.

"Let us then drink to our health, and to our success," said Merlin.

**   **   **

Four people and a Pterosaur looked out over the western edge of the plateau. Gregor was missing. He had decided to stay behind for there was something important he had to attend to.

It wasn't yet noon, and the large, orange Arkatra sun was still climbing high above the eastern horizon. The wizard pointed over to his right, towards a distant hill. "If you look north, beyond the flat scrubland, where the dense vegetation begins, you will see the ground rises up considerably. At the top of the rise there is a track you can't see from here. Beyond that track, the ground rises again, to form a steep hill. Do you see it?"

They all agreed they did.

"Well, that track has been used by herbivores for thousands, maybe millions of years. This is the route we will be taking on our journey west to the Draigoor foothills. It can be dangerous, for predators also use it. They lay in wait to ambush their prey. My friends assure me that most of the predators will be down there, hiding out in the cycad groves or in the lower vegetation surrounding the plains. There they can feed almost at will from the huge number of plant-eaters grazing there. We can only hope they are right."

"Do we *have* to walk through all those frightening creatures down there?" said Chrissie, pointing at the huge animals grazing below.

"Our route would originally have taken us across the foot-bridge, then through the grazing plains to the migration trail I spoke of, but Alexinus has suggested that we should, with his help, fly directly from here to the hill I mentioned. It means we not only avoid having to travel through the herds, but we will save at least one day's march."

"If we 'ave to fly, why don't we just fly straight to ze track?" queried Emile.

"We could do that, but Alexinus requires higher ground to land on, for he needs the thermal currents to enable him to take to the air again. As soon as we are all gathered on the summit, we will make our way down to the track.

**   **   **

Gregor was frantically searching his store house when the group arrived back from the plateau.

"What are you looking for, my friend?" asked Merlin, who suddenly appeared at the door.

Gregor looked up, startled.

"Ahh! So you are back already, Brother Merlin. I did not hear you return."

Merlin was struck by the change in his cheerful friend's demeanour. He seemed worried and preoccupied.

"What is bothering you, Brother?"

"It is nothing of importance, my friend."

"If it is nothing of importance, then why do you look so troubled?"

Gregor looked at him and got up from his knees. "What I am faced with is truly of great importance. I had a vivid dream last night. The Gods appeared as if in the flesh. There were two of them, all dressed in white." Gregor hesitated, searching for words. "They were carrying this large sword between them, it was encased in an engraved silver scabbard and there was a large leather belt attached to it. One of them withdrew the sword from the scabbard and kissed the blade before passing the sword to his companion, who made a similar gesture. They then placed the sword back in the scabbard and, holding it once again between them, turned and walked over to where you were all standing. They went up to your big friend, Emile, and presented him with the sword. They then turned to me, as if to say 'give him the sword'. That's the feeling I had. Then they were gone."

"Excalibur!"

"The very same, my friend."

"But how can that be? Arthur would have taken the sword with him, surely."

"No, Merlin, the sword was brought here on the insistence of Brother Alexinus some weeks after Arthur disappeared. As you know, our brother druid had already been transformed into that flying creature long before King Arthur arrived. Alexinus managed to convince a visiting druid priest of the importance of having the sword brought here to Arkatra. He revealed where Excalibur was hidden, and weeks later it was brought here by another druid. I wrapped it in sheep's hide and concealed it in some safe place, but I have forgotten where."

"Then should we not be asking Brother Alexinus to see if he knows?"

"I have thought of doing so, but I did so want to discover it for myself. You see, it was I alone who was given the responsibility of caring for it.

Please have patience, Merlin," he added. "I shall find the sword."

With that, Merlin left the store house and returned to his friends, who were sitting in Gregor's garden talking with the Pterosaur. "I was asking Alexinus if we could go over on the swing bridge," said Tom, as Merlin sat and joined them.

"Ahh, that is a coincidence, my boy, because it is precisely what I had in mind. I need Brother Gregor's permission to use it, but unfortunately, he has more important things on his mind."

"Where is he now?" said Alexinus, in perfect English.

"He is in the store house," replied Merlin.

"What is he doing?"

"He seems to be searching for something. By the way, Alexinus, I know it was many, many years ago, but do you remember King Arthur's sword being brought here to Arkatra?"

Alexinus responded in his Latin tongue: "The past is an open book to me, Merlin. In my new life as a flying creature, I only have to think about fishing and flying. To keep my brain active I have reflected much on my past life. Sometimes I will spend days at sea just thinking about my childhood, my early education, my life at the druid school, my time at the monastery and my days at King Arthur's court. So yes, I remember well Excalibur. It was taken from King Arthur's secret vault and brought to Arkatra."

"Would you also know where Gregor might have concealed it?"

"Ahh, so that is what our brother is searching for."

"Yes, and he is worried, because he cannot remember where it might be."

"Tell him to look up in the loft. I remember him saying that the air in the loft was warm and dry and that Excalibur would be better protected there."

"Thank you, Alexinus. If Gregor fails to discover it by his own resources, I will tell him where to look. But how did you know about the secret vault? I thought I was the only person apart from King Arthur who knew where Excalibur was kept."

"You were, but that was before I tracked Niddrym and her followers to the Humming Oak. You must realize, Merlin, how worried the king was about his own safety ever since your disappearance; but on that day even more so, for I had forewarned him of bad tidings. He not only showed me where Excalibur was concealed, he also made me promise should he disappear or meet an untimely death, I would remove Excalibur from the vault and take it somewhere safe."

"I understand and I thank you for doing it my friend." Merlin then told him about Gregor's dream.

"It is good news, Merlin. It means our God wants to assist you. Remember, this is your fight, you are responsible. You must defeat her or be destroyed by her. The heavenly one will only protect the boy."

"I understand, Alexinus. It is… "

Merlin was interrupted by an excited cry coming from the direction of the store house. A moment later, he saw the squat figure of Gregor sprinting around the corner of the cottage towards them.

"I have found it! I have found it!" Gregor shouted excitedly, brandishing the heavy sword.

"Found what?" said Alexinus innocently.

"Excalibur! I have found Excalibur after all these years."

"What is Gregor so excited about, and why is he carrying that sword?" asked Chrissie.

"That sword is Excalibur, it has been stored here ever since King Arthur left his realm," explained the wizard.

"You mean the Excalibur sword from King Arthur and the Round Table stories?" said Tom.

"That's correct, Tom."

"I thought those tales were only legends," said Chrissie.

"Legends are a mixture of fact and fable, Christine. Much of what has been written about King Arthur is simply inaccurate, stories emerging from hearsay and wild imaginings. Yet I can assure you my great friend Arthur really was King of all Britain, and I, the greatest of all wizards, was his adviser and the sword you see in Gregor's hands is truly the great Excalibur."

"Can I hold it?" asked Tom, looking longingly at the sword." The wizard grinned. He gestured to Gregor, who slid the sword from its scabbard and offered it to the boy.

"Wow! It's heavy!" Tom exclaimed as the tip of the blade slumped heavily to the ground.

"Yes, Tom, it was not regarded as the heaviest of swords, but certainly the strongest in the kingdom," said Merlin.

"Can I try holding it, Tom?" said Chrissie.

Tom passed the sword over.

"Oh, I see what you mean," said Chrissie, barely managing to lift the blade off the ground.

Merlin, remembering Gregor's dream, invited Emile to take the sword. The big Frenchman had not taken his eyes off the weapon since Gregor had appeared with it.

Now he gingerly took the handle from Chrissie and then, a strange thing happened. The Frenchman strode out in front of the startled group and began twirling the sword above his head as if it was made of balsa wood. He started to lunge and parry as if in combat with some invisible being. This display continued for some minutes in front of the open-mouthed onlookers, until suddenly, the performance ceased as quickly as it had begun. Emile looked around sheepishly at his comrades, then at the sword and said: "I apologise for zat er…stupid display. I do not understand what 'appened."

"Do not be embarrassed, my friend," comforted Merlin. "Excalibur has been lying idle for over fifteen hundred years, it is just er… stretching its wings."

"You make it sound as if the sword is a living thing," observed Chrissie.

"All I will say, Christine, is you are looking at a very special weapon."

"Ze strangest sing is," muttered Emile, "I dreamt I 'ad zis very same sword in my 'and last night. It was so vivid. Zee scabbard, ze belt, even zis engraved 'andle … everysing was… er, was ze same."

Merlin decided not to tell the Frenchman about Gregor's dream.

"Why not put the scabbard on, Emile, for we will be taking Excalibur with us, and you have been appointed to care for it."

Emile, beaming, took the belt and scabbard from the smiling keeper, and, without hesitation, strapped it around his waist.

Merlin then discussed the issue of the bridge with Gregor. After they'd exchanged a few words, Gregor left to go into his cottage. The wizard turned to his companions: "Gregor has agreed for us to use the bridge. He says it is quite safe. He replaced the foot ropes about a year ago. Apart from that, he checks it over at the start of each month. But he insists we eat before we try it out, as it is well past the mid-day."

Chrissie, Emile and Tom had often run along the canal during their early morning exercises, but not as far as the footbridge. During the meal, Merlin explained to his three companions the importance of knowing the whereabouts and structural details of the bridge.

"If anything were to happen to me, or to Alexinus, any survivors would need to find their way to the footbridge to reach safety. Hopefully such a situation will not come to pass, but it is best if we are prepared."

The group reached the footbridge within the hour and Alexinus was already waiting for them on the other side. The bridge straddled a narrow section of the canal, where the rush of the tempestuous waters was accentuated by steep walls. "The lines all look secure over here, Gregor." Alexinus shouted, so as to be heard over the roar of the river.

Gregor's first concern had been the ropes on the far side, especially near where the anchor stakes were embedded into the ground six paces from the river edge. Every so often animals would nibble at the bound ends of the rope and sometimes chew them through completely.

Gregor was the first on to the narrow bridge, carefully examining the structure as he ventured across. The bridge consisted of shoulder high hand rails of thick hessian rope supported by wooden struts. Wooden walking slats about six inches wide by three feet long were fitted into notches in the long planks of timber running the length of the bridge. There was a gap in the last twenty or more feet of the bridge where the walking slats were missing. Gregor was now replacing these from a pile that had been secured nearby. As soon as he had joined Alexinus, he checked the ropes supporting the structure before calling out to Merlin it was safe to cross. Tom was eager to go first. Emile went next, at Chrissie's insistence, for she was unsure of stepping on to the rickety structure.

It took Merlin a few minutes to convince her she would not get tipped into the raging waters below. In the end he went ahead, holding Chrissie's hand. Halfway across she was confident she could walk the rest of the way unaided, but the feel of his hand holding hers stopped her from saying so.

Once over the bridge, Chrissie joined Tom and Emile, who were gazing with rapt attention at a small herd of massive armoured dinosaurs grazing nearby.

"What sort of creatures are they?" asked Chrissie, looking apprehensively at the brown and black mottled beasts.

"They look like Stegosauruses. See the double row of boney fins along its back and those large spikes on the end of its tail?"

"God, they're frightening aren't they?" exclaimed Chrissie. "Are you sure they won't attack us, Tom?"

"I don't think so. I've read they only use their armour for self-defence."

"Well, I sink zey would 'ave no trouble wiz zat big tail," observed Emile.

The trio continued to gaze at the dinosaurs, while Merlin and Alexinus kept a lookout for wandering predators. During the return journey, Chrissie asked Merlin about the wooden slats Gregor had put in place and then removed again on his retreat. He explained it was to discourage large animals from crossing.

"Most of the creatures shy away from the edge because of the noise of the water. Any that are brave enough to venture to the bridge would be deterred by the lack of any visible means of support. It has been successful, to my knowledge."

At the dinner table that evening they were all preoccupied with thoughts of their expedition which was to start the following morning. Days before, Gregor, with Emile's help, had moved the heavy dining table closer to the window where Alexinus rested his head. At first they were a bit disconcerted by his yellow eyes watching them while they ate, but eventually, due to Alexinus' ever growing command of the English language they began to thoroughly enjoy his company. Tonight he was the first to try to lighten the atmosphere. "Emile, pour the wine for your friends and then pass a tumbler over to me."

Everyone looked at the Pterosaur with surprise for he had never shown any interest in the food or drink they consumed. "Why do you look so… shocked?" exclaimed Alexinus. "I might look as if I am not… not capable, but I can… do this if I wish."

Emile passed the tumbler to Alexinus, who took it in his claws. "Let us all drink to the er…our success. I believe good will… triumph over evil. Let us all drink to… VICTORY." With that, Alexinus maneuvered the tumbler to the side of his open beak and with one deft tilt of his head swallowed the contents without spilling a drop. 'To victory', the others chorused tossing the liquid down their throats.

The Pterosaur's stunt had lifted the clouds of worry from the companions. They started to relax and animated conversation began to flow, although the winged druid politely refused further offers of wine. At length Merlin addressed his friends: "Tomorrow, my friends, we start on our quest. It is a responsibility that should rest on my shoulders alone, but it has been my good fortune to have friends who are willing to share this burden with me. I will use all my powers to keep you from harm and pray we will be successful in what has to be done."

The wizard gazed thoughtfully at each of his companions as they contemplated his words. "We will make our way up to the plateau immediately after breakfast. By the time we get there, Alexinus will have arrived. I will take Emile with me and make for the summit of the hill we saw from the plateau this morning. Alexinus will follow with Christine, and then he will return to the plateau to fetch Tom."

Gregor returned to the table with a large hunting knife, which he presented to the wizard. "This you will need, my brother, for it has many uses." Merlin drew the knife from the hard leather sheath. "I had thought about asking you for a knife. Many thanks, my friend."

To the group, he said: "Gregor has supplied us with food, water, blankets and hooded capes in the event of rain. These have already been packed into bags. I have thanked Brother Gregor for all he has done for us. He wishes all of us a safe journey and a speedy return."

Emile addressed the wizard: "Merlin, would you please give Gregor our sanks and appreciation for 'is wonderful 'ospitality, and ask 'im if 'e will join us in drinking 'is 'ealth." Merlin did so and they all raised their glasses in honour of their genial host.

Merlin then rested his dark eyes on each of his three companions. "It is now time for us all to retire, for we need fresh minds and rested bodies to face our coming journey."

His voice suddenly changed to a lower tone. "You will all sleep soundly tonight. Immediately your head touches the pillow, all thought of tomorrow will evaporate from your mind."

Chrissie, Emile and Tom retired to their rooms with Merlin's words still ringing in their ears.

CHAPTER 39

Chrissie, Emile and Tom were awakened by the early morning light. Refreshed from a deep sleep, they were soon dressed and eager to start on their journey. Gregor accompanied the group as they made their last trek up to the plateau, this time with leather bags strapped on their backs. As they approached the western edge, they were a little disappointed to see Alexinus had not yet arrived.

"It is still a little early, so he may be having difficulty taking off," Merlin suggested, as the Arkatra sun began to climb the horizon.

The wizard spoke to Gregor, who nodded and replied in his native tongue.

"I believe Alexinus will be…"

His words were cut short by an excited exclamation from Tom, who had spotted the Pterosaur approaching unexpectedly from the north. It circled lazily around, losing height rapidly as it did so, finally gliding silently in to touch down on its spindly legs.

"I took a flight over that hill, the one you have er… arranged to land on. With extra weight on my back, I have to be sure there is good… landing space for me," Alexinus explained to the wizard.

"I understand. Are you ready to go?"

The big bird nodded his long beak.

With that, the wizard approached Gregor, and as they embraced he said: "We shall be back my brother, I promise you."

The keeper smiled and, with tears gathering in the corners of his eyes, he spoke in his ancient tongue: "May God watch over you, my dear friend. I pray your divine powers will prevail and please tell your friends I will be praying for them."

Merlin then went over to his companions. He grasped the Frenchman's hand. "Just hold my hand tightly, Emile, and whatever happens, do not let go."

Emile nodded, but said nothing.

"Alexinus, you follow with Christine first, then come back for the boy."

The Pterosaur lowered his body to allow Christine to mount.

"But there's no harness," said Chrissie, looking imploringly at Merlin.

"From now on there will be no harness, for no-one will be around to strap you in. Just hold on tightly to his shoulders, Christine, and you will be quite safe. But if you wish, you can remain here with Gregor…"

"I will go," said Chrissie, determined.

"Good!" Merlin smiled.

"Ready Emile?" Emile gave a weak nod. He closed his eyes tightly as the wizard took his hand. A feeling of incredible lightness came upon him as he felt his feet lift off the ground. Minutes later he opened his eyes on Merlin's instruction, only to see they were about to land.

Chrissie turned to the keeper. She hugged him tightly and kissed him on the cheek. "I know you can't understand what I'm saying, but I think you are wonderful." She then eased herself on to the half-prone body of the Pterosaur, grabbed the hard bony shoulders, spread her legs around the body for greater stability, closed her eyes, and said: "I'm ready to go, Alexinus."

She felt her stomach lurch as the bird rose rapidly in the air. Feeling the wind on her face she hung on desperately, but in no time at all she sensed the bird descending as he came in to land.

As soon as Chrissie slid off the Pterosaurs back, he spread his wings again and flew back to the plateau. It wasn't long before they saw Alexinus reappear with Tom perched high on his shoulders.

Assembled on top of the hill, the quartet bade farewell to Alexinus. "Keep listening, my friend, and good luck," came the fading cry from the Pterosaur as he glided away on the freshening easterly breeze. Then the group, led by Merlin, began to make their way down to the dinosaur trail.

The days of training served them well as they began to descend quickly and expertly, sliding at times on shale or jumping from rock to rock as they followed Merlin down the hill. Once on the track, the wizard said: "We will travel two abreast while we can. Tom, you and Christine stay in front, Emile and I will follow. We shall walk swiftly, for we need to reach the Samean caves well before nightfall - any questions?"

"Can we talk to each other?" asked Chrissie.

"Yes, for now. But keep your voices low."

The foursome began their journey into the unknown. Their path was lined to their left with thick and lush vegetation, mainly king ferns and stumpy cycad groves. Behind the verdant fringe lay a bracken-covered swamp. They could see dead or dying trees with their twisted, moss-covered limbs partly submerged in the black stagnant water that was being swallowed up by the creeping undergrowth. Beyond loomed the silent forest, its dark towering conifers giving the place an eerie and menacing feel. The thought of lurking predators was in the back of everyone's mind.

To their right, a gentle slope rose up towards steep, rocky shale. Here, large-leafed vines and ground ferns flourished.

After two hours of brisk walking, Merlin decided they needed to rest. Emile was carrying the largest of Gregor's backpacks, containing a tent made out of hide, which the keeper used to camp overnight during visits to the far side of his island domain. The tent made the pack quite bulky and heavy, so Merlin suggested he and Emile should exchange loads, but the big Frenchman wouldn't hear of it. The bags carried by the others contained two blankets, a leather cape, some chunks of bread, smoked fish, cheese and fruit. Merlin also carried two goatskin bags of water.

Soon they were on their way again. The wizard estimated the caves were still about three to four hours' walk away. He needed to make sure they reached the caves well before darkness to prepare for the night's vigil.

As the companions walked on, the landscape around them gradually changed. The forest on their left started closing in as the swamp had ended, and smaller trees began appearing among rocky outcrops on their right. The further they walked, the more the forest closed in. Eventually, they were forced to walk in single-file. They could now sense movement in the branches, but there were no birds. All they could see were lizard-like creatures of all shapes and sizes.

When they stopped to drink and rest, Tom began to point out some of the tree dwellers to Chrissie. At first she found it difficult to make them out, for the lizards were usually motionless, and, like chameleons, would often blend in with their surroundings. But once she got here eye in, she was astounded.

"They are everywhere!" she cried. "No wonder we cannot see or hear any bird life."

"There are no monkeys here either, Christine," added Merlin. "Alexinus said it's due to the larger lizards and the huge tree snakes that abound."

"With those horrible creatures, it's easy to see why the forest is so silent," observed Chrissie.

Suddenly the wizard's keen ears picked up the sound of chirping. "I might not be correct about the bird life, for I can definitely hear what sounds like birds." Tom was the next to hear the sound. Soon both Chrissie and Emile could hear it too for it was getting louder.

"Whatever they are, they are coming this way," said Merlin, who could hear the chirping turning into a high-pitched, excited grunt.

He was the first to see something. "It is not birds making that sound, it's those big lizards in the undergrowth, do you see them?" Suddenly, a few more of the creatures appeared, their heads protruding above the ferns. Two of the bolder ones ventured close to the track, then disappeared just as quickly back into the undergrowth.

"Those lizards were standing on two feet," Chrissie exclaimed.

"They are not lizards," said Tom.

"What do you mean, Tom?" said Merlin. "If they are not lizards, what are they?"

"They are dinosaurs."

"How do you know?"

"It's their long necks, and I saw their feet. They have three toes and their front legs are like tiny arms, just like the ones in my book."

There now appeared to be a dozen or more of these creatures, although it was hard to tell, for some would dart ahead, while others kept pace with the group, disappearing now and again in the umbrella-like ferns. Three or four of them, it seemed, were always watching the humans. Their shape, Tom thought, was exactly that of the early hunting dinosaur, although their khaki-green bodies and darker green stripes were different from those depicted in the coloured pictures in his book. However, he recognised the distinctive characteristics of the elongated head -

the large yellowish-amber eyes that never appeared to blink, the long mouth with the ends turned slightly upward into the shape of a smile, like that of a dolphin, giving it an expression of benign friendliness.

"They look cute, Tom, what are they called?" asked Chrissie, as three or four more ventured out from the vegetation.

"They look like Coelophysis, but these seem to be bigger."

"What else do you know about them, Tom?" asked Merlin, a slight frown crossing his face as more of them started to appear.

"Well, if they are what I think, they're predators, although they scavenge as well. It says in my book, when they hunt in packs they can be very dangerous."

Merlin didn't comment. He watched the strange reptilian-looking creatures as they grew in numbers and continued to keep pace with the group.

"They walk like chickens!" exclaimed Chrissie, as she watched those nearest jerk their heads forward with each step. Three of them now appeared on the track behind the group.

"Emile, bring out your sword," commanded Merlin, abruptly.

The Frenchman immediately drew Excalibur.

"Be ready to use it as soon as the first one gets close enough. I can freeze a single one in its tracks, but I cannot do it to more than one at a time."

More creatures now appeared on the track close behind. Then, out from behind the verdant fronds, came others to join them.

"Stay together and keep walking," Merlin commanded, softly.

The wizard walked backwards to face the stalking creatures, although to an observer it would have appeared as though he was gliding backward along the track.

"There are more coming over," said Chrissie anxiously. Merlin quickly glanced to his right and saw about six of the creatures had come out from the foliage and were keeping pace about two metres away. Yet others were emerging from the forest fringe. Keeping his attention on the two leading predators who were getting ever closer, Merlin quietly gave instruction to the

Frenchman, who had been glancing backward at every step, but now turned to face the stalking animals.

"Watch closely, Emile. As soon as I transfix this creature, step in and strike it with your sword."

Merlin, still moving backward, waited, watching. Suddenly, like lightning, the nearest predator pounced forward, but the wizard was faster; he pointed a long finger at the lunging figure and the creature froze in mid-attack. The Frenchman immediately stepped forward and struck the creature a sideways blow, almost decapitating it. Not quite realising what had befallen its companion, the second dinosaur lunged forward, but the double-bladed sword in Emile's hand, almost as if it had a mind of its own, was already dealing the creature a swift back-hand stroke, slicing across the side of the gaping head of the predator as it leapt to attack.

As the group hurried on, leaving in their wake two mortally wounded animals, the behaviour of the stalking pack changed abruptly. There was a frenzied rush from every direction as the predators moved in to feast on the two injured creatures. Emile's sword struck again as another predator, in its eagerness to reach the writhing mob, passed a little too closely, bringing it easily in range of the deadly Excalibur.

"Keep walking briskly, Tom, but do not run," instructed the wizard.

As they walked, they couldn't help but glance back at the shocking scene. There must have been twenty or more creatures fighting to gorge themselves on the three bodies beneath them. Occasionally one or more, with their jaws stained with blood, would look up from the melee and gaze after the departing group. Eager to put some distance between themselves and the devouring pack, Merlin hurried them on.

Unnerved by their narrow escape, the group kept a watchful eye out as they continued to walk in single file, with Tom keeping up a good pace in front. Chrissie, quite shaken, kept imagining creatures lurking behind every tree or fern they passed. They were all relieved when, after another two hours, the track began to widen and the thick foliage on their left started to recede. Soon, huge boulders could be seen scattered about, as if they had fallen from the steep rocky peaks which now towered high above them on their right.

CHAPTER 40

"We should be getting near to the caves soon. Alexinus
mentioned some huge boulders close by," said Merlin. Twenty
minutes later the caves came into view.

The Samean Caves were a series of interconnecting
tunnels weaving through the staggered rocky profile of the
Samean Hills. The cave entrances were mostly small, hardly big
enough for a body to slide through, but there were a few that were
much larger.

The group walked on for another ten minutes, with Merlin
noting every cave entrance they passed. Finally, he espied what
he was looking for. The large round entrance to the cave was just
as Alexinus had described. Merlin judged it to be almost two
metres in height and nearly spherical in shape. The wizard
entered first, in case animals had made it their home, but there
was no sign of any creature having recently lived there.

The interior of the cave was quite light and airy, due to the
large entrance and the daylight coming from a narrow opening at
the back of the cave. Merlin beckoned to the others to enter.

"Daylight will leave us soon," he explained. "We will
have a short rest, and then we must prepare for the evening. We
should collect as much firewood as possible, for we need to keep
a fire burning through the night. It will, I hope, keep predators
away."

The druid, who had been taught to use his magic only in
critical situations, judged this was such a time. He jumped up on
to a nearby boulder, almost twice his height, and surveyed the
area.

The wizard called out to his astonished companions:
"Please keep a lookout for pieces of wood flying through the air
for I do not wish to see any of you hurt." Merlin then stretched
out his right arm and pointed at various objects he could see from
his perch. Chrissie and Emile couldn't believe their eyes when
bits of wood, bracken and even parts of a large decayed tree
started sailing in from all directions. Tom had been witness to
many of the wizard's incredible displays of magic in the past, so
he was not too surprised by what was happening.

It took almost half an hour to collect what Merlin thought
would be sufficient firewood to last the night. The daylight was

still with them as they finally had it all heaped into two large piles. The smaller one had been carefully stacked under Merlin's guidance and was placed a little way outside the cave entrance. The much larger stack of heavy timbers had been erected just to one side.

Merlin was just about to prepare himself for lighting the fire when he stood up and gazed skyward.

"Alexinus is close," he murmured.

Chrissie, Tom and Emile scanned the sky, but could see nothing. "Merlin, how do you know?" asked Chrissie.

"He has just told me."

A minute later the gigantic wings of the Pterosaur appeared over the tree tops. Alexinus wheeled southward as soon as he saw his friends below. He would need to turn soon and glide into the light easterly breeze, that way he could approach them at a lower altitude and then use the oncoming breeze to lift him safely up and away.

All eyes were on the Pterosaur. Lower and lower it came, until he was right overhead. Then he let something fall from his jaws before rising up and disappearing into the darkening sky.

"It's a fish!" shouted Tom, who ran over at once to retrieve the silvery creature Alexinus had dropped.

"Ahh, and what a fish!" exclaimed Merlin.

"Let's light the fire, my friends, and soon we will all enjoy a feast of fresh fish, thanks to our dear friend up there." Chrissie watched with the others as Merlin gathered some dry moss and dead twigs and carefully arranged the material in a small mound. He then took a dry slab of grooved timber from his leather bag and, with a carefully selected stick, prepared to make fire.

"Why can't you use your magic to light the fire?" asked Chrissie as she watched him spin the stick in the palms of his hands.

"I use my powers when I have no other choice", he said, looking up. "I needed to collect wood for the fire that way because there might be predators lurking in the foliage, and I could not risk exposing any of us to danger. It is not imperative to use magic to create fire."

While Merlin was busy trying to light the fire, Chrissie started rummaging through her handbag and soon found what she was looking for.

"Why not try this, Merlin?" said Chrissie, holding out a lighter.

Merlin stopped spinning. "What is it?" he asked, examining it.

"It's a lighter; a relic from my smoking days."

"What does it do?"

"I will show you." Chrissie crouched down, flicked the lighter and put the flame to the mound of dry moss and twigs. The material ignited instantly. Merlin, his dark eyes gleaming, grinned. "I am more than happy to succumb to your fire, Christine." She smiled back, inwardly cursing the flame of blushes she knew was rising in response to his words.

Everyone enjoyed their unexpected meal of delicious fresh fish around the fire. Afterwards, Merlin told them of the arrangements for the night: "Although we have the fire with us, we will still need to be vigilant, as we cannot be certain the flames will keep predators away. Emile and I will take it in turns to keep watch."

"I don't think that arrangement is very fair, Merlin," protested Chrissie.

"Oh, and why is that, Christine?" queried the wizard.

"Well, why shouldn't I be part of it, after all I am an adult, or haven't you noticed?"

"It has been a strenuous day, Christine. It is better for you to sleep undisturbed and awake refreshed in the morning."

"But that goes for you and Emile also," Chrissie persisted. "If I do my share of keeping watch, you will both have more time for sleeping."

Merlin sighed. "If it's what you wish, Christine, then so be it. Would it be agreeable if you were to take the first watch?"

Chrissie nodded: "Yes, of course."

"Then you shall keep watch over us for the first two hours, I will take over from you and do the second two-hour watch, then Emile can do the third. Does that suit you, Emile?"

"I will be 'appy to do what you zink is best, my friend," smiled the Frenchman.

"What about me? I'm part of the group, so I want to do a watch as well," piped up Tom.

The wizard looked over at the boy and smiled. "Tom, I know how courageous you are, for you have shown it in many ways, but this is not about courage, it's about being able to stay awake in the middle of the night while everyone else sleeps. It is easier for an adult to do this; they need less sleep than youngsters. We don't know what dangers might be lurking out there, so whoever is on guard has to be vigilant during every second of their watch."

"Well, is it all right if I keep Chrissie company?"

"That's a wonderful idea, Tom," said Merlin, carefully placing some heavier timber on the comforting flames.

"Well, if it is settled, then we might as well relax and enjoy the rest of the evening around the fire."

The evening flew by as the cheerful blaze lifted everyone's spirits, and they reminisced about their eventful first day. It was quite late before everyone was ready to retire.

The wizard reminded Chrissie and Tom not to let the fire go down under any circumstances, and he made both of them promise to wake him immediately if there was anything at all that worried them. Merlin couldn't bring himself to sleep in the cave, for it brought back terrible memories. Instead he settled down to sleep nearby, just out of the glare of the fire.

The night passed without incident. Merlin having done his watch had taken a second one, by relieving Emile for the last session, watching over everyone till daybreak.

CHAPTER 41

The foursome continued their journey much later than Merlin would have liked. The trouble was, they had all overslept. The wizard had decided not to wake the sleeping trio after their demanding day and tiring watch. Much better he thought, for his companions to be rested and alert, than tired and listless. Lost time could easily be made up by walking faster and having fewer rest stops.

He got everyone moving soon after breakfast, a meal that had consisted of bread, cheese and a little of the fruit Gregor had packed for them. Everyone was in a cheerful mood. Chrissie and Tom chatted softly as they walked, while Merlin and Emile kept watch for predators. They had been walking for about ten minutes, when Merlin suddenly called for them to stop.

"What is it, Merlin?" asked Emile.

"It is Alexinus. Please..." The wizard motioned for silence. He stayed still with his eyes closed for a few moments, and then he spoke: "He wants us back. He wants us back in the cave... fast. Quick... run."

All three turned and, without stopping to ask why, ran as fast as they could back to the cave. Within three minutes they were back inside the entrance. Merlin poked his head out to see if he could make out what danger awaited them.

"What is it?" asked Emile, breathing heavily.

"I am not sure, something about a giant serpent... Shhh, I can hear something."

The others listened, but there was only silence. Tom was about to say something, but once again Merlin signaled for silence. Then they heard it. It was a swishing and crackling noise as if something was forcing its way through the dense foliage. It was coming closer, at great speed. Then they heard Merlin's voice, filled with dread. "Oh God! What is this monster?"

Tom couldn't help but run to the entrance and poke his head out at the wizard's words. The boy's jaw dropped in horror at the thing he saw coming towards them along the track. It was a snake of massive proportion. It was still some three hundred yards away, but even at that distance, the loathsome vision would have made the bravest of men tremble.

The monster slithered along the track heading for the cave. "I think it can smell us. Quick, all of you to the back of the cave," ordered Merlin. It was a good ten metres to the rear of the cave, where the tunnel rose up towards the opening. It was what Merlin had seen on first entering the cave. The three had now gathered a good distance away from the entrance when Merlin called out: "All of you; collect your bags, climb up the tunnel and get out through the opening. NOW."

Tom got there first and was soon crawling up towards the opening. Chrissie followed a little way behind. She had seen Tom take off his backpack and stuff it out of the opening ahead of him, and she quickly followed suit.

Emile struggled to get his large pack with the tent through the opening. The wizard, now close behind, pulled it free and tossed it to one side just as the cave entrance darkened suddenly. Emile and Merlin glanced back and saw the gruesome mouth protruding into the cave. The blunt head of the creature completely blocked the opening as it tried to force its way in. The light from the opening beyond the tunnel was enough to see what appeared to be a number of small, snake-like parasites hanging from the top lip of the monster. Underneath, they could see the fangs inside the snake's cavernous mouth.

Emile crawled quickly to the top and managed to get much of his torso through the opening when he got stuck again. At that moment a blood-chilling roar echoed around the cave.

"Some zings caught… I cannot move," he said in desperation. Merlin immediately saw the problem. "It's the sword, Emile!" said the wizard.

Merlin quickly unbuckled the belt, allowing the scabbard to come away in his hands, then ordered the Frenchman to move. Emile responded fast for such a big man, and within seconds he had thrust the rest of his body up and out of the opening. Tom, crouched by the side of the opening, quickly grabbed the scabbard offered up by Merlin. By now, the monster had managed to cram its repulsive head through the entrance and was moving rapidly towards the scent of its warm-blooded prey. The wizard crammed his bag through the opening and quickly followed, just as the enormous forked tongue of the snake flickered towards him.

Outside, Merlin ordered his companions to move well away from the opening while he searched the area. To his left and above, the hard rocky exterior of the cave jutted straight up, to about thirty feet, before disappearing into thorny vegetation. The terrain on his right was also quite rocky, but appeared to flatten out beyond thick foliage. Merlin pushed through the vegetation and saw the ground banked steeply downward and the track they had been walking on the day before lay a mere few feet at the bottom of the incline.

Hearing a horrified cry from Chrissie, the wizard hurried back to his companions. Jutting out from the opening was a huge purple-pink tongue, easily as thick as a man's thigh. The glistening appendage with its forked tip flickered wildly, sensing the close proximity of its prey. It moved purposefully towards them. Merlin pulled his comrades back even further into the foliage at the top of the bank. The gruesome tongue now began to swing from side to side in a desperate attempt to locate them.

The wizard turned to Emile. "I might need to call on you, my friend, so be ready. You and Excalibur might be of great help."

The Frenchman felt for the hilt of his sword. Then he remembered, he had not retrieved it after emerging from the cave. Everyone had been too engrossed in watching the slithering tongue.

Without thinking, Emile made a desperate dash for Excalibur, for he caught sight of it, leaning against a rock near the opening. Grabbing it quickly, he turned and started to race back to the group, but he didn't make it.

His leg was touched by the quivering tip of the snake's tongue and in a flash, it had entwined itself around the leg, toppling the big man. Chrissie let out a loud scream as she watched the tongue starting to pull Emile towards the opening. In a split second, Merlin had the sword in his hand. With three strides he was at the opening and, striking down hard on the huge tongue, he severed it. Amid appalling high-pitched screams from the cave, they pulled Emile safely away; then, with everyone's help, the Frenchman frantically began trying to pull the gruesome piece of tongue from his leg. Although its vice-like grip had loosened somewhat, the severed end was still difficult to remove. Prising it away, Merlin noticed its underside was covered in suckers, like those of an octopus.

The screaming from the cave had subsided and now all that could be heard was a low rattling hiss. Suddenly, Tom yelled and pointed again to the opening. There, emerging tentatively from the opening was the tip of a forked tongue.

"It's grown a new tongue!" yelled Tom. "The new part's pink!" The group watched in amazement as the bright pink appendage flickered in search of them.

Merlin again turned to his friends. "I have a plan. If it succeeds, this monster will not trouble us again. I need you all to stay where you are, for my success depends on the snake keeping its attention on trying to force its way out. It will only continue doing this if it can sense you." The wizard turned again to Emile. "I will not be far away, the track is just down there." Merlin pointed to the slope. "Listen for my call, my friend, for I might need you." The wizard disappeared.

It was the round shape of the boulder Merlin had stood on the previous day that had given him the idea. It was about ten feet high and a good ten paces from the cave entrance. Merlin wondered if his powers would be sufficient to move the huge thing, but move it he must.

He went to the side of the boulder facing away from the cave. He stared intensely at a spot on its surface and with a long forefinger pointed to that same spot. He stood motionless for about two minutes, when suddenly the boulder began to move; just a fraction at first, and then it stopped. The wizard, as still as a statue, remained focused, his finger fixed on the same spot. The boulder moved again, this time rolling slowly and inexorably towards the cave entrance. When it was half way there, Merlin's concentration was interrupted by a sudden movement. It was the snake's tail, eight or more feet of it still protruding from the cave.

Merlin quickly called Emile, and almost immediately the Frenchman appeared on the track beside him. "The tail, Emile... Quickly!" cried Merlin, who took up his position once more behind the boulder. Emile wasted no time, he struck the gristly tail with all his strength, almost severing it. Another unearthly scream erupted from the cave before the remnant of the tail disappeared inside.

Merlin, deep in concentration, was intent on only one thing. He had to move the boulder another three or four feet at least to accomplish his task. Slowly but surely the boulder began once more to move, while Emile looked on in amazement. The blood-chilling sound from inside the cave grew louder and louder. "It's turning back toward us," shouted the Frenchman. He raised his sword and waited.

The boulder was still feet from the entrance when the snake struck. The boulder shook but didn't stop and Merlin, unwavering, kept the massive stone moving towards its final resting place. The Frenchman, still waiting with his sword raised, watched as the quivering tongue emerged from the ever-diminishing gap, but before Emile could bring his sword down upon it, it withdrew as it felt the boulder closing in.

When the rock was finally in place, Merlin and Emile stood side by side listening to the muffled screams which still sent a shiver down Emile's back. They heard the serpent strike again and again at the boulder, but to their relief, it did not yield an inch. "I have handled many snakes, Emile," said Merlin quietly, "and my experience tells me that this monster may be no different, in some ways, to its little cousins in our world. The frontal part, or the nose of a snake, is most sensitive to hard pressure, and I think our ghastly friend in there has the same problem. I am sure we can safely assume it is now well and truly trapped."

"I 'ope you are correct, my friend," said Emile, smiling.

Merlin then called the others.

"Was that in one of your dinosaur books, Tom?" Merlin asked when Tom and Chrissie slid down the bank to join them. "No, nothing like that. Boy, what a monster!" he exclaimed excitedly.

Chrissie was gazing at the huge boulder that was blocking the entrance.

"How... how did you move that?" she asked, wide-eyed.

"Ahh, well, let's call it er ....a simple example of mind over matter," said the wizard, smiling.

"You don't think there might be another one of those... those horrible monsters out there, do you?" said Chrissie, imploringly. Merlin studied her closely. He realised how petrified she must have been throughout the ordeal. His uncanny ability to understand the human mind gave him an insight into Chrissie's underlying fears, and he realised her concerns were as much for the safety of Tom, for whom she felt completely responsible.

"If there is another out there, Christine," said Merlin kindly, "I am sure Alexinus will let us know.

"But now, I think, we should move on, for we have lost so much time. Alexinus informed me before we left, we have a long march from the Samean Caves to our next safe haven, so I'm afraid we must forego any rest."

CHAPTER 42

After an hour of brisk walking, Emile came up alongside Chrissie. "Chrissie, I 'ad to leave my bag back in ze cave, so I would be 'appy to carry yours, if you wish."

"Thank you, Emile, but no. I'm quite capable of carrying it," said Chrissie, haughtily. But when she noticed Emile's slightly crestfallen expression, she touched his arm and smiled up at him. "It's really sweet of you, Emile, but honestly, it is very light, I hardly know I'm carrying it. Anyway, I'd like you to look out for horrible monsters instead."

Emile smiled, nodded and turned back to rejoin Merlin.

The group walked on for another hour or so when, suddenly, a shadow passed over them. They looked up to see the great wings of the Pterosaur as it glided silently above. Then, just as quickly, it disappeared over the dense forest ahead. Merlin stopped to listen while his companions took a much needed break.

"Alexinus says we have a long march through the forest before coming to a large clearing," Merlin said at last. "There we must turn north and walk on for quite a distance. He will meet us somewhere along this part of the journey."

"I zink I also picked up a little message, Merlin," said Emile. "Somezing about fishing?"

"You are right, my friend. He said he was going off to fish again."

As they entered the shadows of the dense forest, they began to walk faster, for the brooding atmosphere unnerved all but Merlin. The sooner they could get out into the open again, thought Chrissie, the better. They trekked on in silence for a considerable time, until they came upon a massive tree that had fallen across the track; its trunk's diameter was at least ten feet. They paused in front of the fallen colossus, when the sound of squealing and snorting reached their ears. Merlin jumped up on to the trunk to find out where it was coming from. After a few moments, he quietly called down to the others to join him. The remains of branches and stumps made the climb relatively easy, and soon they were all gathered on top of the huge trunk.

"What are those creatures over there, Tom?" asked Merlin.

The boy looked where the wizard was pointing. There were about fifteen dinosaurs burrowing around the sprawling root system of a massive podocarp tree that stood thirty feet away. Their rotund bodies were supported by thick, muscular legs and their greenish-grey skin had dark stripes running from the back of the neck to the base of the broad tail. The three metre long bodies had the typical dinosaur shape, although they were not as sleek as those stalking them the day before.

Their broad parrot-like beaks appeared to be digging under the roots in search of something edible. Occasionally, one or the other would stand upright, rising four feet or more and look around for signs of danger.

"They look like Dryosaurus," said Tom, observing the large sombre-looking eyes and the horny beak.

"Like what?" said Chrissie, trying not to smile at the ease with which Tom pronounced the word.

"Like Dryosaurus," he repeated.

"Oh, I see" said Chrissie, impressed.

"Are they dangerous, Tom?" asked the wizard.

"They aren't supposed to be," explained Tom. "They're foraging plant-eaters mostly, and the forest is their normal habitat."

"I see. If that is so then we will continue with our journey."

Merlin was just about to jump down on to the other side of the trunk, when Tom whispered urgently: "Wait…! Look Merlin, do you see them?"

The wizard looked where Tom was pointing and spotted a number of larger, yellowish creatures moving like shadows through the trees as they advanced towards the burrowing Dryosaurus. Suddenly the stalking pack froze. Then, moving as one, they crept silently forward again.

The group watched as the stalkers stopped once more. Then the attack came from all sides. The speed and agility of the predators was frightening. The plant eaters didn't stand a chance. They responded instantly, moving with surprising speed, but for most it was too late. Within two short minutes the horrified watchers counted at least ten dead or dying herbivores lying among the sprawling roots of the giant podocarp.

"What are these terrible creatures, Tom?" asked Merlin quietly, as he watched the pack feeding frenziedly.

"They look like Deinonychus. Do you see the one closest to us? It has that large claw, shaped like a sickle on its foot. I think the word Deinonychus means 'terrible claw'."

Tom paused, looking intently at the carnivores. "They could be velocaraptors, but I don't think they're big enough. Anyway, see how their jaws are much longer and their eyes are larger. I read that Deinonychus are meat eaters and they always hunt in packs. Oh yes, and they are supposed to be very intelligent. It says in one of my books, that packs of Deinonychus would even hunt down a tyrannosaur."

"What are they likely to do if they see us while feeding?" questioned Merlin.

"They'd probably do what any predator would do, I suppose," said Tom, in a matter-of-fact sort of way.

"And what is that?"

"They'd take no notice and just keep feeding."

"Well, let's hope these creatures respond the same way. Stay where you are, all of you, and please, whatever happens, don't make a sound."

Merlin jumped lightly to the ground and started to make his way along the track. The three looked on as he walked casually forward, making no attempt to tread silently. There were twelve or more predators feeding near the podocarp tree only a few metres from the track. A few others were gorging on a single carcass a little further away. The three watched with bated breath as Merlin neared the feeding pack.

The sound of a broken twig made the predators raise their long necks and look over towards the track. They peered with casual interest at the moving figure, but within seconds, all but two of the yellowish creatures crouched back, continuing to fill their stomachs. The other two, not wanting to lose out, quickly followed suit.

Merlin strolled back, this time drawing no more than a quick glance from one of the meat-eaters as he passed. Back at the fallen tree, the wizard quietly requested his companions to climb down from the trunk as quickly as they could. Once gathered, Merlin spoke again: "We shall walk along the track together, but we will not go too fast. Emile and I will keep a sharp eye on them, just in case they have a change of mind about attacking us. Let us move now." Merlin was about to ask Emile to draw his sword, when he noticed the big Frenchman had already done so.

The foursome started walking leisurely along the track. Chrissie and Tom both held their breath as they drew near the feeding predators. They were so close, they could hear the sickening crunching of bones and the occasional scuffle as one or another of the pack fought over a choice morsel. The few seconds it took for them to move past the frightening creatures seemed to last forever. Merlin heard a muffled sob from the front. He knew it was Christine. Once again, the predators raised their heads, but gave them nothing more than a cursory glance.

The group pressed on for some distance before they started to relax a little. Tom explained to Chrissie that most carnivores will gorge themselves until they can eat no more. Then they will usually find some suitable resting place and sleep for a long time to help digest the food. The companions were hoping the Deinonychus might be doing just that, but they still walked as fast as they could to get out of the dark and depressing forest as soon as possible.

CHAPTER 43

At last the trees began to thin out and soon they found themselves on a stretch of open ground bordered on both sides by forest. It looked like a giant causeway, stretching as far as the eye could see to the far off grazing plains.

The wizard studied the churned-up, reddish soil at his feet, realising a multitude of creatures must have passed through recently. It had been a migration trail for millions of years, he mused. The two forests had probably been one and over countless centuries an ever- widening trail had been cut through it by herds heading from the north to the rich grazing lands of the south.

Merlin urged his companions on. They turned to the right to head north, as instructed by Alexinus, and made their way down the wide trail toward the distant hills. The group hurried on, now walking abreast and chatting freely with one another. As they walked, Merlin told his three companions about his theory on the existence of the huge path they were walking on. They all agreed with the wizard's hypothesis, and Tom thought what a great sight it would be to see huge herds of large herbivores streaming through the gap during their seasonal migration. Chrissie and Tom felt more relaxed, now they were away from the depressing forest, although Merlin had felt great comfort there, moving among the huge trees, for it reminded him of home and of his youth. He now felt uneasy in open terrain and warned his friends to remain watchful.

"It is possible that hostile eyes may be watching us at this very moment. So be vigilant."

They walked quite a way before Merlin finally called a halt.

"I was hoping we might have a chance of reaching the river island Alexinus mentioned, but it still seems to be a long way off. By the position of the sun, I estimate nightfall is not too far away, so we will prepare to bed down here in the open."

The wizard looked towards the forest from which they had recently emerged. "I will need to gather wood once more. Again I cannot take the risk of having any of you help collect the wood, for we do not know what danger may be lurking in the forest. You can all help by gathering it up as it falls, but one of you should watch out for predators."

Merlin then flew over to the forest edge and started searching for suitable timber. Soon, firewood of all shapes and sizes was once again raining down a little distance away from them. At times Merlin would return to see how much wood he'd gathered before flying over to another section of forest to collect more. While away on his last wood collecting jaunt, he heard an excited cry from Tom. He looked around and saw the Pterosaur landing on the trail. Merlin arrived back to see his druid friend surrounded by his three companions.

"Good to see you again, Alexinus, my friend. I thought it was difficult for you to take to the air from this flat land?"

"Ahh, this is often true, Merlin, but a good breeze will lift me as easily as the thermals. This track between two high forest lines becomes a wind tunnel, even in the slightest breeze. The signs are, that tomorrow the winds are going to come from the north and this is unusual. But it means the breeze will increase for a time in the morning, so I will have no difficulty in rising up against it."

"Look, Merlin, Alexinus has brought us another fish and it's even bigger than the last one," said Tom, proudly picking up the silver creature for the wizard to see.

"That's wonderful!" said Merlin, smiling at the boy. He then looked up again at Alexinus, whose wings were now folded in the shape of a narrow tent.

"So we will have the pleasure of your company tonight, my friend." Merlin spoke in the old tongue.

"Yes, and it will be my pleasure also, for, apart from giving you the benefit of my knowledge on the last part of your journey, I hope to talk with you and your friends to improve my understanding of their language."

The group had set about collecting the timber Merlin had sent over, and had just finished heaping up the second pile of firewood when the dark Arkatra night descended upon them. With the help of Chrissie's lighter, they soon had the comfort of a roaring fire. No-one complained about having fish for the second night running. Merlin had wrapped it in some large leaves and cooked it slowly in the embers at the edge of the fire. The hungry group delighted in the taste and texture of the perfectly cooked fish. There was still some fruit, a portion of smoked fish and a little cheese remaining in their bags, but Merlin was eager to ration the last of their supplies to tide them over the rest of their journey.

The group told Alexinus about their horrifying experiences during the day, and the gigantic snake Merlin had managed to trap in the cave. "Thank you for the warning, my friend", added Merlin, smiling up at Alexinus. "You saved our lives."

Chrissie, Emile and Tom, soon started to doze in front of the warm, comforting fire, and none of them put up any objection to the wizard's suggestion that they should all get some sleep.

Alexinus then invited anyone who might feel cold during the night to shelter under his wings. Back in the village, Tom had noticed how Alexinus would partly open his wings when he was sleeping. The couched wing membranes looked like two large tents.

"Can I look, please?" Tom asked enthusiastically.

"Please do," said Alexinus.

Tom spotted a pyramid shaped gap where the outer part of the wing folded over the inner part, and proceeded to crawl in. "It's great in there, Chrissie!" exclaimed Tom as he emerged from the winged canopy. He grabbed the leather bag with his belongings and crept back into his new shelter.

Merlin arranged to take the first watch, and Alexinus the second. Emile had agreed to take the third and then wake Chrissie from her slumber to take the watch through 'til daylight.

Once the two druids were alone, Alexinus spoke with Merlin about the rest of the journey. He talked about the coming hazards his friends might have to face, and described the safest route they would need to take if they were to reach the castle unharmed.

Chrissie was into the first few minutes of her early morning watch when Tom crawled out from under Alexinus' wings and sat down beside her.

To ward off the early morning chill, they sat close to each other and the still burning fire. Like this, they silently watched as the rising sun cast its first orange tinge on the purple-blue sky above, heralding the beginning of another beautiful summer's day. After a while, Tom started talking about all the things that had happened to them since starting out. As Chrissie sat there listening, she was amazed how the boy could talk with so much enthusiasm and excitement about it all. It was almost as if he'd enjoyed the terrible experiences.

Chrissie had not slept well. She was unable to rid her mind of the day's horrifying events. In her restless sleep she had visions of the monstrous snake's gruesome forked tongue as it slithered out of the cave opening and then coiled itself around Emile's leg. Suddenly, it wasn't Emile's leg, it was her own. She woke up in a terrible sweat, just as she was being pulled through the cave opening. She pictured time and again the dreadful attack by the predators on the harmless plant-eaters, and the sheer speed and cold-blooded efficiency of these monsters. Worst of all was the memory of the utter terror she felt when the four of them walked past the predators as they gorged on their prey.

Chrissie still had great trepidations about what might lie ahead.

CHAPTER 44

The companions felt the warmth of the morning sun as they prepared to journey on for another day. Alexinus turned to the wizard and addressed him in his own tongue. "From this moment on, Merlin, I will need to turn my mind to the whereabouts of the Perodors. Much of the day you will be in open terrain and easily seen by them during their regular patrols of the area. I will try to locate them and lure them away by flying towards the castle. Once I have them on my tail, I will turn towards the southern ranges. Hopefully they will then remain in the south, well away from you."

The Pterosaur then spoke to the group in his newly acquired language: "May the Gods watch over you all."

Then he strutted away on his ungainly legs to find the space he required to take off into the northerly breeze.

It was Tom who saw them first. "Look! Over there! They're coming this way!"

All eyes turned where Tom was pointing. Large, green, motley creatures had appeared from the opposite forest and were running at great speed towards the Pterosaur. Tom's warning call alerted Alexinus who immediately saw the danger, and propelled himself into the freshening breeze just in time, for the predators were closing in fast. The first two to arrive under the rising bird made an almighty leap into space, colliding with each other as they did so, in their effort to bring the bird down. It was the collision which saved Alexinus, for the outstretched claw of the leading animal was closing in on the Pterosaur's long trailing legs when the body of the second struck the leader, knocking him sideways.

The dinosaur pack watched as the Pterosaur gained height. But then they turned their attention to the four people standing only thirty metres away. They approached cautiously, their heads jerking forward with each step, just like chickens. They slowly circled the group as they tried to gauge what these unfamiliar beings were.

"Stay still and calm." said Merlin quietly. He then turned to the boy. "What do you know about these creatures, Tom?"

"I am sure they're Velociraptors, but they look as if they have feathers on their backs."

"Forget about that Tom, what are they likely to do?" questioned the wizard, as the predators continued to circle them cautiously.

"Well, they are the most dangerous of all the meat-eating dinosaurs, 'cos they're the most intelligent... and... and... I think... I think they're going to attack us soon, sir."

Tom had seen how the eight foot high predators were moving ever closer, and were now less than ten feet away.

"Is there anything you know that might frighten them, Tom, because they seem... unsure of us."

"Don't know, maybe we could try shouting. I don't know... don't know what else," said Tom, worried.

"I 'ave a strong voice," said Emile. "Shall I try?"

"Please do," said the wizard.

Emile let out a loud roar, and instantly the carnivores backed off. The alien sound confused them, but soon they began to circle the group once again.

"What are we going to *do,* Merlin... Please do something," came the frantic cry from Chrissie, who was holding Tom close. She remembered how the other predators had attacked the plant-eaters in the forest the previous day with frightening speed. These creatures were much larger, and she sensed their deadly intentions.

Merlin, swiftly assessing the situation, had already singled out the leader. Slightly larger than the other predators, the animal was easily recognised. It had a long whitish scar running down the left side of its neck, ending in a heavier scar on the breast. It was also the one that had almost brought down Alexinus. The wizard quickly pointed the predator out to the Frenchman, who was standing close by with his sword drawn.

"Emile, be ready! I will have to halt this one before they get any closer. From what we have seen, these creatures seem to attack simultaneously and if that were to happen we wouldn't stand a chance. We have to attack first, it's the only way."

Just as the wizard had finished speaking, a dark mass suddenly materialised above them. It was Alexinus. He had seen his friend's dilemma and was desperately trying to intimidate the Velociraptors in the only way he could. He glided dangerously close over their heads, frightening them with the sheer speed of his approach. By the time they had recovered, Alexinus was already soaring up into the sky, preparing to repeat the tactic. His second approach received almost the same reaction from the dinosaurs, but his third drew only a minor response, and soon their attention was again riveted on the four strange beings in front of them.

The pack, led by the scarred velociraptor, started to move forward. Merlin repeated his order to the Frenchman and was about to freeze the leader in its tracks, when suddenly the large creature stopped and turned his head away from the group. Almost in unison, the pack looked northward, down the trail. Suddenly, they all turned as one and sped back towards the far forest from which they had emerged.

"What made them go?" asked Christine, who could still feel her heart beating madly.

"I am not sure, but it looked as if they sensed easier prey."

CHAPTER 45

Merlin peered intently along the trail.

"Wait! Look there!" cried the wizard, pointing northward.

"What is it, Merlin? I see nozing," said Emile.

"A dark line in the distance, do you see it now?"

"I see it! I see it! It looks like a long dark cloud," exclaimed Tom.

"Listen!" said Merlin.

"Can't hear a thing," said Chrissie.

Merlin remained silent, then commanded: "Quickly, run for the forest, they're coming this way."

The four ran as fast as they could back to the forest they had been so relieved to leave only yesterday.

"I hear it now," said Tom, still breathless. "It sounds like thunder."

"It's the migration from the north Alexinus was talking about last night. Many animals are leaving the northern grounds because the grazing is exhausted and there is much flooding. It happens every year about this time. Because of the distance they have to travel and the type of foliage they need, herds arrive at different times. Alexinus believes that some years the migration period can last three months or more."

The noise increased rapidly as the fast moving mass of huge herbivores approached. Seconds later, the herds arrived in a dense cloud of choking red dust. The deafening noise continued for almost an hour as the animals streamed past. Finally the pandemonium was over. Only the drumming of hoofs from the occasional straggler disrupted the welcome silence.

After a few moments, Chrissie asked: "Why were they going so fast?"

"Hunger, I suppose. Probably been without food for days," said Merlin.

"But zere must 'ave been 'undreds of zousands of zem," said Emile, amazed.

"I've read there were hundreds of different species of dinosaurs at their peak, and they reckon some of the plant-eating herds numbered in their thousands," Tom explained enthusiastically.

"But they were so huge. What sort of creatures were they?" queried Chrissie, again impressed by the boy's knowledge.

"They looked like Corythosaurus, going by the duck-bill and that funny sort of helmet on their heads. They're bird-footed dinosaurs that lived during the Jurassic period."

Chrissie turned to Merlin. "Where do you think they were going in such a rush?"

"They are going down there, to the great southern plains. Alexinus said some of the southern grazing plains take hours just to fly over."

"Well, all I can say is they must have been darned hungry," said Chrissie, glad they were gone.

"They also probably saved our lives," said Merlin. "It's obvious the predators were waiting for their arrival when they saw Alexinus. Pterosaurs are probably familiar prey and they possibly couldn't resist going after him. Would that be right, Tom?"

"Yes, in one my books it actually shows a colour picture of a predator attacking a large Pterosaur on the ground."

"Those carnivores about to attack us, Tom, what did you say they were?"

"I am sure they were Velociraptors. I don't remember reading anything about them having feathers, though."

"Well, feathers or not, I think we need not worry about them in future. All the predators will be able to fill their stomachs more easily from now on," said Merlin, waving a finger southward. The group continued their journey at a brisk pace for they realised they had lost much time. The deep red soil underfoot was like powder from the millions of hoofs that had just passed over it.

They had not been walking long, when their attention was drawn towards some activity near the far forest to their left. A mob of feathered Velociraptors were feeding on two large carcasses.

"So zat's what zey were waiting for," said Emile.

"Seems they were just waiting to pick off the stragglers," said Merlin.

It took some time to reach the end of the wide tract, but finally the forest petered out on both sides and they found themselves in open scrub land. A little way ahead lay the first of the foothills of the Draigoor Mountains and in the distance ahead, they could see faint columns of steam rising upward into the orange sky, creating a mushroom shaped vapour cloud. To the left was a single narrower trail. It was the one Alexinus had instructed Merlin to follow.

After another hour of fast walking, Merlin decided it was time to rest. He had seen a large grove of cycad trees up ahead, so as the late afternoon sun was getting uncomfortably hot, they made their way there to rest awhile and lunch on another meagre portion of Gregor's food.

They were about three hundred metres away when Tom spotted something.

"Look! Can you see them? Above the trees!"

They did. There seemed to be rodents with large eyes moving high among the cycad crowns. Only as they got nearer, it dawned on them they were actually the heads of gigantic creatures standing on the other side of the grove and feeding on the leaves. The quartet approached the grove quietly so as not to disturb the grazing monsters. They sat down and listened to the extraordinary sounds coming from above. There was a constant, almost rhythmic rubbing sound, like moving screwed-up newspaper over a wash board. At regular intervals, a long, rumbling groan reverberated through the thicket.

Merlin made a sign for everyone to eat, so Chrissie opened out a blanket and laid out some of the remaining food. Tom finished eating first, and then asked Merlin if he could go through to the other side to find out what type of dinosaurs they were.

"Do you think it is quite safe, Tom?" said Chrissie.

"They're harmless herbivores, Chrissie, the only thing they can hurt me with are their tails, and if I stand close to the trees they won't even see me."

"I will come with you Tom," said Merlin.

"And I," said Emile.

Not to be left behind alone, Chrissie joined them as they started to creep softly through the grove towards the grazing monoliths on the far side.

They all gaped at the incredible sight that greeted them as they stood within the last line of cycad trees. There were six of these huge creatures with skin that appeared to be the texture of coarse sandpaper. Three of them had fawn coloured bodies that merged into a whitish colour on the lower chest and belly. The fourth dinosaur was quite a bit larger than the others and its skin was much darker. The other two were quite a bit smaller. "Maybe they are the young ones," Chrissie ventured.

"I think that big one is the female," whispered Tom. Much of the time the dinosaurs perched on their solid pillar-like hind legs, using their incredibly thick, long tails to balance themselves as they reached thirty to forty feet into the tops of the cycads. Now and then an animal would drop back to the floor with a ground-shaking thud, as its forelegs hit the ground. Looking up, the observers could see the large white belly, five to six feet above their heads. At times, one or another of the gargantuan feeders would push in closer in order to raise itself up to reach further into the uppermost branches. It was then almost possible for the onlookers to reach out and touch the white belly of the awesome creature.

Too soon, the time came for them to leave. Merlin quietly called them back to pick up their bags so they could resume their journey.

He decided they should skirt the cycad grove, allowing them to see the huge creatures in their entirety, before rejoining the game trail.

"I could never imagine such incredibly large creatures," said Emile, shaking his head in wonder. "What sort of dinosaurs are zey, Tom?"

"Most of the giant plant-eaters are Sauropods. I think these ones are called Diplodocus because they have a row of spines running along the top of their body. See how long the tail is, and see how it thins out, almost like a whip."

The group moved swiftly on. Eventually the trail took them through a shallow pass and into what Merlin guessed was the start of the Draigoor foothills. The rising terrain took its toll on Christine and Emile who, despite their newly acquired fitness, struggled to keep up. As they neared the summit, the sound of rushing water could be heard, and an unpleasant smell like rotten eggs reached their nostrils. From the brow of the hill they could see, far below them, a wide turbulent river. On both sides of the river and on the scrubland beyond, a number of narrow shafts of steam could be seen springing up through vents.

"Pooh! What's that smell?" said Tom.

"It's Sulphur, I zink," said Emile. "I've experienced ze same odour in zermal activity areas around on Earz.

"Me too," said Chrissie. "I visited my sister in New Zealand once, and she took me to a place called Rotorua, it had the same distinct smell, but you got used to it quite quickly."

Merlin's gaze swept along the length of the river and he immediately found what he was searching for. "Do you see that small island in the middle of the river down there?" he said, pointing. "That's where we will be staying tonight. Alexinus assured me the island is very safe, as predators find it almost impossible to cross the turbulent waters. He also said the ground is quite warm as there is thermal activity close to the surface. So you should all be quite comfortable tonight."

It took a little under an hour for the group to reach the river's edge closest to the island. "If its impossible for predators to cross, my friend," said Emile, scrutinising the area, "'ow are we to get across?"

"You are forgetting my formidable powers, Emile," Merlin retorted with a smile. "Remember how I transported you from the plateau?"

It wasn't long before the wizard had ferried the four adventurers on to the island. He had put them down on an area of pale green, broad leaf grass that reached almost to the gravelly foreshore. Nearby, here and there, pools of greyish-brown mud bubbled away, releasing pent-up heat from below the Arkatra surface. The higher ground was covered in conifer trees and below the forest fringe, thickets of stumpy swamp-cypress grew, their leaves mostly grey-white.

Merlin had selected a wide flat area to set up for the night, as far away as possible from the mud pools "Hey, the ground is really warm!" exclaimed Tom, who was feeling the ground with the palms of his hands. Chrissie crouched down to feel the soil. "Well, we won't be cold tonight," she said with a smile.

"Alexinus will be with us soon," advised Merlin. "Hopefully he will have another fish for us for we have little left to eat."

"There's quite a bit of drift wood around, can we start collecting it?" asked Tom.

"Yes, I think it's safe enough this time," said Merlin.

Everyone set about the task, and it wasn't long before there was enough firewood to last the night. There was still an hour to go before nightfall. Late enough, Merlin thought, to start the fire, knowing how quickly darkness closed in. He again watched with a mixture of amusement and wonder as Chrissie used her lighter to create a flame. As the fire began to flourish, Tom caught sight of the Pterosaur as it flew over the hills and swooped down towards the island.

"Here comes Alexinus!" he cried, as the Pterosaur glided toward them. "I don't think he's got a fish this time."

All eyes were on the massive bird as he approached rapidly from the south and landed skillfully no more than twenty metres away from the watching group.

"No fish today then, my friend?" said Merlin, as Alexinus approached them.

"Not this time, Merlin, yet I have had a most satisfying day."

"It started with your bravery this morning", said Merlin. "I think I speak for us all, when I say how thankful we were for your help with the predators," said Merlin, "Your brave action was enough to distract them from attacking until they sensed the approaching herds."

Alexinus nodded in acknowledgement, before responding.

"As soon as I realised you were safe, I began to fly towards the great ocean for I needed food. You see, during our nine-month winters fish migrate to deeper water, so I have to fly further to find them. I take the fish bag and catch as many as I possibly can. Gregor smokes and salts the fish, then packs it away to help us through the long winter. But I had only flown a short distance from you, when I saw the Perodors. They were far below me and flying in your direction."

He explained to Merlin of his worry the Perodors might find his friends in the open. He had flown low, making the Perodors turn to attack him. He lured them towards the southern hills and while they were close on his tail, he tried to take advantage of the thermals, only to find the up-draughts he was seeking were not there.

He told how he led them through the mountain pass towards the Great Southern Ocean, and how, by bouncing off the foothills on either side of the pass, using what little thermals there were, he eventually reached the sea, with the Perodors closing in on him. Once over the sea, he dived down to take advantage of the cushion of air just above the ocean surface, which only a Pterosaur with its huge wing membrane could ride. The Perodors, being land birds, and unable to fly low over the water, eventually gave up the chase and turned back towards the safety of the land.

"But then," said Alexinus, "a strange thing happened. It is something I have only experienced a few times during all the years I have been flying. I saw a huge white cloud rushing down the mountain side. It came upon the sea like a powerful tempest. I could see the white foaming water approaching from the shore and as soon as I realised what it was, I used all my power to get up to a great height for safety. Looking down I saw the wall of wind reach the perodor flock, they had no chance against it. Some were tumbling into the turbulent water while others were being blown helplessly out to sea. Being land birds, they could not possibly have survived so, as a result, this flock of deadly Perodors no longer exists."

Merlin grinned up at his friend. "Well, Alexinus, that is one worry off our minds, it seems this God is truly watching over us."

Alexinus nodded. "Maybe so, my friend, but he was of no assistance in helping me find fish, for I spent the rest of this day searching without success."

Merlin's thoughts now turned to finding food. "We have to find something to eat, Alexinus. I want our friends to be nourished and fully rested for I believe tomorrow will be another trying day for them."

"I think I saw something down river as I was about to land. It might be just what you need," said Alexinus. The flying druid then described the small creatures he had seen down by the river's edge. "Come with me, my friend, I will show you."

The group watched as Merlin leapt on to the Pterosaur's back and flew with him down the river. Christine, Emile and Tom sat by the blazing fire and chatted while they waited for Merlin and Alexinus to return. Just as night was about to close in they saw the Pterosaur approach. As soon as it had landed, Merlin approached holding something that looked like a fat, light brown lizard. He took the hunting knife from his bag and went down to the river's edge, accompanied by Tom.

"Have you seen anything similar to this animal in your books, Tom?" asked the wizard as he prepared to skin the carcass.

"No, not really," he answered. "They mention about lots of fossils and bones of smaller dinosaurs being found, but the books mostly show pictures of the large ones."

It wasn't long before portions of leaf-wrapped dinosaur meat were being slowly cooked on glowing embers raked away from the blaze. The meat was cooked to perfection and turned out to be extremely tasty, yet, after everyone had had their fill, more than half of it still remained.

"We will save that for tomorrow," said Merlin, "for we will need to have it cold for breakfast and possibly for the mid-day meal also."

"You have about half a day's march to the castle from here," advised Alexinus. "Much of it will be up the steep hill lying to the west. From there you will come to a ridge where the ground drops away steeply on your right. On reaching the ridge you will see a beautiful valley and there, on the western hills above the valley, lies the castle."

"Will we see you again during the day, Alexinus?" asked the wizard.

"Of course you will, my friend. I will meet you on the ridge. It is the best place to stop and rest before the journey down to the castle."

Tom stayed with the others longer than he should. He just loved to sit staring into the flames and listening to all the interesting talk around him. It was Chrissie who finally coaxed him into seeking a place to sleep. She laid down beside him on the warm ground, listening to the soft voice of Merlin. She gazed up at the two moons climbing from different directions into the star-filled sky and wondered why she couldn't help being so attracted to this man. She pushed the thought from her mind as concerns about the coming day and the terrors it might bring took over until she fell into a fitful sleep.

Merlin had decided to let his three companions have a good night's sleep. Alexinus had offered to stay alert, and Merlin planned to feed the fire now and then through the night. That way they would all get as much sleep as possible. The wizard had noticed both Chrissie and Emile were looking tired and strained.

He understood why. Their bodies were not accustomed to the physical demands being placed on them. The grinding physical routine with Gregor back at the village and the last three days of physical and mental stress were starting to take their toll. Tom was the only one who appeared to thrive under the conditions, for even in the scariest of situations, Merlin noticed how calm he appeared to be.

It was still dark when Merlin gently roused his sleeping compatriots. "By the time we have eaten, dawn will have arrived. It is best, I think, if we set out early today, for there is much to achieve." Alexinus roused himself near the dying fire. "I will fly now to Gregor. He will be worried, for he was expecting me yesterday. I need to inform him of your progress and will then return to our meeting place on the ridge before you arrive." With those words the Pterosaur rose easily from the ground on the warm thermals and soon disappeared over the shadowy eastern hills.

As dawn arrived the group was preparing to leave their night's resting place. The remains of the meat had been packed into the leather bags, along with the goat bladder pouches filled with river water. Once these were secured on willing backs, Merlin set about taking his comrades over the river to the far side of the bank. He decided to take Tom over first. The boy was always keen to be the first; it was a trait Merlin admired. After depositing Tom on the mainland well beyond the river bank, he flew back for Emile. Lowering the Frenchman to the ground, Merlin noticed Tom wandering towards the river bank. There, the constant fallout of moisture from the steam vents invited the growth of dense lush foliage and thickets of tall swamp cypresses. Merlin quickly returned to the islet to fetch Chrissie, and took her to where Emile was waiting.

Tom was walking back from the cypress grove when Chrissie screamed. Almost at once there was a blood-curdling roar from behind him. Tom turned, and tearing out of the high thicket came the most terrifying creature imaginable. Tom started sprinting, but he tripped and fell. A mere second later the massive beast was standing over him. Chrissie and Emile were paralysed with shock, but Merlin moved swiftly. His action shook Emile out of his stupor and with his sword drawn the Frenchman quickly followed the wizard.

Tom felt the hot, foul breath of the beast as it lowered its head over him. He looked into the gruesome mouth as putrid smelling saliva dripped on to his face Watching the slimy black tongue recede, he was conscious of only one thing - huge yellowish teeth that were about to descend upon him. Tom closed his eyes and prayed. Merlin was now only ten metres away. The huge creature, distracted by the movement, raised its head. This was the wizard's chance! He pointed his finger at the monster to stop it in its tracks. Nothing happened. The dark-skinned, scarred leviathan just peered down at them. Its pale amber eyes held Merlin's gaze for just a few seconds before turning its attention once more to the boy. As Merlin and Emile began moving closer, another petrifying roar came from a different direction. The creature looked up, peered across the scrubland and responded with a deafening bellow. There was another distant roar, louder this time, making the hulking brute turn away from its intended prey and with a another deep, reverberating bellow, it moved quickly towards the sound. Merlin immediately pulled the boy to his feet and with Emile beside him, raced back to where Chrissie was standing.

"Quickly, let us move," ordered Merlin, ushering his comrades across the scrubland towards higher ground. They ran fast, fear driving them on, until they reached the incline. They could still hear the terrible deep-throated roaring as they raced up the slopes of the Draigoor foothills. The group soon lost sight of the scrubland as they rounded a hill that lay to their left, but they continued to run until, with Emile and Chrissie gasping for air, they were eventually compelled to walk. Soon they passed an area allowing them another view of the scrubland and the dense vegetation near the river. The scene confronting them stopped them in their tracks.

Two monstrous behemoths were locked in deadly battle. One had his wide jaws around the other's huge muscular neck. The other, who was the larger of the two, had managed to get half of his adversary's face into his lethal maw and was clawing at the other side of the face with his powerful short right arm.

"What sort of horrible creatures are they, Tom?" said Chrissie.

"They are the Tyrannosaurus Rex."

"My God, they're awful!" said Chrissie, quietly.

"They reckon they were the kings of the Cretaceous Period, but I've read a predator called Spinosaurus has been discovered that was even larger than the Tyrannosaur."

Chrissie couldn't help but admire the youngster by her side. Less than half an hour ago, he had been lying helpless on the ground, almost being eaten by that horrible creature, and here he was, calmly talking to her about pre-historic dinosaurs.

"Look! Ze large one 'as ripped ze ozer one's belly open," exclaimed Emile.

They all saw the entrails like writhing purple-black snakes hanging from the lower greyish-white belly, but the wounded dinosaur continued to hang on to the neck of its larger adversary, shaking its head violently as it did so.

"I think that's blood coming from the big one's neck," observed Tom.

"Looks like iz going to be a fight to ze deas," Emile added.

"This is a territorial dispute, is that not so, Tom?" asked Merlin.

"I think so, 'cos they were very territorial, and their territories covered a very wide area. The big one is probably female, you see they always grow larger than the male. They're also more territorial, except when they are on heat. So my book says, anyway."

Chrissie put her arm around his shoulder. "You are just amazing." she said. And she meant it.

"We are still not safe," said Merlin. "It is possible one of those down there might finish the other off quickly and then come hunting for us. It is best if we keep moving."

Reluctantly the three tore themselves away from the gruesome scene and began the long trek up the Draigoor foothills. After about two hours, Merlin decided a rest was needed. It was getting warm. Most of the terrain was uphill, but now and again they would find themselves walking down into a shallow valley of sparse vegetation, before climbing up yet again.

"We will rest, eat and drink," said Merlin, "for the steepest climb is yet to come."

They all looked up at the ridge Alexinus had mentioned. They noticed the sharp drop to the right of the ridge. It was as if the side of the hill had just fallen away.

Emile thought how useful their training had been. Had it not been for that brief physical regime, he might not have lasted the distance. He viewed the steep ridge with confidence, for he knew now he had the stamina to reach it no matter what the distance.

Soon they were on their way again. The stiff ache in their limbs from the short rest quickly disappeared as they warmed to their task. Half way up, Tom called the group's attention to a band of horse riders watching them from the brow of a hill. Merlin stopped to look at the motionless horsemen. He recalled Alexinus' words about the black knights and knew without doubt these were the very same.

"I 'ave not got a good feeling about zem," said Emile, as he walked back towards Merlin.

"They're all dressed in black... even their horses. Makes me feel creepy," commented Chrissie. As she spoke, the horsemen started galloping down the hill towards them.

"Merlin ... they're coming down... what are we going to do?" came the frantic cry from Chrissie. Merlin refrained from answering and continued to watch their progress. The gold-framed crests adorning the chests of the horsemen were flashing in the sunlight. They were now less than two hundred metres away, and closing in fast.

"Let us run, Merlin, or zey will drive us over za cliff," said Emile, watching the twelve riders raise their swords. "We 'ave no chance against zese black warriors."

The riders were now less than fifty metres away. Merlin could make out King Arthur's red dragon emblem within the shield-shaped crest. He knew what these people were. His decision was instant. "All of you, stay where you are. Face these knights and do not move." The wizard's commanding tone compelled the three to do as they were bid. Chrissie watched in sheer terror as the black riders charged towards them at full speed. She glanced behind her at the sheer drop only a few feet from where she stood. The thundering hooves and the clashing of metal became almost unbearable as the riders came at them. They were so close now, Chrissie could see the white-rimmed red eyes of the steeds and the clouds of steam pumping from their nostrils. She closed her eyes, grabbed hold of Tom's hand and stood there, petrified. Quite suddenly, the clamour ceased and all was quiet.

Chrissie waited, not daring to open her eyes, until she felt Tom shake her hand.

"Where… where are they? Where did they go?" she said, looking around her.

"They were never here, Christine," said Merlin. "They were phantom knights brought down upon us by Niddrym. It was only fear in your minds that made them appear real. Many of our trials in life spring just from our minds. You will not see them again, for fear is no longer within you."

Merlin suggested a rest was in order, allowing everyone to regain their composure. Then they pressed onwards and upwards. They were not too far from the top of the ridge when they saw a familiar shape coming towards them. They watched as the Pterosaur landed on the ridge.

Tom was the first to reach the small tussock-strewn plateau where the tall figure of Alexinus the Pterosaur was waiting. Far below them, on the other side of the ridge, the most beautiful valley could be seen, and there, on its western slopes, just as Alexinus had said, stood the castle.

"What a beautiful castle!" exclaimed Chrissie. "It's like the one you often see in fairy tales."

"This is no fairy tale," said Merlin quietly, as he looked down upon the imposing structure.

When they had all gathered around, Alexinus described the best route to the castle, starting with an animal track nearby. He then turned to his old friend: "This is where we shall meet, my friend, when your business is done."

Merlin addressed his travelling companions. "I do not know what dangers we will meet down there," he said, gesturing in the general direction of the castle, "so if any of you wish to stay here and wait for my return, I will not think any the less of you."

"We 'ave been srough many dangers togezer, Merlin," said Emile. "I for one wish to see zis srough to ze end. Excalibur also might feel a little disappointed if we were to give up now." The wizard smiled at the big Frenchman's remark.

"I want to come, 'cos you'll need me," said Tom, "and your God said he would keep me from harm."

"Well, he didn't help much when that horrible beast was about to eat you," said Chrissie.

"I am not sure you are right about that, Christine." said Merlin. "Do you not think it unusual for the other Tyrannosaur to be where it was at precisely that moment? After all, Tom said these creatures had a very large territorial range, so another Tyrannosaur appearing on alien territory must be quite a rare coincidence."

"Anyway, if Tom goes, I go," said Chrissie, "and after all the horrible things we've been through together, it would be something of an anti-climax to stop now."

"What is an anti-climax?" asked the wizard.

Chrissie looked at Merlin, thinking he was making fun of her again, until she remembered he had only recently become familiar with her language.

"I suppose it means, becoming frustrated or disappointed over the expectation of something."

The wizard let her words sink in. "I think I understand," he said, smiling at her.

Merlin looked up at the Arkatra sun. "It is not yet noon. If you are all ready, I think we should start right away." He turned again to Alexinus. "Farewell, old friend, and do not worry. Next time we meet, Niddrym will be no more." Alexinus nodded his beak. "I almost forgot. Gregor has asked me to tell you he has prayed daily to God to keep you safe. Good luck, my friends. I shall remain here to watch over you."

The group rounded the side of the hill in silence, engrossed in their own thoughts. They followed the animal track down the steep valley, then rested about half way before continuing on their long downward trek. The castle appeared much closer now, its beautiful spires and figurines clearly visible in the late afternoon light.

"Look! It's even got a moat and a drawbridge," said Tom. The travellers noticed a high stockade encompassing a good part of the valley around the castle. The top of each post had been honed to a sharp point to keep large animals from entering. The wizard continued gazing down at the castle for some time, in deep thought. He then slowly turned to the boy. "Tom, I'm going to transfigure you," he said quietly. "Do you know what it means?"

Tom hesitated before answering. "I think so, sir. You want to change me into something."

Merlin smiled at the boy's response. "Well, not all of you, just your face – like I did with your hair – remember?" Tom nodded.

"You will be the same person,, but you will appear much older. The reversing process is quite simple, and this will be done when the time is right. Do you understand?"

Tom nodded.

"I wish to do this now," explained the wizard. "Are you ready?"

"Yes… yes, sir, I'm ready."

Merlin looked at the boy with intense concentration.

Chrissie and Emile watched in amazement as, as little by little Tom's face began to show a series of fine wrinkles, his mouth began to droop and his brown hair become thin and grey. Soon they saw the face of a small elderly man staring at them.

The wizard scrutinised his handiwork. "How do you feel, Tom?"

"Alright, I think. I don't feel any different,"

The wizard laughed. "And now, Tom, your hooded cape, please put it on." The boy opened up the leather pull-string top to withdraw the cape. The capes had come in useful, not during the day for there had been little rain, but most nights when keeping out the chill.

"Keep wearing the cape, but leave the hood off. There may come a time when I need you to put it up, but I will tell you when. Is that understood, Tom?"

"Yes… yes, I understand."

"Thank you my boy," said the wizard, smiling down at Tom.

CHAPTER 46

The animal track they were following had turned into a ditch,
countless cloven hooves having worn away the top-soil over the
ages, and the going was tough. Eventually, the foursome came up
against the timber ramparts of the castle grounds. Merlin, after a
careful survey of the surroundings on the other side, carried each
of his friends across. Walking silently, they soon came upon the
moat surrounding the castle.

Music could now be heard coming from inside. Merlin
recognised the instrument as the medieval flute, a sound he had
often heard at King Arthur's court. The wizard led them in single
file along the bank of the moat behind the castle. He kept
stopping to listen, but he could hear nothing but the music. He
peered cautiously around the corner before waving everyone
forward towards the front of the castle. The drawbridge was up,
but crossing the moat would not a problem thought Merlin.
However, the castle walls might well be.

He studied the high walls. He knew he could get each one
of his companions up and over the walls, but the chances of being
seen were high. Also, during the ferrying process, each of his
friends would be without his protection, both inside and outside
the castle walls. It was something Merlin was not willing to risk.
At that moment he caught a fleeting glimpse of a fair-haired
woman disappearing from the castle's parapet.

Suddenly, a loud snarl behind them made them all turn.
The most fearsome looking dog was walking stiff-legged towards
them. Its froth-speckled lips were drawn back to expose
enormous teeth and its yellow, half open eyes gleamed with
malignant intent. Merlin realised the beast's attention was riveted
on Chrissie, for she had been standing a little apart. The wizard
quickly stepped in front of her and, just as the animal was about
to leap, he pointed his finger and rooted the creature to the spot.

"Your sword, Emile"

The Frenchman, without hesitation, stepped forward, and
with one deft swipe, sliced through the creature's throat. At that
moment, the clanking of heavy chains could be heard as the
drawbridge started its ponderous downward movement.

As it slowly settled across the moat, the sound of bolts
being drawn could be heard. The two heavy carved castle doors

slowly opened inward to reveal a group of people in medieval attire standing there. The first to draw the eye was the beautiful blond woman. She was standing beside a tall handsome man. A little way behind them were three other men, all armed, with their hands on the hilt of their swords.

"Welcome, Merlin. We have been expecting you." The woman spoke in the Latin tongue.

"Greetings to you, Lady Guinevere."

The wizard turned his attention to the elegant man by her side. "Greetings, Sire. It has been a long time."

Arthur nodded briefly. "Greetings to you also, Merlin."

The wizard then smiled at the three men. "Greetings to you Ramon, you Borich, and you Ortella, it is good to see you all again."

The three smiled, but looked uncomfortably at each other.

"Our greetings to you Merlin," said Ramon, but the smile had gone from his face.

"You may bring your friends, they are also welcome," said the woman.

"How did you know I was here?" asked Merlin, remaining motionless.

"I saw you as you were coming over the stockade wall. I happened to be on the roof listening to my husband playing the flute. He plays it well, do you not think so?"

"He always did," replied the wizard.

"I see you have lost none of your powers, Merlin," said the woman, looking beyond them at the decapitated dog.

"If you knew we were about to call, it is strange we received no warning about your pretty watchdog."

"You gave us little time," said the lady.

"You must come and enjoy our hospitality, Merlin," said King Arthur, interrupting the discourse. "You have long been forgiven."

"Forgiven for what, Sire? Many years have passed and the events have escaped my mind."

"You deserted me, Merlin, remember? Those important years when I needed your support and the benefit of your wisdom, you deserted your king, to follow your own selfish ends."

"Is that what you have been told Sire?"

"Yes. My lady Guinevere told me of your treachery, but it is a Christian act to forgive and I offer it to you now."

"I accept your forgiveness and your kind invitation, Sire, but please, may I tell my friends of your invitation, for you see, they speak in an alien tongue and cannot understand what has been said."

"Please do so, Merlin. We are looking forward to your company, as we have very few visitors these days." The wizard turned to his three companions. He briefly explained the situation and what had been said.

"Cor! Is that really King Arthur?" said the elderly Tom, his eyes wide with astonishment.

"She is really beautiful," said Chrissie, still staring at the fair-haired woman.

"Do not be deceived, Christine," said Merlin. "It is nothing more than a mask to hide the evil within. Now listen carefully, especially you, Tom. I need you all to do what I ask."

Tom nodded his aged head. "I'll be ready, sir," he replied gravely.

Merlin addressed his hosts. "My friends would be pleased to avail themselves of your hospitality, sire."

With that, the companions followed King Arthur as he led the way with his queen up sweeping steps and into the banqueting hall. Emile, Chrissie and Tom looked around in wonder at the fine carvings and statues. Chrissie caressed the heavily embroidered silk curtains hanging in drapes down the sides of the large stained glass windows.

"Your taste is as good as it has always been my lady," said Merlin.

"Oh, please, Merlin, call me Guinevere as you always used to."

"Thank you, my lady, I will make the effort."

"Would you like to see the rest of the castle?" asked the woman, ignoring the wizard's remark. "My husband and I would gladly show you. It was built especially for us, you see." She smiled sweetly, leaving Merlin with the feeling she was playing with him, like a cat with a mouse. She was biding her time, but so was he.

They eventually came out on to the parapet where they gazed upon the most wonderful panorama. "We call this place

Camelot after our wonderful domain on Earth," said the queen, waving a slender, heavily ringed hand at the scenery. It was indeed a sight to behold. The valley was carpeted in lush grass with flowering shrubs and a wide variety of ferns growing everywhere. Groves of miniature conifer and cycad trees clustered on higher ground and a small stream sprang from the hills, its sparkling waters feeding a beautiful, azure lake in the middle of the valley.

Here and there goats were busily chewing on bramble-like vegetation and a small flock of sheep could be seen grazing on pastures near the lake. The high walls encircling the castle somewhat marred the breathtaking scene.

"I think I shall arrange to have the dog buried," said Arthur. "Otherwise it could attract those horrible scavenging birds. I will leave you to entertain our visitors, my dear."

As soon as Arthur had gone, the woman moved silently up to the wizard's shoulder.

"I would like to speak privately with you, Merlin."

"There is no need, my lady, for my friends speak in an alien tongue and therefore cannot be privy to your words."

"I have no way of satisfying myself you speak the truth. This could be trickery, so please, let us talk in the privacy of my chamber."

Merlin turned to Christine, who was close by.

"Christine, the lady wishes to talk with me in private, please stay close to Emile and Tom while I am gone. I will be back soon."

"But is it safe for you to go with her?"

"I am aware of the dangers, Christine, and I can assure you I will come to no harm."

The wizard followed the woman along a wide passage to a large ornately carved door. Once inside the lavishly furnished bedroom, she turned to confront her stepbrother.

"Why did you come, Merlin?"

"You know why I am here. I have come to take possession of the staff, the sacred staff you have taken from me."

"It seems you must have forgotten the words of my spell, my dear Merlin. If I remember aright, you were almost asleep at the time, such a shame!" The woman smiled sweetly. Merlin shrugged. accepting her sarcasm. He was more concerned about finding his staff. He commented on the large four-poster bed, with its pale green silk cloth draped over it in generous folds. The false Guinevere looked lovingly at the bed, allowing Merlin to quickly scan the room. She then walked over to the balcony. "What do you think of this?" she asked, casually waving her slim hand at the luxuriant landscape down the valley.

"It is a most beautiful scene, but you must have required much labour to achieve all this," said the wizard.

"Of course, over the years there were many artisans, tradesmen and labourers working here."

"Where did they come from?" he questioned.

Niddrym hesitated, half closing her eyes as she scrutinised her hated stepbrother.

"From our lands in Britain, of course! They were all volunteers for they realised they'd have a better life here than in their own world."

"And where are they now?"

"All dead and gone," she said, "except our butler, Ramon, Ortella, our cook, and Borich, our gardener."

"I remember them well, for they were regarded as the most loyal of all Arthur's knights. So why have you demeaned them in this way?"

"We are just a very small family. In reality, there is just the king and I to consider. It is all I ever wanted. And anyway, this is not Britain, and the men might easily have become bored, so I allotted them each an essential duty. However, they still regard themselves as aides to their king and spend much of their spare time in his presence. "

"I see you have no ladies-in-waiting."

"That is so. They would have been a distraction to the men and I could never have allowed it."

"So, only the five of you have had access to the sacred well?"

"That is so."

She looked at Merlin for some moments before speaking again. "I am disappointed in the perodor flock, for they should have found you and warned me of your coming."

"They no longer exist, my lady."

The woman's eyes narrowed as she heard his words.

"And the serpent, my lady, your creation, I imagine?"

"Yes," she answered proudly, "it took much of my power to bring this… this thing… this serpent from the netherworld."

"Then you will be pleased to hear that your precious serpent has been rendered harmless, my lady. At this very moment it is trapped and will slowly starve to death."

Niddrym's hooded gaze rested on her half-brother. "Why do you not take your friends and leave Merlin. Leave Arthur and I in peace. If you do this, I will see no harm comes to any of you."

"Do you think I could ever trust your word, after what you have done to me and others? Your tongue is as forked as that of the giant serpent; the creature you hoped would destroy us."

"So be it!" she hissed. "But remember, you can do me no harm, for the staff is in my possession. Also, you would have Arthur to contend with, for he would fight to the end to avenge my death." Niddrym hesitated and smiled. "I do not think you would relish a battle with your king and long-time friend."

"It would not come to that, once he knew you were not his beloved Guinevere."

"I am sure you know he would never believe you, no matter how eloquent your words or persuasive your manner."

With that, she turned and swept out of the room. Merlin followed her as she regally descended the sweeping flagstone stairs.

"What were you both talking about?" queried Chrissie, when Merlin rejoined them.

"I will explain later, Christine," said the wizard quietly. The group soon found themselves back in the castle grounds. Merlin let the false queen's small talk wash over him, while Chrissie, Emile and Tom hovered around the grounds. The wizard appeared relaxed, but his mind was continuously assessing the situation. He recalled the words of Alexinus, when he described the events of that terrible day when he and his two druid colleagues were all but destroyed by Niddrym.

Alexinus had said the witch had appeared above them and he had noticed the sacred staff in her hand. It meant Niddrym must have addressed her druid captives from the castle's parapet, for her bedroom balcony faced away from the courtyard. Alexinus also said she ordered the men who had captured them to leave and 'remained silent for some time'. Merlin deduced she had waited until the men were safely out of earshot before casting her deadly spells. This means, thought Merlin, she will go to great pains to make sure no-one in the castle is witness to her sorcery. If so, then her need to get Arthur and the men away from the castle would be foremost in her mind now.

Niddrym beckoned towards a large, heavily timbered table near the steps to the banqueting hall. "Please ask your friends to rest, Merlin. They must be tired and hungry from their arduous journey. Ramon, will you go and prepare some food for our guests."

The knight nodded, turned and left without a word. It wasn't long before the food was on the table. It had been prepared quickly, for it consisted mainly of fruit, thick dark bread and goat's cheese. On another plate was a portion of dark meat that had been cut into small slices. There was also a ceramic jug holding a yellowish-brown liquid. The four travellers were the only ones seated at the table. Merlin stood up and looked down at his comrades. "Do not eat yet."

The wizard then turned to Arthur, who had just returned from attending to the dog. "It is the custom in my companions' world that the hosts partake of the food before the guests. I would be grateful if you would honour this tradition, for then my comrades can begin to enjoy their meal."

"'Tis a strange custom, Merlin, but I shall be happy to comply."

The king sat down, took some bread and a little cheese from the platter and began to eat. The wizard turned to the woman. "You too, my lady."

When the woman was seated, Merlin addressed Ramon: "Would you be kind enough to fetch another two tumblers, so the king and queen can drink with us."

Merlin returned to his seat at the table. He watched as the witch slowly began to eat a small portion of bread and some meat. He then gave a sign to his friends to commence eating, helping himself to some bread and cheese. As soon as Ramon had placed the extra tumblers on the table, the wizard began to pour the liquid into each container.

"What is this we are about to drink?" he asked.

"It is a delightful drink, Merlin." Arthur replied. "It is a special concoction devised by Ramon. I am not sure how it is brewed, but I do know the main ingredients are apple and honey."

"Then please, Sire, you must also drink first."

After the king had drunk from the tumbler, Merlin and the others did the same.

Merlin turned to the king. "It is a delightfully refreshing drink, Sire. I think we might try and steal the recipe from Ramon before the day is out." Arthur laughed.

"Our friends must stay and eat with us this evening," Niddrym said as Ramon began clearing the table. "What do you think my husband?"

"I think that is an excellent idea," said the king, smiling at the group.

"It would be fitting to provide fresh venison or boar for the table, would it not?" said Niddrym, taking her husband's hand.

"Ah yes, I feel ready for an exciting hunt. We caught a glimpse of wild boar two days ago, they were rooting around in the thick foliage near the cypress grove.

"Would you go now, my husband, for there is not much time until dinner?"

"Of course my dearest. We will go immediately."

Merlin already knew her plan. He was also beginning to read her mind, and he knew he would have to work fast. He quickly turned to the king. "Would you mind if I told my friends about your kind invitation for us to dine with you tonight? Also, my big friend, Emile, may wish to join you on your hunt. I also would enjoy it."

The king beamed. "Certainly Merlin."

Merlin turned to his friends, who were still seated at the table. He had been conversing in Latin, so all of them were anxious to know what was being said.

"I have not time to explain, but now I want you all to listen carefully. First you, Tom," said the wizard. "Have you ever seen anyone have a seizure?"

"Do you mean having a fit, sir?

"Yes, I believe that is the word."

"Yes sir, at school… at assembly. I saw him on the floor having an epileptic fit."

"Can you remember his actions?"

"Yes, I remember everything, 'cos he was a friend of mine."

"Ahh then, so be it. When the time is right, I will want you to stagger to one side, fall on the floor, close to the queen's feet and act as if you are having a fit. Can you do this, Tom?"

"Yes sir, I think so."

"The most important thing is you must make sure your hood is placed over your head beforehand and see it remains on. Also, Tom, make sure you keep your face to the floor. Can you remember all I have said?"

"Yes sir," said Tom.

Merlin looked at Chrissie. "As soon as Tom hits the floor I want you to count to five, then go and cover most of his body with yours, while you stroke his head. Do you understand, Christine?"

"Yes... yes I do," she said softly.

"Emile, you must be ready to use your sword when I tell you. Do not draw it until I tell you to do so. Is that understood?"

"Understood, my friend," replied the Frenchman.

"Listen, Tom. I will cough twice. That will be the sign for you to begin having your seizure. Do you understand?"

"Yes sir," the boy said quietly, nodding his elderly face in agreement.

Merlin got up from the table, followed by his three friends and approached Arthur. "My big friend Emile and I would like to join you in the hunt."

"Of course Merlin. It will be like old times, will it not?"

The king turned to his wife. "That would be wonderful, would it not, Guinevere?"

She smiled and nodded to the king, but her eyes were filled with hatred as she gazed at the wizard. The time was right, thought Merlin, for Tom was now standing almost opposite the woman. He fervently hoped the boy had remembered what to do. He coughed twice. Tom hesitated for a moment, then staggered forward three paces and fell to the floor, his body twisting and shaking violently. Christine came forward, and leaned over the prone body as if to comfort him. She made soothing noises while stroking his head.

"What is the matter with him?" queried Arthur, looking worried.

"It is just a seizure. He will recover soon. Pay no attention," explained Merlin.

Niddrym had already looked away, for she found any kind of sickness distasteful. The wizard, wishing to detract Arthur's attention away from the shaking body, turned to the king. "Are you and your domestic animals not troubled by the wild predators, for in our travels we have come across many?"

"We have little trouble, for you see there are very few plant-eaters in the valley. Those that did come around were easily scared off by Rake, our wild dog, the one you have now killed. Also, our fence is high and sturdy. Some smaller ones climb over at times, but we soon catch and kill them before they cause us too much bother. So you see, if the plant-eaters are not about, then the meat-eaters do not come."

Merlin was acutely aware that neither the woman nor Arthur had noticed the change happening to Tom's face under the body of Christine. Merlin had moved slowly to the side of Emile to prevent the two knights having a clear view. The move went unnoticed. Ramon had come out from the kitchen, but was standing away by the table where they had all just eaten. The wizard, realising Tom's face was back to normal, spoke to the pair on the ground. "You may leave him now, Christine... Tom, please remain still."

He then addressed Niddrym: "Guinevere, my lady, you always loved to attend the needs of the sick and the weak. It was your kindness to those less fortunate that attracted the attention of our king those many years ago. Do you remember?"

The woman looked at her husband with a smile, before gazing once more at Merlin with hooded eyes. "Yes, I remember it well."

"Then would you care to help my friend to his feet? His ailment has now passed. He is just resting, for the seizures always tire him."

"I... I do not think I should. Why... why does your woman not do this?" she spluttered, looking over at her husband.

"She will gladly help him, but my old friend would love nothing more than to be comforted by the queen." Merlin looked appealingly at Arthur. "He would treasure that moment for the rest of his life."

"Yes, help the poor man, Guinevere. Merlin is right." The woman looked at her husband and smiled, then turned and went to Tom who was still lying face down.

"When she lifts you, Tom, look straight into her eyes," said Merlin.

"What did you say?" said the woman who was desperately trying to understand what her stepbrother was up to.

"I just told him the queen was about to help him, and he must not be too much of a burden."

The woman once again looked over at the king, who just smiled his encouragement. Hesitantly, she bent to help lift Tom to his knees. The boy slowly raised his hooded head and met the woman's eyes. She held his gaze for a moment before the sickening realisation dawned. Merlin had tricked her. She turned away from the boy's stare with a soft groan.

"What is it, my dear?" questioned the king.

Crouched on the floor, she made no answer. Instead, she stared back at the wizard with undisguised hatred.

"'The boy who saves you I must see, before thy staff is returned to thee.' Do you remember those words, Niddrym, or had you forgotten? It was such a long time ago, wasn't it?"

"What are you saying, Merlin?" said Arthur, stepping forward.

Merlin turned to the king. "This is not your beloved Guinevere, my Liege. This woman you see before you is Niddrym, my half-sister.

"Kill him, Arthur. Have him killed now," Niddrym screamed. Merlin saw the three knights go for their swords.

"Hold, men!" ordered Arthur. "This is my fight."

The king stepped forward and turned to face Merlin. "I forgave you for your treachery and invited you into our home, and in return you insult my wife and accuse her of being your evil half-sister. You were once my greatest friend. Therefore I will allow you to defend yourself with the sword. It shall be a fight to the death... your death, my friend."

"If that is your wish, my Liege, but as you can see, I am unarmed."

"Then take the sword from your big friend."

"I wish him to remain armed, Sire. After all, his weapon might be my companions' only defense against the three swords held by your knights."

"Ramon! Hand Merlin your sword," the king ordered.

The knight started to protest, but one look from his king made him decide against it. He begrudgingly handed his sword to the wizard.

Niddrym rose to watch with unconcealed relish as the two men clashed swords. This was a far better outcome, she thought, far better for her husband to kill her hated stepbrother. She would then only have the others to deal with, and without the protection of their precious wizard, their fate would be sealed. However, she was not prepared for Merlin's sword fighting skills. Neither were Chrissie, Emile and Tom, who stood open-mouthed, amazed at the speed and agility of the wizard.

"You have lost little of your combat skills, Merlin," said Arthur, as he parried the thrust of Merlin's sword.

"You seem to have forgotten, Sire, it was I who taught you those same skills."

Merlin pushed Arthur away and, with a lightning fast backhand strike, dealt the king a blow to the ribs. It was Merlin's intention to wound, nothing more. Again Arthur parried, struck at Merlin's neck, but the wizard effortlessly deflected the blow. In the same move, Merlin ran his sword down half the length of Arthur's blade, twisted his weapon, sending Arthur's sword flying from his grasp. As the wizard waited for the king to retrieve his weapon from the ground, he happened to glance at Niddrym and was taken aback by her changed appearance.

Merlin turned to Arthur, who was advancing once more. "Look, Sire. This woman is not your lovely Guinevere, look at her,… gaze upon her."

Niddrym frowned as it slowly dawned on her something strange, something unthinkable was happening. She glanced at her tresses hanging down over her left shoulder and realised with dread her locks were no longer fair. The classic beauty of Guinevere's face had already begun to dissolve into an ugly visage.

"Look, Sire. Surely you can see this is not your beautiful queen."

The king looked confused. "Guinevere, Guinevere what is happening. Tell me…" A snarl issued from the witches' mouth as she glared with malevolence at her half-brother. For a moment she stood looking at the king as if to say something, but then she turned and rushed out of the hall. Merlin wanted to follow and stop her from getting to the staff, but he couldn't risk leaving his friends. Without him, they could be at grave risk from the three knights.

Arthur, his sword hanging limply in his grasp, appeared bewildered. He looked towards the doors as if expecting his beloved Guinevere to reappear. The three knights watched their king, waiting for his commands.

Suddenly Emile pointed to the roof balcony. "Zere! Zere up on ze roof." They all cast their eyes upward. There stood Niddrym, a terrible expression on her face as she pointed the sacred staff towards them. She looked down upon them, then started laughing and gradually the laughter became a hysterical cackle as she crazily waved the staff in the air. Then suddenly she became quiet and looked down at them without a sound. Then came the evil voice of Niddrym: "Whoever possesses the sacred staff is the one with power, and it is I, Merlin, it is I, Niddrym, who has that power." The woman screeched the last few words.

"Twice you have betrayed me, Merlin, but now your time has come. You are the first to die." She let out a maniacal laugh as she pointed the staff at the wizard. Suddenly Merlin felt himself being held by invisible bonds.

"Just a few words more and my world will be rid of you forever."

As she started her incantation, Merlin used all his spiritual force to break free, but to no avail. He realised now he should have followed and overpowered her before she had a chance to retrieve the staff. But now it was he, Merlin, who was the being overpowered. He also knew, should he succumb, his friends would meet a terrible fate.

No-one had noticed a silent shape gliding in from the hills. Niddrym, engrossed in her evil work, was unaware of the huge flying creature speeding towards her. It was the strange rushing sound that broke her concentration, and then, a fraction of a second later, she felt the staff being torn cleanly from her grasp.

Everyone watched in amazement as the Pterosaur flew away at speed, then made a wide turn and banked into the wind for a slower approach towards his waiting friends.

"Look! Alexinus has got the staff in his mouth," shouted Tom. Merlin, now released from Niddrym's spell, rose up in the air to meet the approaching bird. Alexinus glided in slowly over the wizard's floating form and with great precision dropped the staff into his hands. The Pterosaur then glided across the valley to take advantage of the warm up-draughts on the eastern hills, allowing him to soar to a great height before gliding effortlessly down to the village, to convey the good news to the waiting Gregor.

All eyes were on Merlin as he dropped lightly to the ground. He looked closely at the staff, slid his hand down its length, lovingly touching the intricate engravings, before his thoughts turned once more to Niddrym. He looked up to the balcony, but the sorceress had disappeared. He then turned to his one-time friend and king.

"I am terribly sorry, my Liege, but this had to be done."

Arthur studied Merlin gravely for a few moments. "This terrible happening I have witnessed is almost beyond belief. Did my eyes not deceive me? Did my ears hear the truth? What of my lovely Guinevere? Please, my dear friend, you must reveal all, for I am a desperately unhappy man."

Suddenly they felt a severe jolt. It was followed by a loud rumbling sound that seemed to be coming from deep under the ground.

"What was that?" said Arthur.

"Have you never experienced such turbulence before, Sire?"

"Never! Never in all our days here."

"Then it must be a warning - an omen. We must leave here quickly."

"But where? This is my home, Merlin. I cannot leave."

It came again; another jolt, worse than before. Everyone tried to steady themselves on the swaying ground.

"You must come, now. All of you." Merlin's voice had a fearful and desperate edge. They quickly ran to the stockade and, without waiting, Borich quickly unbolted the heavy gate.

"Now go, leave as fast as you can! Tom, you lead the way and make for the ridge."

Half way up, Tom stopped and waited for the rest to catch up. Once gathered, Merlin, who brought up the rear, urged everyone to keep moving for they still had a long climb. At that moment the earth shook with such force that most were knocked off their feet. A violent cracking noise followed; it was so loud, they thought their ears would burst.

They hurried on, but Arthur was finding the climb strenuous and his loyal knights would not desert him, even now. Merlin drew level with Arthur. "Take my hand, my Liege," he ordered softly. Two minutes later, he lowered his passenger on to the ridge. He then flew back down, setting himself down near Chrissie and Emile, who were struggling up the hill.

"You are both weary and we need to hurry. Christine, you shall be first. Take my hand." She did not hesitate and in no time at all she found herself standing next to the legendary King Arthur. The wizard returned for Emile and before long, everyone was gathered on the ridge.

"Look at the castle!" said Tom. They all looked down at the cataclysmic events below. Around the castle, huge jets of steam were shooting high into the air and a terrible grinding noise could be heard. The ground, even where they stood, shook violently again and again. Suddenly there were gasps as they watched a vast gaping hole appear in the grounds to the side of the castle. Then ear-splitting claps of thunder resounded off the hills, making the onlookers wince and cower back.

Molten rock and fire began cascading from the abyss, and gradually, as if in slow motion, they saw the castle begin to tilt. Then, like a huge sinking ship, the edifice slowly sank into the fire and brimstone enveloping it.

There came another thunderous sound accompanied by an enormous eruption of molten rock, lava spouting a thousand feet or more into the air. The remains of the castle were now completely wrapped in smoke and steam. But gradually, the awful sounds diminished and the ground stopped shaking. And as the smoke lifted, they saw the castle had completely disappeared

The onlookers stood in silence. Finally, Tom said: "Core!"

Alexinus broke the daze of those around him. "Do you not think it would be wise to return to the village, Merlin? After all, Gregor is waiting impatiently to welcome us."

"Yes, of course. There is nothing more to do. Take Tom with you and give Gregor the good tidings."

"I will do that, my friend," said the Pterosaur, lowering himself to the ground. "I will return as soon I can, to collect the others."

After they had gone, the wizard went to sit beside Arthur. His friend sat with his face in his hands. "I did not realise…After all those years…I did not realise…That was my home! Gone… Everything… My castle… Camelot and my beautiful Guinevere."

"Your beautiful Guinevere died a long time ago, Sire. She was murdered by Niddrym less than two years after your marriage." Arthur remained silent as he digested Merlin's words. "What about my people beyond the valley? She would take me there. I saw the crowds. They were my people. They cheered whenever we went by."

"The woman was an evil sorceress, my Liege, and would have created the illusion of cheering crowds in order to keep you happy yet under her control." Arthur looked the wizard in the eye before speaking. "Are you telling me my realm…my people are not out there?"

"Your kingdom here has never existed, my Liege. Niddrym deprived you of it fifteen hundred years ago."

"But how can that be? If it were so, I would… we would no longer be alive."

"My Liege, you were under her spell and knew nothing. You drank daily from the Sacred Spring of Eternal Life. I speak the truth," Merlin assured him, "no matter how unimaginable the truth might be."

"It is difficult for me to comprehend everything, Merlin… so difficult…" Arthur's voice trailed off.

"It will be, for some time to come, my Liege. But once we are back at the village everything will be explained; only then will you possess the true knowledge and the ability to accept the awful truth." Merlin gave the dejected figure a reassuring hug, then rose, took Emile by the hand and flew him back to the village.

318

CHAPTER 47

The squat figure of Gregor was there to welcome each one as Merlin and Alexinus ferried them in. They gathered around the table in the back garden, where the keeper had laid out refreshments. For a while, little was said. The shock of the earth-shattering events of the day took its time to wear off, even in the tranquility of Gregor's little paradise.

At last Merlin broke the silence. "We have done it, my friends." Looking at each of them in turn, he said: "With your help great evil has been expunged from this world. I will never be able to thank you enough." The companions looked at each other, smiles beginning to light up their faces as gloom gave way to elation at what they had achieved together.

"We must zank you, Merlin, for letting us share your quest," countered Emile. "I believe all of us will remember zis adventure for ze rest of our lives." Chrissie and Tom just beamed in agreement.

Gregor, meanwhile, had gone to fetch his bow and arrows, for tonight of all nights they would celebrate with a feast.

Merlin turned to Tom. "He's going to hunt for dhuka for dinner. Would you like to go with him?" The boy nodded enthusiastically, and soon the two of them were heading for the nearby forest. At the edge of the trees, Gregor stopped, looking one way, then the other. The foliage here was quite dense with an abundance of ground ferns, club mosses and horsetails fighting for space. The keeper turned to his left, moving forward, slowly and carefully. Tom followed three paces behind.

Suddenly, the druid turned to the boy and put a finger to his lips, motioning Tom to stay still. Quietly he placed an arrow in the bow and with a slow, deliberate movement drew the arrow back and waited. Tom was still trying to make out what he was aiming at when he heard a loud squeal and watched as Gregor, with lightning speed, rushed to the spot, drawing out a wriggling fat rodent. Deftly, he broke the animal's neck and pulled the arrow from its still shaking body before putting the carcass into a leather bag attached to his belt. He handed it to Tom and started looking for another victim.

Within the hour the duo were making their way back to the village with Tom proudly carrying the bag containing four dhuka carcasses, skinned, gutted and ready for cooking.

Merlin and the others had not been idle and had already lit a big fire outside the cottage. Now they watched as the keeper wrapped the carcasses in large green leaves and placed them on stones the size of large potatoes on to the deep glowing embers on one side of the pit. The meat was covered with skins and a layer of smaller stones.

With the comforting scent of roasting dhuka in their nostrils, everyone now sat around the fire gazing into the flames, lost in their own thoughts. Alexinus stood crouched with his wings folded in such a way as to cradle his long, light torso. In front of him sat Merlin, Arthur and the three knights.

"It's going to be lovely," said Chrissie, her eyes glued to the flames, " just going into a comfortable bed without worrying about being attacked during the night, or fretting about the dangers tomorrow might bring."

"Yes, like being eaten by a Tyrannosaur," said Tom. They all laughed.

"Well, it was ze greatest adventure of my life," said Emile gravely. "And I believe I h'ave lost much weight also."

"You certainly have, Emile," laughed Chrissie. "Me too, I think!" she added.

"You look wonderful... doesn't she, Tom?" The boy looked at the Frenchman nodded, then grinned.

Gregor, who had been preparing the rest of the food in his cottage, emerged with a woven bag full of vegetables, portions of which he again wrapped in large leaves and spread over the hot stones. He covered them with another skin and a layer of sand. Having turned the carcasses, he went to fetch a huge black pot of thick brown soup, which heralded the start of their sumptuous repast. Soon the hungry adventurers were tucking heartily into exotic vegetables and generous proportions of tender meat, followed by fruit and nuts.

"I wish we could get dhuka down on Earth," said Chrissie, after the meal was over. "The meat is delightful."

"It could ave a lot to do wiz ze way it was cooked," suggested Emile.

"Yes, I think you are right, Emile, I remember seeing a Maori tribe in New Zealand cook their food the same way," said Chrissie.

Everyone was gazing in silence at the flames when a question from Tom stirred them from their reverie. "Merlin, now you have the staff back, why can't you turn Alexinus back into a real person?"

The wizard was taken aback by Tom's remark, with everything that had happened, he had completely forgotten about his friend's dilemma.

"Alexinus, please forgive me!" he cried. "Amid all the excitement, I had given no regard to your predicament." He went over to Alexinus and pointed his staff at the Pterosaur.

"Merlin, wait!" cried Alexinus. "We need to think carefully about this."

"But surely, my friend, this must be what you have longed for during all these endless years."

The Pterosaur rose up on his spindly legs without answering. He looked down at the wizard, searching for the right words to convey his feelings.

"Merlin," he said, addressing his friend in Latin. "Our young friend Tom tells me I am an Ornithocheirus, the largest of all Pterosaurs that once existed on Earth, and I must confess I have come to enjoy my life as that bird."

Alexinus paused, looked around at his friends before continuing in English. "You must understand - I have enjoyed life in two different worlds. When conditions are not suitable for flying, I enjoy the company of Brother Gregor here in the village. At other times I can revel in the freedom of the skies. If I wish, I can climb to great heights and glide for a thousand miles or more without once flapping my wings. I can travel over lands on the other side of the Great Southern Ocean and see the highest of mountains and the deepest of canyons. I can glide on the apron of approaching storms and be pushed effortlessly, and at great speed, over sea and land. I have gazed at breathtaking sunrises on a winter's morning and seen glorious sunsets on a late summer's evening, and I never cease to be enraptured. I see my lofty world through human eyes and human understanding, and the wonder and freedom of this life often fills my heart with utter joy."

Alexinus turned his head to look down on the keeper. "You, Gregor, must know, for you have never heard me complain."

The keeper looked up and smiled. "In all the many hundred years I have known you, Alexinus, I cannot recall ever hearing you utter a negative word."

"Except about the Perodors", the Pterosaur quipped.

"But I also reap joy in many other ways. In the winter, during the rains, when I cannot raise myself aloft, you and I spend many happy times together, talking about old times or about the sights we've seen. When the weather is fine, you often ride with me over the great ocean to fish. Just think, my friends, two or three times a week there is fresh fish on the table, and often, before the summer has ended, we manage to store such a great supply, it lasts us all winter. How would all this be possible if I were to revert back to my human form?"

Merlin and Gregor looked at each other, lost for words.

"Now there will be more mouths to feed," continued Alexinus, "and I will find great satisfaction in bringing more fish. I also look forward to the days when I can relax here with you, and also Arthur and his companions, basking in the warmth of your company.

So you see, my friends, not only do I exist in two different worlds, but I also live life to the full in each of those worlds, and if one or the other was taken from me, my life would be the poorer for it."

The wizard smiled up at Alexinus. "We accept what you say, my friend. It is, as you describe, a wonderful life you live, although I am sure Niddrym never intended it to be this way."

"I am sure that is so," replied Alexinus, with a gleam of humour in his large amber eyes.

Later, sitting by the fire, the drone of two languages could be heard. Merlin, Gregor and Alexinus were in serious conversation with Arthur and his knights, while Chrissie, Emile and Tom sat reminiscing about their incredible adventures. None of them noticed the gathering clouds or heard the first soft rumbles emanating from above. It was the sudden vivid flash of lightening in the night sky, followed by a deafening clap of thunder, that made everyone look up to the heavens.

They knew the signs. A sky-rending flash of lighting had them all on their feet, fearful of the maelstrom developing above them. Then the booming voice they had heard once before said:

MERLIN... THE DEED IS DONE... AT LAST YOU HAVE DESTROYED THE EVIL ONE. YOUR ACTIONS TOOK MUCH COURAGE AND FORTITUDE... YOU ARE ABSOLVED FROM YOUR TRANSGRESSIONS OF THE PAST... BE A WORTHY HOLDER OF THE SACRED STAFF AND USE ITS GREAT POWER WISELY.

Silence reigned for a few moments before more grave words resounded from the heavens.

GREGOR... TAKE HEED... YOU ARE NOW FREE TO PROCEED WITH AGEING, FOR YOUR RESPONSIBILITIES AS KEEPER OF THE VILLAGE HAVE BEEN FULFILLED... ARTHUR AND HIS COMPANIONS MAY RESIDE AT PEACE IN YOUR VILLAGE,... THEY WERE UNDER THE INFLUENCE OF THE EVIL ONE, AND INNOCENT OF ANY WRONGDOING... THEY MAY NOW LIVE OUT THEIR DAYS HERE IN PEACE AND HARMONY.

With that, the clouds began to disperse and within a few minutes the stars shone again in the tranquil night sky.

Everyone fell back into their seats, as the exhaustion of the last few days finally took hold. Chrissie took a sleepy Tom by the hand and led him to his bed, before seeking her own. The others followed one by one.

CHAPTER 48

Chrissie and Tom were the first to rise. She was eager to shower, and as soon as she saw Gregor emerge from his cottage, she relayed to him her wishes in sign language. With a smile, the keeper disappeared into his store cottage, to emerge a minute later with a bundle of chopped wood. Soon he had a fire going under the water tank feeding the shower.

Breakfast was a piecemeal affair of delicious pancakes made from a sort of bran and a selection of fruit. Arthur and his three comrades had talked with Merlin, Gregor and Alexinus into the early morning hours and were now feeling the effects.

"Is it true we are going back to Earth today?" Tom asked Merlin, as he joined them at the table.

"That is correct, Tom. It is time for us to leave. Also, Gregor has no additional beds or bedding for the new arrivals, therefore it is good for all if we leave today. Now please, what is the time back on Earth? All three looked at their watches.

"Mine's not going," said Tom, anxious.

"I'm not surprised," said Chrissie, "your Tyrannosaur friend almost ate it!" They all laughed.

"Ze time on Earth is precisely 4.35am," said Emile.

"Mine's about the same," said Chrissie.

"Then we shall depart after the mid-day meal. We should be back on Earth some time between nine and ten in the morning," declared Merlin.

The wizard thought for a moment. "And do these marvelous watches of yours also show what day it is?" he asked, looking with admiration at the small objects on their wrists.

"Yes, of course," says Chrissie. "It is Thursday, August the twenty first."

"That would mean we've been away for just over three weeks!" she exclaimed.

"Yet on Arkatra, only eighteen days have passed," said Merlin.

"Oh my Goodness!" she added, holding her forehead. "I completely forgot, I'm due back at work on Saturday."

After lunch, Merlin and his companions said their goodbyes. Alexinus folded Tom into a winged embrace. "You are a very brave boy. Be proud of yourself… and come and see us again one day."

Merlin translated Gregor's parting words, the keeper's winning smile enveloping each in turn. "Gregor says he is extremely grateful for the bravery you have all shown in helping me in my quest. He wants you to know all his love and prayers will follow you for the rest of your days."

Emile whispered something to Merlin, then quickly disappeared. He returned moments later with Excalibur. Holding the sword in both hands, he presented it to King Arthur.

"My good friend, Emile, returns this sword, the great Excalibur, for I believe it is yours," Merlin told him.

Arthur's eyes lit up at the sight of the weapon encased in its ornamental sheath. He turned to Merlin. "I did not think I would ever see my beloved Excalibur again. How did it come to be here?"

"You were not aware Emile was armed with it in the castle yesterday?"

"I noticed and admired what appeared to be a fine weapon, but no, I did not recognize it."

Merlin explained how Alexinus had retrieved it from the secret vault in the castle and Gregor had kept it safe. Arthur, who had heard all about Alexinus' deeds, turned to the large bird. "Alexinus, I do not know how I can ever repay you for your help and loyalty over all these years. And you, Merlin, how can you forgive me for thinking the worst about your disappearance? I can only express my deepest regret and offer you my most humble apology."

"Knowing you will be enjoying the rest of your days here with Gregor and Alexinus will be sufficient reward for us both, Sire," said Merlin.

"Thank you for your kind words, my friend, but take heed. I was once ruler of Britain, but that was in the distant past; since then my kingdom has been nothing more than an illusion, a sham. I no longer wish to be referred to as King, Sire, My Liege or Your Majesty, but simply as Arthur. Is that understood?" Everyone had no choice but to agree.

Then the four made their way back to the forest.

"How different this place is," observed Chrissie, looking around her. "I don't remember seeing any birds or monkeys at all in the forests on the mainland."

"Yes, it's as if ze Creator made zis island as a 'aven for small, less 'armful creatures of ze pre-'istoric era, if Andrew's zeory is correct."

"We know all about the extinction theory," answered Chrissie, "but surely it means one day the cataclysmic event that wiped out the dinosaurs is yet to come."

"Yes, I think that's exactly what will happen," Tom said.

Before long they reached the Humming Oak. Here Merlin wasted no time. He asked everyone to join hands and embrace the tree. After some simple words of advice, they closed their eyes and before long they stepped back into their own world.

Back in the New Forest, the subdued companions started their walk back to where they had come from, with Merlin leading the way. It was as if he had some homing device, thought Chrissie, as he made his surefooted path through the trees. Chrissie turned on her mobile phone. She had turned it off on the first evening at the druid village and was pleasantly surprised to find it still had plenty of charge. But there was no signal. They walked for some considerable time before emerging out into open park land. Here they found a well-trodden path, which took them to a forestry building. Further on they saw cars parked and nearby a café in a delightful, tranquil setting under some trees.

They decided to stop here for some refreshments and found a table outside in the shade. Chrissie discovered she now had signal on her phone, so she ordered a taxi to take them back to the hotel. While in the taxi she made a call her boss. Robbo was relieved to hear from her and was anxious to have her back for he had much to tell her. She then called the Forest Inn Hotel, where they had stayed the night before they left, to see if they had any vacancies.

"Unfortunately", the proprietor said, "we are fully booked, it's high season." He was helpful however, offering to phone around to see if he could find suitable accommodation for them. Fifteen minutes later he called back to say there were vacancies at the Oakdene Hotel.

Meanwhile, Emile, who had promised to phone Andrew on his return, finally got through to him. The Scotsman was overjoyed at hearing Emile's voice and knowing everyone was safe. "Emile, I'm coming down to bring you all back. You must be exhausted. I will leave at first light tomorrow, so I should be with you around lunch time. I cannot wait to hear all the news!"

At the Oakdene Hotel, the friends were soon ensconced in the two rooms reserved for them.

Remembering Robbo's words about Tom, Chrissie went out to get a copy of The Mail. "There's an article about Tom's disappearance," she said, passing the newspaper to Merlin. "They've set a date for the hearing. It's being held in Saltridge at 11.30am next Thursday.

"My boss said there had been articles over the last three to four weeks and the rest of the tabloids have now got in on the act, including the Saltridge Echo. It's also been featured a lot on TV."

The Mail's piece was headed WHERE IS HE? Next to the story, there was a photograph of Tom and underneath, in bold capital letters, the location and date of the forthcoming family court hearing.

The wizard read the article, before passing the paper to Emile. "They are hoping Tom will make contact."

"Yes, Merlin, that's right," said Chrissie, "because usually in family court cases, the child concerned has to be interviewed. If they don't hear anything, they're likely to postpone or cancel the hearing."

"I see," said the wizard. "Then please, Christine, would you ask at reception for some plain paper and an envelope?" Chrissie left, returning a little while later with a pad and envelope. "The hotel's paper had their logo on it, so I went out and bought some," she said, handing the stationary to the wizard. Merlin thanked her and asked for a pen, before calling Tom, who had been quietly gazing into the large fish tank in the corner of the lounge. Merlin wrote down the address of the newspaper man he had sent Tom's letter to some weeks ago from Long Acre Farm.

He handed the pen and pad to the boy. "Tom, I want you to write 'I will be there' in your normal handwriting on a separate sheet and also address on the envelope."

Once the boy had sealed the envelope, the three friends looked on curiously as Merlin laid the letter flat on the palm of his hand. They saw him stare at it for some seconds, then watched as the letter slowly began to vibrate, until, moments later, it became nothing more than a blur. Chrissie and Emile could only stare with incredulity, when, in the blink of an eye, the letter vanished. They continued looking at Merlin's empty hand, not quite believing what had just happened. Tom, of course, had seen it all before.

The wizard smiled. "It will reach the editor much faster this way," he said casually.

**   **   **

Andrew arrived at the hotel earlier than expected. The prospect of seeing them all again and hearing their news had prompted him to leave home earlier than planned, and by 11.45am he was parked in the hotel grounds.

On their way back to Scotland, Andrew kept bombarding them with questions and their exciting tale made the miles fly by. Before they knew it, they were approaching Craigemere.

CHAPTER 49

John Nielson fingered the note delicately, and then looked again at the envelope before scrutinising the handwritten note once more. At that moment Paul Mac'Veer entered his office.

"This has really got me beat, Paul," the editor said, waving him to a chair. "It arrived just like the other one. No stamp or anything; just sitting on my desk when I got here this morning. Miss Carr cannot give me an explanation and apparently Mrs Berendson didn't turn up to clean, because her mother has suddenly taken sick, so it rules her out."

"I suppose you're checking the CCTV again, just in case," said Paul.

"No.... I mean I would, but I can't. You wouldn't believe it! The blasted thing wasn't working at all last night or this morning, due to a technical fault of some kind or other. My secretary is getting to the bottom of it right now."

"Can we include this in the article?"

"Include what?"

"Well, the strange way these two notes from the boy appeared on your desk."

"Absolutely not Paul. You can imagine what everyone would think if we printed that, especially the people we know would love to take my job. They'd all be saying I was either going doolally, or the job was getting to me, or we were going for sensationalism. No, let's forget about it. I'm letting the police have the note for analysis, in return they have promised not to put out a press release until we've published."

"So you just want a sensational article created by yours truly, declaring to the world we have received a note from Tom Watson in response to our thoughtfully planned series of articles?" said Paul, putting emphasis on the word 'sensational'. John Nielson returned Paul's grin. "You've got it in one, Paul. Let me have a look at your masterpiece when you've got it together. By the way, here's a copy of the boy's note," he said, passing a folded paper to his chief reporter.

The editor waited until Paul had left before studying the offending articles once more. He frowned slightly because something else had been worrying him. For some inexplicable reason he had known the note was going to arrive! Even the short phrase, 'I will be there', and the name, 'Tom Watson', signed in free hand, had been pictured clearly in his mind. Now that was strange, weird even! He couldn't divulge that sort of thing to anyone, not even to his long-time friend, Paul.

Something else was on the editor's mind. He had promised a persistent lady he would call her immediately if there was any response from the boy. With little enthusiasm, John Nielson pushed a button on the intercom and asked his secretary to contact Lady Emma Woodford.

**   **   **

Ann Roper drove through the beautiful Sussex countryside. She enjoyed the scenery, and would have enjoyed it even more if she hadn't been so preoccupied with the reasons for Emma Woodford's phone call. She was sure it would be about Tom Watson, but her ladyship had been reticent. She had just said she wanted a little chat about things.

And the lady took her time before coming to the point, indulging in a little small talk after she received Ann in drawing room. Finally, she said: "I've recently had word from the press, Ann. They've received another note from Tom Watson." Lady Woodford remained silent for a few seconds, letting the news sink in. "The editor told me he wanted to 'keep it under wraps', as he put it, until the article is published in tomorrow's paper. It's why I couldn't say much over the phone, after all, you never know who might be eavesdropping, do you."

"That's wonderful! What does the note say?"

"There are just four words, 'I will be there' and the boy's signature."

"Yes!" Ann beamed, but added "I would imagine there'll be even more spotlight on this case, when that gets published."

"I believe so, but Ann, it proves you were right. Congratulations! As for the publicity, we'll just have to ride with it."

Lady Emma Woodford took a couple of sips of her favourite chardonnay. "I have spoken to James Hickfield; he's the judge whose been assigned to the case. Jim was an old friend of my husband. He's not happy about the publicity; as he sees it, it could jeopardise fair and impartial judgement. He also says he will refuse to adjudicate if there are no transcripts of official interviews with the boy."

"But we have nothing, you know that, Lady…er Emma."

"I know Ann, but he did say this; he would not adjourn until the last moment. When I asked him his view on the hypothetical scenario of the boy turning up on the day, he said, if that were to happen, he might allow the boy to appear before him in private, before the start of the hearing, but it would be highly irregular."

"This is an exceptional case, Emma."

"I understand that."

"It would be a bit of a shame if the boy turns up and the court case is postponed, it might take weeks to arrange another hearing."

"I heartily agree Ann, and I will do my best to prevent that from happening. Imagine the publicity! The TV and the tabloids would have a field day."

"I think they will anyway, whether the case is postponed or not, especially when that article is published tomorrow."

"Mmm, you're right. By the way, Ann, will you be attending court on Thursday?"

"Yes of course, and Kathy Simmons, the young lady who was escorting the boy to his home when he absconded from the car."

"Absconded… or abducted," mused the hostess.

"I suppose we'll know the answer to that if and when he shows up."

Lady Woodford looked thoughtfully at her guest for a few seconds. "I don't suppose there's any chance of the stepmother giving up her rights of legal guardianship? It might save this entire hullabaloo?"

"I'm afraid not. She's determined to keep the boy. Could be out of sheer malice, who knows, but she is adamant."

"Yes, I thought as much," said Lady Woodford. "But it might not hurt to have another word with her."

"We'll arrange a visit, but it's wishful thinking, I think."

"Yes, Ann, as you say… wishful thinking." They both laughed.

CHAPTER 50

By the time Chrissie Flowers reached her parents' place in Woodford it was already late afternoon. She had stayed overnight at Brae'mar House, in Craigemere, as a guest of Andrew and Monica Robbins. On her way down south she decided to visit her parents again, mainly to see her father and apologise for the way she had spoken to him on her last visit. Her good intention to stay calm and detached, however, flew out of the window, as once again she found herself snapping at her mother. She came away almost grinding her teeth in frustration at the way her mother took advantage of her father's good nature. She almost wished she had not gone to see them.

She would be home within the hour. She couldn't wait to have a shower, put on her faded blue towel dressing gown and have a cognac on the veranda. She would steer her thoughts away from tomorrow, her first day back at work, but she wasn't sure she could keep a certain man out of her mind.

Chrissie got to work at 8.15am. It was Saturday. Her boss had requested an early start as he needed to brief his star reporter on a number of matters. The first thing Robbo did was comment on Chrissie's tan. "You look great, Chrissie. You must have been out in the sun every day to get a tan like that."

"Almost," said Chrissie.

The editor briefed her for almost an hour, then asked his secretary to have coffee brought in. Halfway through the coffee break, Robbo handed over an A4 sheet of paper.

"It's from John Nielson, editor of the Mail."

"I know who he is, Robbo," admonished Chrissie, "but when did he get this?"

"I'm not sure. Yesterday I'd guess. He's giving us a run on it prior to the release, 'cos he knows the story originated from here."

"Well, it's the least he should do. So the boy has been waiting for court action, after all." said Chrissie, innocently.

"It looks that way, doesn't it? Anyway, the Mail is printing an article featuring a copy of the note on today's front page. You're familiar with this kid's situation, so have a good look at it all. Oh, and Chrissie, remember this story happened on our patch, so let's put out an emotional humdinger for our readers on this one."

She needed to think about how she was going to write an article about a boy she felt so deeply about, so at lunchtime she slipped out of the office. She sat in the park to eat her lunch and then made a call to Brae'mar House. She engaged in small talk with Monica before asking to speak to Merlin. She disguised the thrill she felt at hearing his voice by talking about the forthcoming hearing and their intended arrival in Saltridge. Merlin told her that Andrew and Monica were driving down to Portsmouth on Thursday to catch the morning ferry, as Emile had invited them to join him for a holiday at his chateau in Brittany. He and Tom would be dropped off in Saltridge on the way.

"That sounds great," said Chrissie, "but you'll need to be here at least an hour or more before the court's due to sit." Merlin said he'd give Andrew that message. She desperately wanted to say more - to say she was looking forward to seeing him again, but instead said "Goodbye" and hung up

On Wednesday evening Chrissie phoned Brae'mar House once more and Andrew answered. She brought up their forthcoming journey south and gave directions on how to get to Saltridge. She then spoke with Tom, pointing out where he and Merlin should go when they reached Leneaton Square. "You realise there will be many reporters and photographers there, don't you?" she warned.

"Yes, I thought there might be," he said

      **   **   **

Andrew parked briefly in Saltridge high street. They were running a little behind schedule for the ferry, so they decided to say their goodbyes to Merlin and Tom right there. Monica embraced the boy and then joined Andrew and Emile in wishing Tom good luck with the hearing.

"It will go well for you, you'll see," the Frenchman added.

Monica gave the boy another hug. "You know I am going to miss you. Tell your aunt Kate you must all come up and stay with us soon."

"Do not forget, Merlin," said Emile, as the car was about to pull away from the kerb, "it will be my pleasure to 'ave you stay at my chateau. I will show you many beautiful tings in my country."

"I will not forget, Emile. And thank you." Then, as the car started to pull away, the big Frenchman opened the back window. "You too, Tom!" he called.

Merlin and Tom soon found Leneaton Square, the main feature of Saltridge Town, which consisted of a grassed square in the middle of a pedestrianised area. In its centre, stood three life-size bronze statues of helmeted infantry soldiers. It was the town's cenotaph, honouring those from the district who had fallen during the First and Second World Wars.

Tom pointed to a café ahead of them. "That's the one!" he exclaimed, seeing the name and recognising the dark green awning that Chrissie had mentioned.

"Do you have any money, Tom?" Merlin asked as they walked towards the café.

"Yes, I got twenty pounds from Uncle Bill before I left the farm. I've only spent three pounds of it and Mrs Robbins gave me another twenty after we got out of the car."

"Well, you must be rich! Let us go and have something to eat. You wouldn't want this poor wizard to go hungry now, would you?"

"No, of course not," said Tom, returning the wizard's smile.

It had been a few hours since the start of their trip that morning and Tom was feeling quite hungry. He glanced at the menu and quickly decided to have a full English breakfast. Merlin ordered a jacket potato with smoked salmon and salad. When Tom's meal arrived, Merlin stared at it in disbelief. "You cannot possibly eat all that."

"I can," said Tom, sprinkling liberal doses of tomato sauce on it before grabbing his knife and fork. During their meal, Merlin kept glancing at the clock hanging slightly askew on the wall behind the counter. It said 11.05am.

"I hope that is the correct time," said Merlin.

"It's about the same as that one," said Tom, pointing to the large clock on the other side of the square.

"It must be the council building Christine mentioned," observed Merlin.

The sandstone structure was conspicuous with its unpretentious 1920s architecture, but it was the adjacent building that drew their attention, for there, surrounding the wide concrete steps hovered a large crowd of people with microphones and cameras at the ready. Suddenly Merlin caught sight of Chrissie standing a little apart from the expectant throng. A tall gangly man with a camera around his neck stood next to her. The man was looking at an attractive woman positioned near the entrance to the court house with a microphone in her hand. Chrissie's eyes were riveted on the café.

Then Tom's face broke into a grin. "Look Merlin, there's aunt Kate and uncle Bill... and look! Fliss is with them as well."

The wizard looked over to the court building and saw Tom's relatives, in the company of a man with a briefcase, trying to wend their way through the horde of clamouring journalists.

"I imagine they will be excited to see you again, Tom."

"Me too," he replied.

Merlin was sure Kate and Bill would recognise him, for although he had erased all memory of his visit, he knew the spell was only temporary. In fact, it was only when their solicitor rang to inform them of the forthcoming court hearing that memories of Merlin's visit began to resurface. And then, after reading the article in The Mail, and seeing Tom's handwritten note, everything came back to them.

The wizard glanced at the clock again. "Christine said you should start to make your way over there at 11.15, Tom. Do you remember everything she said?"

"She just told me not to answer any of the questions the reporters might ask. I've just got to say I am Tom Watson, but otherwise be polite and tell them, 'I have nothing to say'." The wizard smiled at the boy. "This will be nothing compared to facing that Tyrannosaur, eh Tom?"

Tom grinned. "No Sir, that was pretty scary wasn't it?" he said, spearing the last sausage onto his fork. Chrissie said I've just got to head for the entrance to the court house over there and she will try to get to me before they do."

"Yes, Christine said the same to me. She cannot make it obvious she knows you, otherwise other reporters might be suspicious and start thinking she is involved in your disappearance."

"I know," Tom replied.

At 11.15, Merlin looked around the café to make sure no-one was watching, and proceeded to alter Tom's appearance. The boy sat there unaware his fair curls were turning back to his own straight brown hair.

"I have changed you back to your normal handsome self, Tom. Go now, I will watch from here."

Chrissie saw the boy emerge from the café and quickly moved across the green towards him, tugging at the sleeve of her photographer. She was about half way across the square and close to the cenotaph when the others saw him.

"There he is!" came a female voice. "Over there!" a man shouted. There was an excited gabble of voices behind her, but Chrissie had already reached the boy's side.

"Are you Tom Watson?" said Chrissie, winking at the boy as she approached him.

"Yes, I am," he replied. The thin young photographer started walking backwards, rapidly clicking as he went. Chrissie put her arm around Tom's waist and quickly steered him towards the court entrance. A number of journalists and photographers began crowding in on them and a clutch of microphones appeared around Tom's face.

"Who have you been staying with Tom?" came a female voice.

"I'm sorry, but I cannot say."

"Where have you been, Tom?" questioned a man, thrusting his microphone nearer.

"I'm sorry, but…"

"Who was the man with the beard, Tom?" asked another reporter. Chrissie held Tom closer as she came up to the wide steps of the court house. More photographers were waiting half way up, barring their progress, cameras flashing.

"Please let the boy through," shouted Chrissie.

"Awe, come on, Chrissie, stand aside so we can get a shot of him," said a familiar voice.

"Yes, we just need a picture without you in the way!" came another.

"Here we are!" said Chrissie, ignoring the jibes. A tall, balding court official in a black uniform came to help steer Tom through the open double doors. "Good luck, Tom," Chrissie said as the doors closed behind him. In the quietness of the interior, the official led Tom by the elbow down a short corridor and stopped outside a panelled, varnished door. He knocked twice.

"Tom Watson, sir," he said as the door opened.

"Come in, Tom," called a voice.

The boy walked into the room.

"Come and sit down at the table, Tom," said the same voice.

Tom instantly assumed the speaker was the judge. The man's face was quite lined but it had, Tom thought, a kindly expression.

The scene that confronted him was not what he had imagined. He had thought he would be ushered into a large court room with lots of officials everywhere. He was certain his stepmother would be there and more especially his aunt Kate and uncle Bill, maybe even Fliss. But there were only five men and women sitting casually at a round table, and at a small desk, a middle-aged woman was typing on a machine.

As if sensing the boy's confusion, the older man said: "Tom, we are just here for a short while to introduce ourselves to you, and then hopefully ask you a few simple questions. Is that ok with you?"

Tom felt a little more relaxed at the older man's manner and sat down in the proffered chair.

**   **   **

Merlin watched the throng of newspaper people crowding around Tom and Chrissie as they made their way up the steps towards the council chambers. The wizard idly sipped on a cup of black tea, for which he was beginning to acquire a taste, while he contemplated his immediate future. At the conclusion of the court hearing, he would, he thought, return to Arkatra. The thought of relaxing in the company of Gregor and Alexinus and renewing his relationship with Arthur, appealed to him, especially now he had appeased the gods.

A young woman approached the table and asked the wizard if he would like another cup of tea. Merlin smiled and declined the offer. He continued to sit there, thinking of the future. He hadn't noticed Chrissie hurrying across the square until she was almost at the door of the café. She pushed open the door and walked over to where he was sitting.

"I can't stay, Merlin," she said as she withdrew a gift-wrapped object from her handbag. She sat it on the table in front of the wizard, then hesitantly bent and kissed him on the cheek. "It's a little gift as a reminder of the days we had together on Arkatra." Before he could say anything, she turned and quickly walked out of the café. "Damn, damn!, she muttered to herself. Why did I walk away so quickly? He might have stood up, put his arms around me, thanked me for the watch then kissed me. Damn!"

Merlin studied the rectangular object for a few moments before gingerly picking at the bow of gold ribbon. He unwrapped the shiny red gift paper in the same deliberate manner, and, folding it neatly, he placed it on the table by the ribbon. He gazed at the black velvet box for a few more seconds, before slowly lifting the lid. There, cradled in a bed of black velvet, was a gold watch. Merlin's eyes widened at the sight of it. Carefully taking it out of the box, he placed it in the palm of his hand, gazing in wonder at the beauty of the thing. He turned the watch over and on the back he noticed an inscription. In a simple scroll, the words read: 'To Merlin ~with love~ from Christine.'

The wizard had observed people tended to wear their watches on the left wrist, so he careful slid the strap over his left hand. He stretched out his arm to study the small, wondrous thing, at the same time glancing at the clock on the wall of the café to reassure himself they showed the same time. He was delighted to see they were a perfect match.

**   **   **

Tom, this is Mrs Roper," said the judge. "She represents SOCAR, an organisation attached to the Social Welfare Department. It's there to provide help and guidance for certain 'children at risk' cases. Your situation has been deemed to be in that category."

Ann Roper gave a little wave of her hand: "Hello Tom."

"And this young lady is Miss Simmons. From what she tells me, you've already met."

Tom instantly recognised the woman as the one who had been in the car with him on the day he had left with Merlin.

"Hi Tom, I'm Kathy, remember?" she said, smiling.

"Hi Kathy," said Tom, a little sheepishly.

"This gentleman is Mr Malcolm. He is here to represent your stepmother, and this gentleman is Mr Leach. He will be council for your uncle and aunt."

"Hi Tom," they both said in unison, reaching over to shake the boy's hand.

"The lady at the desk is Miss Grey, and she is here to type out everything said in this room." Miss Grey smiled and waved.

"And my name is James Hickfield and I will be presiding over today's hearing."

The judge extended his hand for Tom to shake.

"Now, Tom, first of all I think you should know I am not going to question you on where you have been and who you have been with. Those details have no bearing on the essentials of this case. All I need from you is an honest answer to three simple but important questions. Is that okay with you?"

Tom nodded. "Yes sir."

"Okay! Well, the first question is: "What was the reason behind you leaving the car at the petrol station?"

Tom thought a moment. "I just didn't want to go back to my stepmother."

"I see," said the judge. "Could you have stayed in the car if you had wanted to, or did the man with the beard entice you away?"

"No, Mer… I mean the man would have let me stay if I had really wanted to."

"Mmm, I see." The judge jotted something down on a pad in front of him. He then started looking through his paperwork.

"The report I have from your school states your academic work has deteriorated over a period of two years, and during that time you played truant on numerous occasions and mixed with some unruly elements at the school. Why was that, do you think?"

Tom took a little time to think before he answered.

"I just lost interest… I got... I got bored."

"And why was that, do you think?"

"No-one was interested in me, I suppose."

"Who's no-one, Tom?"

"My stepmother," said Tom, after a slight hesitation.

"What about your uncle and your aunt, were they interested?"

"Yes, sometimes my aunt came to my school to see the headmaster. But they live too far away."

Another quick jot on the pad by the judge.

"My third and last question is: If you could choose, where would you like to live?"

"With my aunt Kate and uncle Bill, on the farm." Tom replied without hesitation.

"Why?" pursued the judge.

"Because... because I feel happy there, I suppose."

"Any other reason?"

"Uhmm ...because I think ...I think they love me."

"Okay Tom, that's all. I will ask Miss Simmons to stay with you while I adjudicate your case in court. You won't run away from her this time, will you?" The judge said with a smile.

"No sir," said Tom.

**   **   **

Judge James Hickfield took his place at the bench.

"The court will rise," said the usher.

After the initial procedures were gone through, the judge settled down to hear the submissions from both lawyers.

Most family court hearings were not open to the public or the press and this case was to be no different. This meant only those closely involved were allowed to be present, along with their counsel. Apart from Social Welfare and court officials, all other personnel had no authority to attend. The judge listened patiently to the submissions from both counselors. Occasionally he would interrupt to clarify a point or quickly jot something down for reference.

Finally, Judge Hickfield summed up:

"This has been a very unusual case, due to the extraordinary action resorted to by the lad in question, Thomas Watson. The issues surrounding the lad's circumstances have been clouded and distorted by the considerable publicity these matters have received over the last few weeks. Nevertheless, due to the unique nature of this case, I have spent additional time studying all aspects of this situation in order to arrive at the right

340

and proper decision. I need not reiterate the submissions presented by each counsel, nor expand on the comprehensive report from the Child Welfare department, although my comments will touch on each one of these.

"I have, as you know, interviewed Thomas Watson in my study prior to the court hearing. Both counsels and two representatives of the Child Welfare department were present. The interview has also been recorded, so a copy of it can be obtained at any time. Both counsels should ensure their clients know the correct procedure for acquiring this information."

The judge glanced down at some papers he had in front of him. "There is no doubt Tom's physical needs have been met by his stepmother, Mrs Cynthia Watson. He has been well nourished, clothed and housed. But children need more than this. After all, children can have all their physical needs attended to in an orphanage, but there will always be something missing. That something is the need to belong, and the comfort and the feeling of security that comes from knowing you are with those who love and care for you.

"From the substantial amount of evidence I have deliberated over in the past few days, I have come to the conclusion Tom did not have those emotional comforts in the home of his stepmother. It must be remembered that the boy, first of all, lost his mother when he was no more than a toddler. Then, after another three or more years, he was taken from his aunt, who had become his surrogate mother, to live back with his father, who had recently married again. About three and a half years later, his father was taken from him in a tragic accident. Since then he has been in the care of his stepmother, who although tending to his physical needs, has disregarded the essential psychological, emotional and spiritual needs of the boy.

"I think this is borne out by his school records, which show a high academic standard of achievement while his father was alive, but almost from the time of his father's tragic death there was a steady decline, leading to constant truancy and a total disregard for school and education. Again I must emphasise I have carefully perused substantial material, including child welfare and SOCAR reports. I have listened to the eloquent address from both counsels and questioned the lad carefully before the start of this hearing.

"I will now give my decision on the matter of guardianship of Thomas Watson, but before doing so, I will ask the lad be brought before the court to hear what I have to say. I realise this is an exceptional measure, but this has been an exceptional case and the lad himself has, by his own actions, highlighted his unhappy situation, one that has brought about this hearing today."

The judge quietly said something to the lady below him. She passed the message to the court official standing by the side door, who then left the court room. When Tom appeared with Kathy, he was escorted to the centre of the room. The SOCAR official then returned to her place next to her senior, Ann Roper.

Tom cast a quick glance to his left where his stepmother sat with a young blue-suited man. Cynthia Watson looked up briefly at her stepson, smiled, then looked away. Tom looked over to his right. His aunt Kate smiled and gave a quick wave of recognition. His uncle beamed at him, poking his thumbs in the air, and Fliss could hardly contain herself; she stood and waved two hands at Tom until her father quickly pulled her back down onto her seat.

"Tom," said the judge, "I have reached a conclusion regarding your future wellbeing. It is a con…"

The judge stopped in mid- sentence. "Who is that gentleman sitting in the back of the courtroom?" Everyone turned their heads. It was Merlin. The uniformed official, who had been standing just inside the main courtroom door, looked at him in surprise.

"Who are you sir?" enquired the judge, "Do you not realise this is a private hearing?"

Merlin stood up. "I am…"

Before the wizard could say more, Tom's uncle interrupted: "He is Tom's godfather, sir," he said, standing up as he spoke.

The judge turned to the speaker. "That still does not give him the right to attend this court, Mr Watson."

"I understand sir, but he has been very close to my nephew and has been of enormous help to him during this period."

The judge looked back at the stranger and sighed, before addressing the court. "There have been a number of irregularities involved in this case, I suppose one more will make little difference."

Judge Hickfield turned his attention again to Merlin. "You may be seated, sir."

The wizard smiled at the judge and sat back down.

Kate glanced at Bill, a little surprised by her husband's quick thinking.

"Tom… as I was saying, a conclusion has been reached regarding your future welfare. It must be understood before a legal guardianship can be revoked, strong irrefutable evidence must point to the disadvantages the current guardianship might have for the child's wellbeing. Conversely, the party that applies for a new guardianship must be able to prove beyond doubt that they can meet all the needs of the child. The child's own wishes must also be taken into account.

"I believe, in this instance, we have irrefutable evidence that the boy, Thomas Watson's, wellbeing would be better served living in the care of the applicants. I propose therefore to rescind the current legal guardianship forthwith, and allow temporary guardianship to be given to Thomas Watson's only blood relative, his uncle, Mr William Watson, and his wife, Mrs Kathleen May Watson.

"During the period of temporary guardianship, the appropriate welfare officials will be granted access to interview the boy, Thomas Watson, six months from this date. They will also, at that time, interview Mr William Watson and his wife, and visit the boy's school to record the child's academic progress, and to see how he has settled into his new school. The inspection process will be repeated again six months later. If all evidence indicates the child is being well cared for, then the guardianship will be made permanent."

Judge Hickfield smiled down at the boy. "Tom, you may join your relatives now, if you wish."

As he hurried away, Tom glanced over at the wizard and grinned. Merlin nodded and smiled, raising a slim hand in response. Aunt Kate, her eyes brimming with tears, embraced her nephew while his beaming uncle ruffled the boy's hair. Felicity jumped up and down in pure joy. "Does this mean Tom will stay with us forever?" she said, looking up at her mother.

"Well, for as long as he wants to, my darling."

Tom broke free from his aunt's embrace. "Can Merlin come over?" he asked.

"Of course he can. Your uncle and I have a lot to thank him for."

The boy turned to beckon Merlin, but his happy expression changed to a bewildered frown.

"Aunt Kate... he's not there... he's gone!"

They all looked over to where Merlin had been sitting. The wizard had vanished.

THE END

If you have enjoyed reading 'Merlin, please write a review to amazon.com or amazon.co.uk. Thank you.